JELLABY

"A simply wonderful tale of friendship and whimsy,
masterfully constructed with depth and moxie."
—Kirkus Reviews

"Sophisticated and thoughtful,
this comic also has plenty of child appeal."
—School Library Journal

"I'm addicted to Jellaby! Kean Soo's
storytelling is irresistable."
—Scott McCloud, author of *Understanding Comics*

"Jellaby will win your heart."
—Jeff Smith, creator of *Bone*

Eisner Award nominee
for Best Digital Comic

Joe Shuster Award winner
for Best Comic for Kids

Monster in the City

Kean Soo

CAPSTONE
www.capstoneyoungreaders.com

Acknowledgements:
Special thanks to Calista Brill, Roberta Pressel,
Judy Hansen, Hope Larson, David & Nicolas Seigneret, Ben
Hu, Jason Turner, Clio Chiang, Kazu Kibuishi, and of course,
all my friends and family for their love and support
over the years. A very special thank-you to the Canada
Council for the Arts for their support of this work.

Jellaby is published by Capstone
1710 Roe Crest Drive
North Mankato, Minnesota 56003
www.capstoneyoungreaders.com

Text © Kean Soo 2014
Illustrations © Kean Soo 2014

Cataloging-in-Publication Data is available on the Library of Congress website.
ISBN: 978-1-4342-6421-3 (paperback)

Summary:
Ten-year-old Portia Bennett and her friend Jason continue their journey
through the city of Toronto. They're one step closer to finding the home
of their lost friend, a sweet, silent creature named Jellaby. Unfortunately,
dangers await, including a tentacled beast with a taste for children. To succeed
in her quest -- and save her friends -- Portia must step up and
kick some monster butt.

Cover Design: Kean Soo & Kazu Kibuishi

Printed in the United States of America in North Mankato, Minnesota.
112014   008614R

Foreword

As a kid, I didn't spend much time in "the city." My family lived in an apartment complex just barely within San Francisco city limits, and my parents preferred suburban conveniences like ample parking and large supermarkets. City visits were reserved for special occasions like my grandparents visiting from Hawaii, or going to see the lights at Christmastime.

One year, during a field trip to see a play downtown, my classmates decided it would be funny to ditch me. They took off down the street, leaving me in a crowd of tourists, cable car noise, homeless people, and utter confusion. I still remember how terrifying it felt to be alone in the center of the city. A friend would've come in handy right about then.

Thankfully, the people I surround myself with now are a little kinder. I've known Kean since 2004, by way of comic conventions, Livejournal posts, and message boards. We forged a bond over our love of comics, as well as our shared interest in food. Some of my fondest memories involve riding around Toronto in the backseat of Kean's tiny Volkswagen, listening to indie rock and looking for the best ice cream, sushi, or Hungarian meat stacks. Conversation usually steers back to our work, and we've spent many hours discussing braces, monsters, and middle school.

My readers constantly look to me for graphic novel recommendations, and despite the kids' graphic novel boom of the last decade or so, I'm often hard-pressed to come up with age-appropriate titles that have that perfect combination of great art, solid cartooning, and wonderful storytelling. Jellaby is the complete package, and I'm unabashedly pleased to recommend the book you hold in your hands.

Get ready to soar over the city, explore its dark underground tunnels, and find yourself among friends.

~ Raina Telgemeier,
creator of Smile and Drama

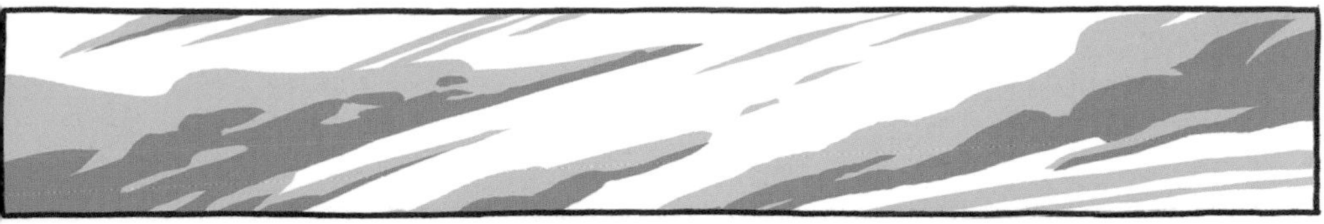

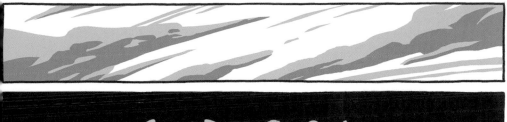

CHAPTER ONE

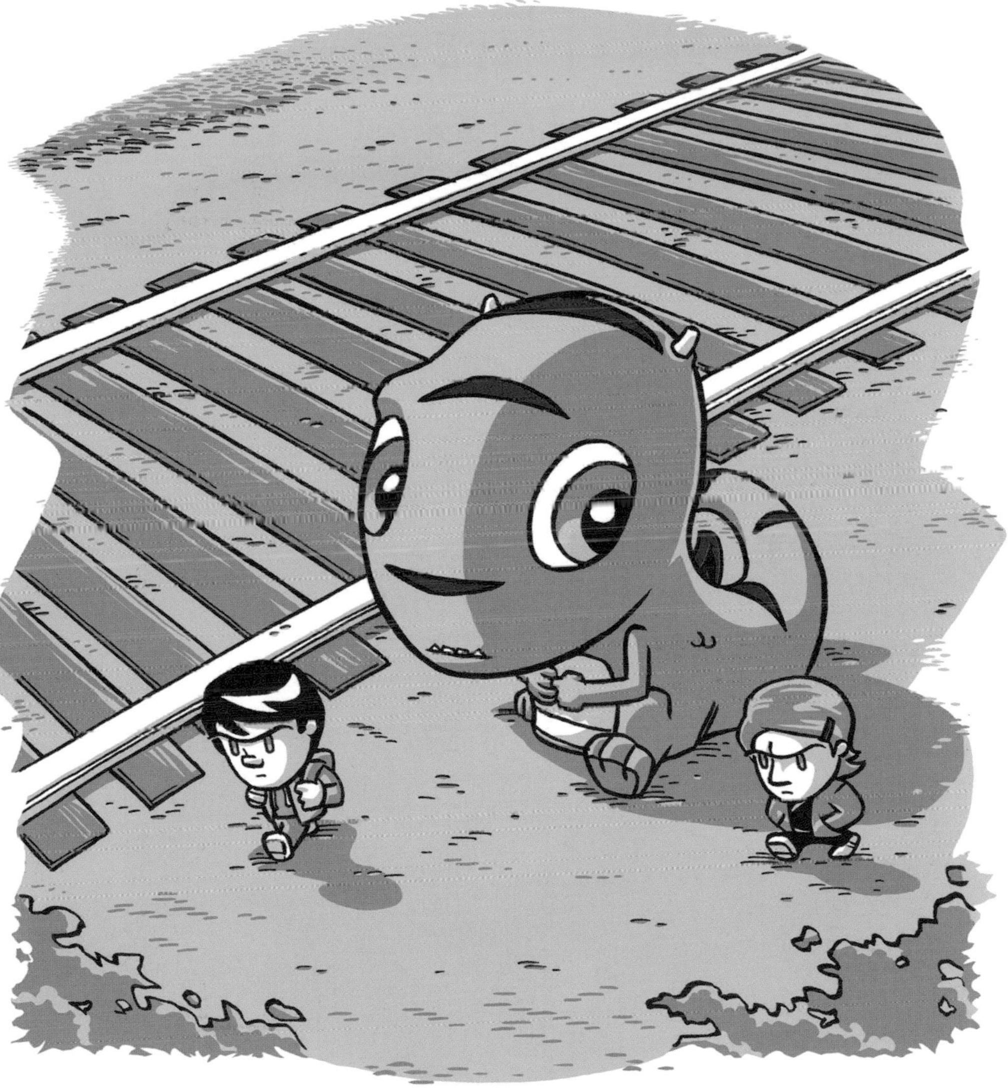

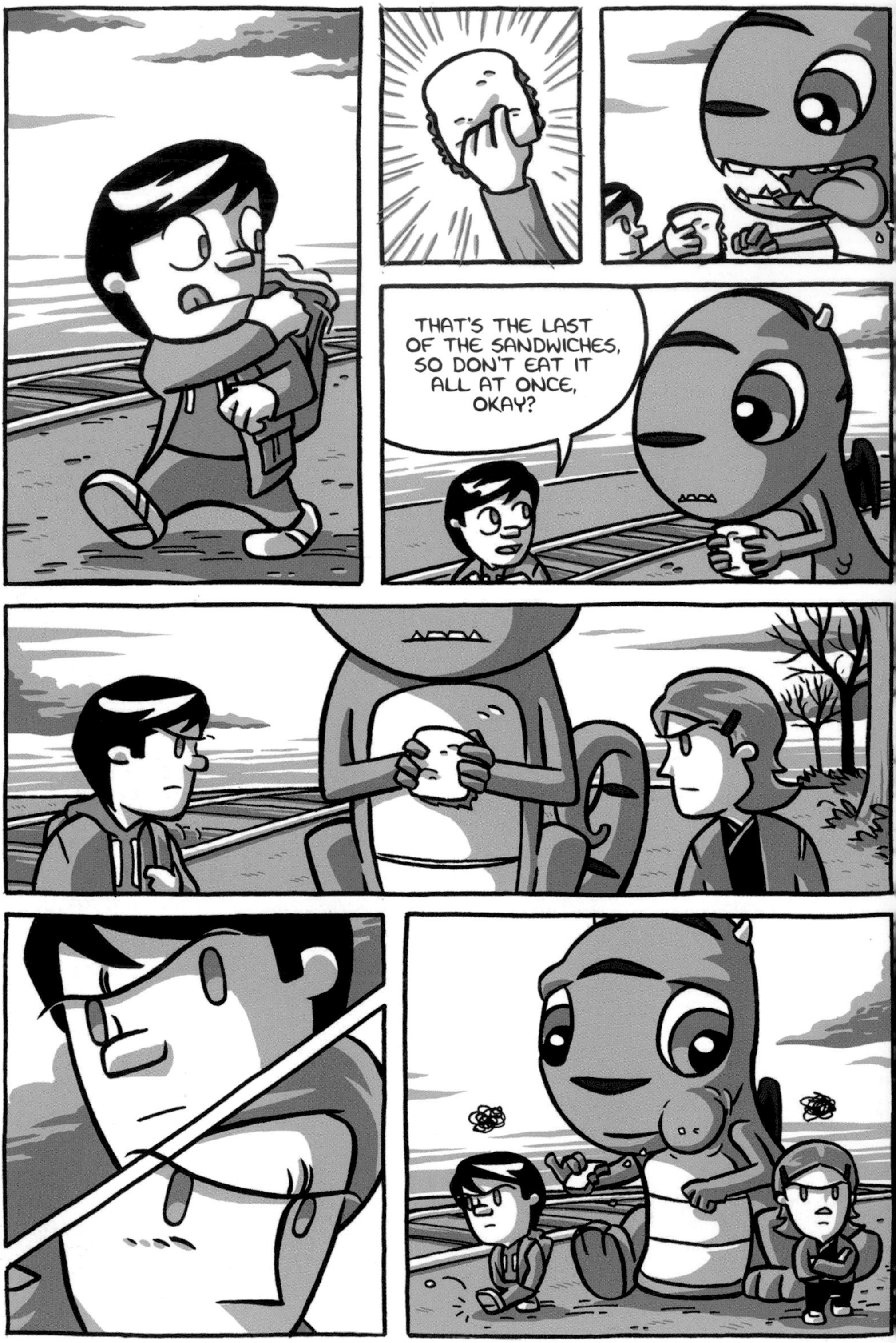
THAT'S THE LAST OF THE SANDWICHES, SO DON'T EAT IT ALL AT ONCE, OKAY?

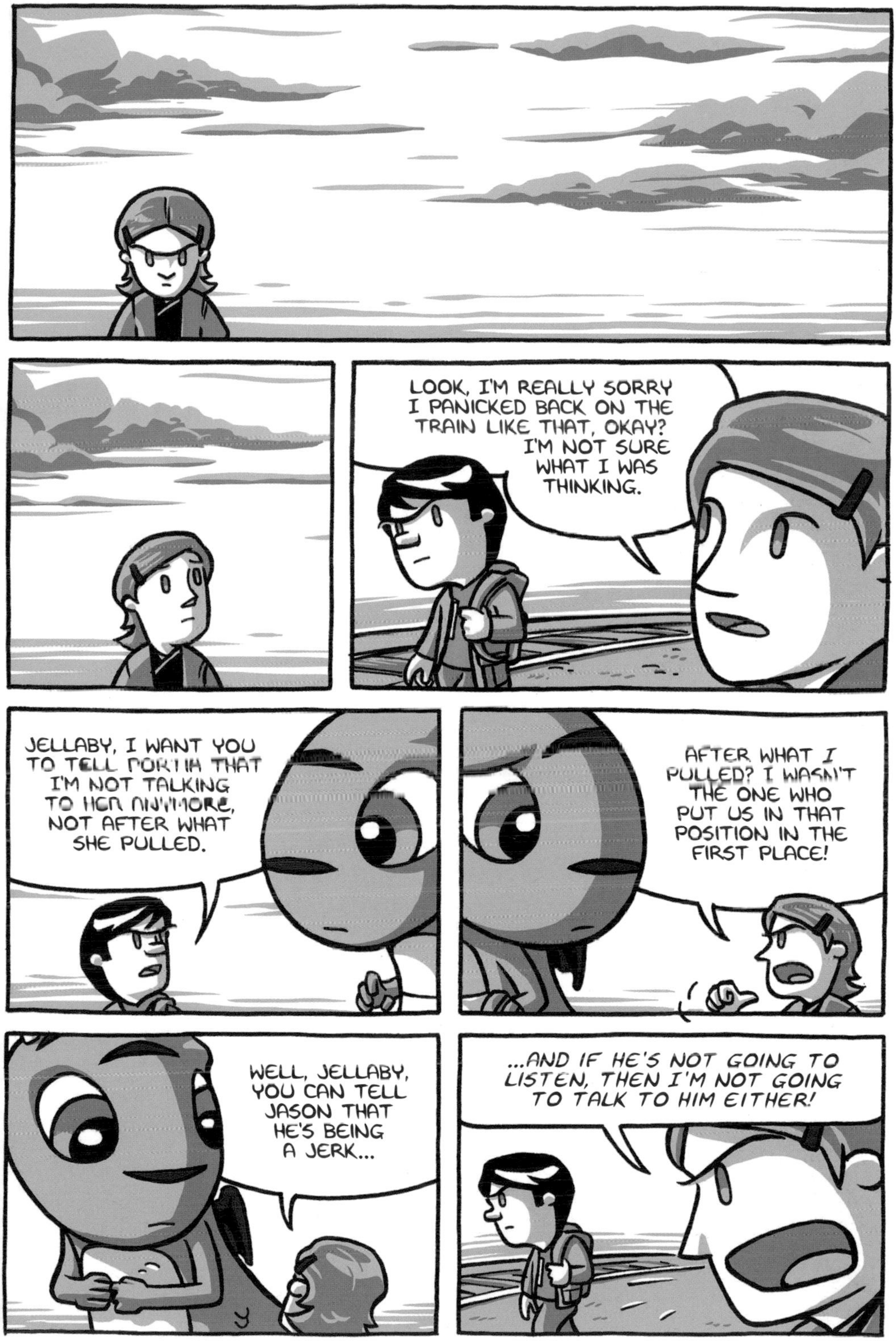
LOOK, I'M REALLY SORRY I PANICKED BACK ON THE TRAIN LIKE THAT, OKAY? I'M NOT SURE WHAT I WAS THINKING.
JELLABY, I WANT YOU TO TELL PORTIA THAT I'M NOT TALKING TO HER ANYMORE, NOT AFTER WHAT SHE PULLED.
AFTER WHAT *I* PULLED? I WASN'T THE ONE WHO PUT US IN THAT POSITION IN THE FIRST PLACE!
WELL, JELLABY, YOU CAN TELL JASON THAT HE'S BEING A JERK...
...AND IF HE'S NOT GOING TO LISTEN, THEN I'M NOT GOING TO TALK TO HIM EITHER!

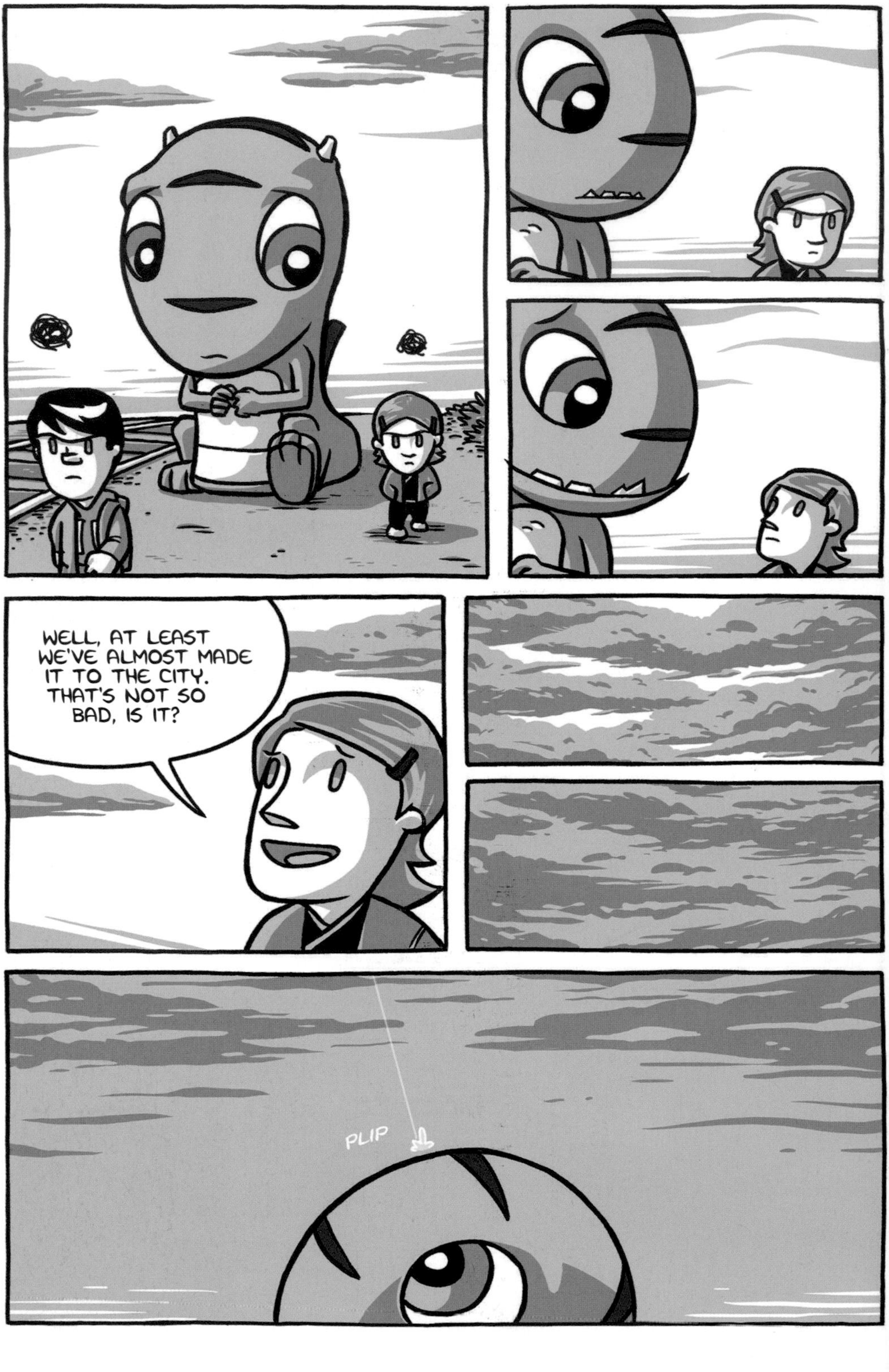
WELL, AT LEAST WE'VE ALMOST MADE IT TO THE CITY. THAT'S NOT SO BAD, IS IT?
PLIP

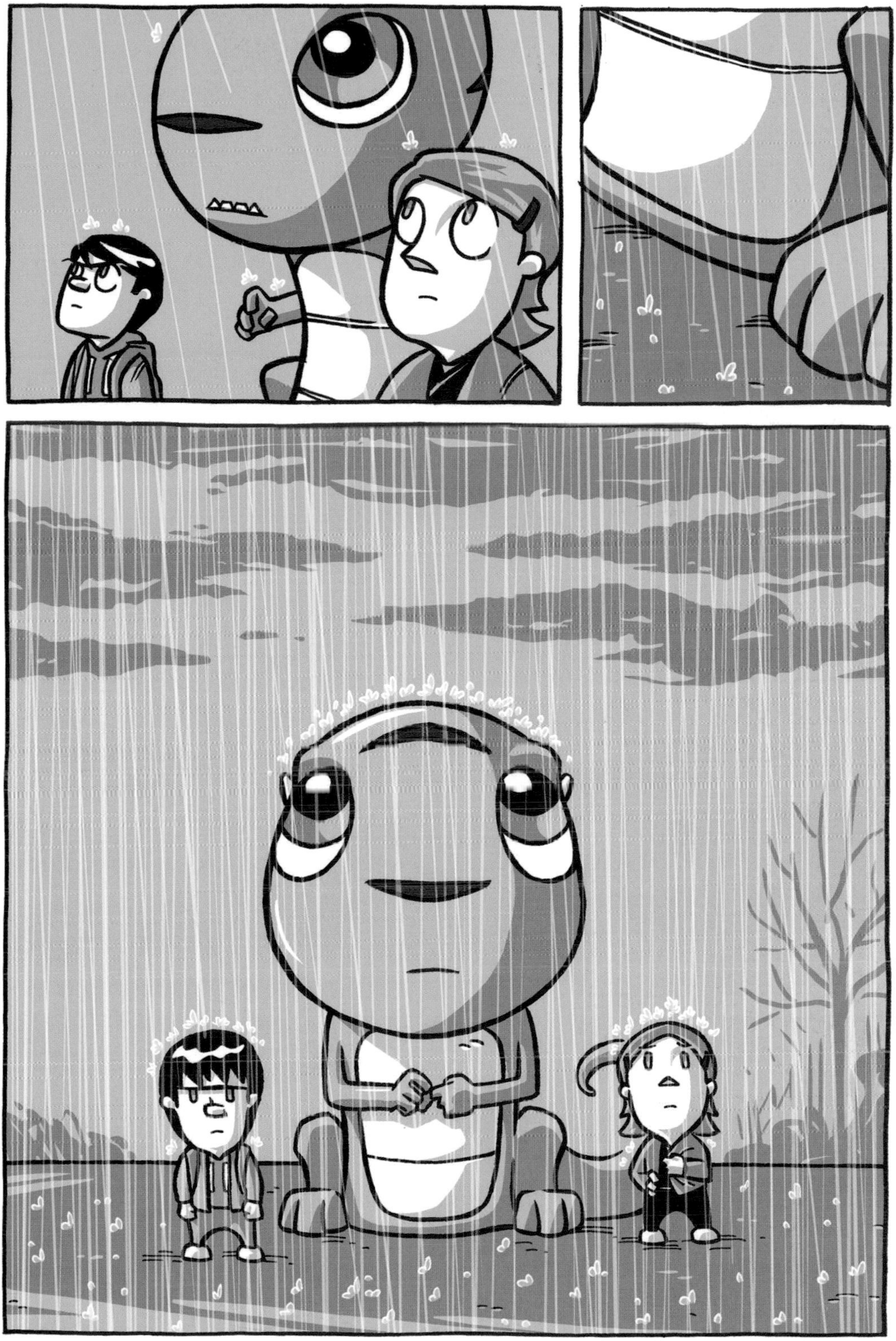

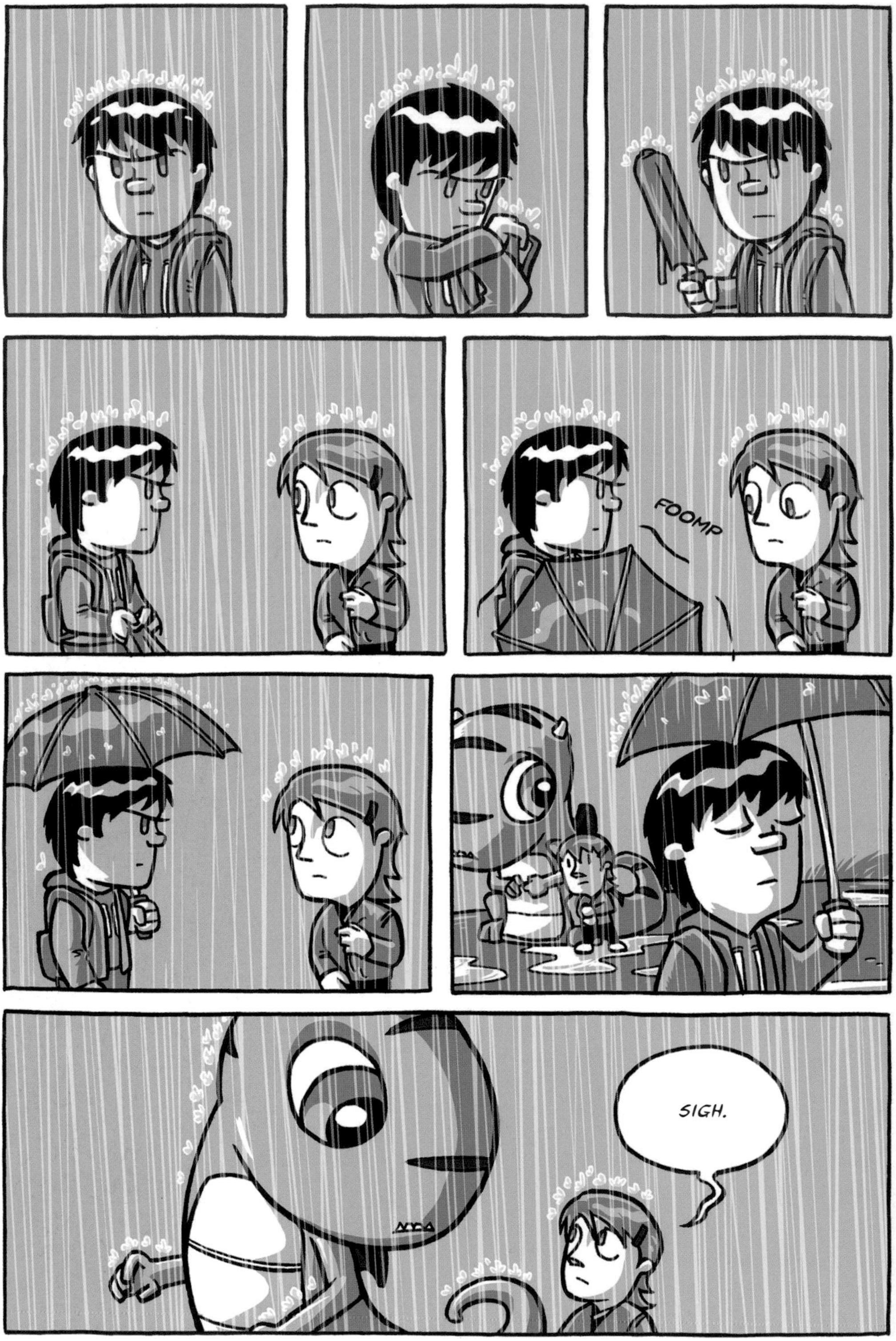
FOOMP
SIGH.

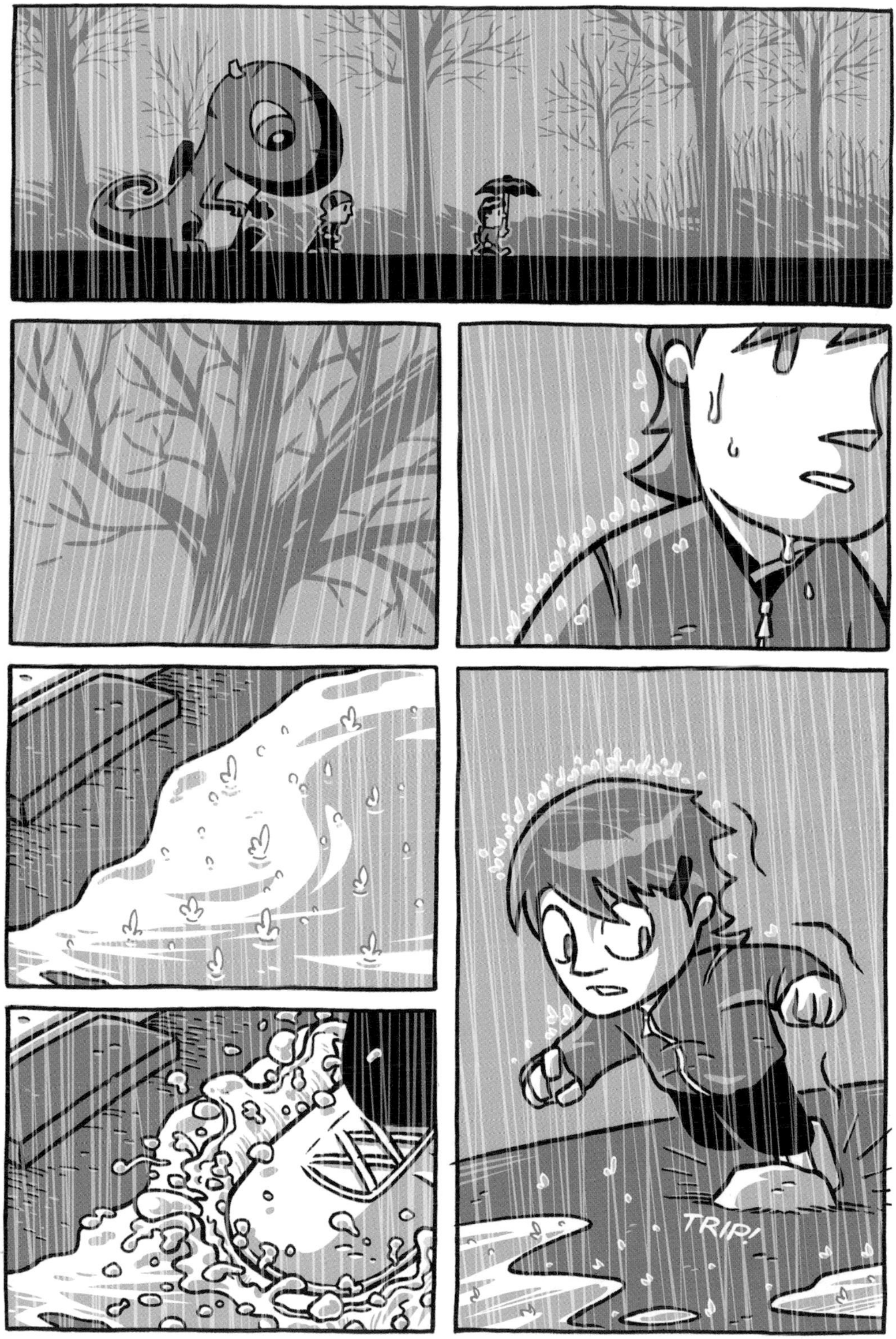
TRIP!

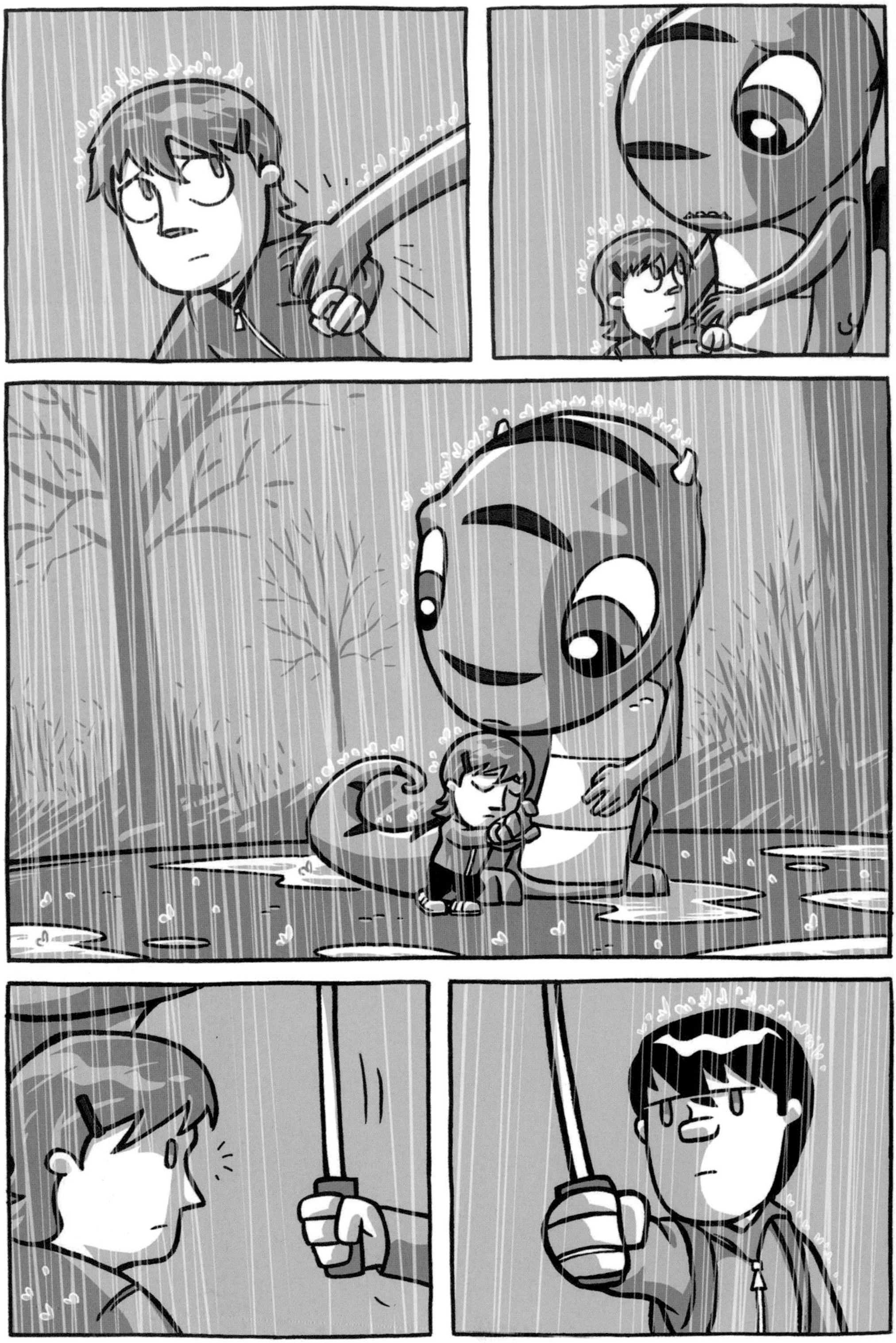

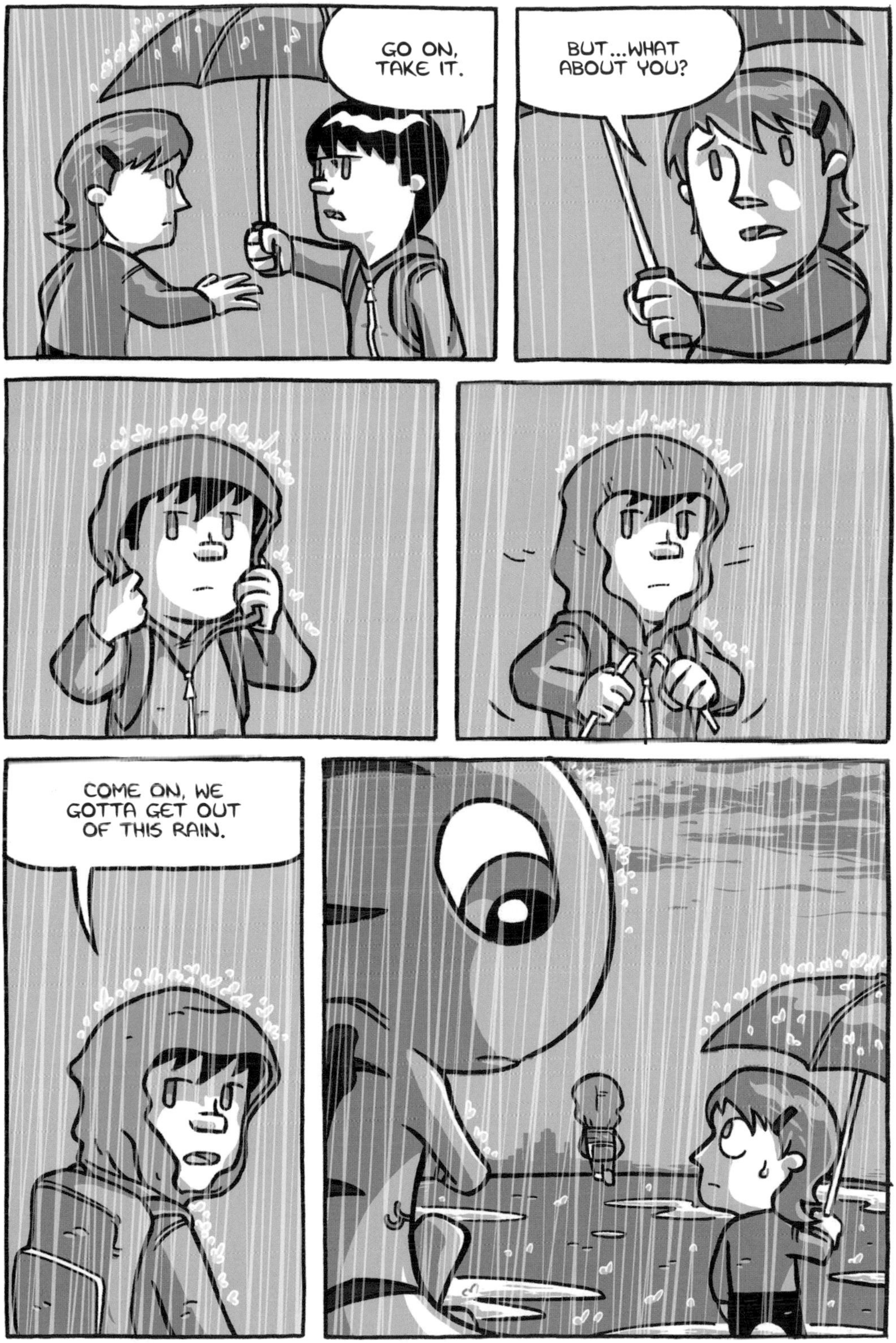
GO ON, TAKE IT.
BUT...WHAT ABOUT YOU?
COME ON, WE GOTTA GET OUT OF THIS RAIN.

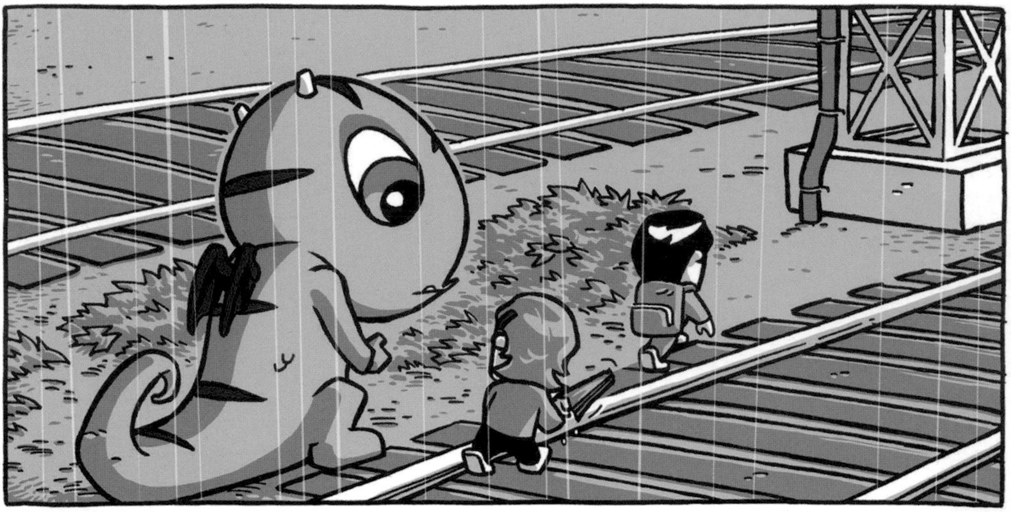

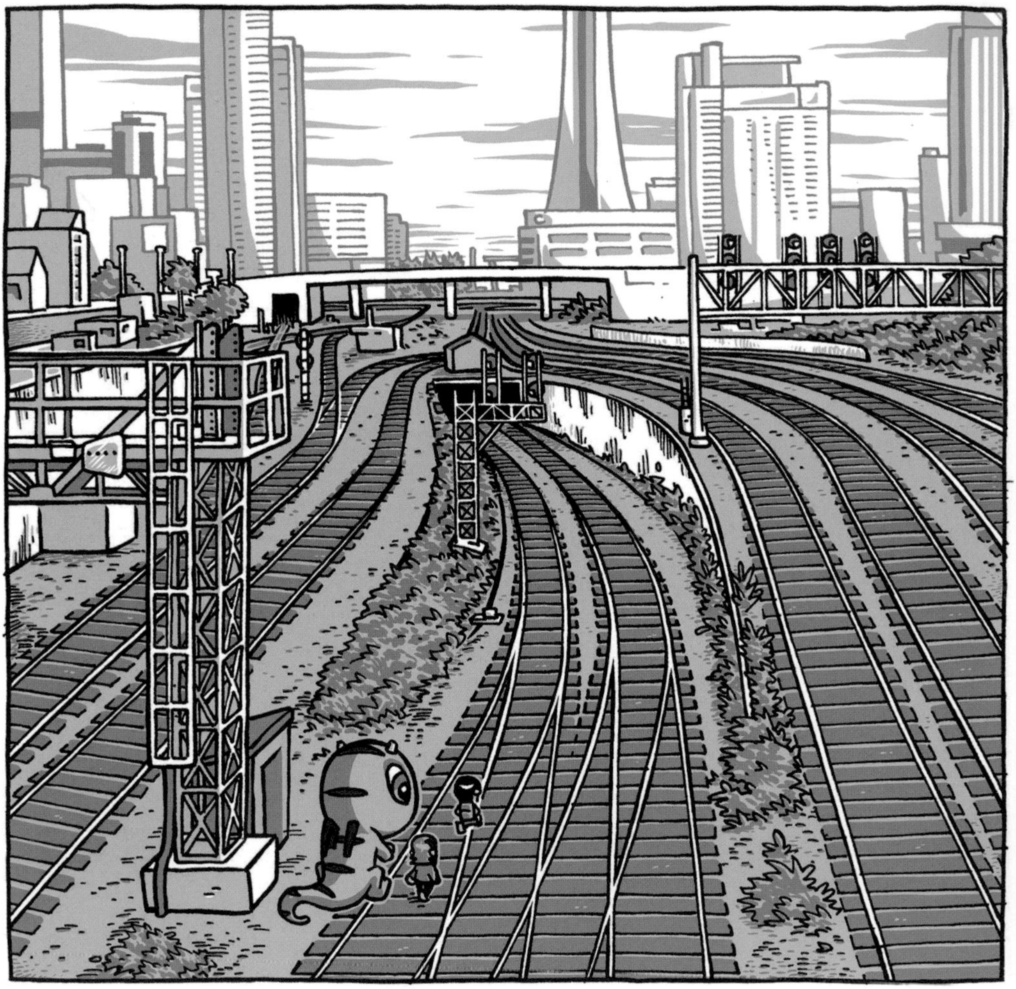

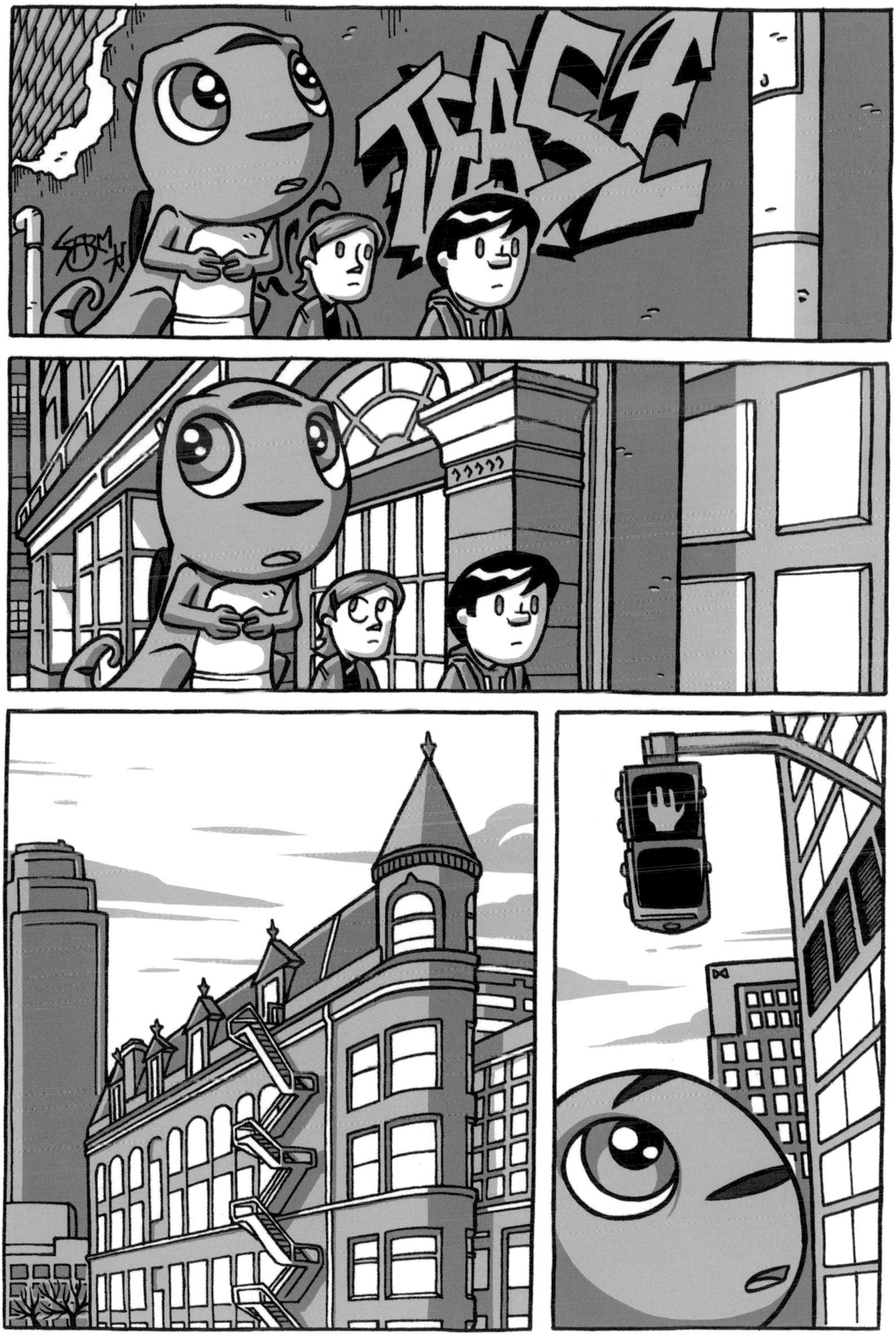

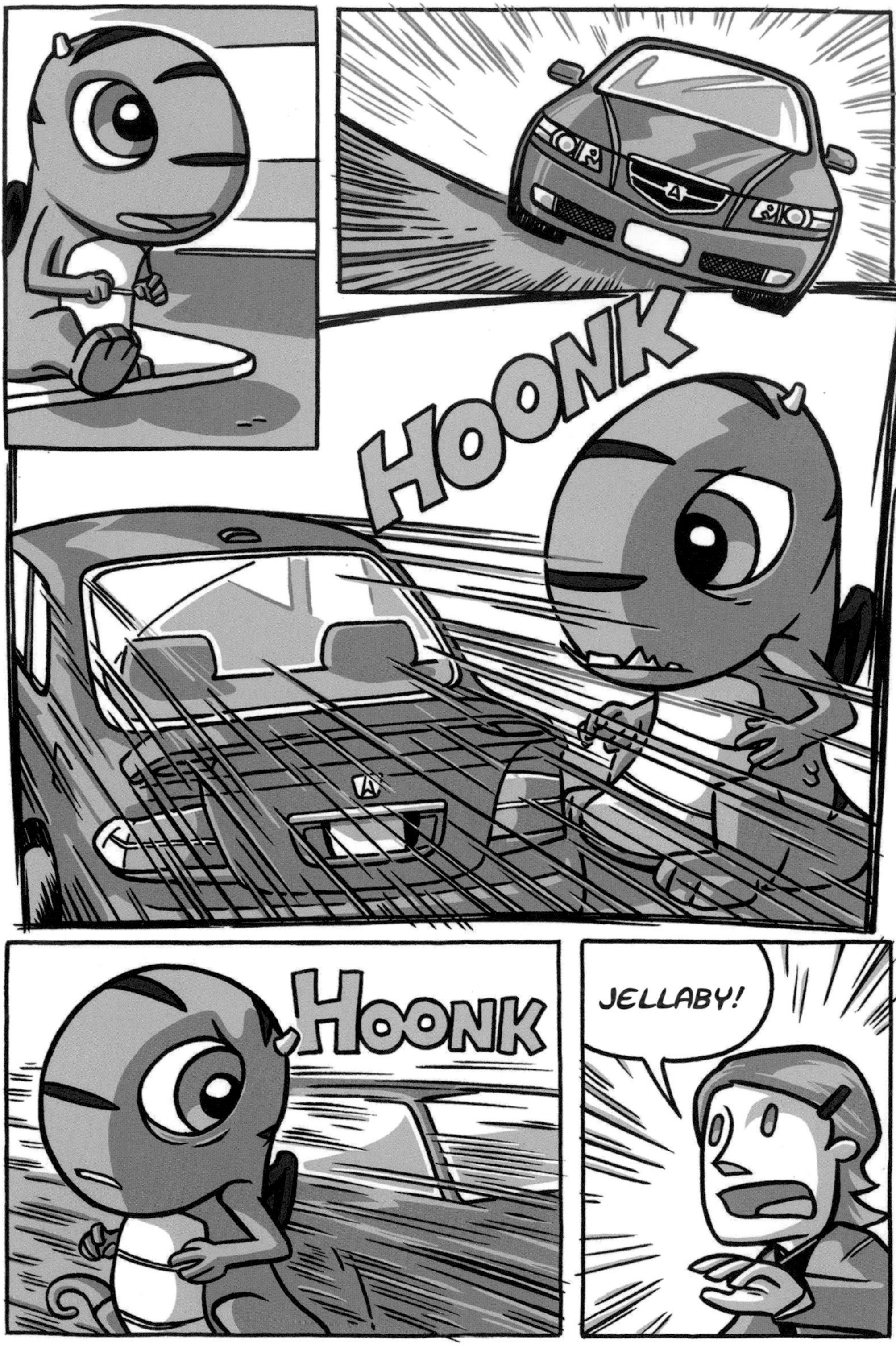
HOONK
HOONK
JELLABY!

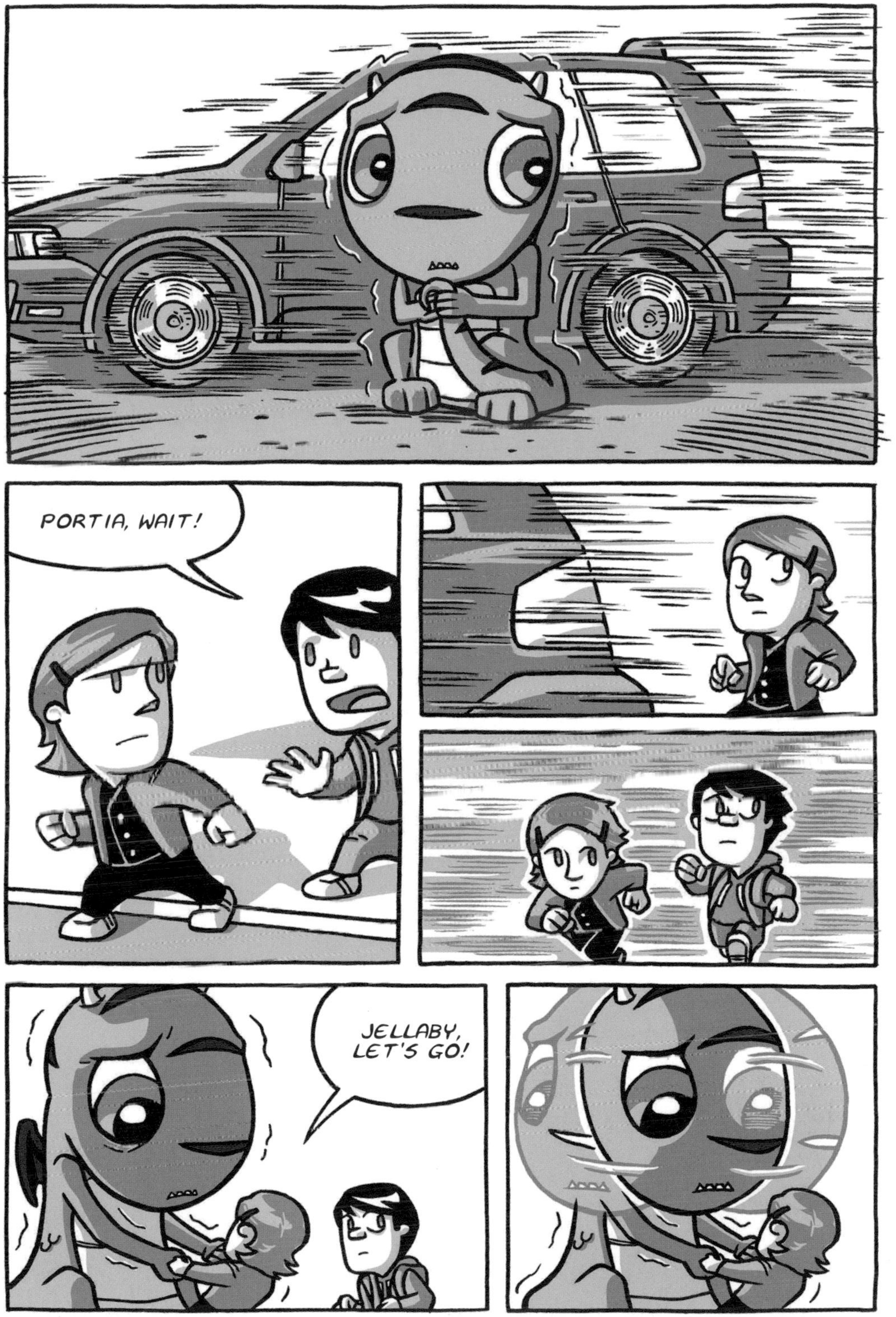
PORTIA, WAIT!
JELLABY, LET'S GO!

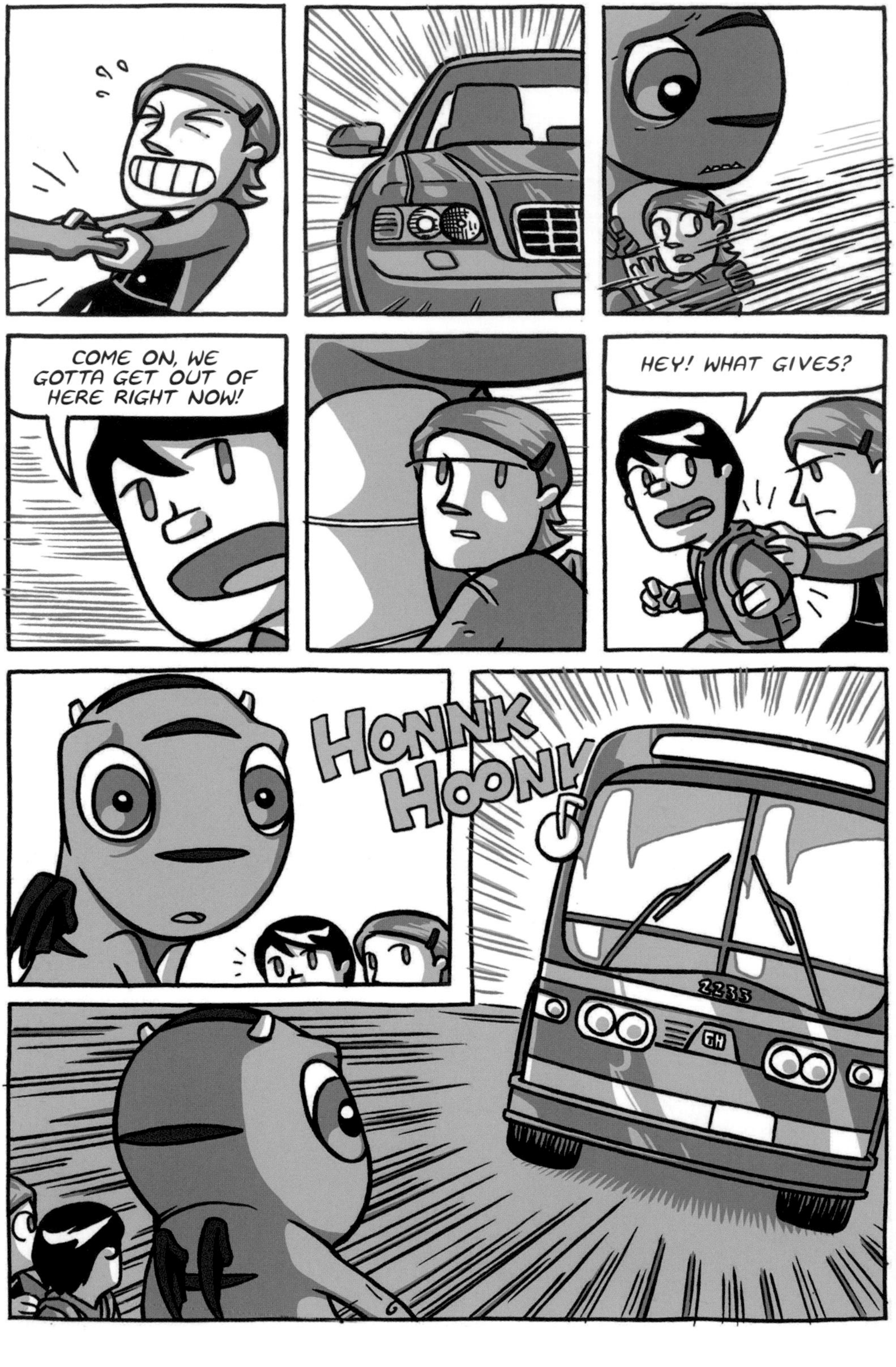
COME ON, WE GOTTA GET OUT OF HERE RIGHT NOW!
HEY! WHAT GIVES?
HONNK HOONK
2235

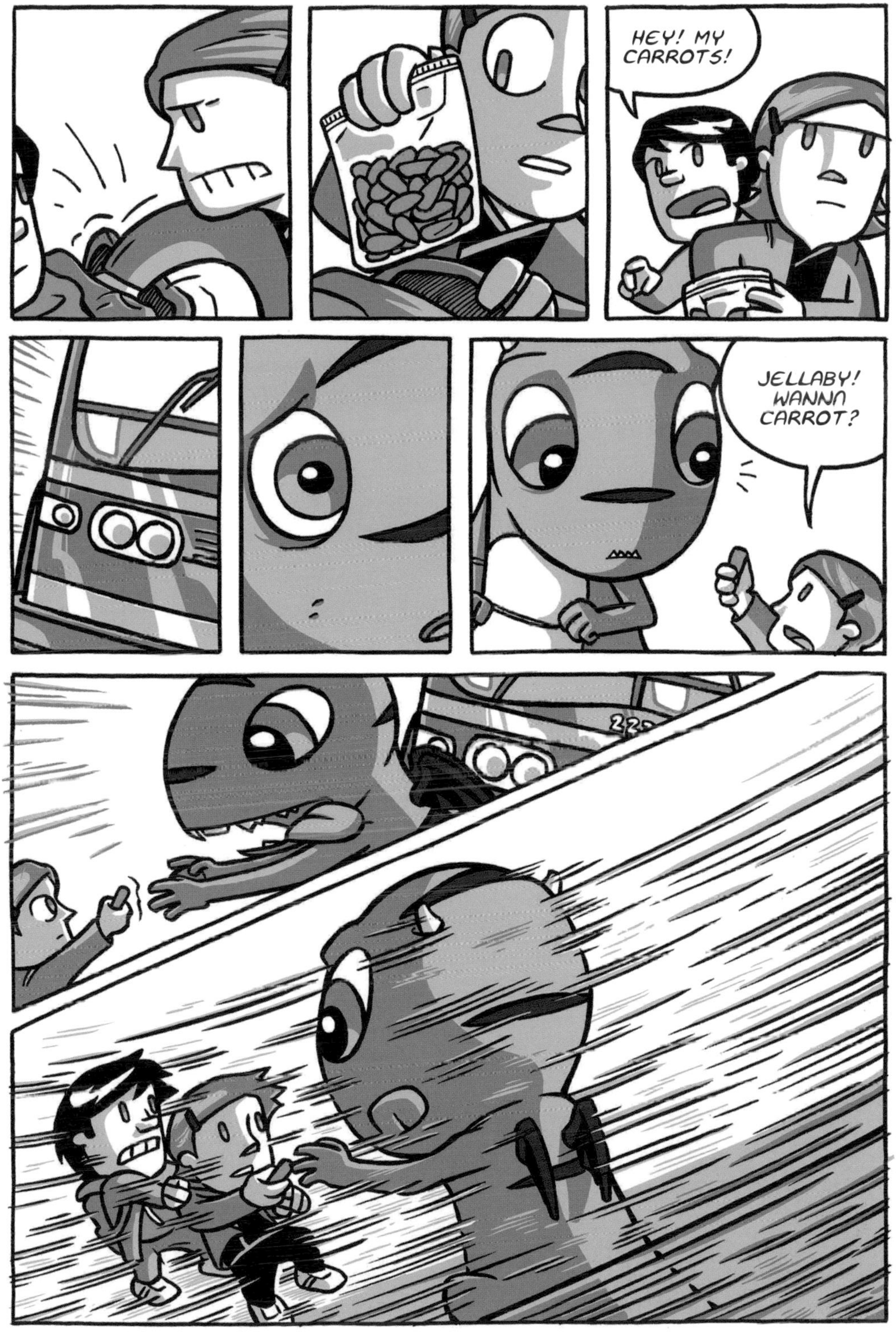
HEY! MY CARROTS!
JELLABY! WANNA CARROT?

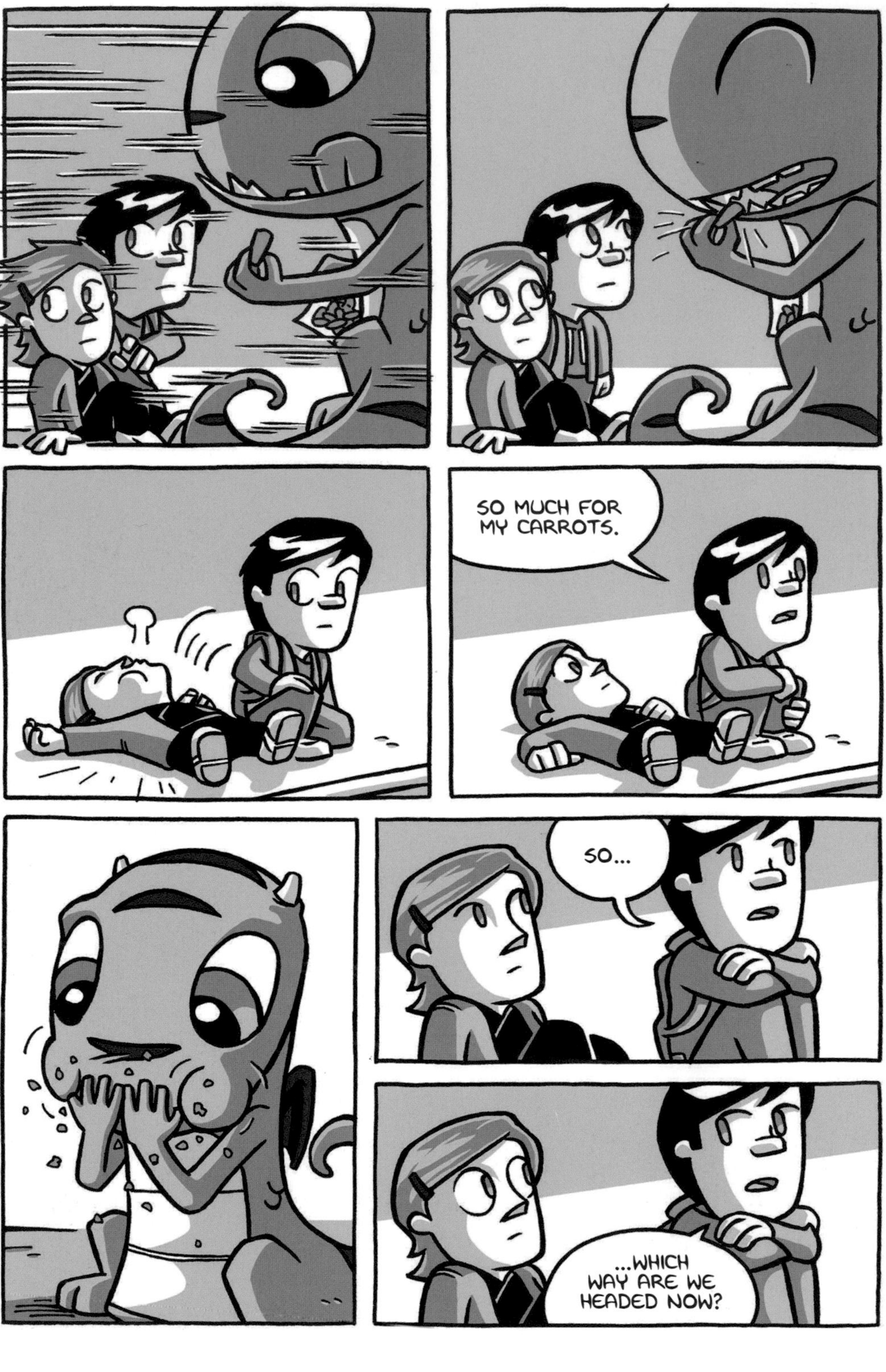
SO MUCH FOR MY CARROTS.
SO...
...WHICH WAY ARE WE HEADED NOW?

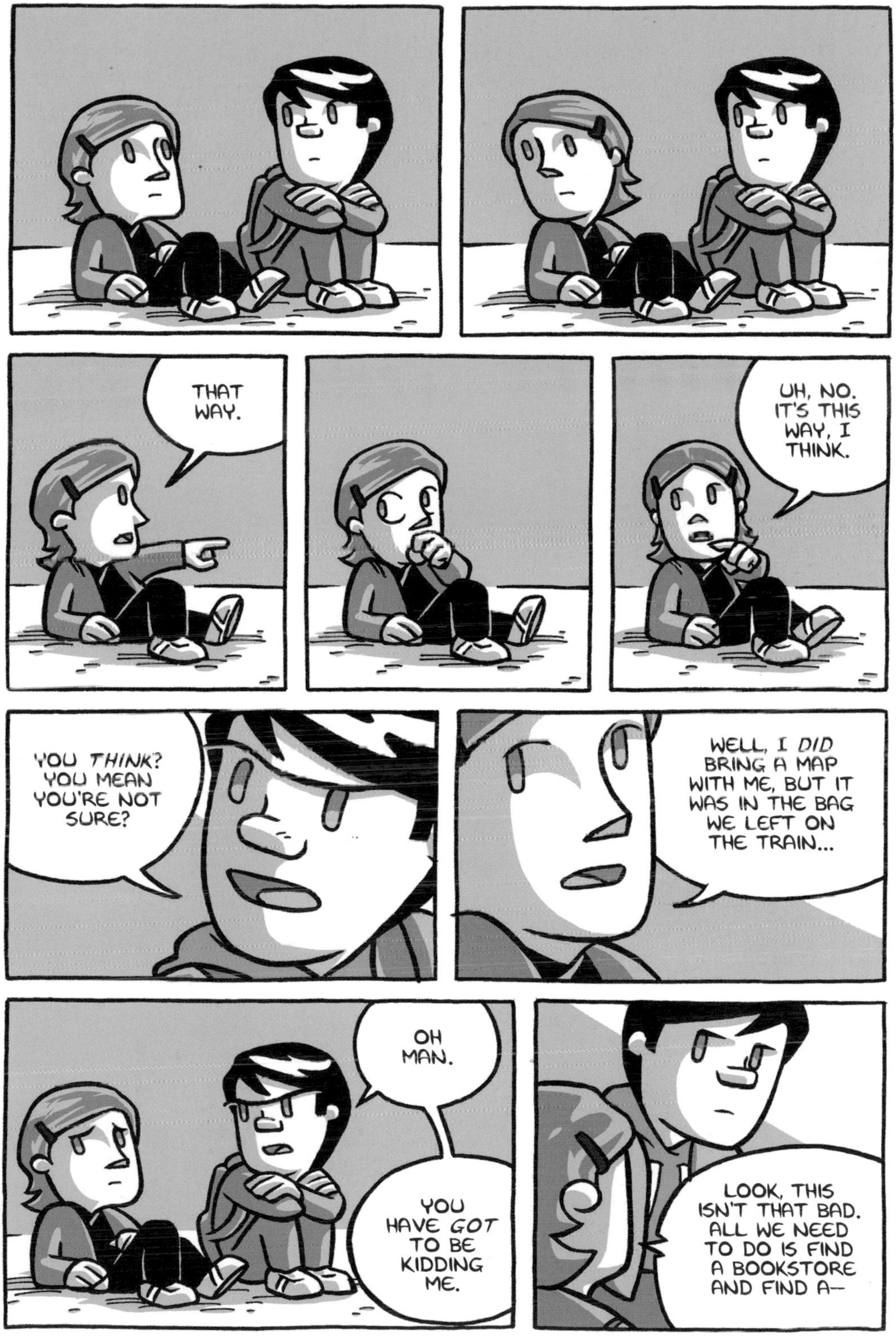
THAT WAY.
UH, NO. IT'S THIS WAY, I THINK.
YOU *THINK*? YOU MEAN YOU'RE NOT SURE?
WELL, I *DID* BRING A MAP WITH ME, BUT IT WAS IN THE BAG WE LEFT ON THE TRAIN...
OH MAN.
YOU HAVE *GOT* TO BE KIDDING ME.
LOOK, THIS ISN'T THAT BAD. ALL WE NEED TO DO IS FIND A BOOKSTORE AND FIND A—

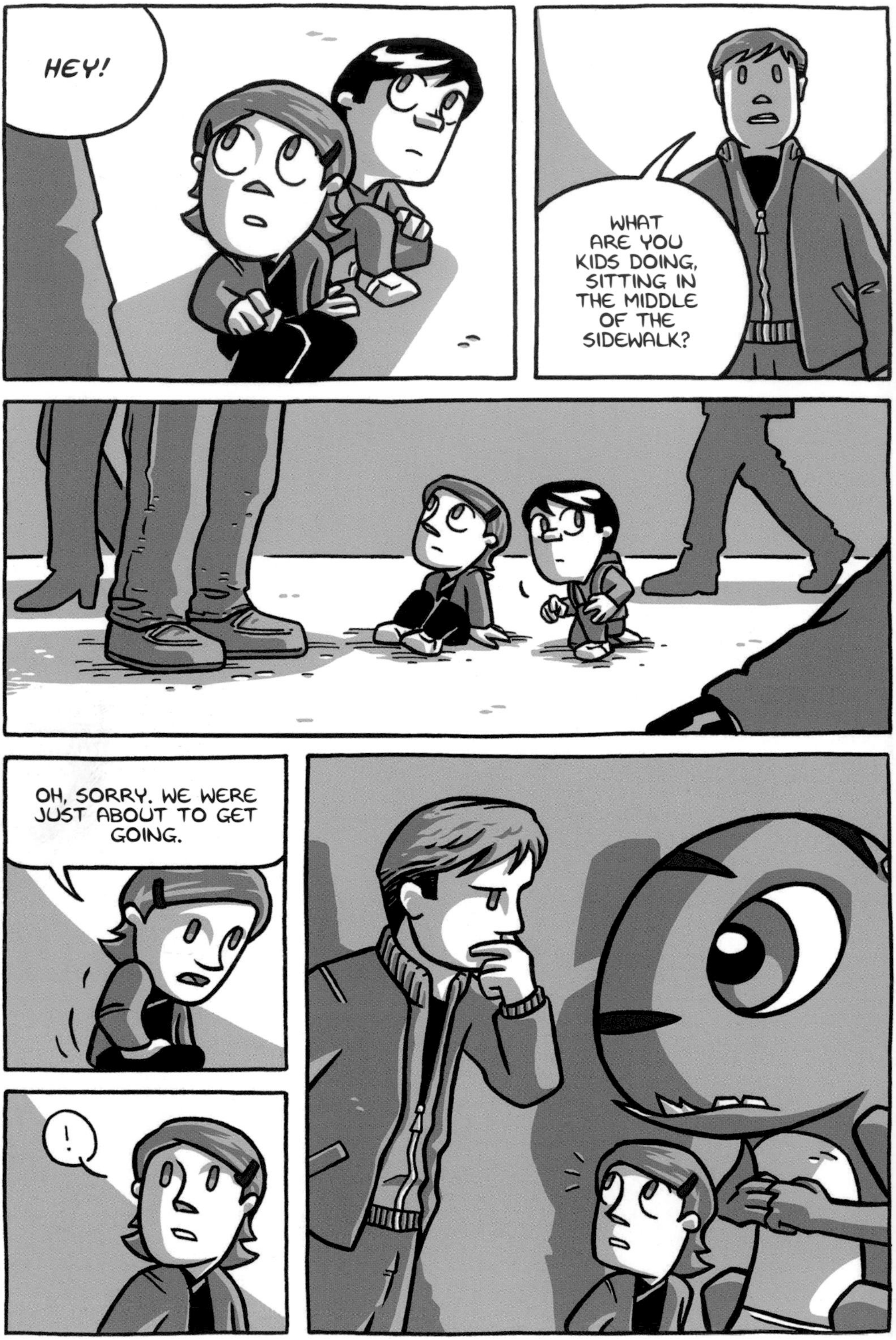
HEY!
WHAT ARE YOU KIDS DOING, SITTING IN THE MIDDLE OF THE SIDEWALK?
OH, SORRY. WE WERE JUST ABOUT TO GET GOING.
!

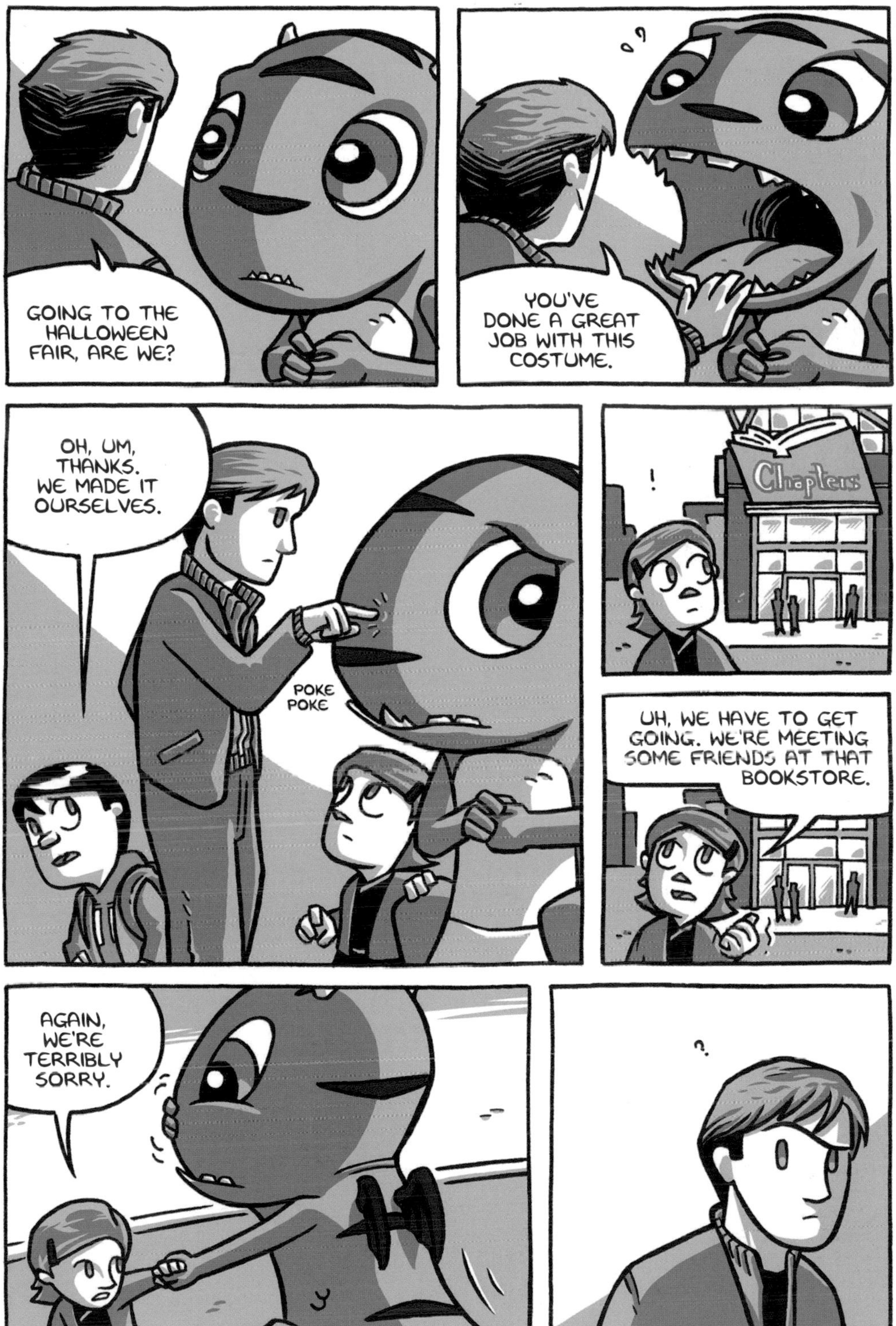
GOING TO THE HALLOWEEN FAIR, ARE WE?
YOU'VE DONE A GREAT JOB WITH THIS COSTUME.
OH, UM, THANKS. WE MADE IT OURSELVES.
POKE POKE
!
Chapters
UH, WE HAVE TO GET GOING. WE'RE MEETING SOME FRIENDS AT THAT BOOKSTORE.
AGAIN, WE'RE TERRIBLY SORRY.
?

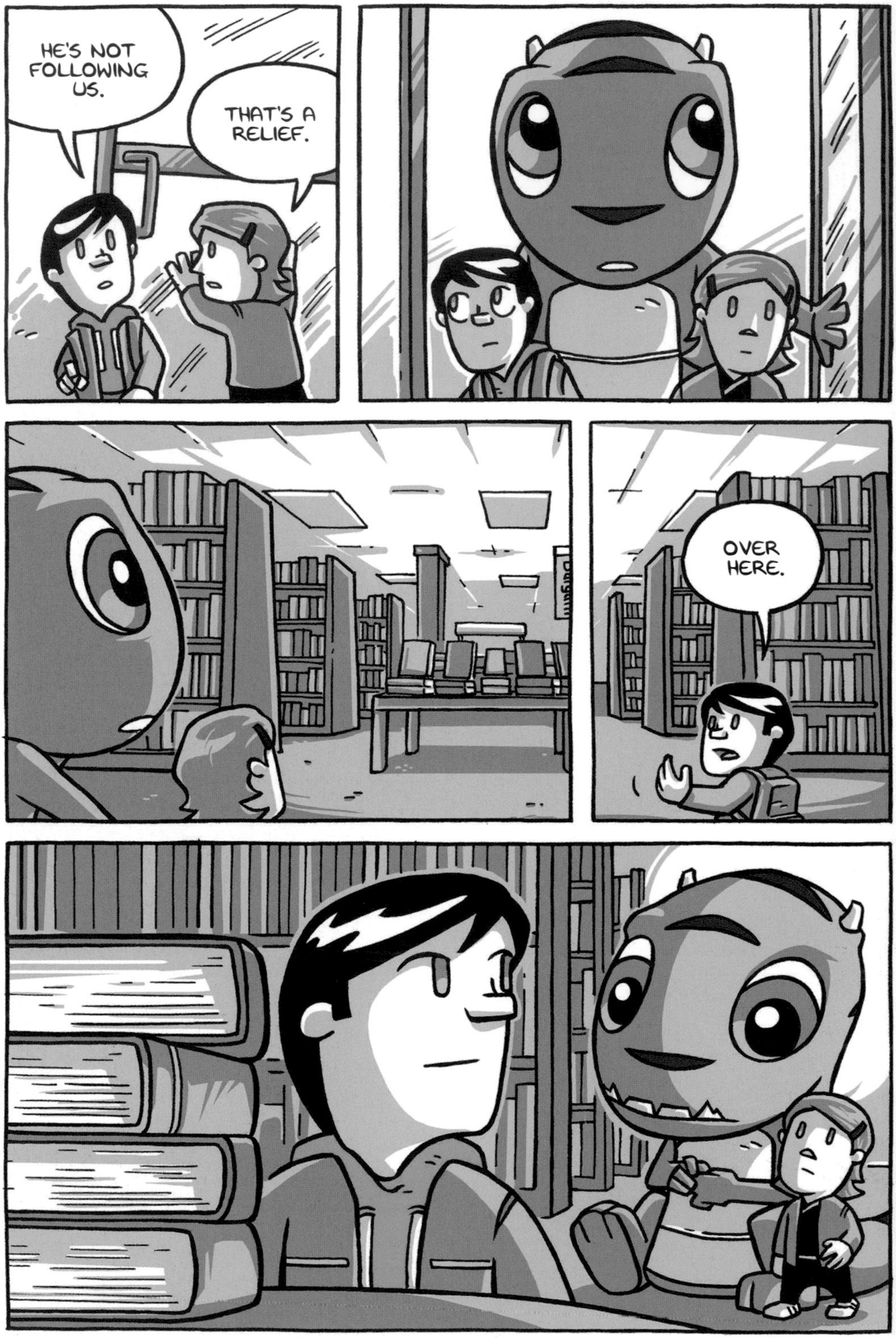
HE'S NOT FOLLOWING US.
THAT'S A RELIEF.
OVER HERE.

CREEEEAAK

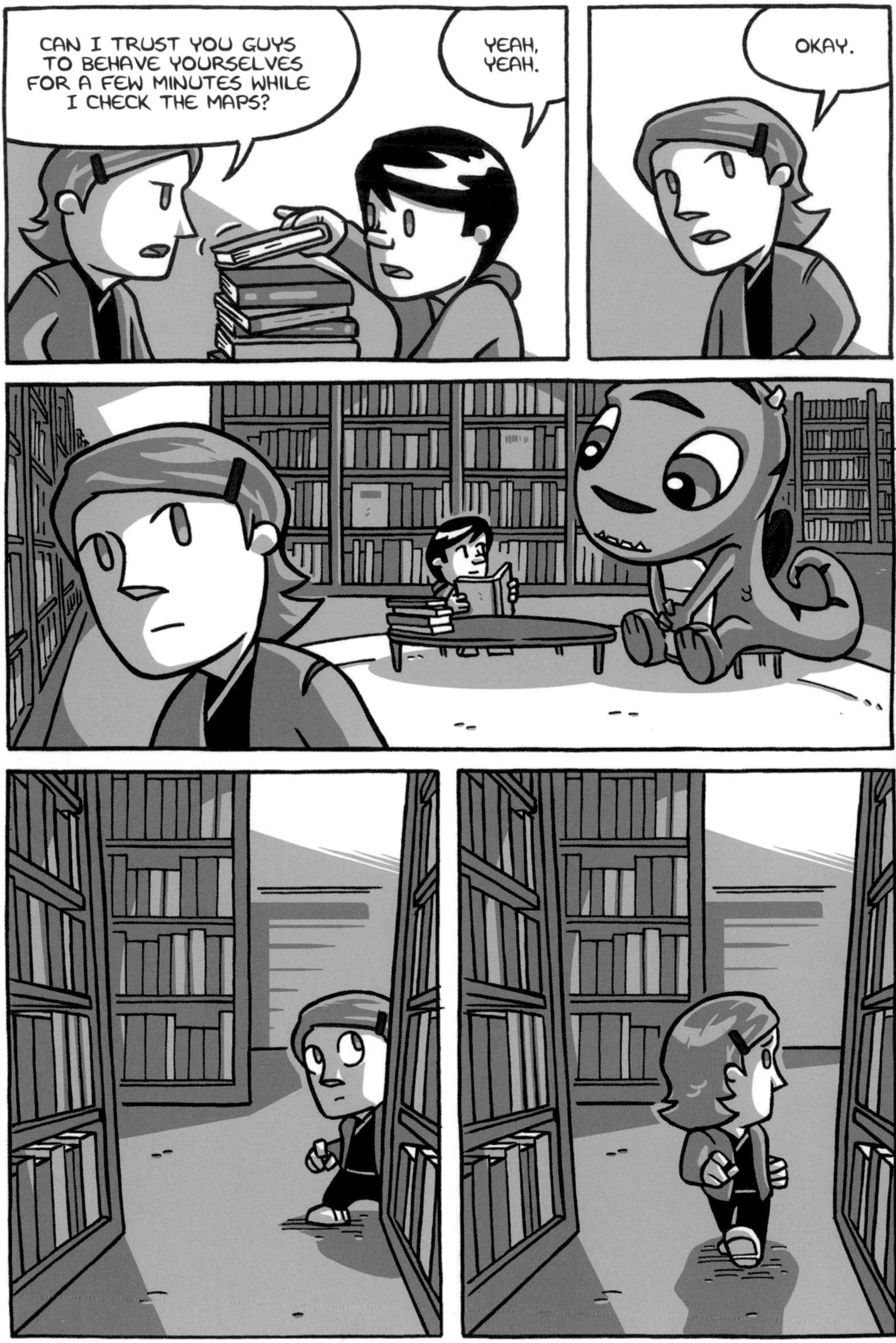
CAN I TRUST YOU GUYS TO BEHAVE YOURSELVES FOR A FEW MINUTES WHILE I CHECK THE MAPS?
YEAH, YEAH.
OKAY.

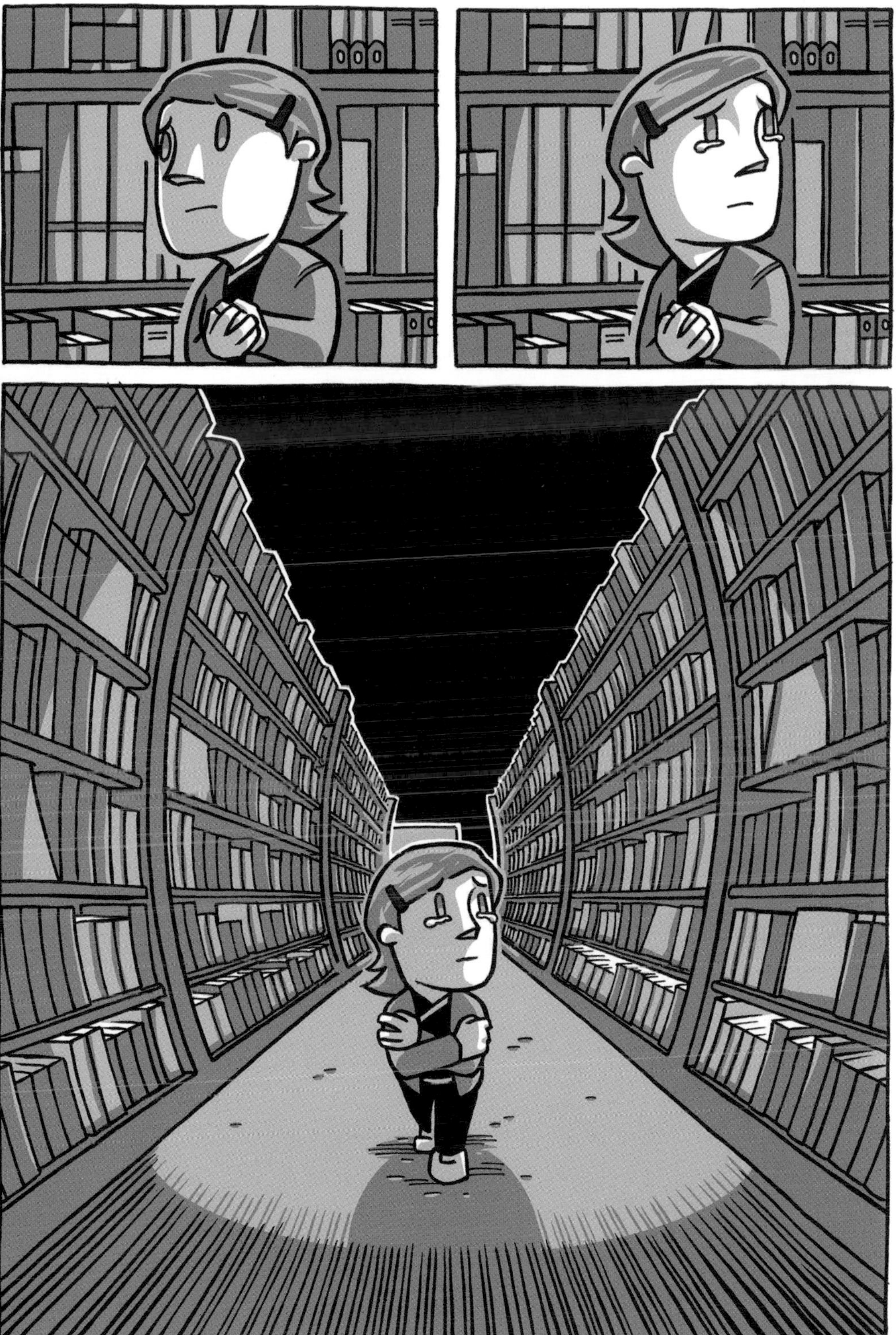

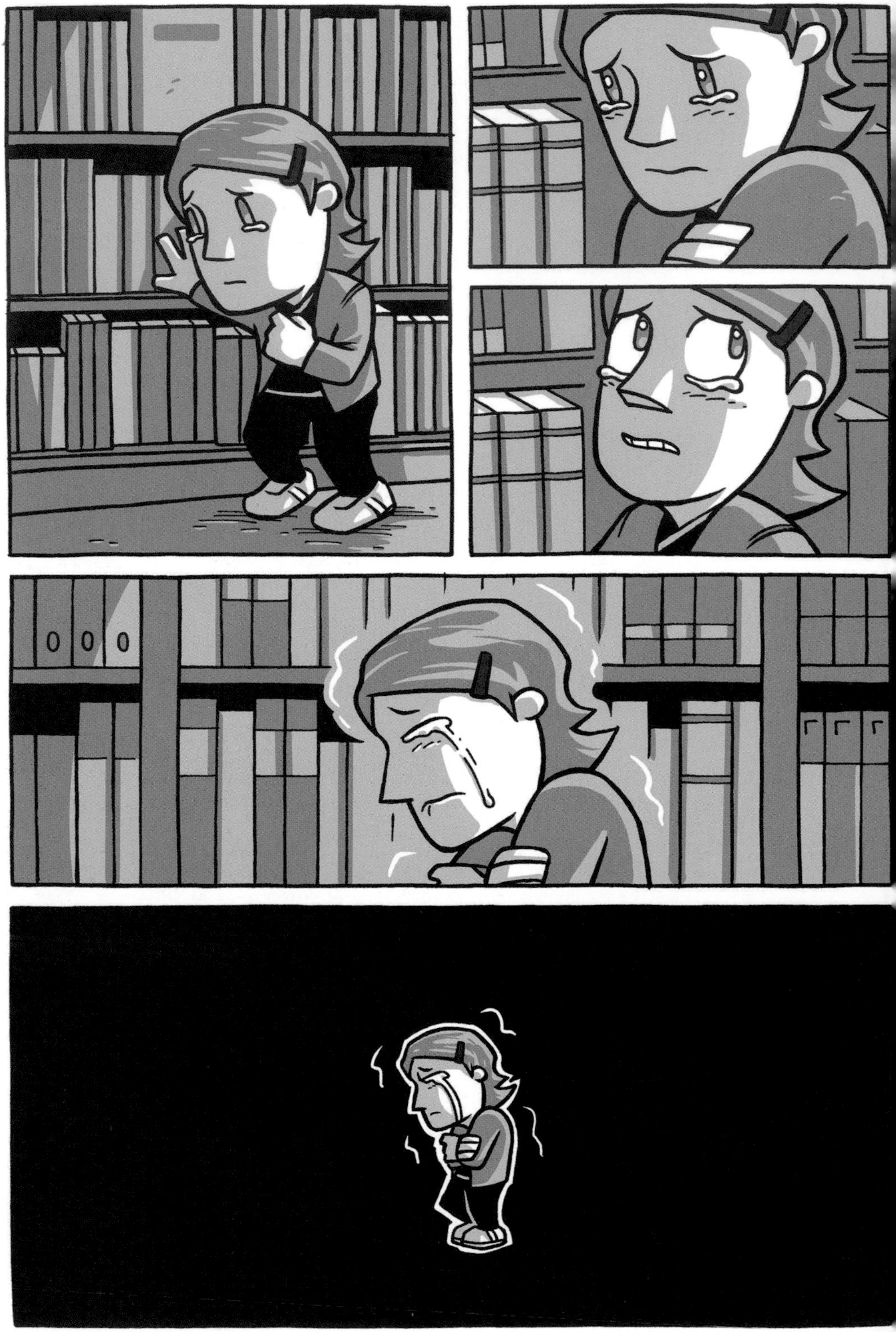

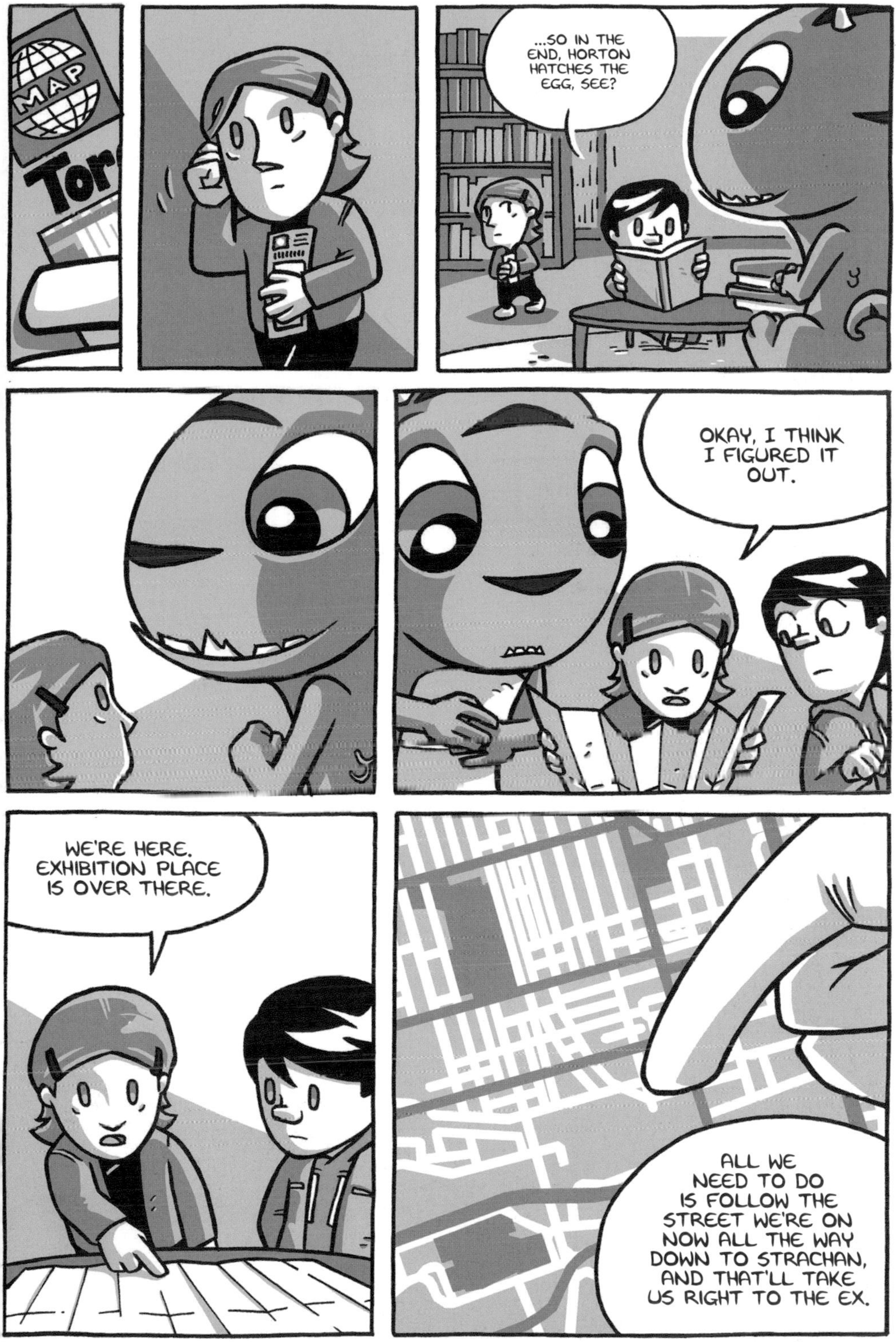
MAP
Tor
...SO IN THE END, HORTON HATCHES THE EGG, SEE?
OKAY, I THINK I FIGURED IT OUT.
WE'RE HERE. EXHIBITION PLACE IS OVER THERE.
ALL WE NEED TO DO IS FOLLOW THE STREET WE'RE ON NOW ALL THE WAY DOWN TO STRACHAN, AND THAT'LL TAKE US RIGHT TO THE EX.

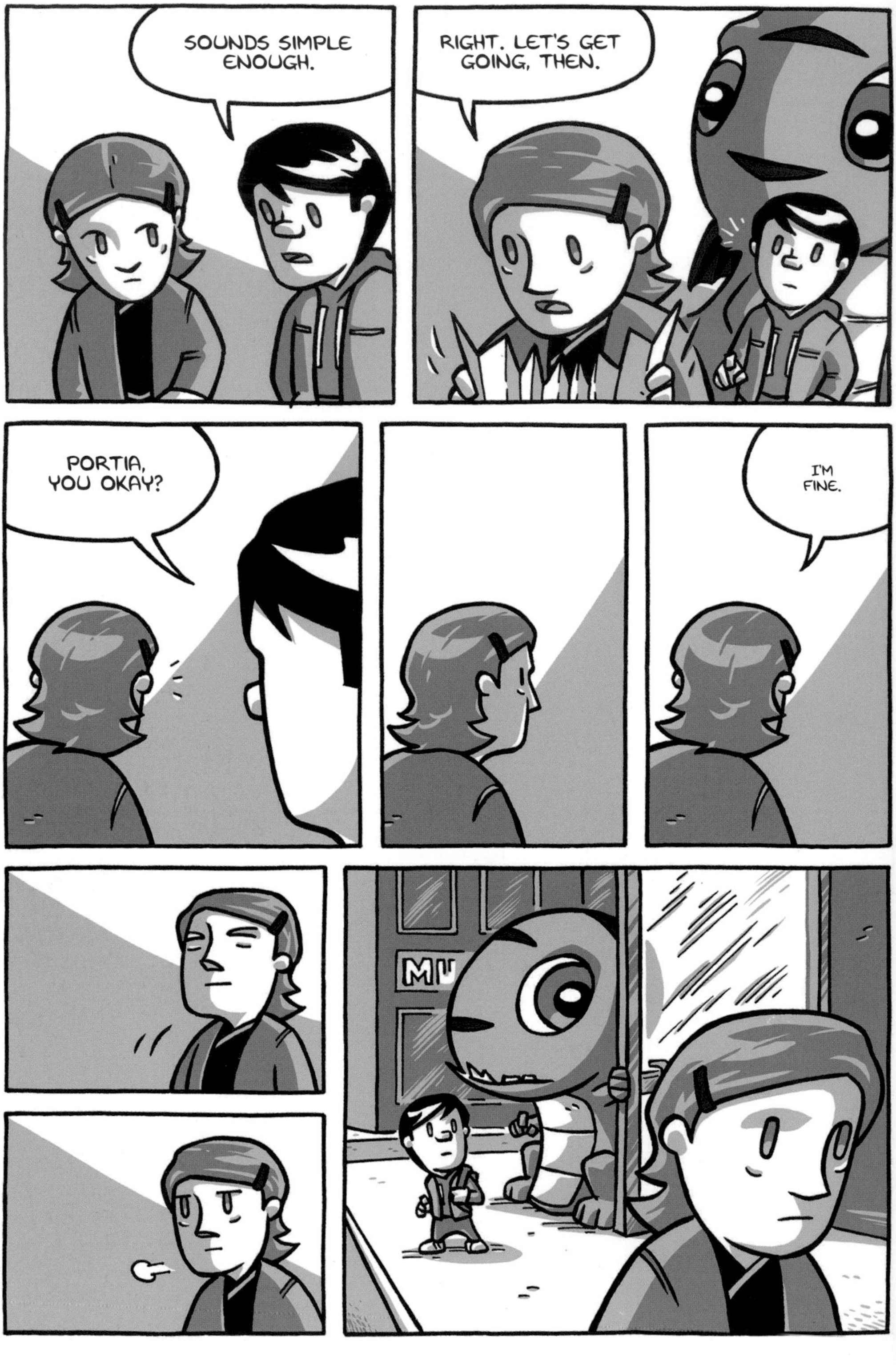
SOUNDS SIMPLE ENOUGH.
RIGHT. LET'S GET GOING, THEN.
PORTIA, YOU OKAY?
I'M FINE.
MU

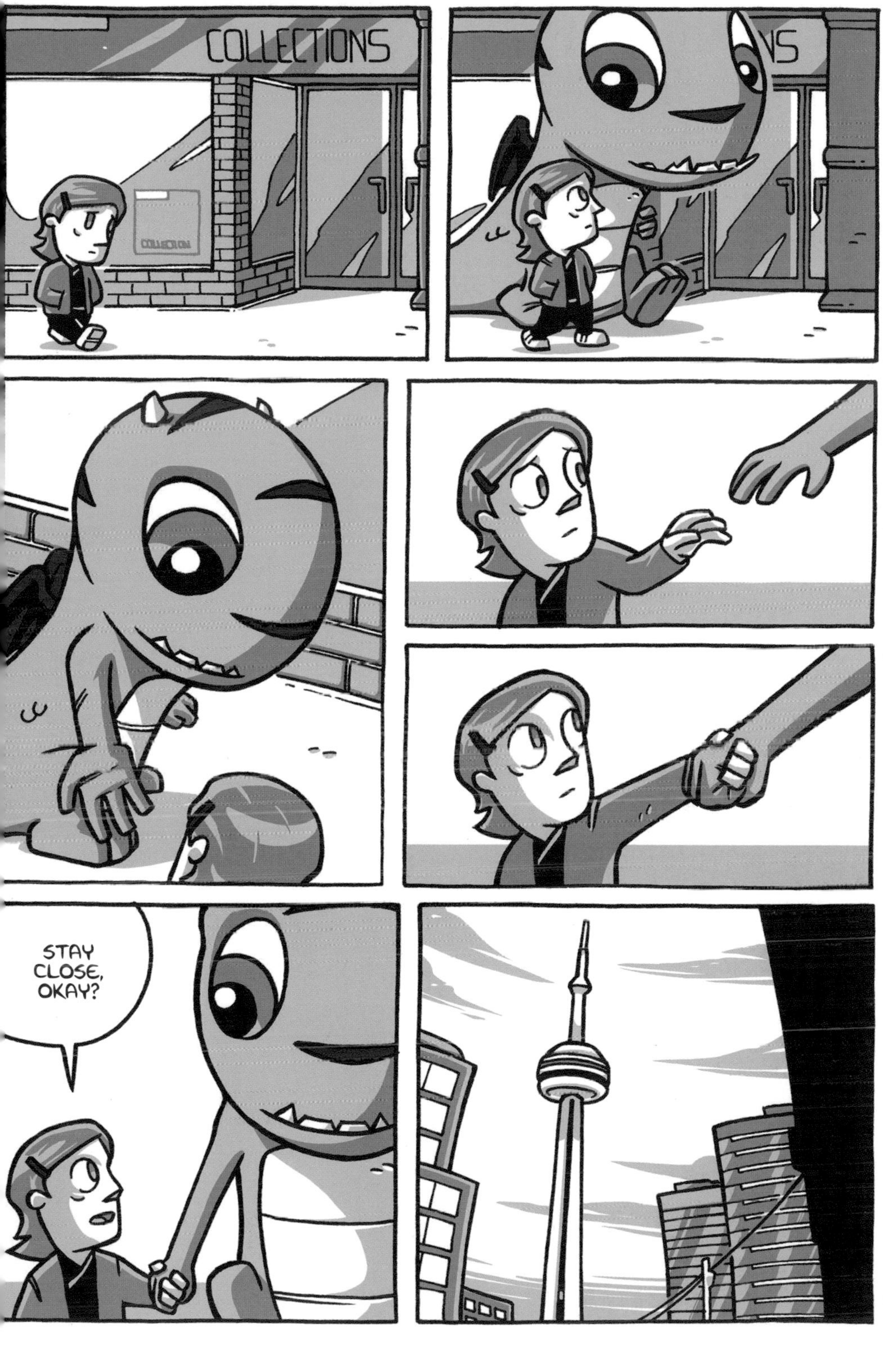
COLLECTIONS
COLLECTION
STAY CLOSE, OKAY?

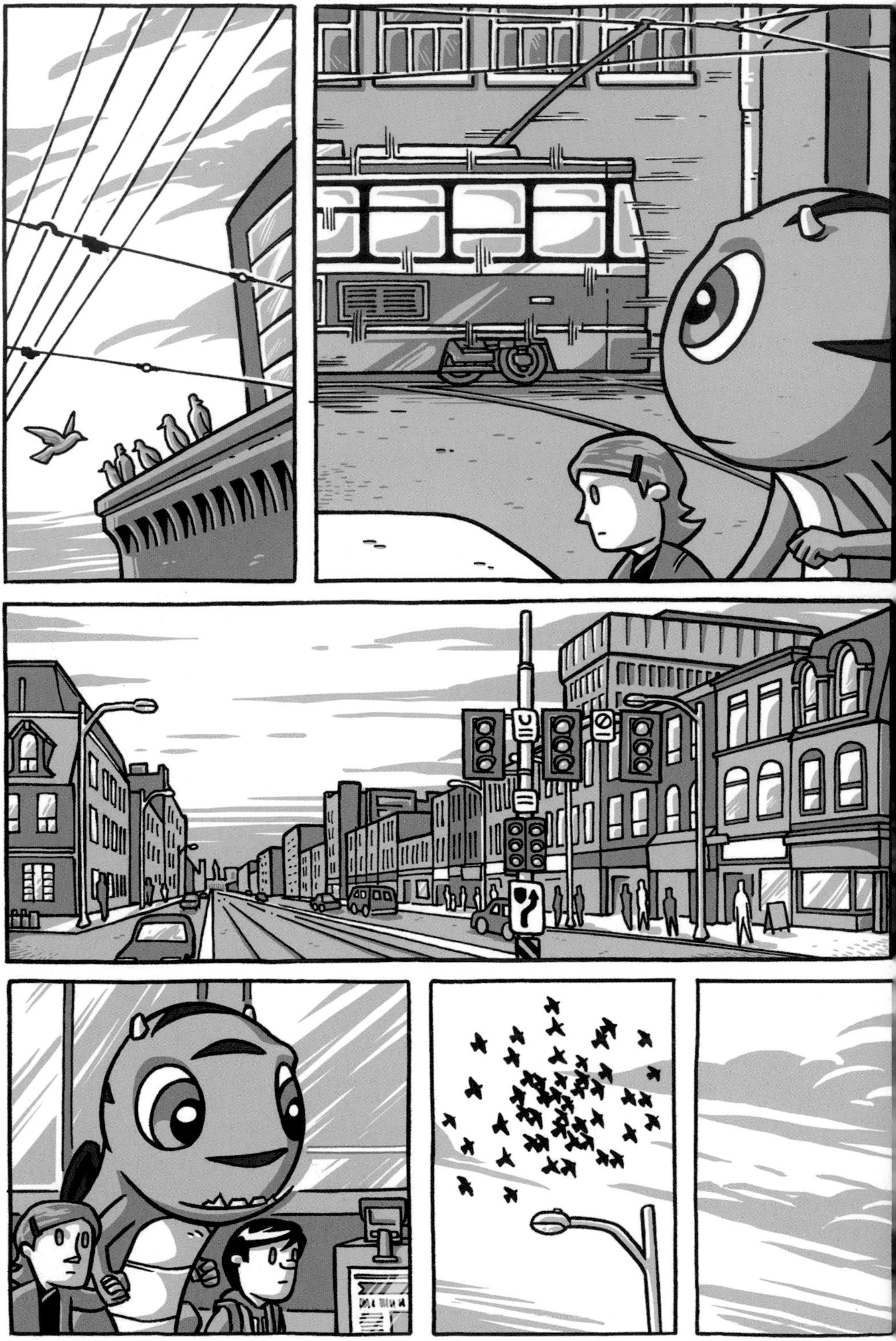

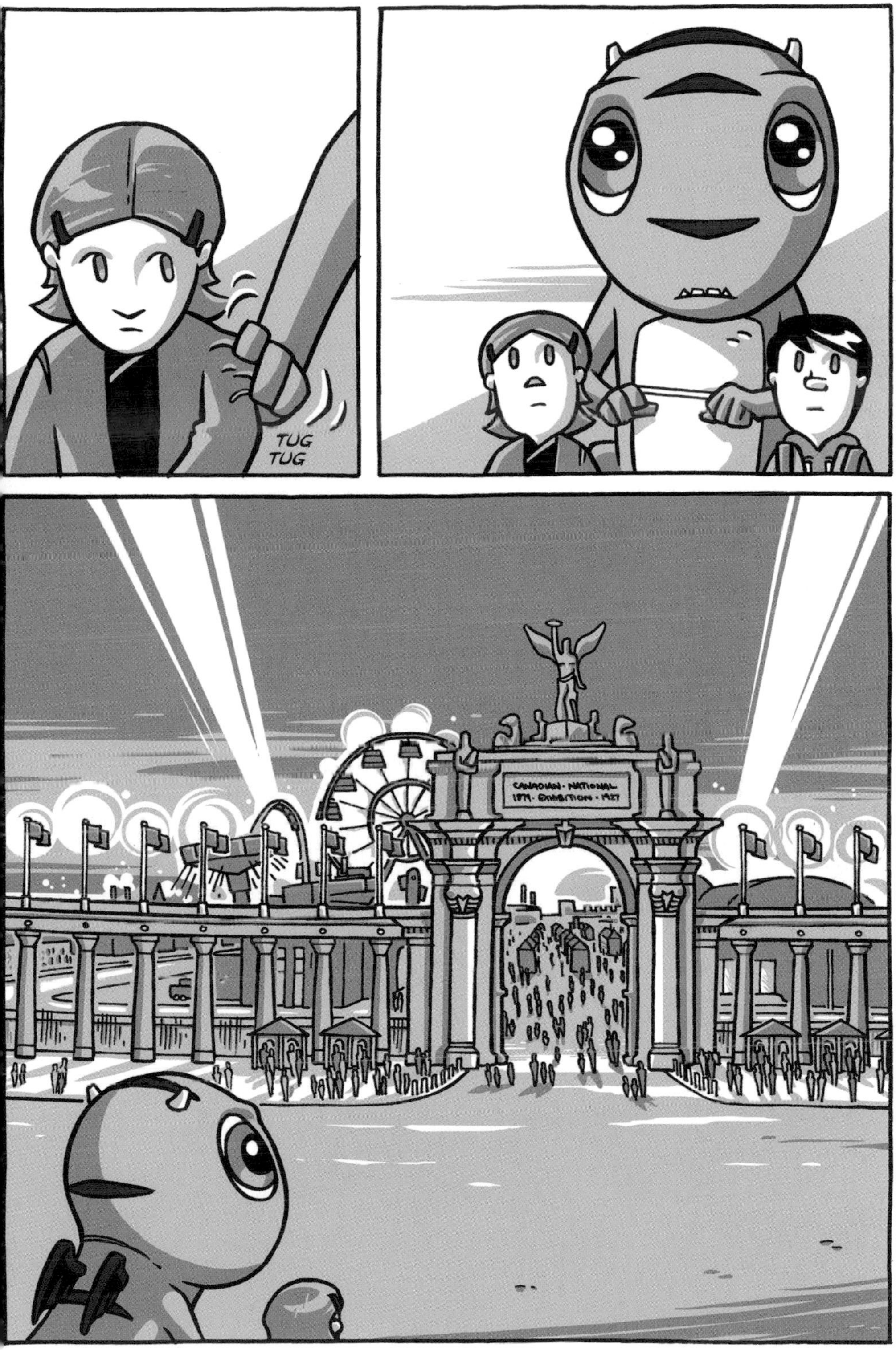
TUG
TUG
CANADIAN · NATIONAL
1879 · EXHIBITION · 1927

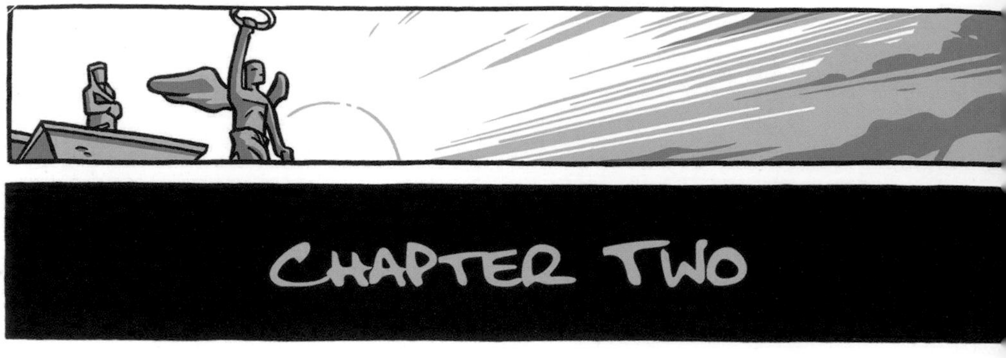

CHAPTER TWO

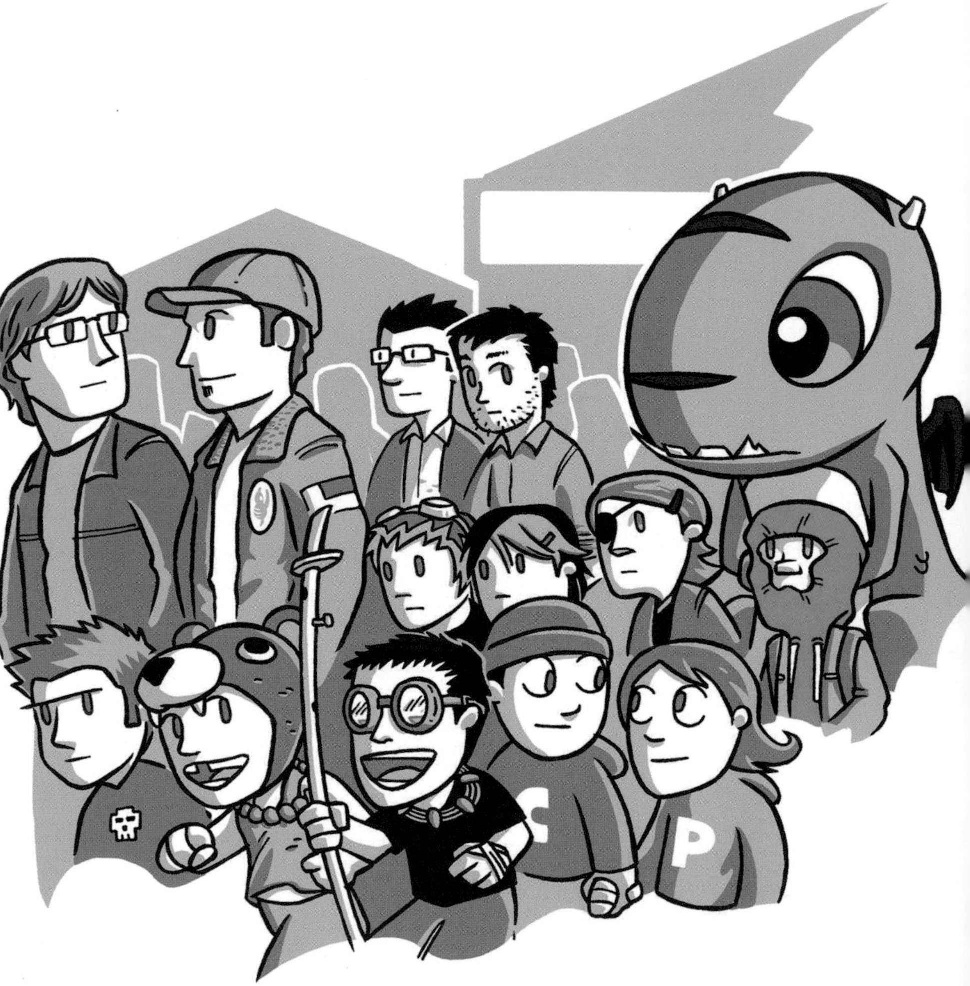
C
P

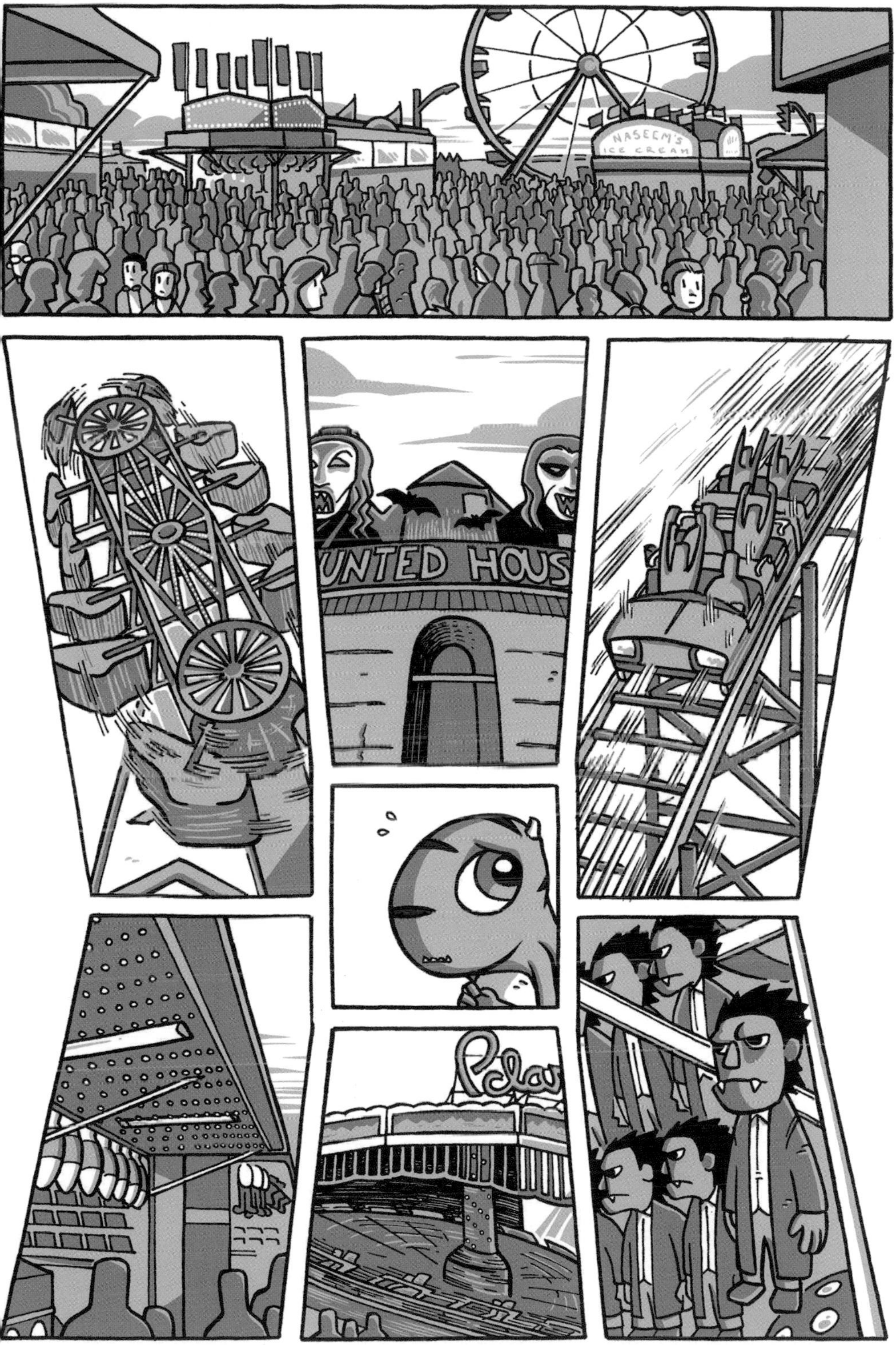
NASEEM'S
ICE CREAM
UNTED HOUS
Pcla

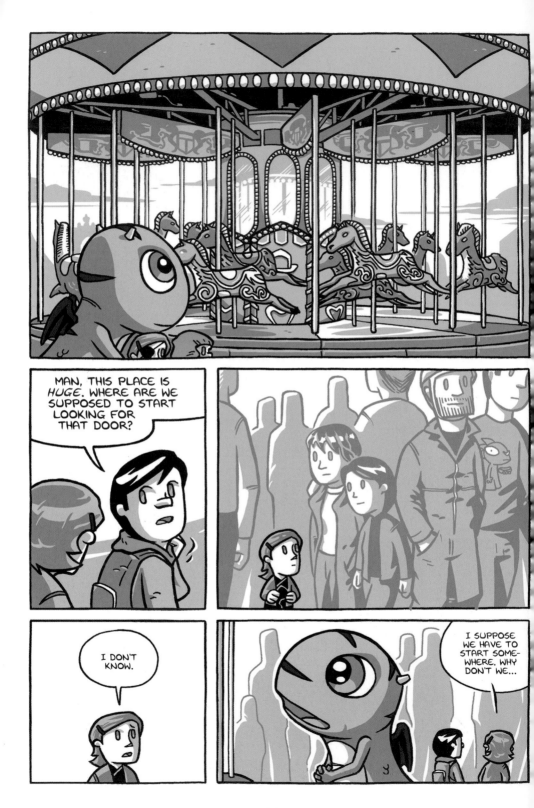

MAN, THIS PLACE IS *HUGE*. WHERE ARE WE SUPPOSED TO START LOOKING FOR THAT DOOR?

I DON'T KNOW.

I SUPPOSE WE HAVE TO START SOME-WHERE. WHY DON'T WE...

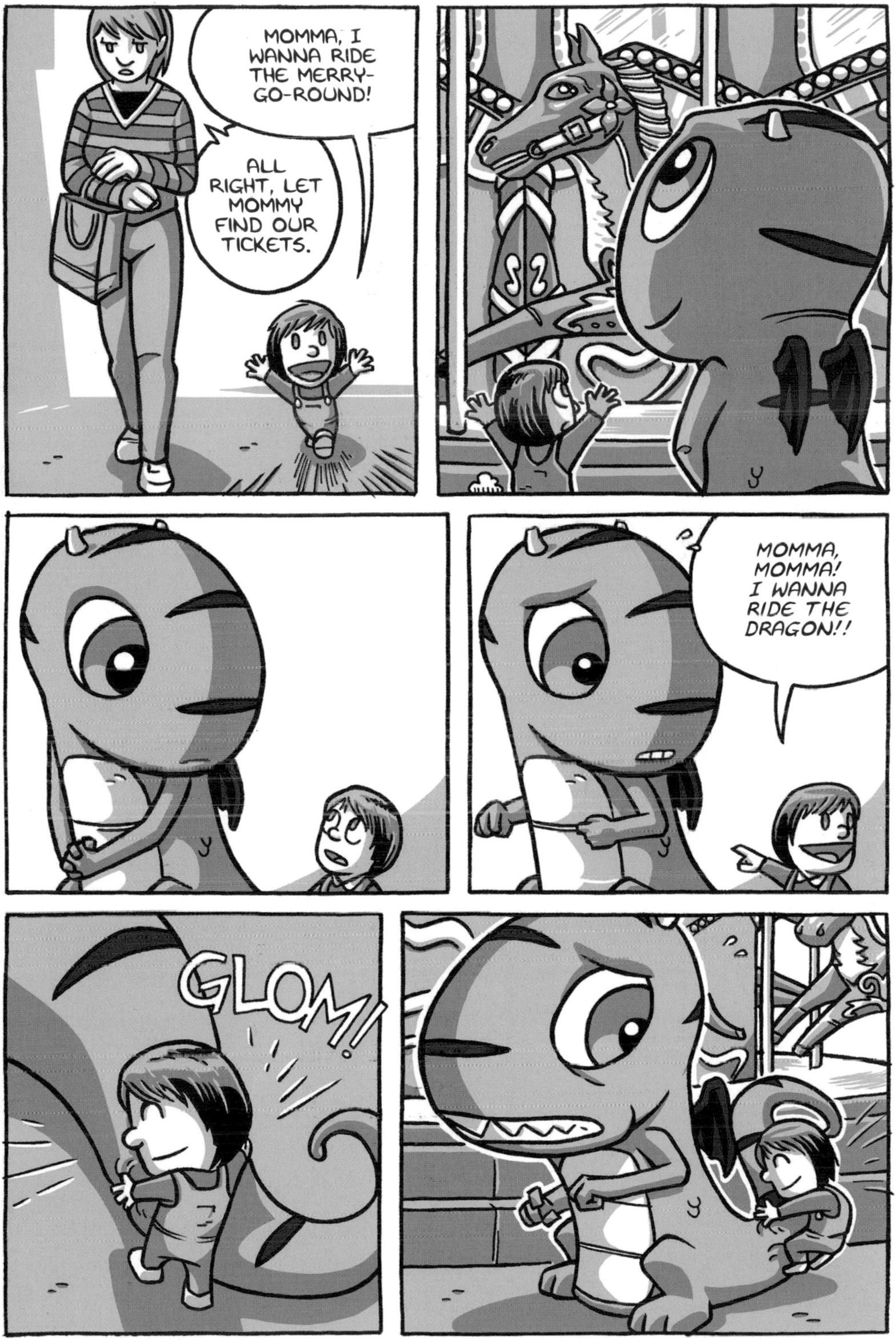
MOMMA, I WANNA RIDE THE MERRY-GO-ROUND!
ALL RIGHT, LET MOMMY FIND OUR TICKETS.
MOMMA, MOMMA! I WANNA RIDE THE DRAGON!!
GLOM!

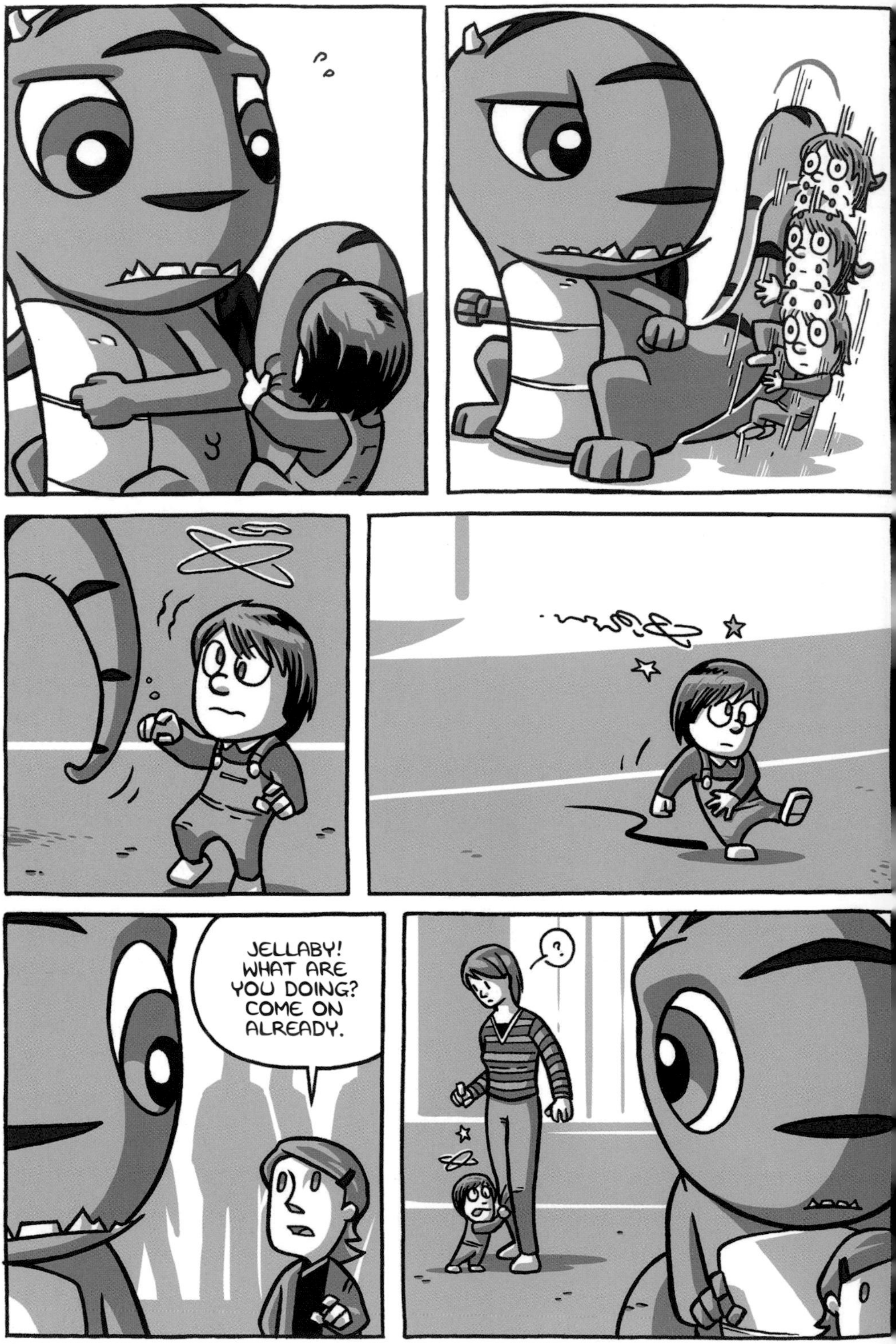
JELLABY! WHAT ARE YOU DOING? COME ON ALREADY.

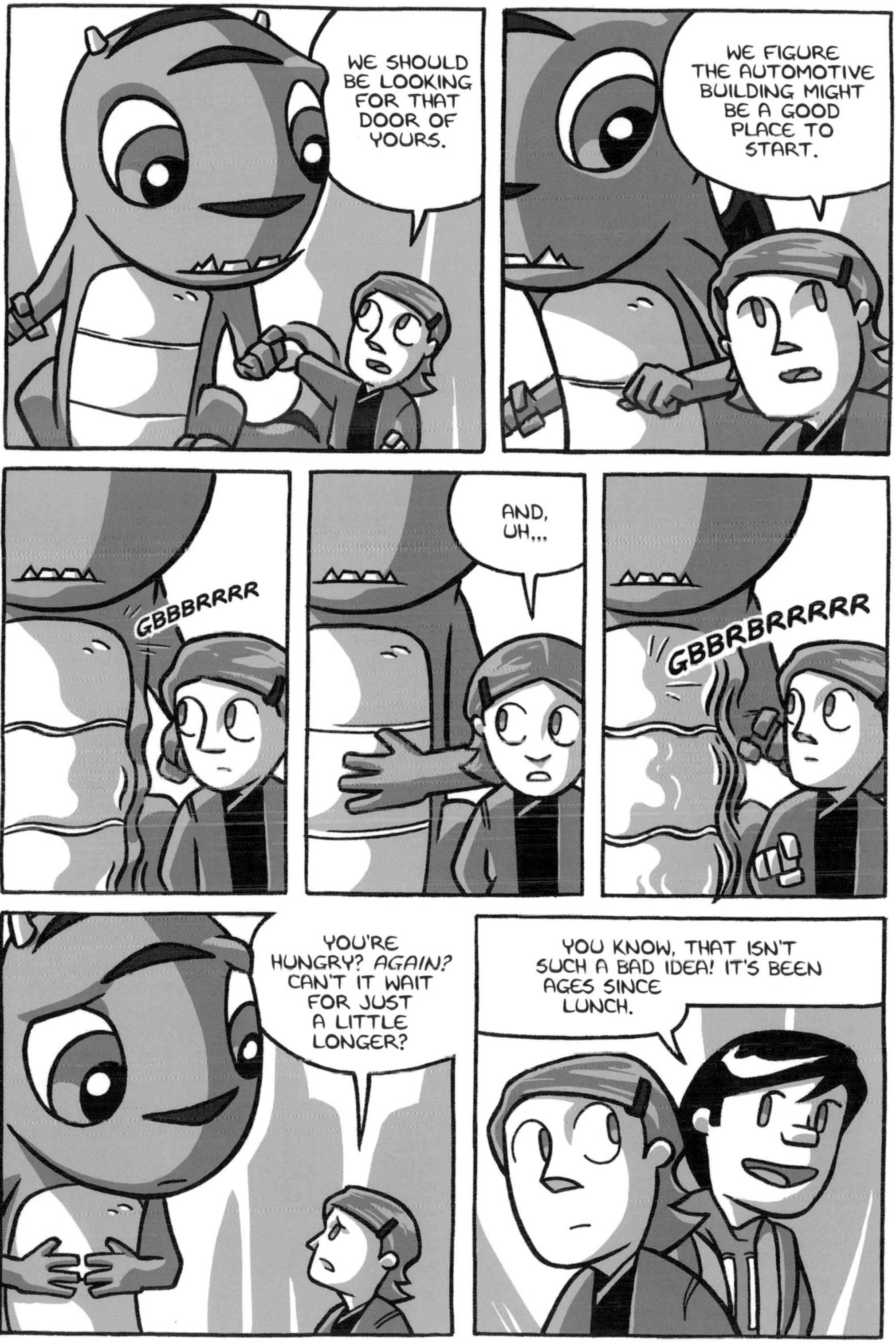
WE SHOULD BE LOOKING FOR THAT DOOR OF YOURS.
WE FIGURE THE AUTOMOTIVE BUILDING MIGHT BE A GOOD PLACE TO START.
GBBBRRRR
AND, UH...
GBBRBRRRRR
YOU'RE HUNGRY? *AGAIN?* CAN'T IT WAIT FOR JUST A LITTLE LONGER?
YOU KNOW, THAT ISN'T SUCH A BAD IDEA! IT'S BEEN AGES SINCE LUNCH.

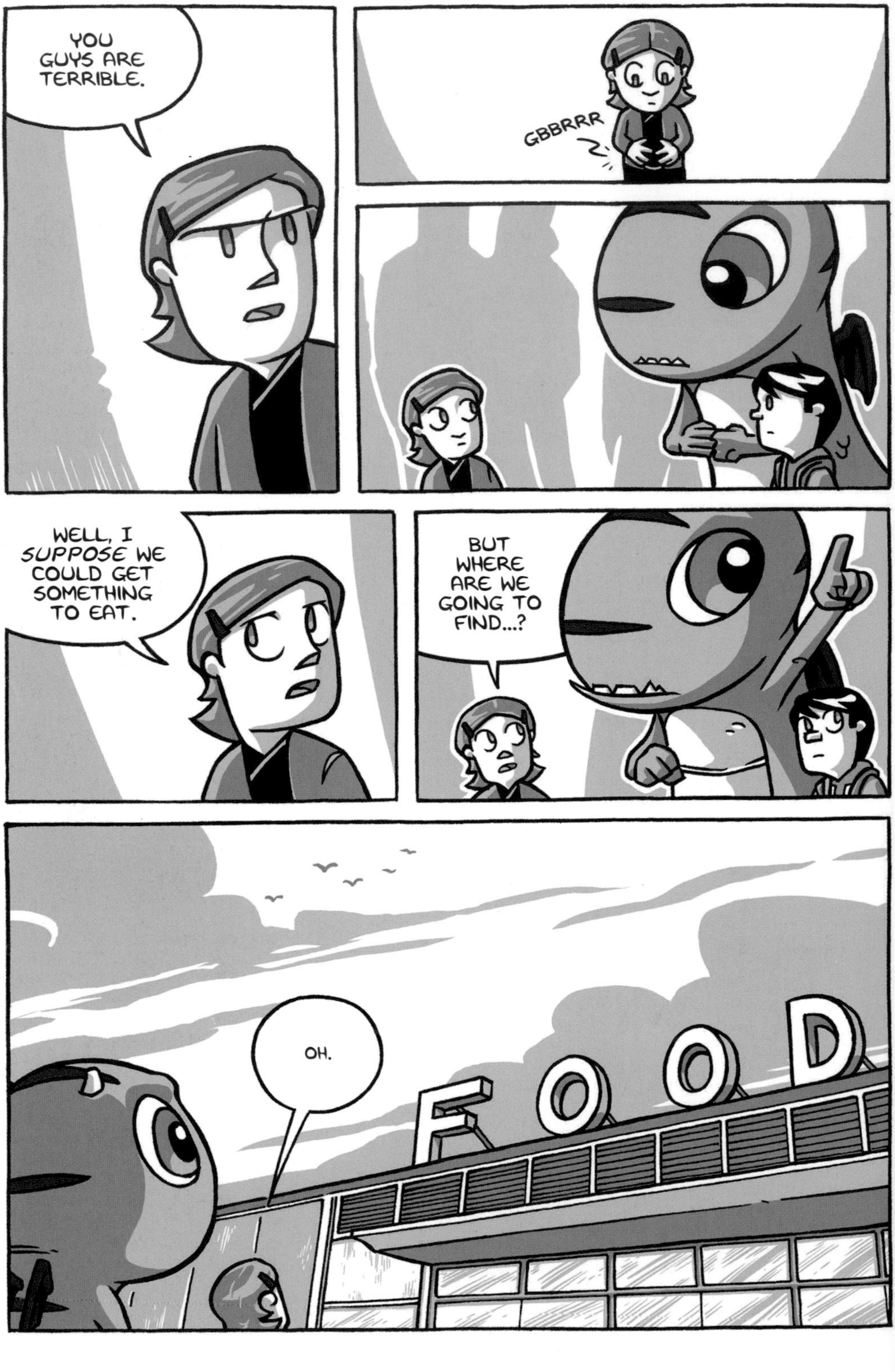
YOU GUYS ARE TERRIBLE.
GBBRRR
WELL, I SUPPOSE WE COULD GET SOMETHING TO EAT.
BUT WHERE ARE WE GOING TO FIND...?
OH.
FOOD

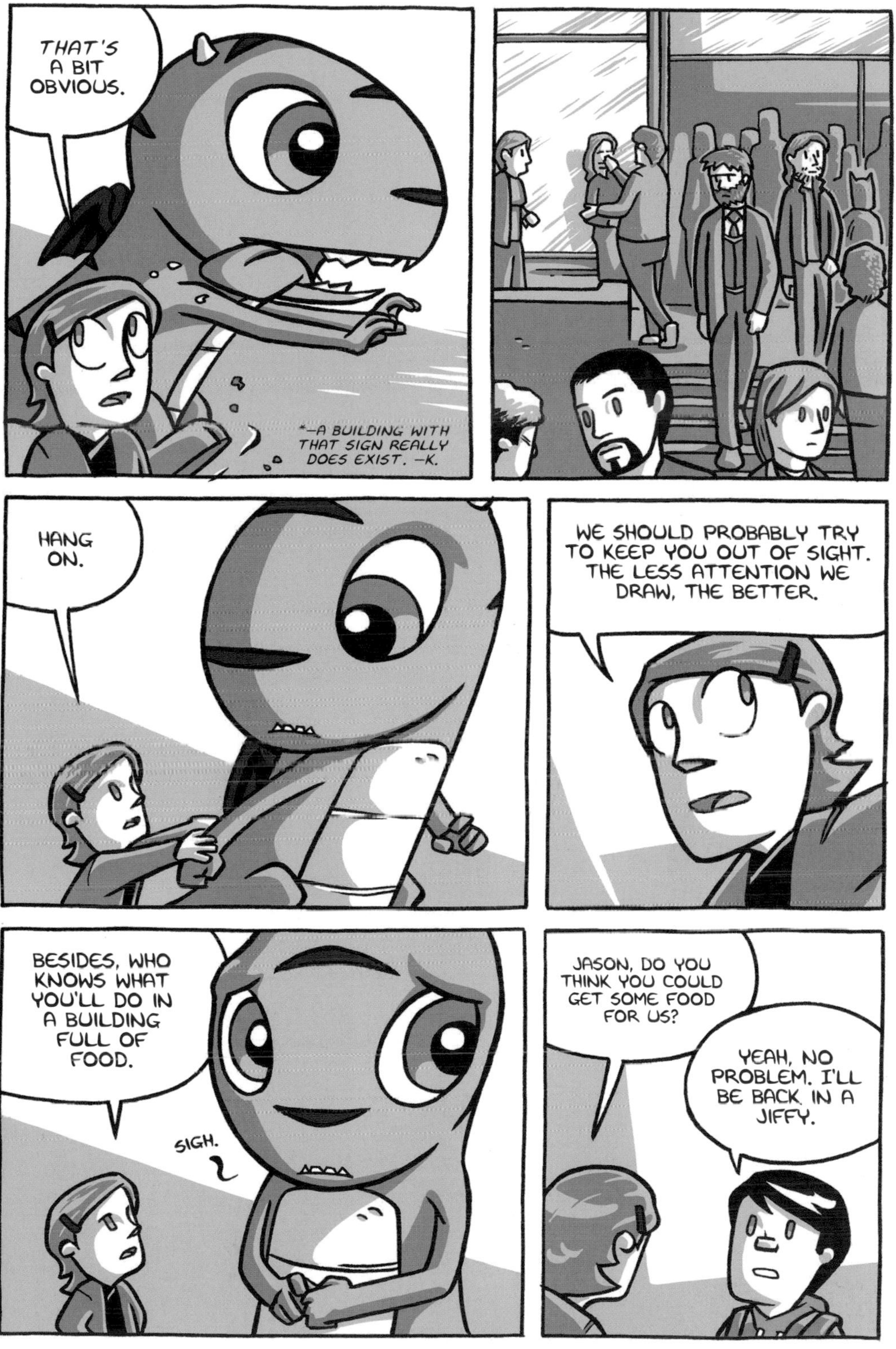
THAT'S A BIT OBVIOUS.
*—A BUILDING WITH THAT SIGN REALLY DOES EXIST. —K.
HANG ON.
WE SHOULD PROBABLY TRY TO KEEP YOU OUT OF SIGHT. THE LESS ATTENTION WE DRAW, THE BETTER.
BESIDES, WHO KNOWS WHAT YOU'LL DO IN A BUILDING FULL OF FOOD.
SIGH.
JASON, DO YOU THINK YOU COULD GET SOME FOOD FOR US?
YEAH, NO PROBLEM. I'LL BE BACK IN A JIFFY.

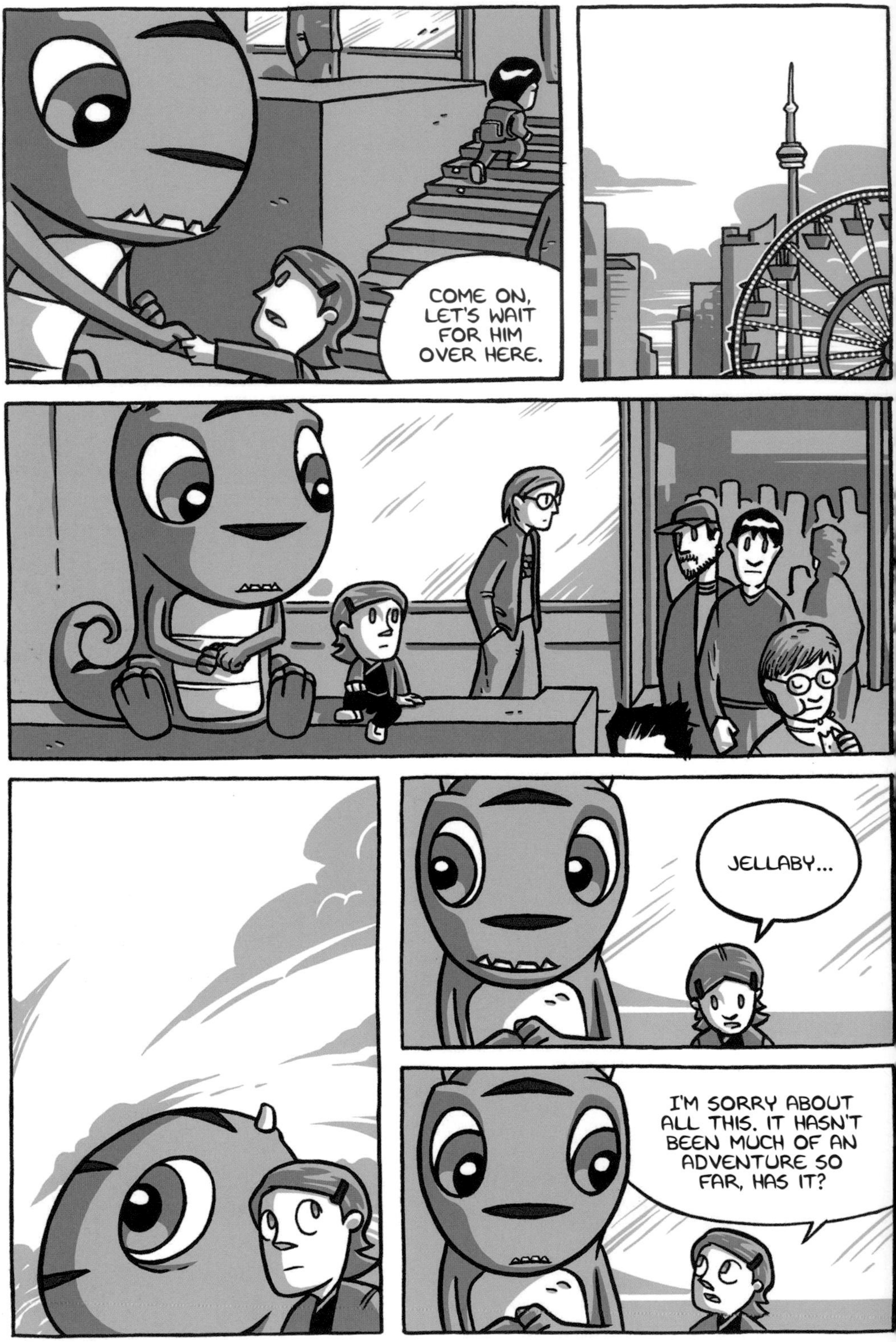
COME ON, LET'S WAIT FOR HIM OVER HERE.
JELLABY...
I'M SORRY ABOUT ALL THIS. IT HASN'T BEEN MUCH OF AN ADVENTURE SO FAR, HAS IT?

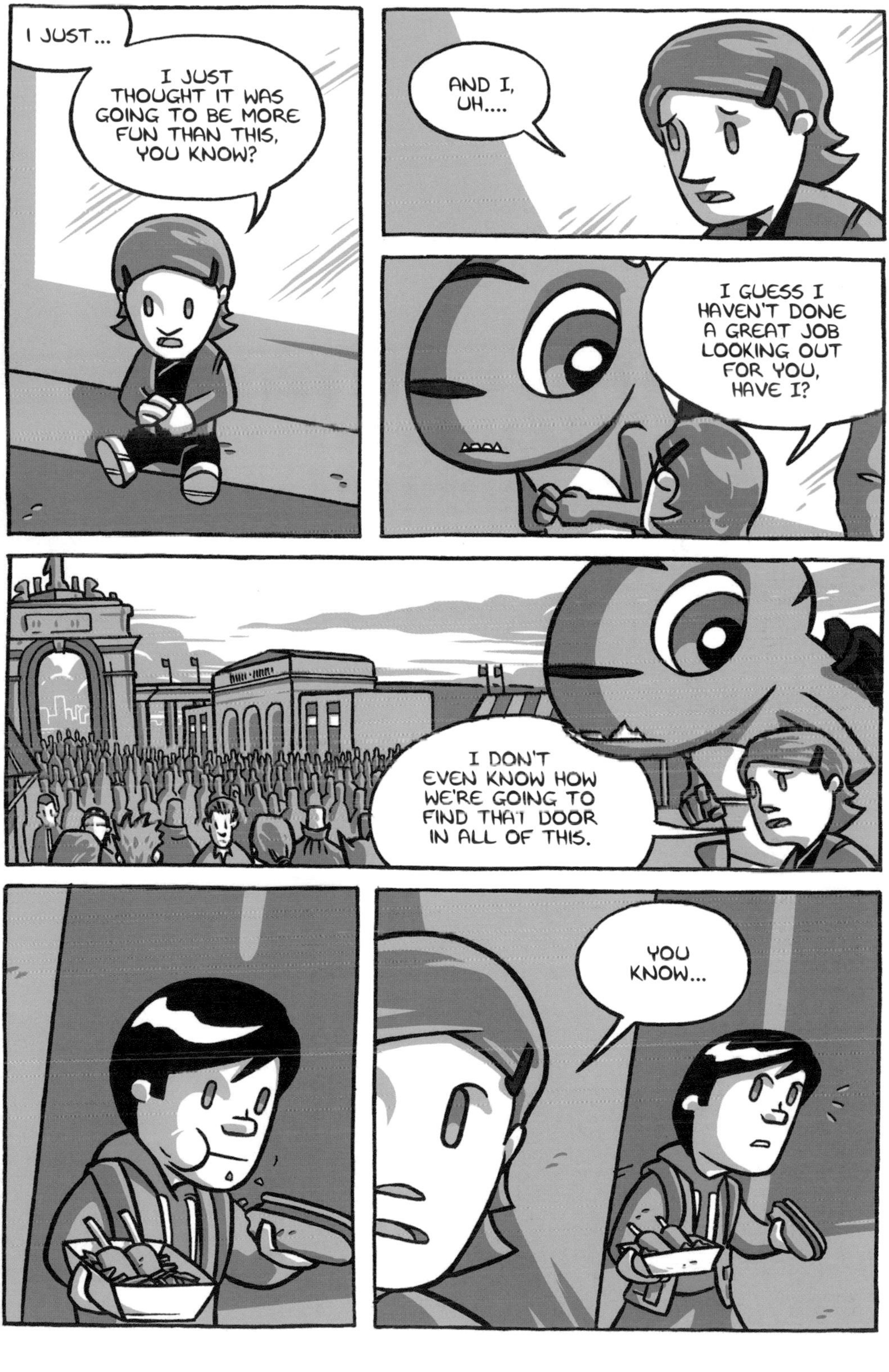
I JUST...
I JUST THOUGHT IT WAS GOING TO BE MORE FUN THAN THIS, YOU KNOW?
AND I, UH....
I GUESS I HAVEN'T DONE A GREAT JOB LOOKING OUT FOR YOU, HAVE I?
I DON'T EVEN KNOW HOW WE'RE GOING TO FIND THAT DOOR IN ALL OF THIS.
YOU KNOW...

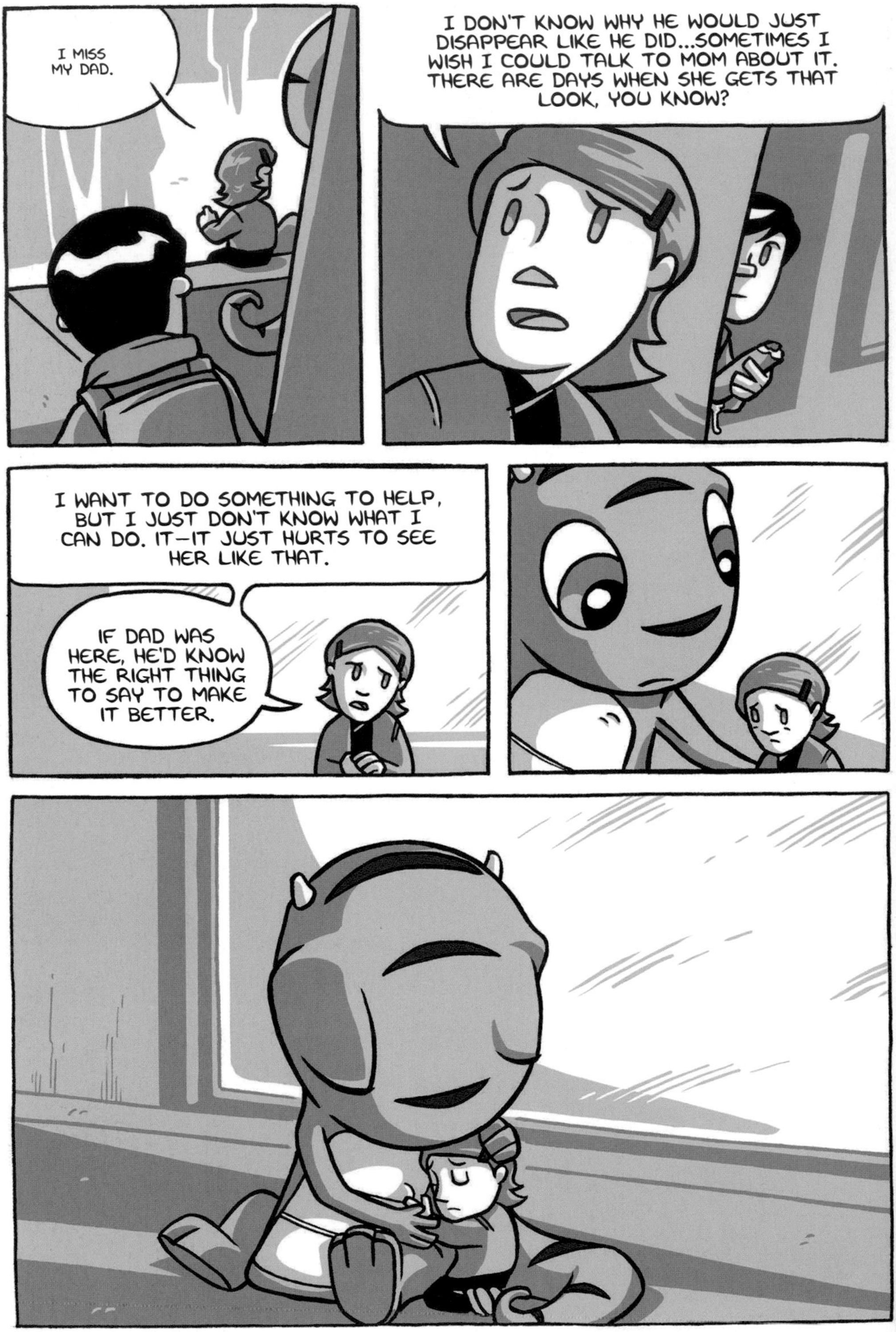
I MISS MY DAD.
I DON'T KNOW WHY HE WOULD JUST DISAPPEAR LIKE HE DID...SOMETIMES I WISH I COULD TALK TO MOM ABOUT IT. THERE ARE DAYS WHEN SHE GETS THAT LOOK, YOU KNOW?
I WANT TO DO SOMETHING TO HELP, BUT I JUST DON'T KNOW WHAT I CAN DO. IT—IT JUST HURTS TO SEE HER LIKE THAT.
IF DAD WAS HERE, HE'D KNOW THE RIGHT THING TO SAY TO MAKE IT BETTER.

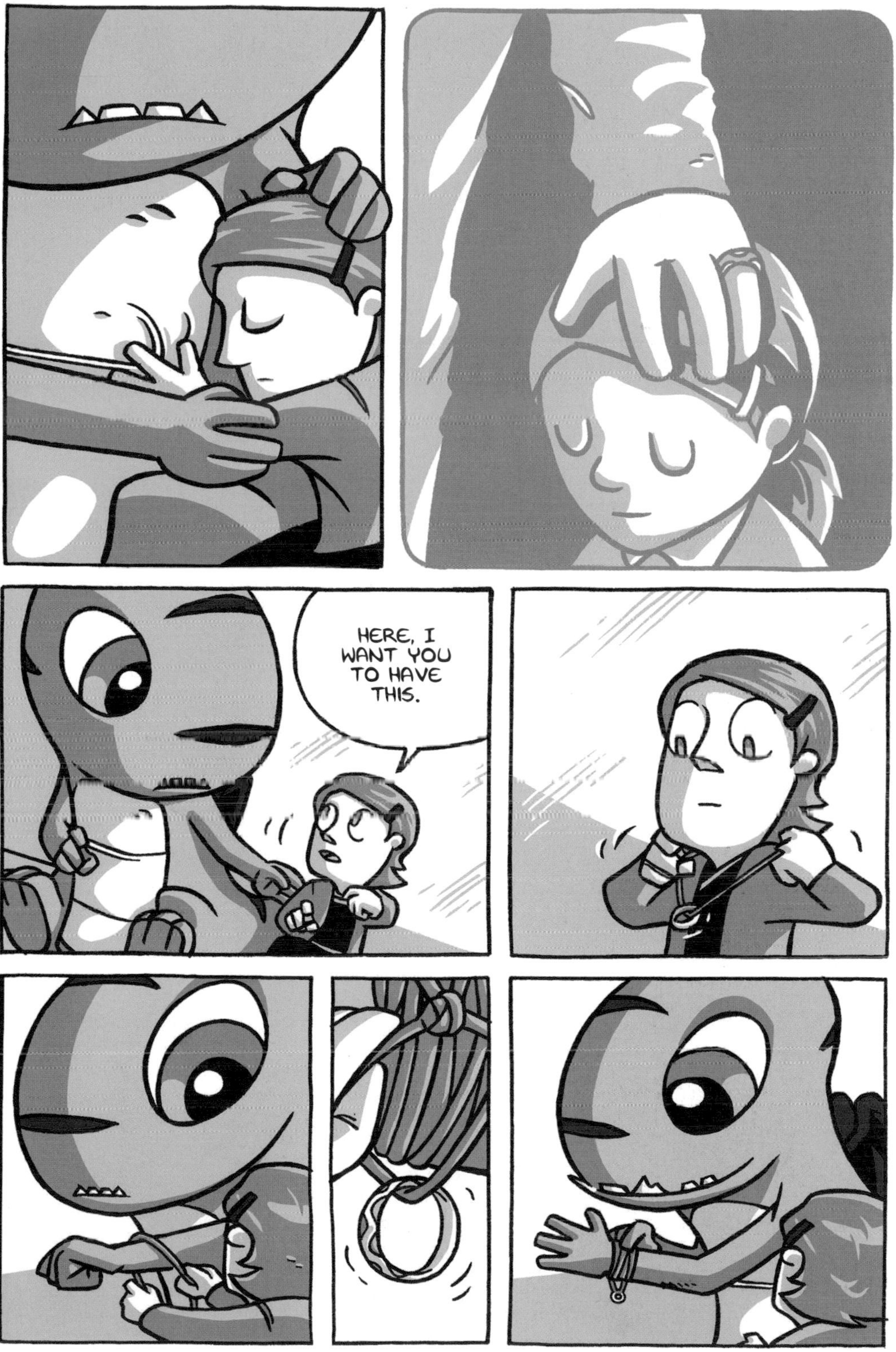
HERE, I WANT YOU TO HAVE THIS.

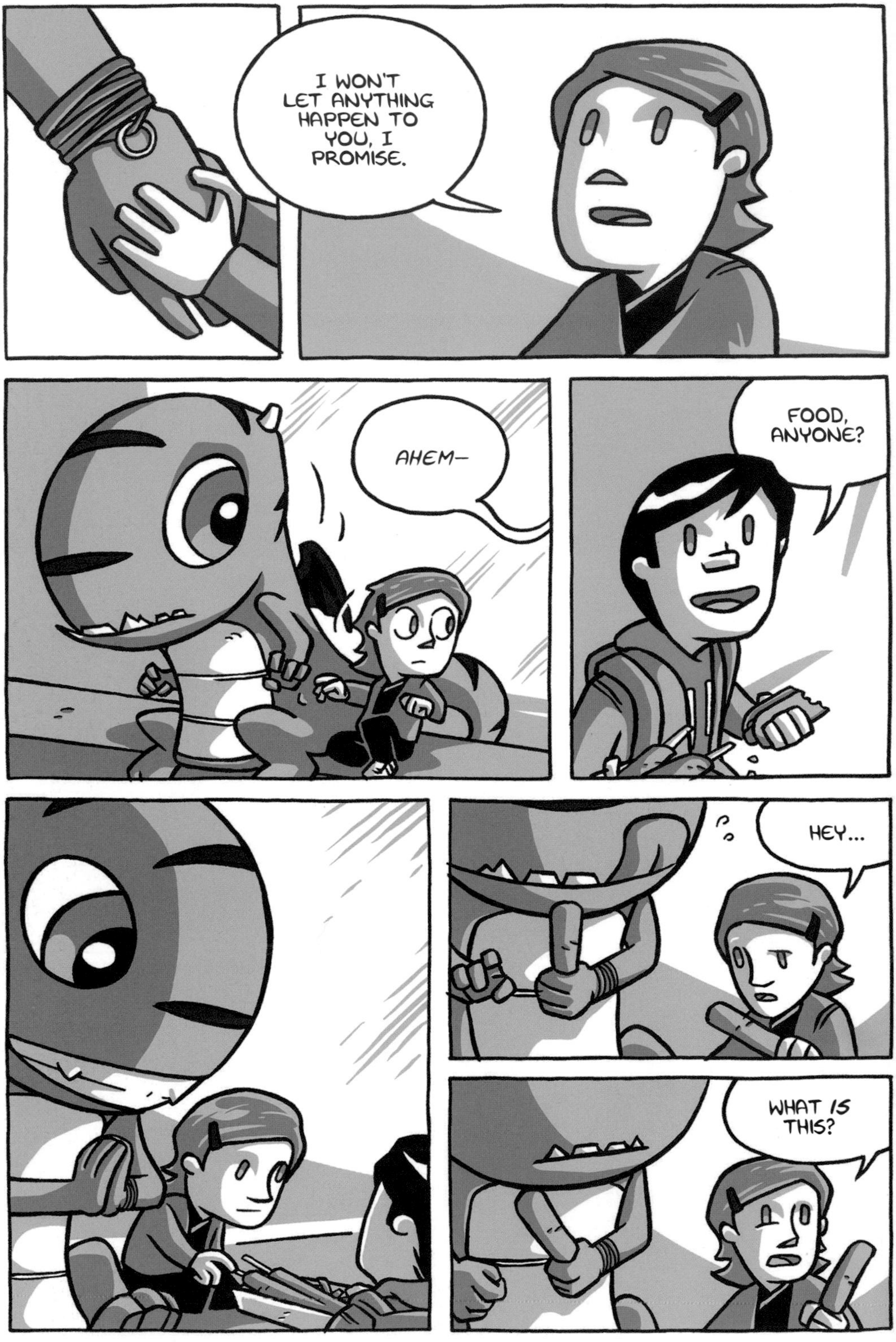
I WON'T LET ANYTHING HAPPEN TO YOU, I PROMISE.
AHEM–
FOOD, ANYONE?
HEY...
WHAT *IS* THIS?

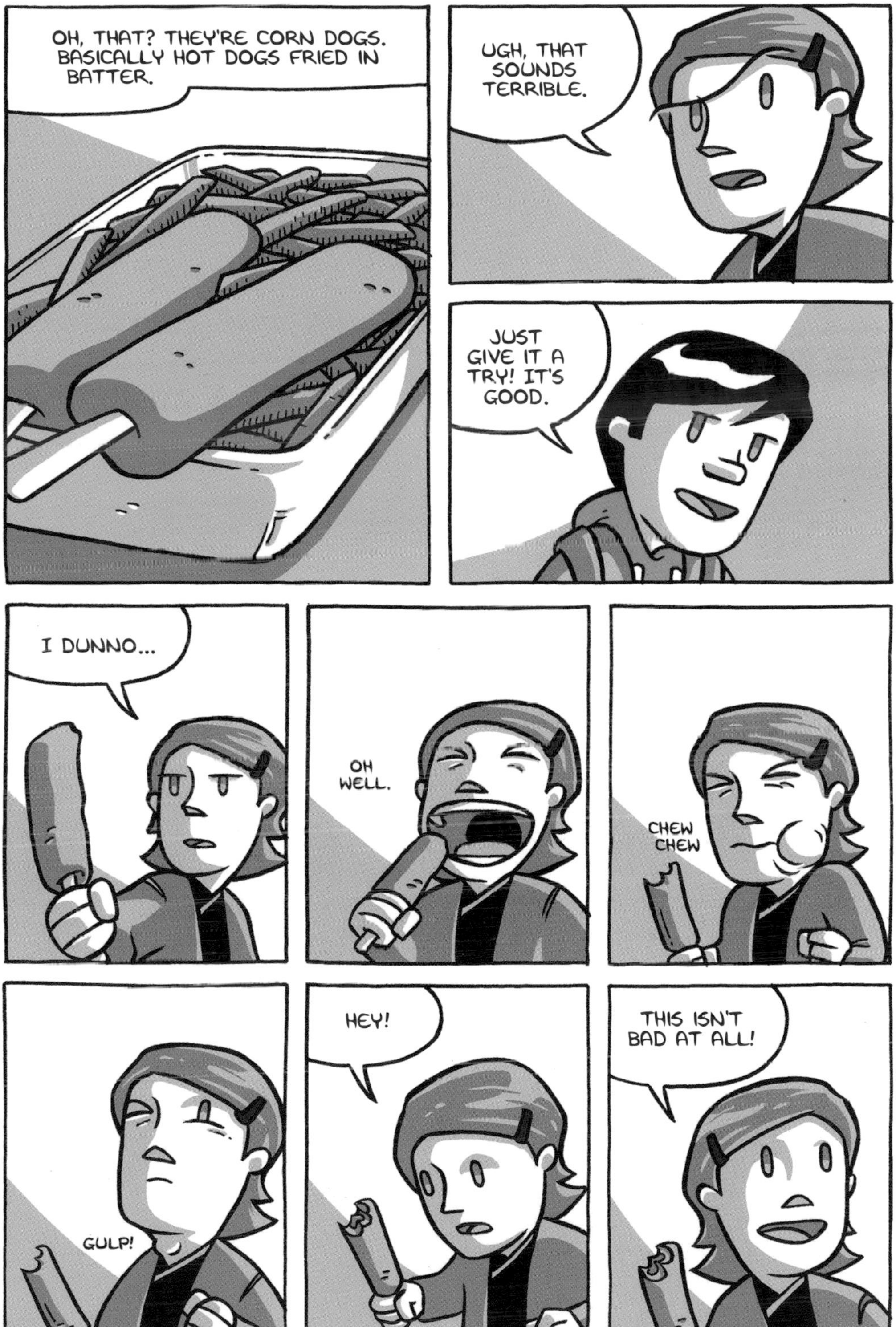
OH, THAT? THEY'RE CORN DOGS. BASICALLY HOT DOGS FRIED IN BATTER.
UGH, THAT SOUNDS TERRIBLE.
JUST GIVE IT A TRY! IT'S GOOD.
I DUNNO...
OH WELL.
CHEW CHEW
GULP!
HEY!
THIS ISN'T BAD AT ALL!

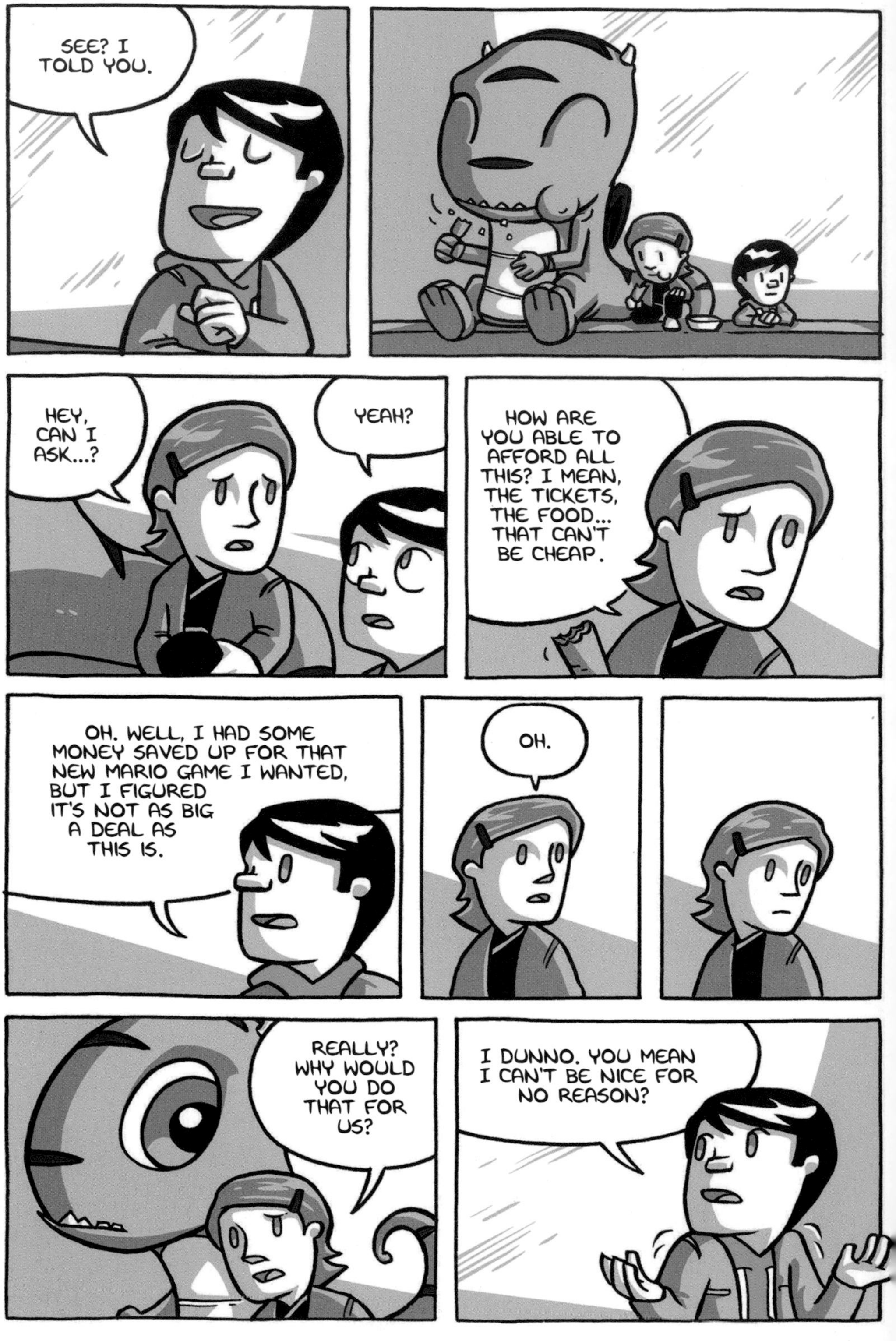
SEE? I TOLD YOU.
HEY, CAN I ASK...?
YEAH?
HOW ARE YOU ABLE TO AFFORD ALL THIS? I MEAN, THE TICKETS, THE FOOD... THAT CAN'T BE CHEAP.
OH. WELL, I HAD SOME MONEY SAVED UP FOR THAT NEW MARIO GAME I WANTED, BUT I FIGURED IT'S NOT AS BIG A DEAL AS THIS IS.
OH.
REALLY? WHY WOULD YOU DO THAT FOR US?
I DUNNO. YOU MEAN I CAN'T BE NICE FOR NO REASON?

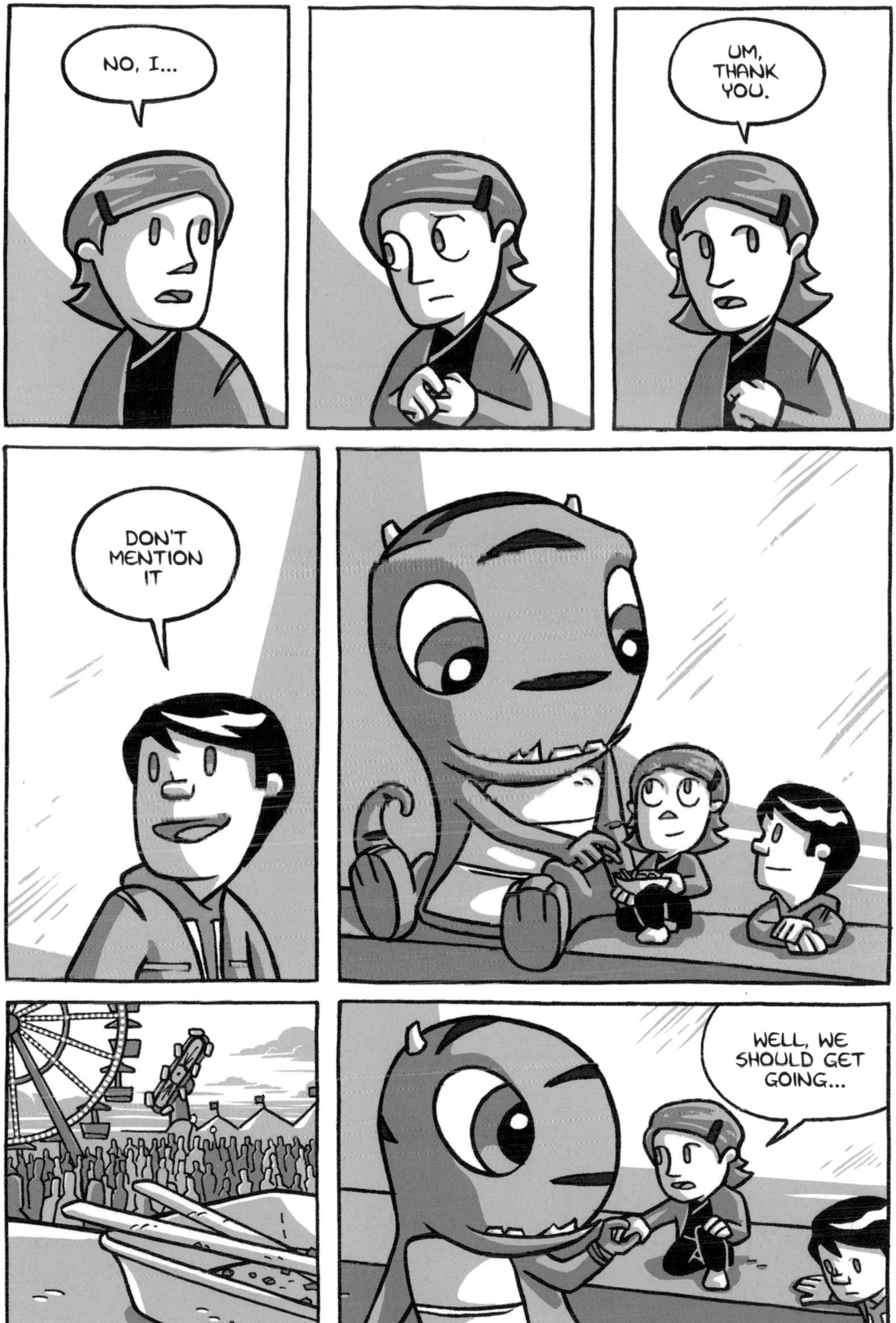
NO, I...
UM, THANK YOU.
DON'T MENTION IT
WELL, WE SHOULD GET GOING...

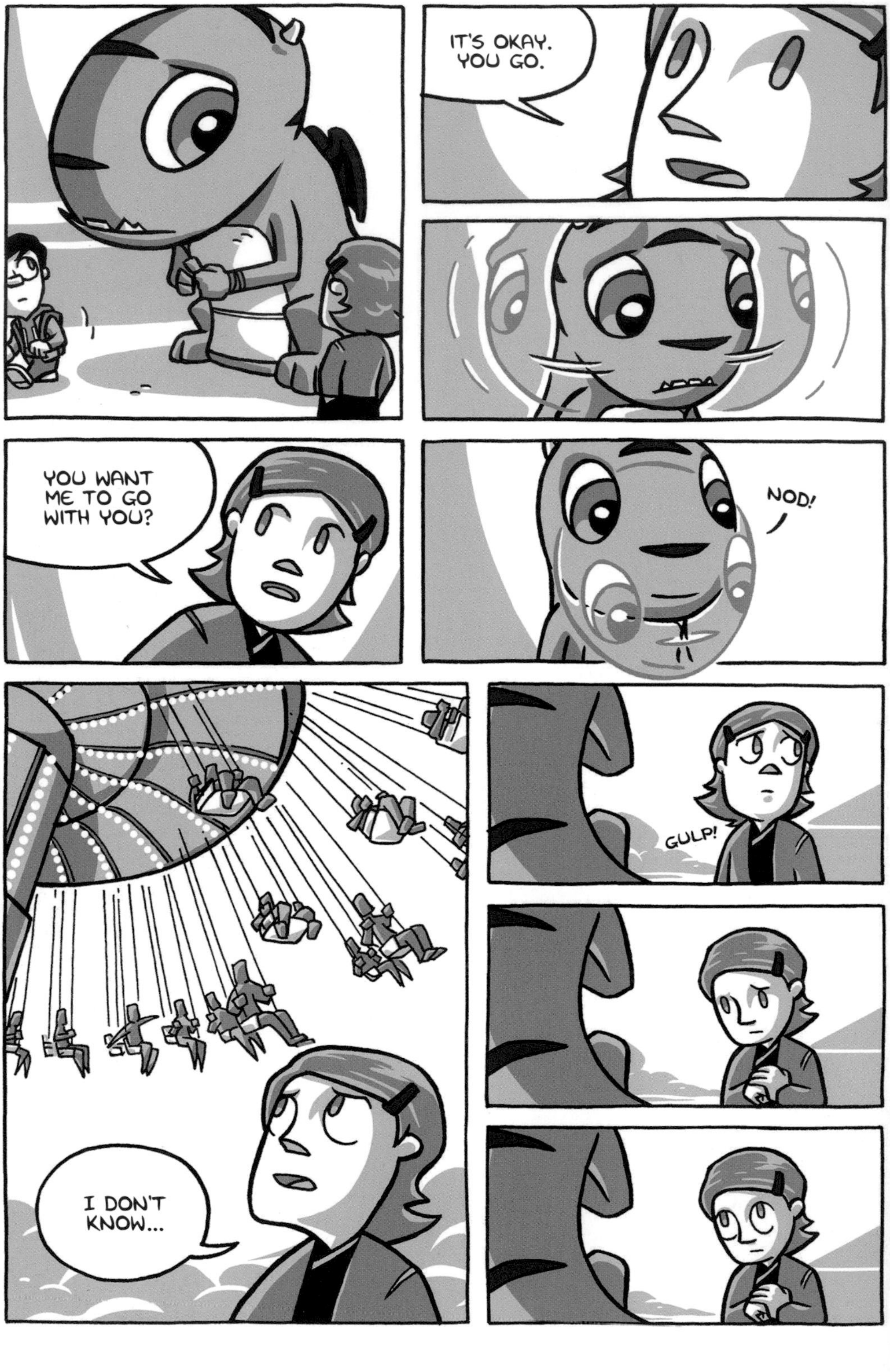
IT'S OKAY. YOU GO.
YOU WANT ME TO GO WITH YOU?
NOD!
I DON'T KNOW...
GULP!

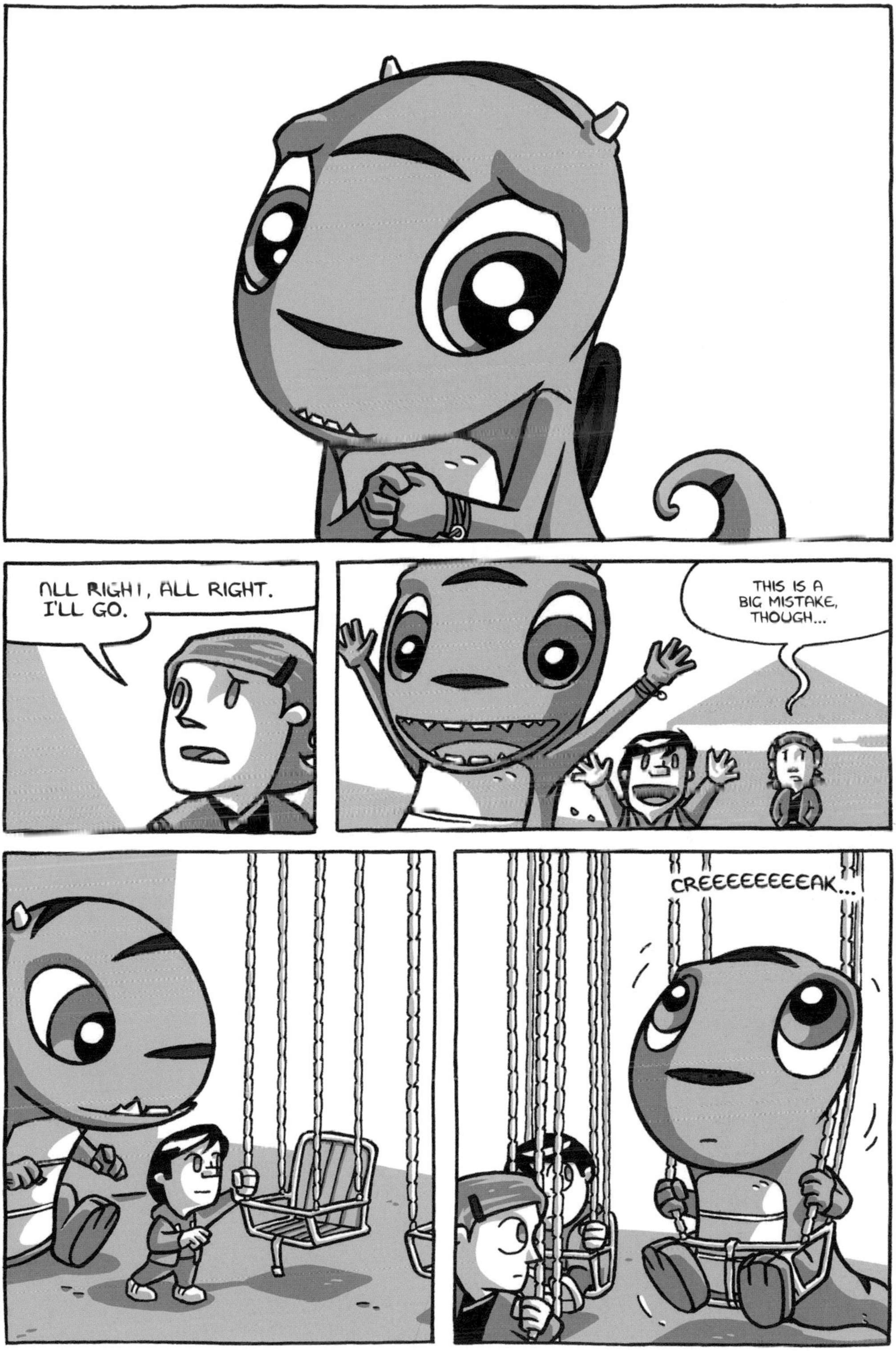

ALL RIGHT, ALL RIGHT. I'LL GO.
THIS IS A BIG MISTAKE, THOUGH...
CREEEEEEEEAK...

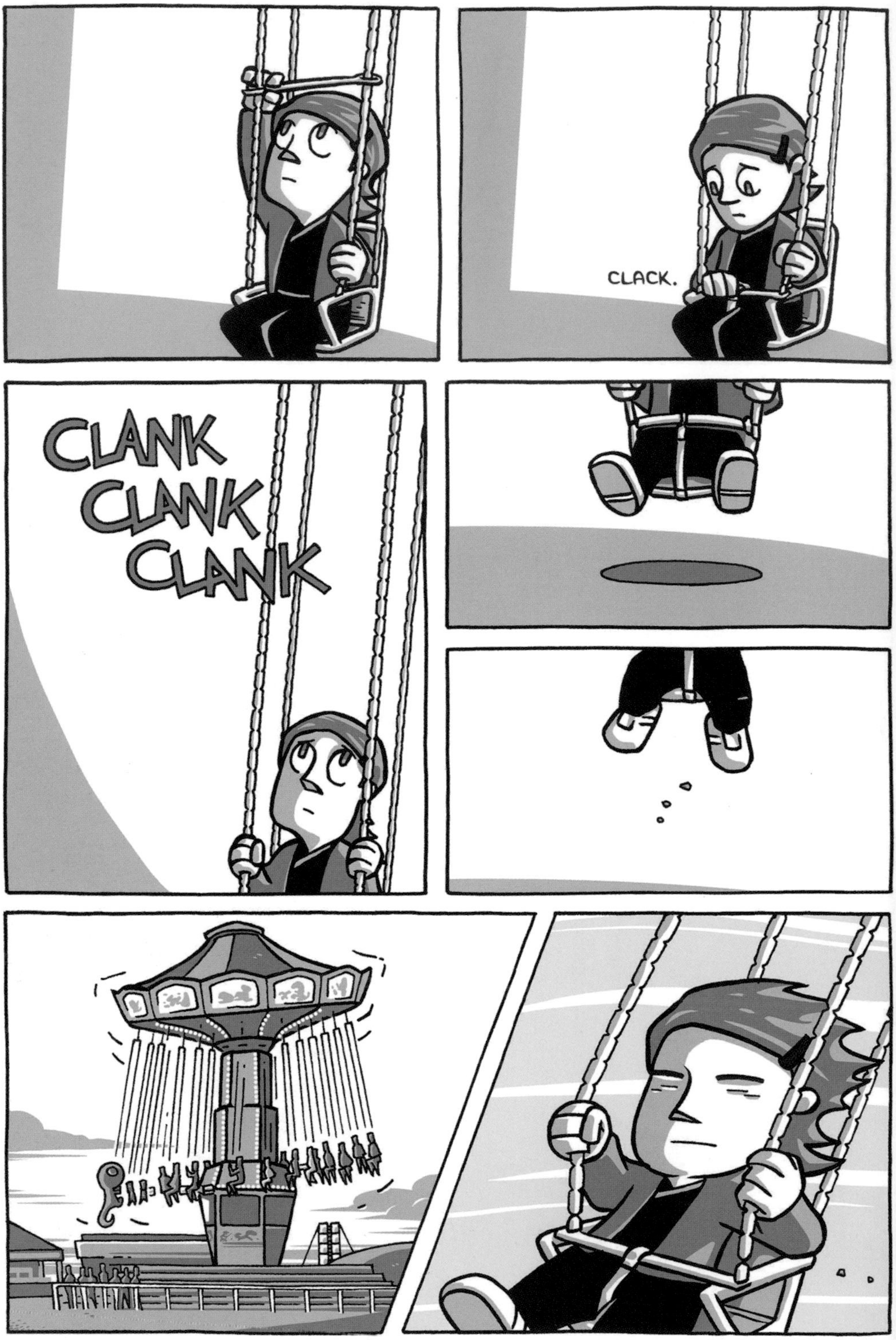
CLACK.
CLANK
CLANK
CLANK

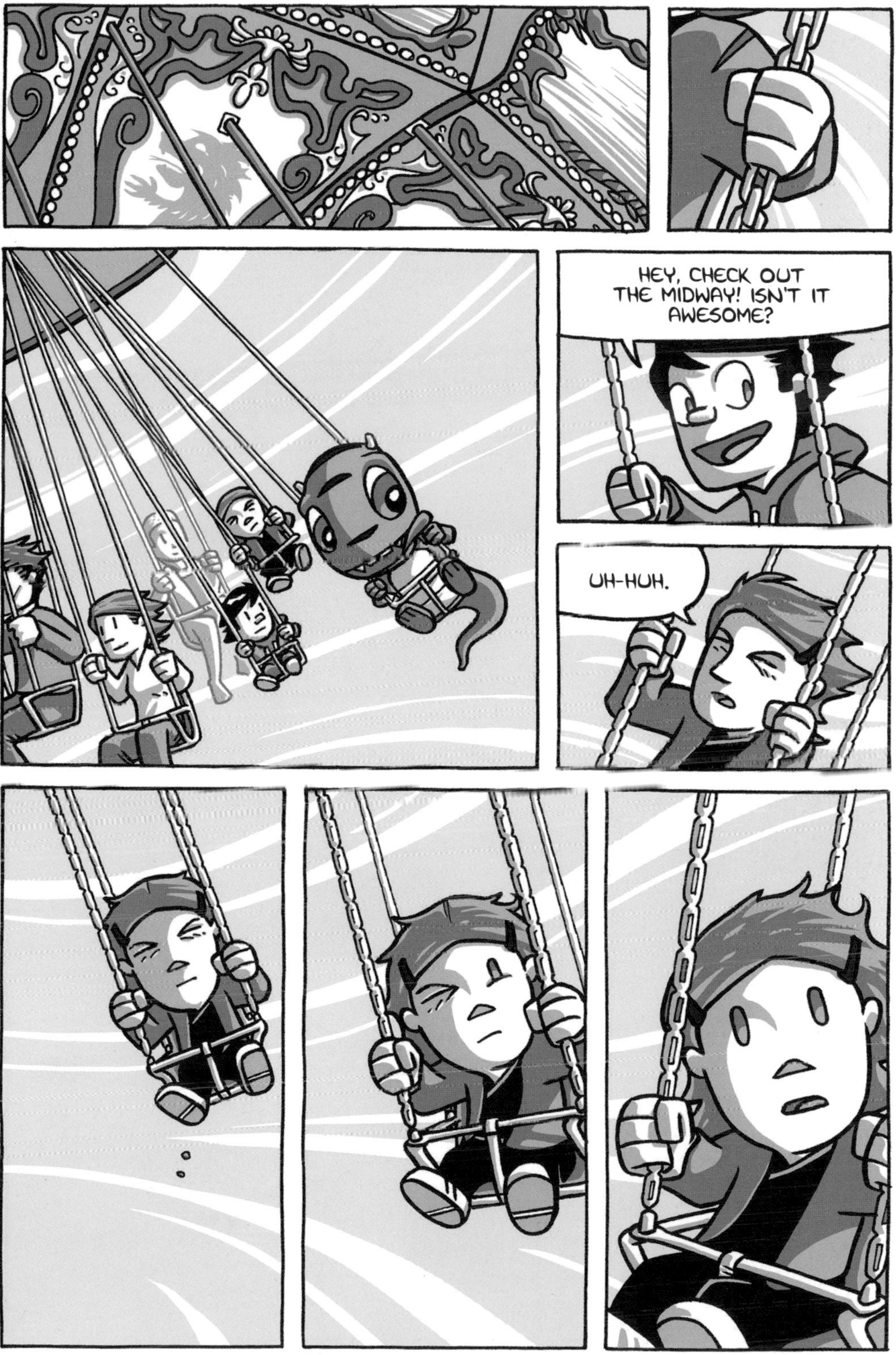
HEY, CHECK OUT THE MIDWAY! ISN'T IT AWESOME?
UH-HUH.

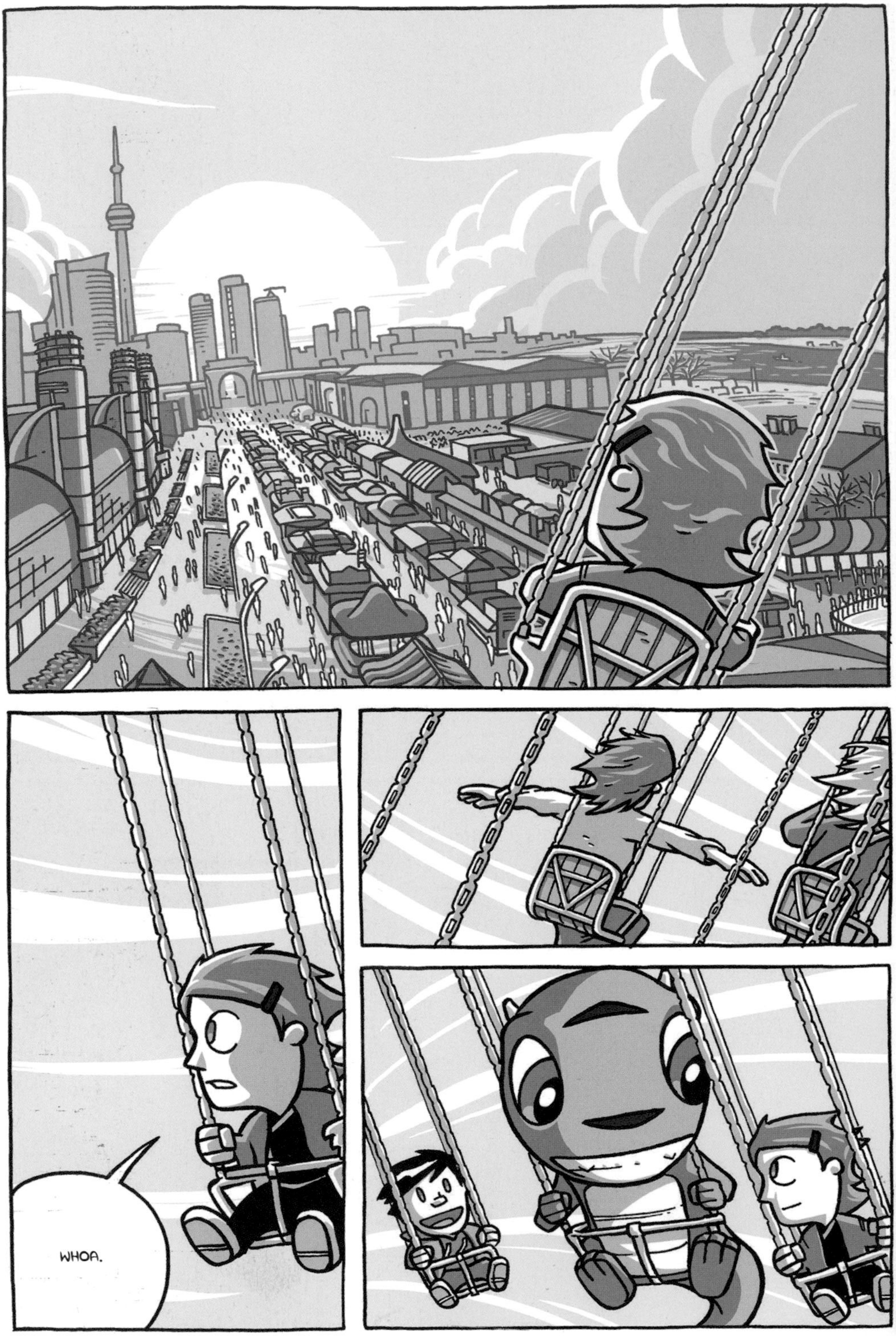
WHOA.

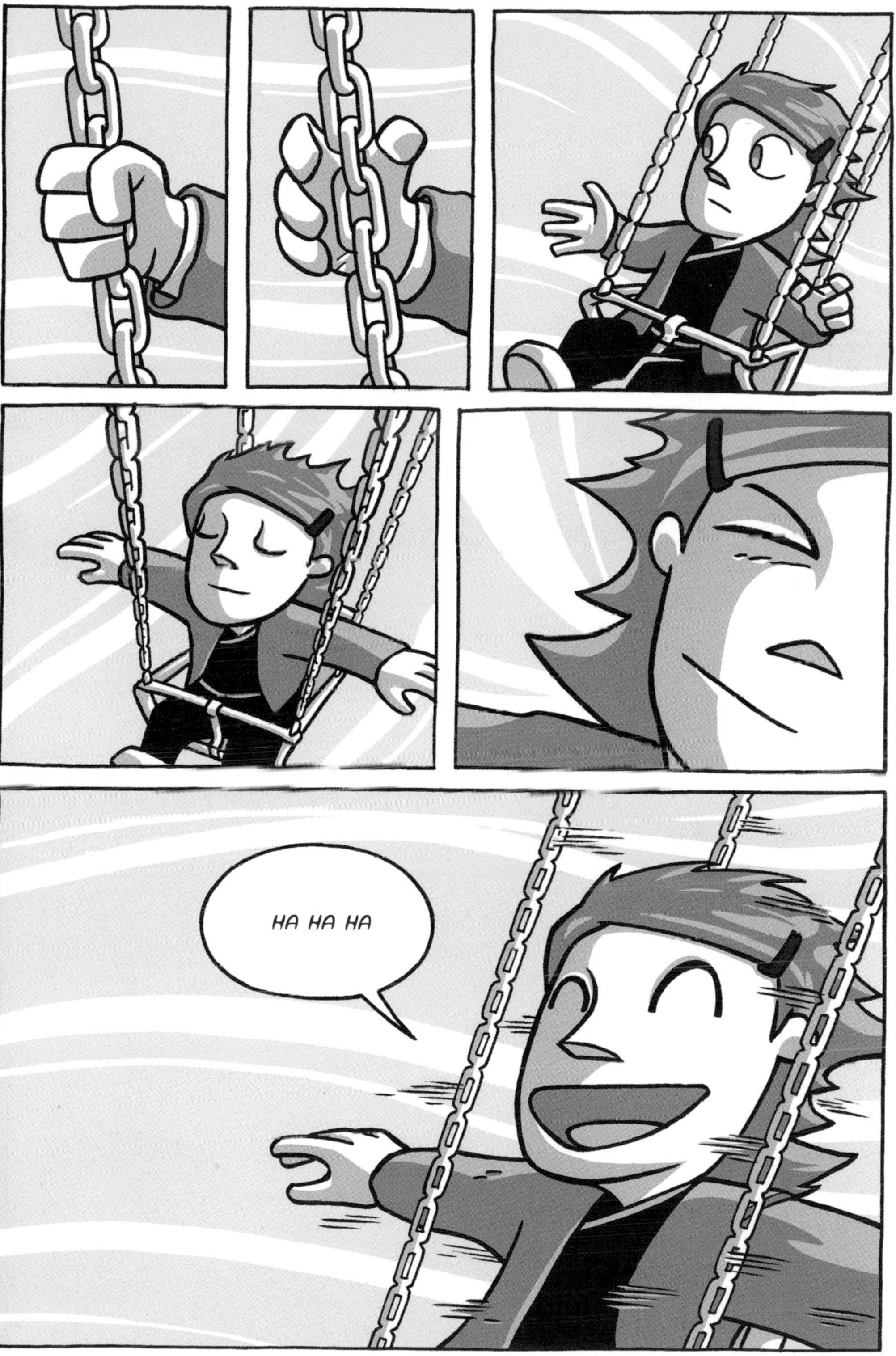
HA HA HA

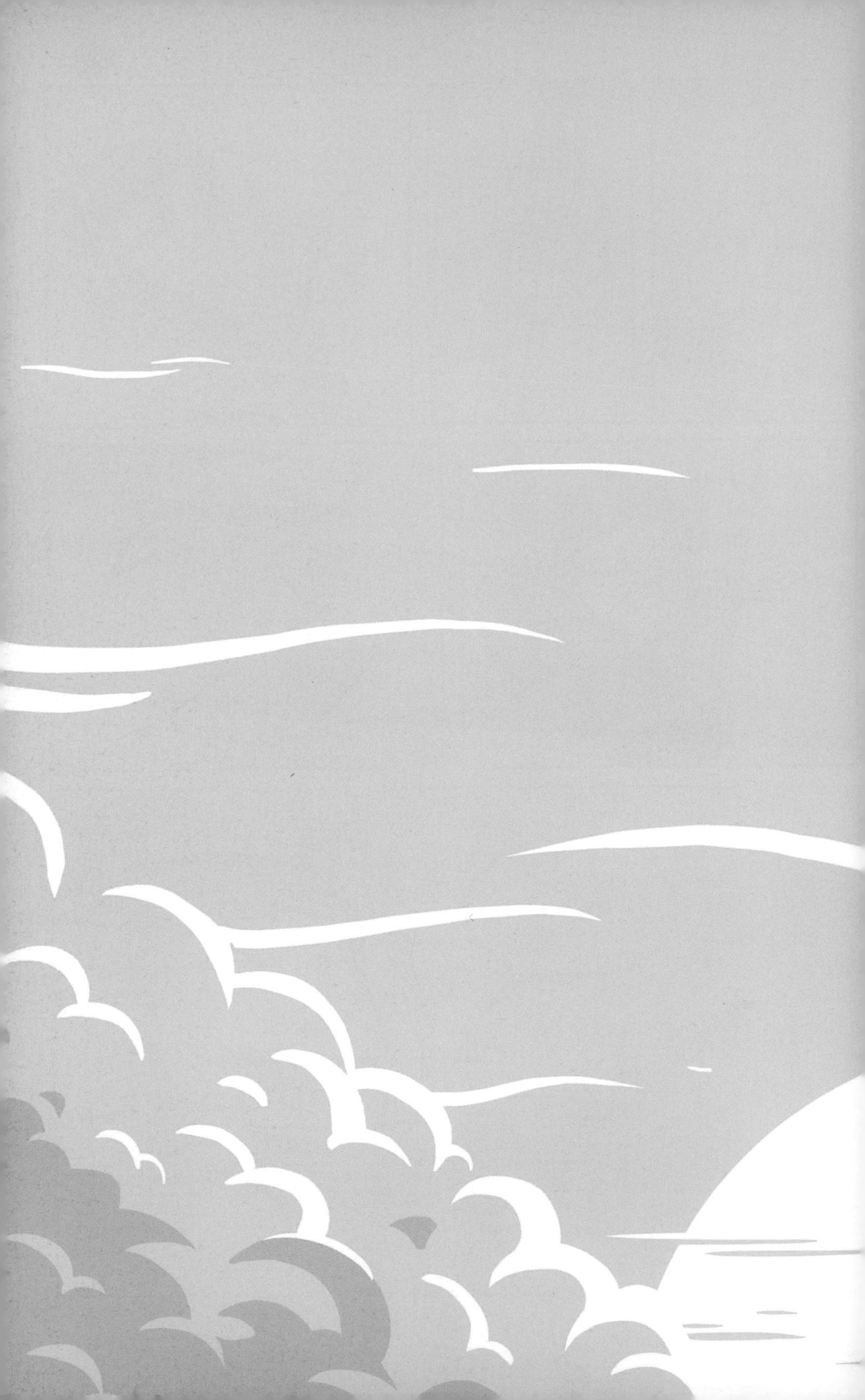

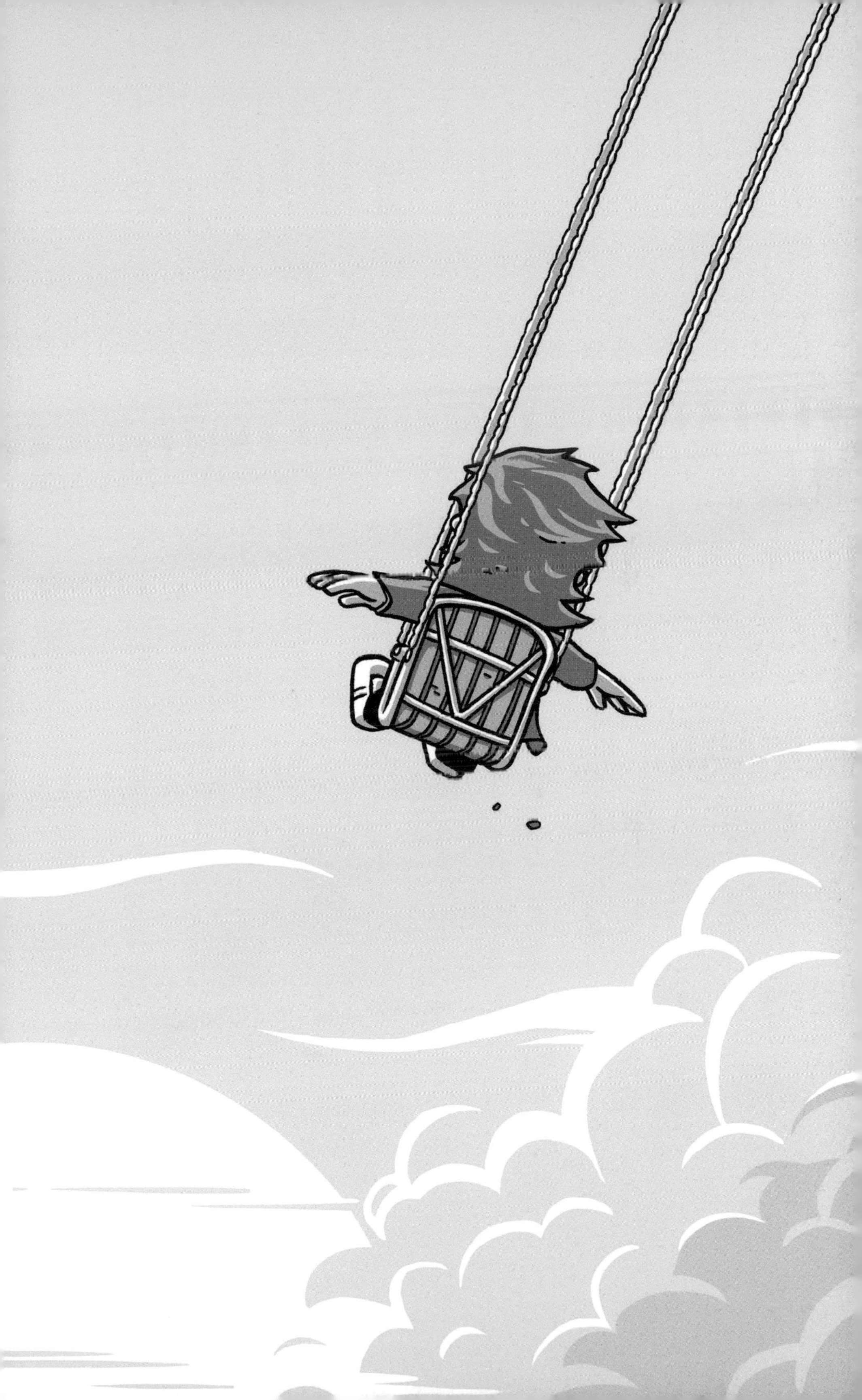

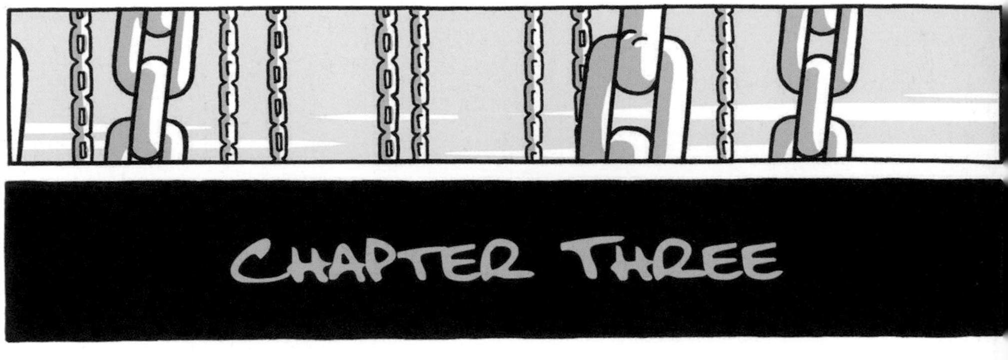

CHAPTER THREE

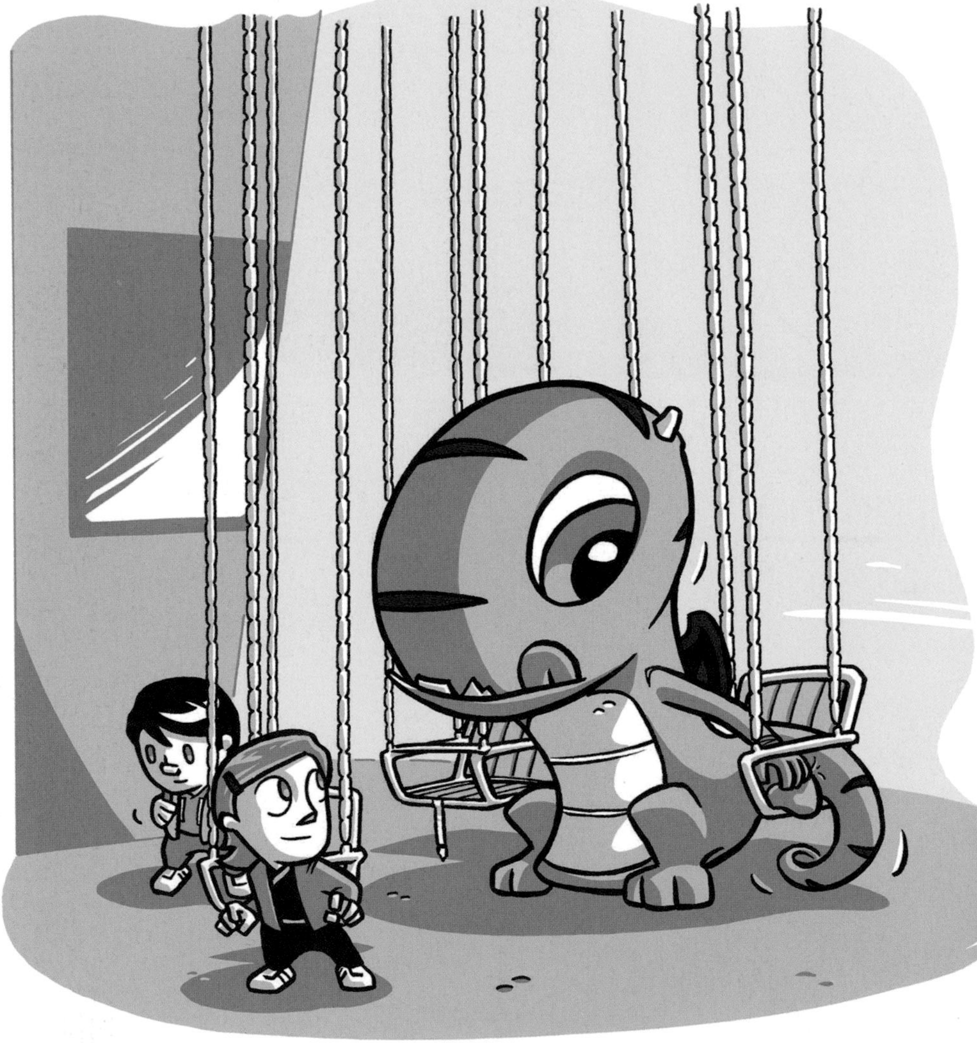

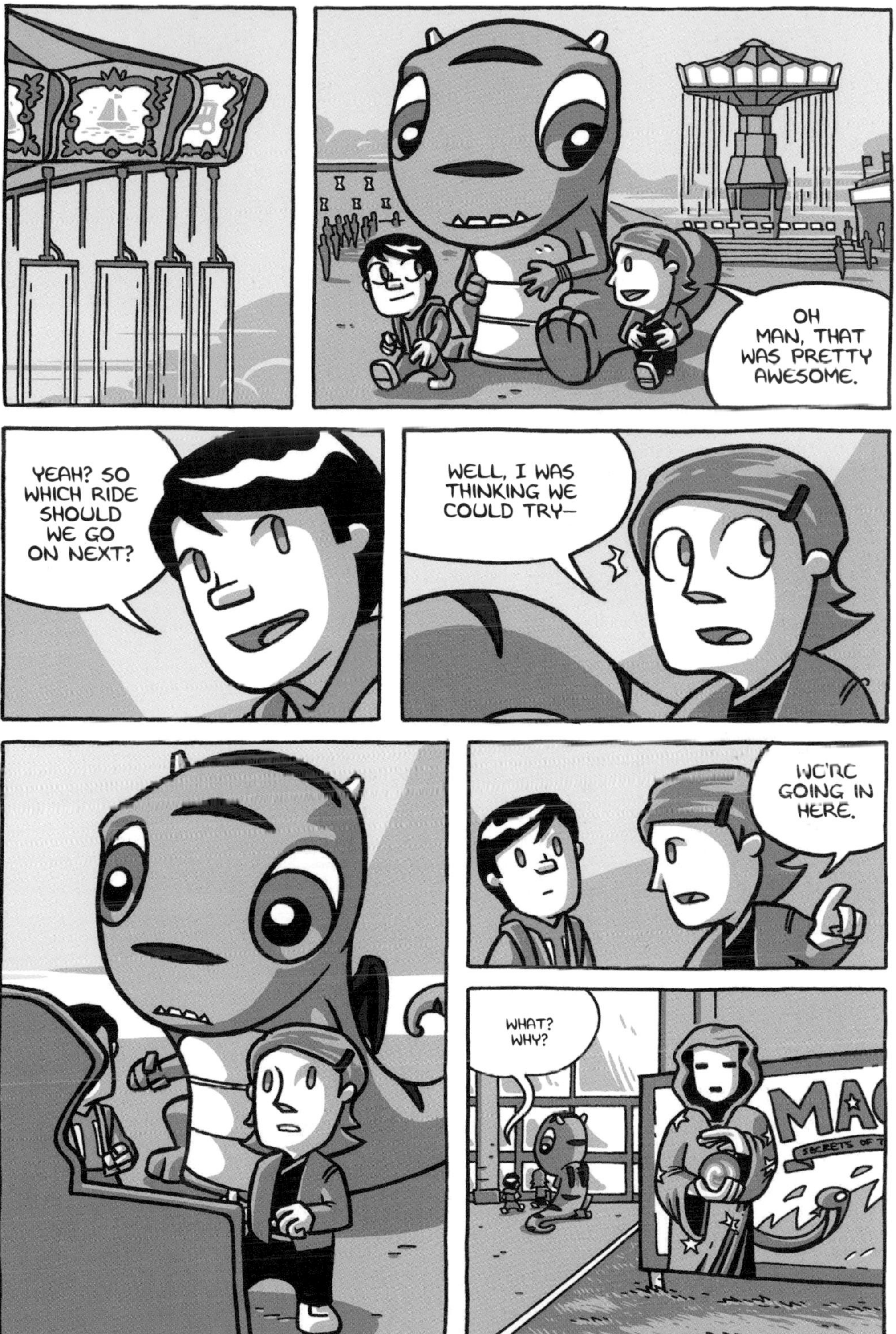
OH MAN, THAT WAS PRETTY AWESOME.
YEAH? SO WHICH RIDE SHOULD WE GO ON NEXT?
WELL, I WAS THINKING WE COULD TRY—
WE'RE GOING IN HERE.
WHAT? WHY?

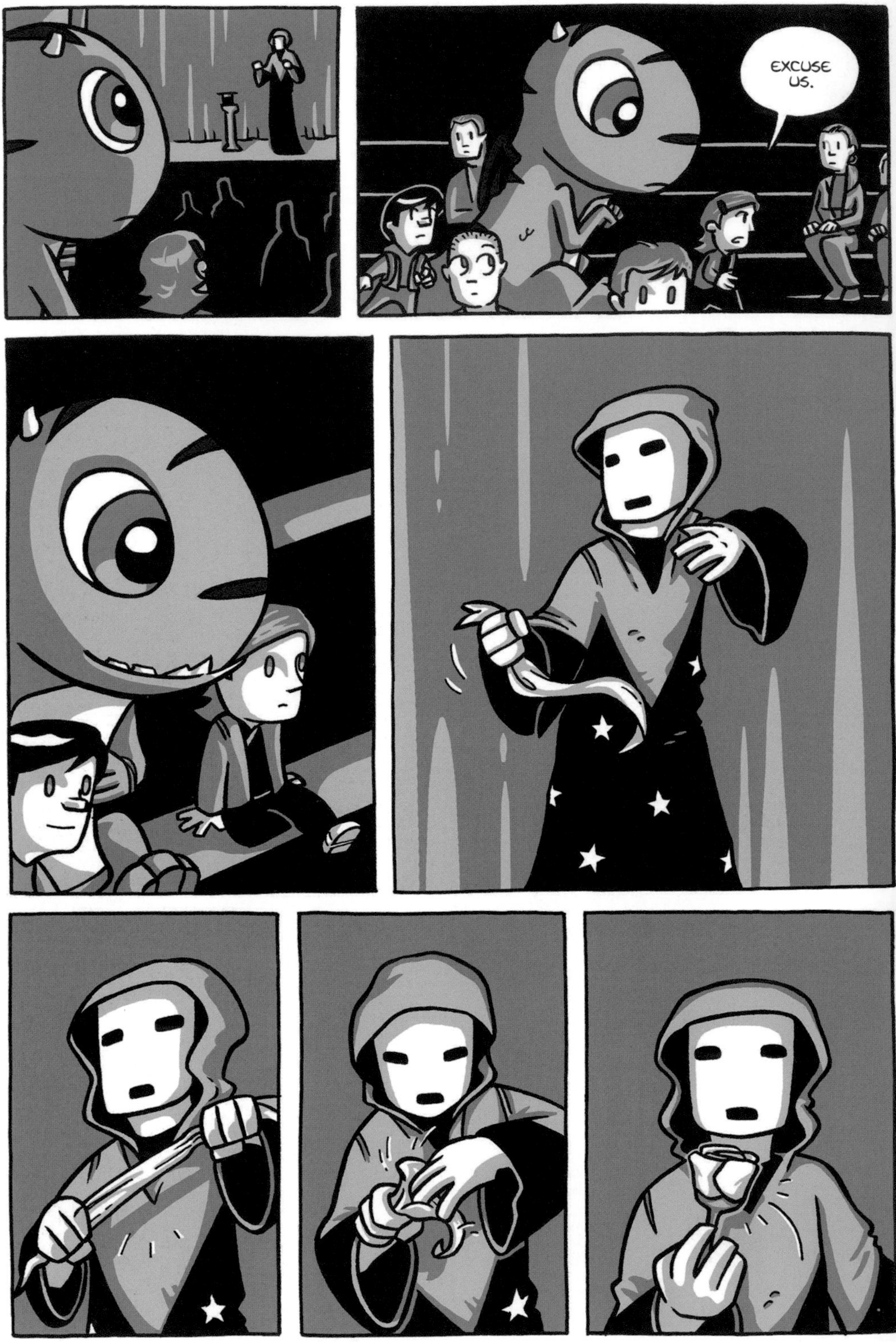
EXCUSE US.

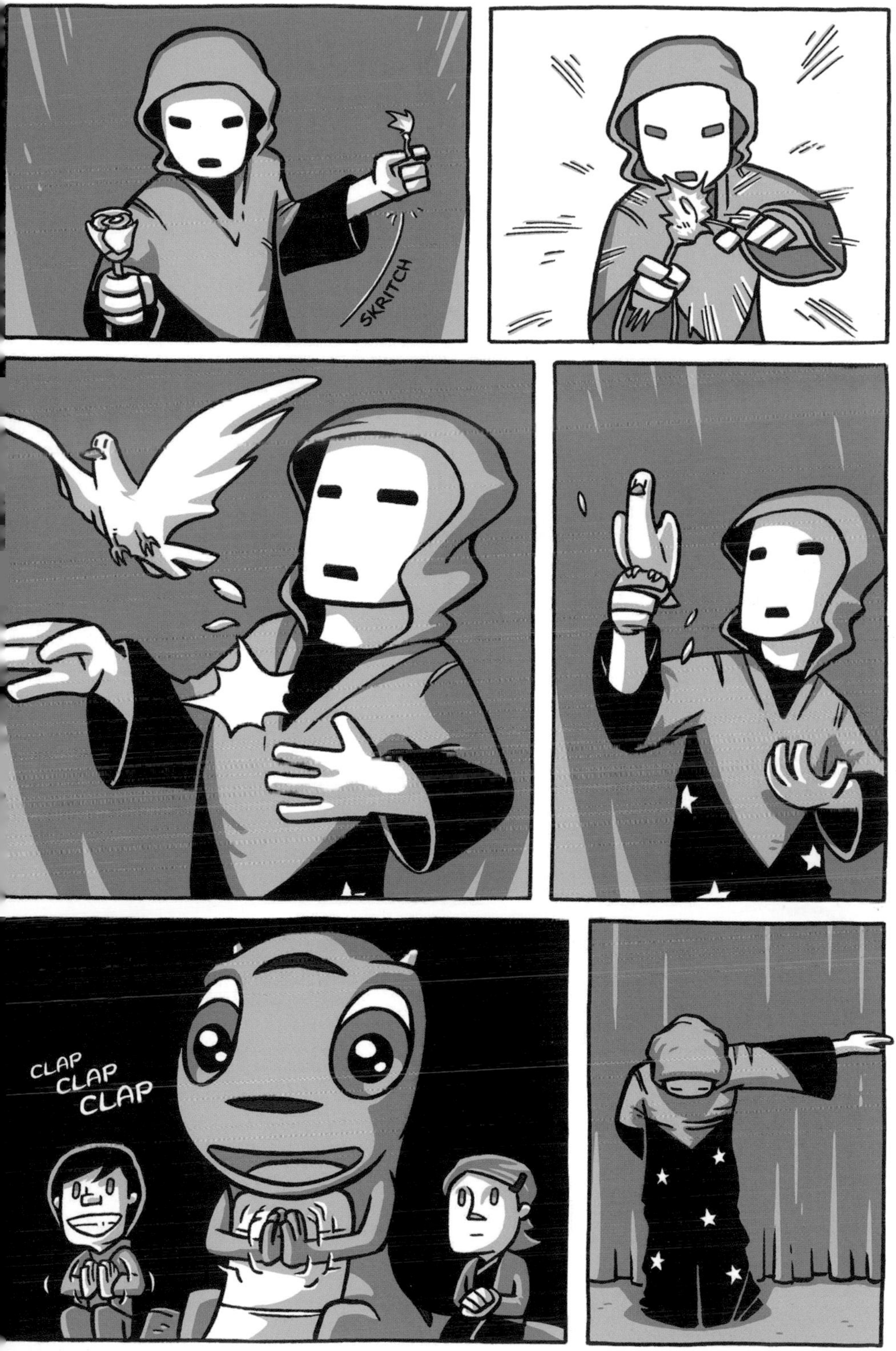
SKRITCH
CLAP
CLAP
CLAP

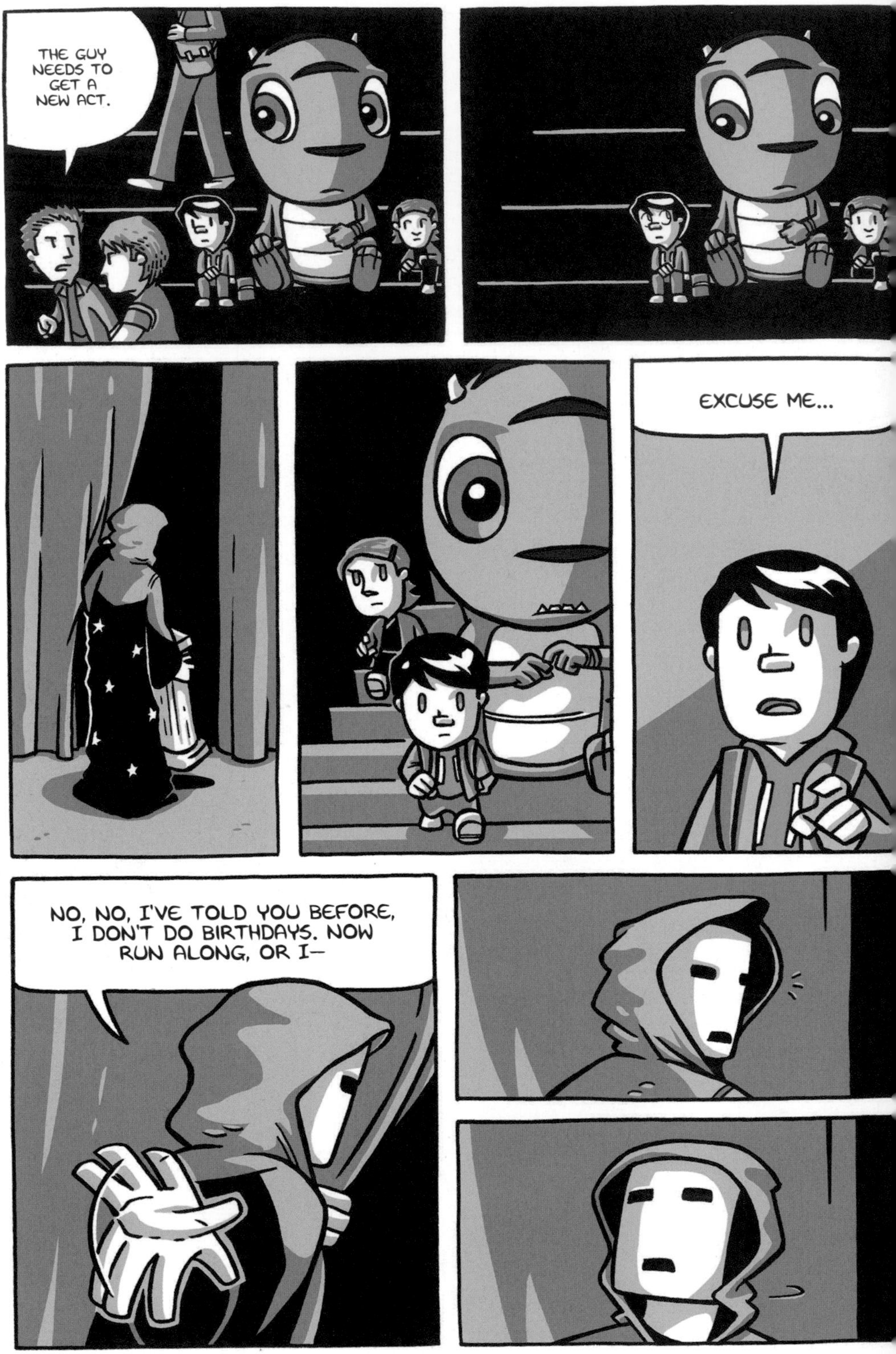
THE GUY NEEDS TO GET A NEW ACT.
EXCUSE ME...
NO, NO, I'VE TOLD YOU BEFORE, I DON'T DO BIRTHDAYS. NOW RUN ALONG, OR I—

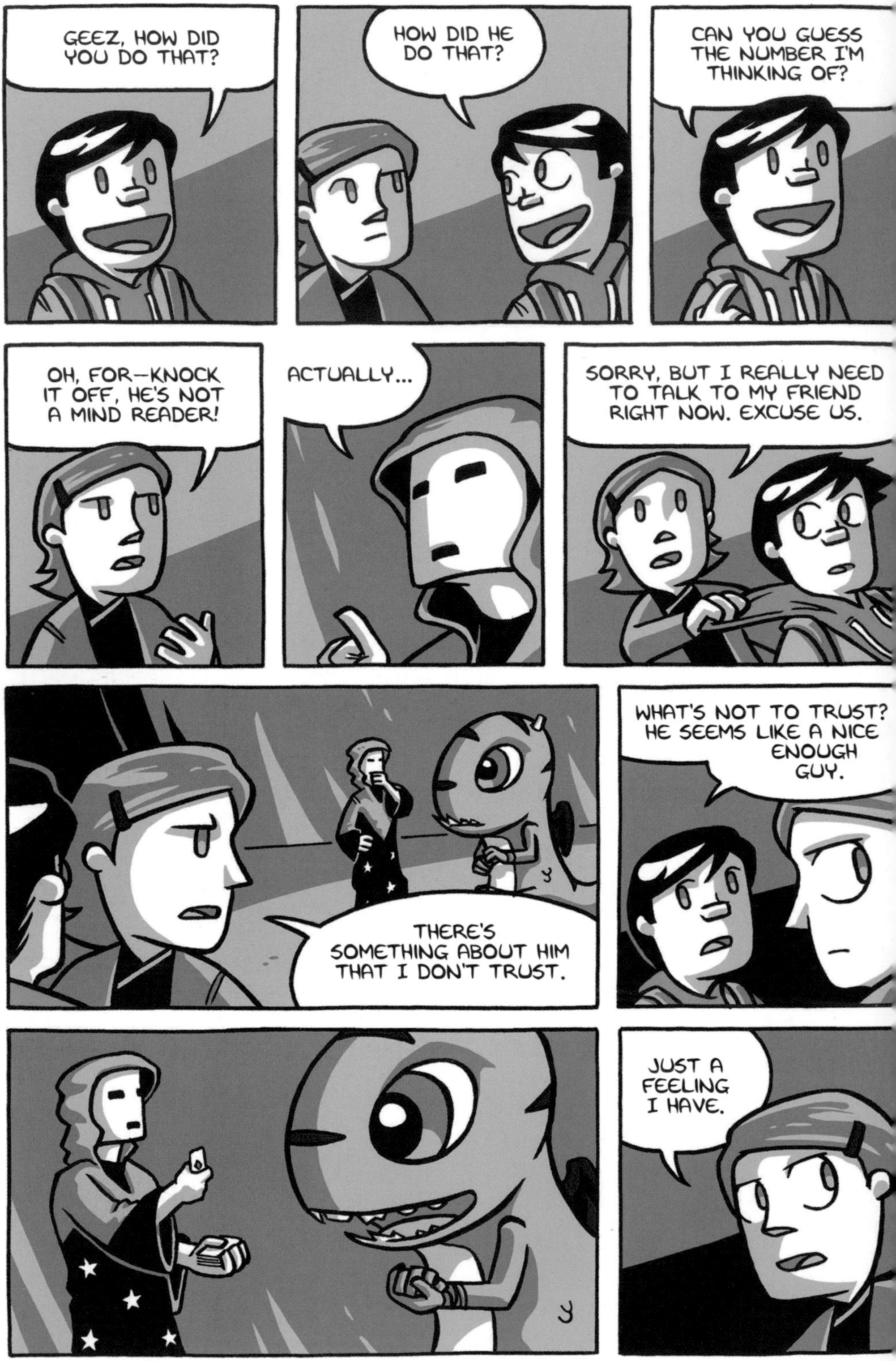
GEEZ, HOW DID YOU DO THAT?
HOW DID HE DO THAT?
CAN YOU GUESS THE NUMBER I'M THINKING OF?
OH, FOR—KNOCK IT OFF, HE'S NOT A MIND READER!
ACTUALLY...
SORRY, BUT I REALLY NEED TO TALK TO MY FRIEND RIGHT NOW. EXCUSE US.
THERE'S SOMETHING ABOUT HIM THAT I DON'T TRUST.
WHAT'S NOT TO TRUST? HE SEEMS LIKE A NICE ENOUGH GUY.
JUST A FEELING I HAVE.

69

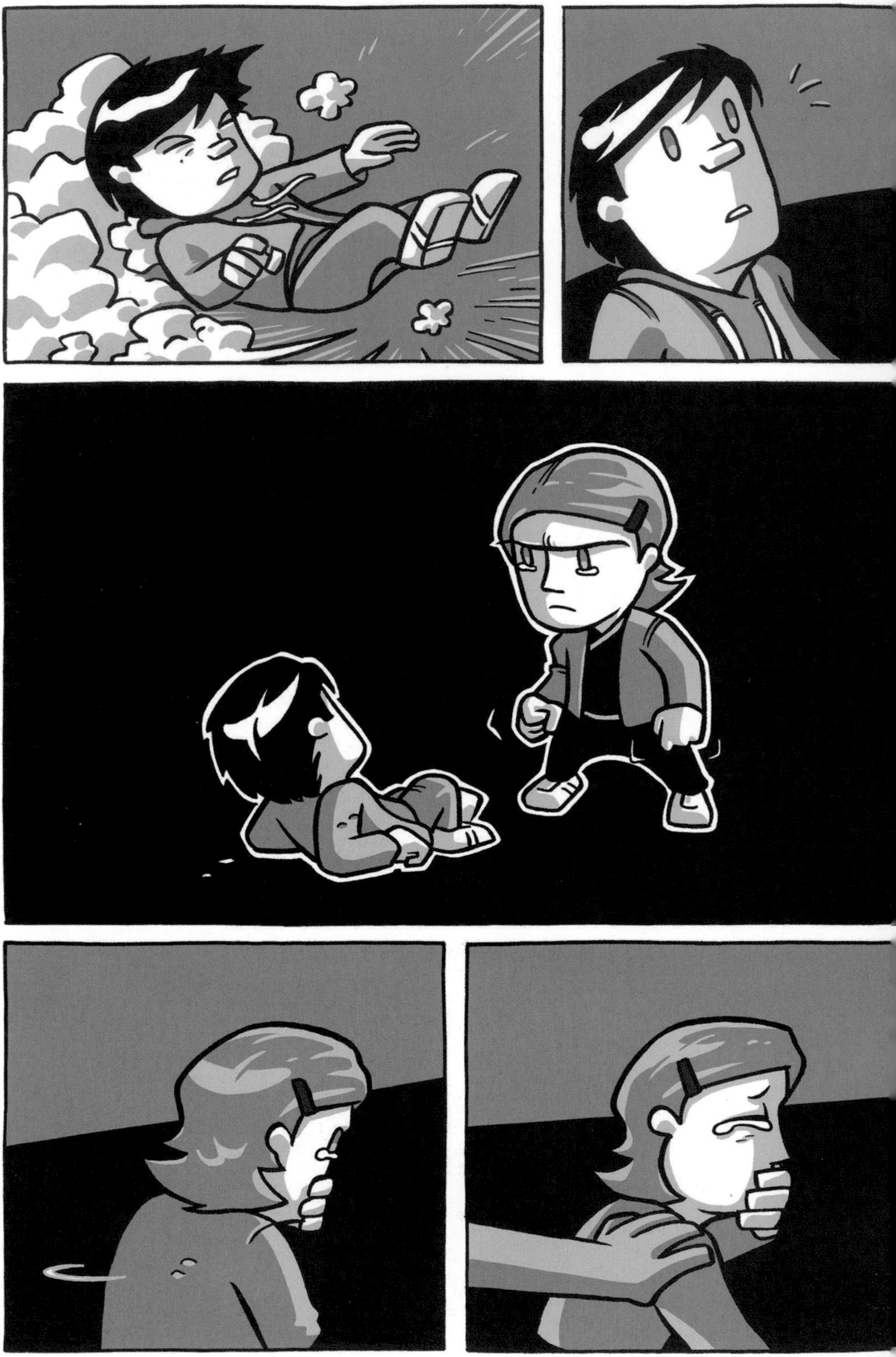

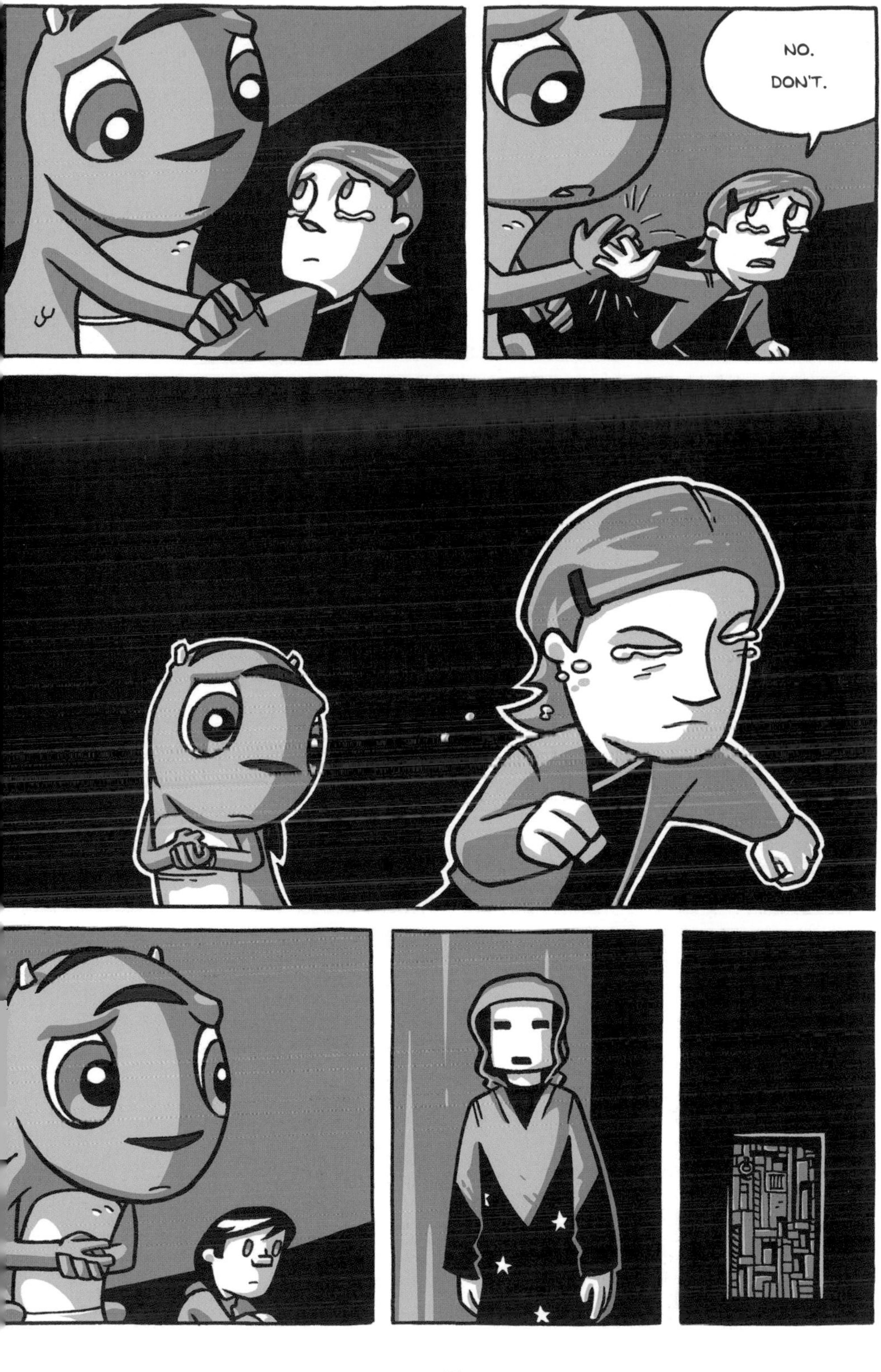
NO.
DON'T.

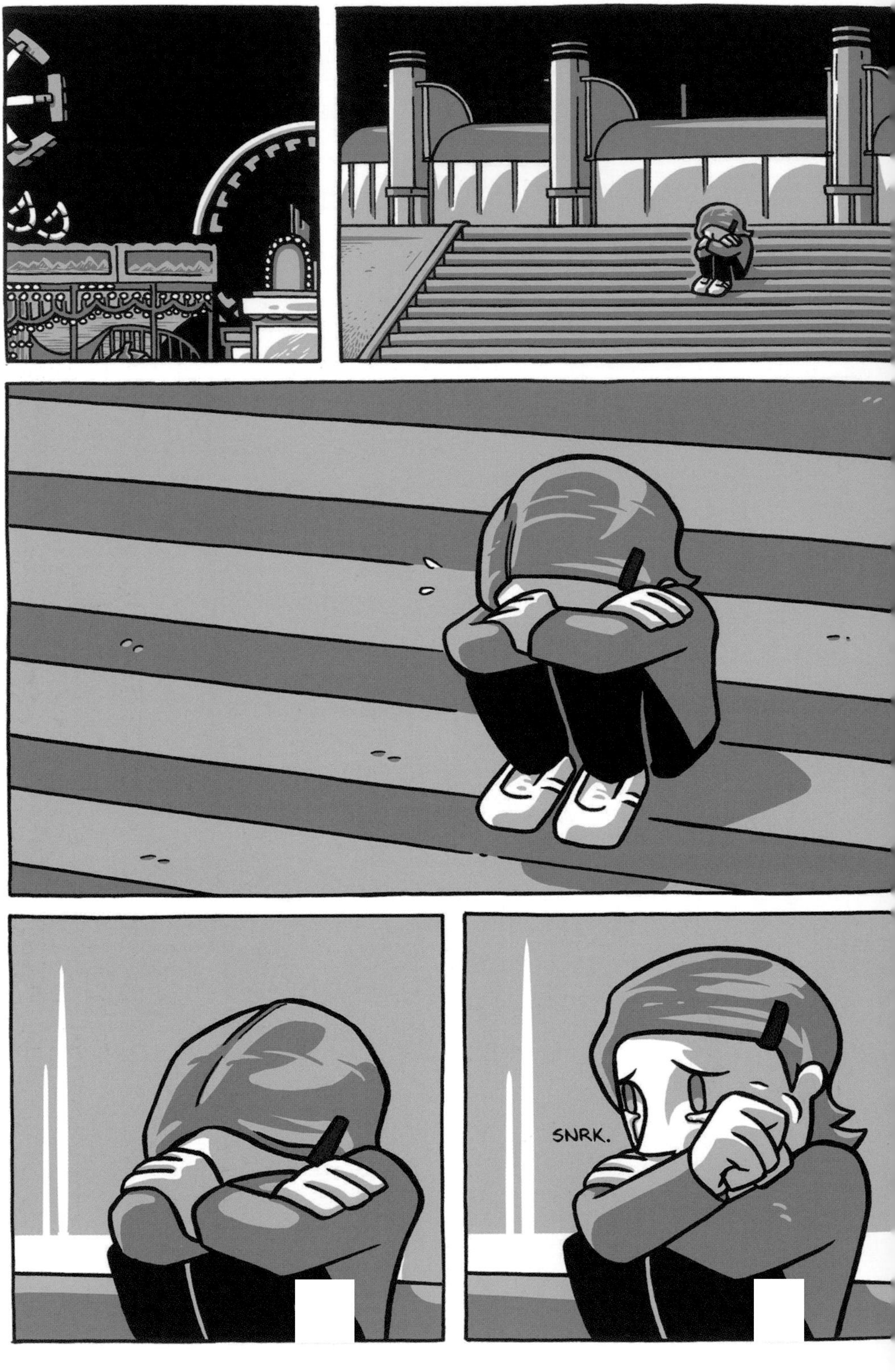
SNRK.

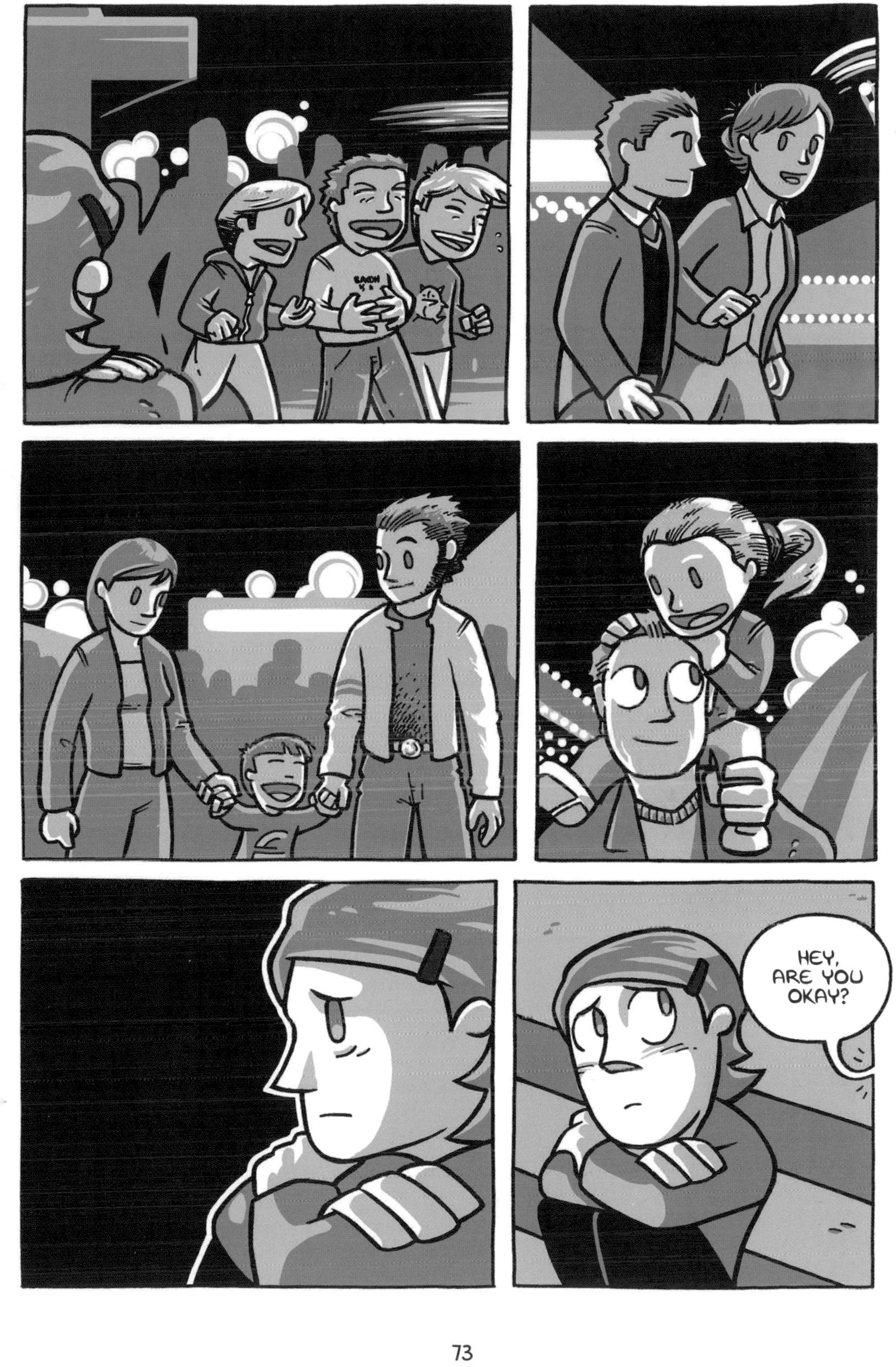
HEY, ARE YOU OKAY?

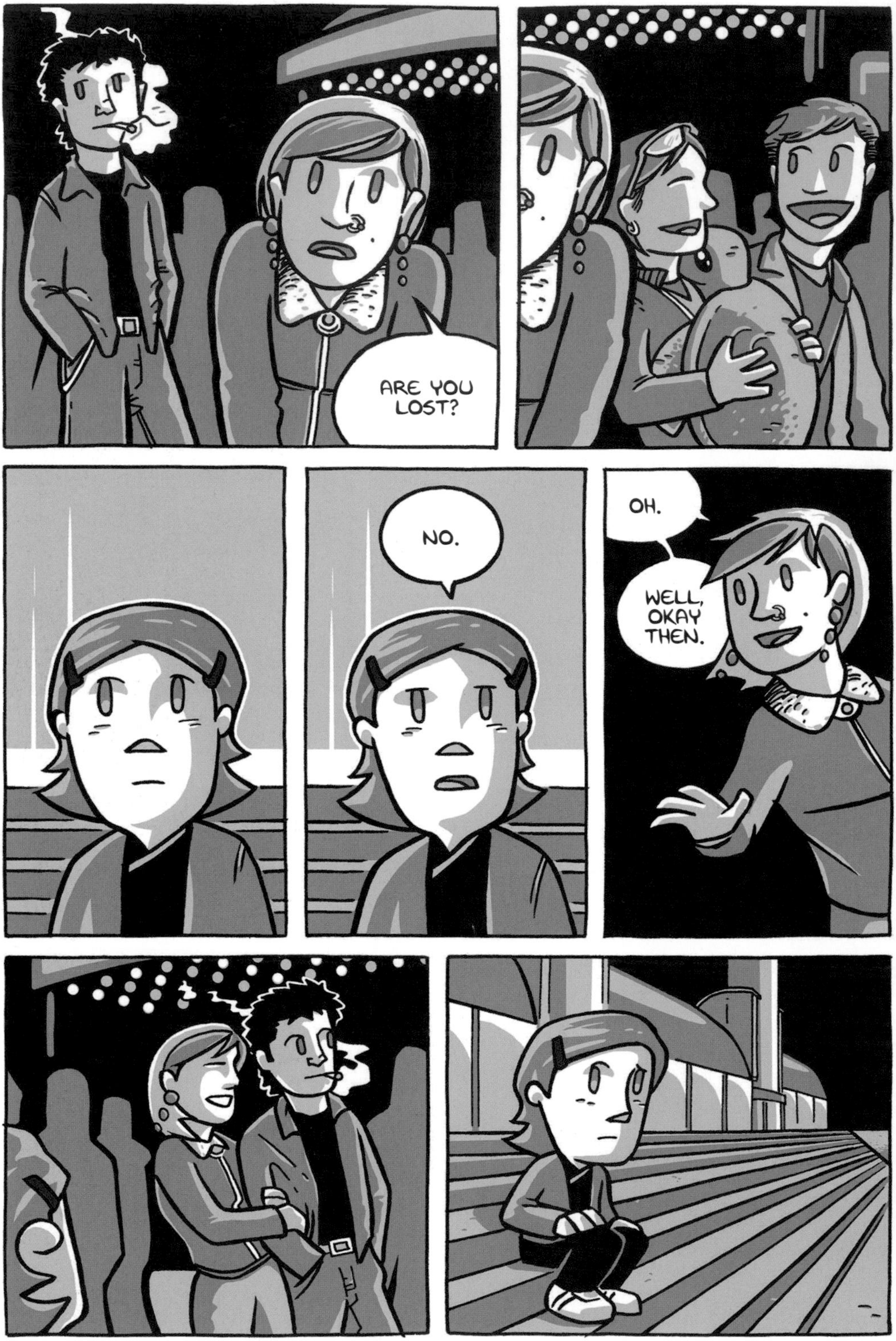
ARE YOU LOST?
NO.
OH.
WELL, OKAY THEN.

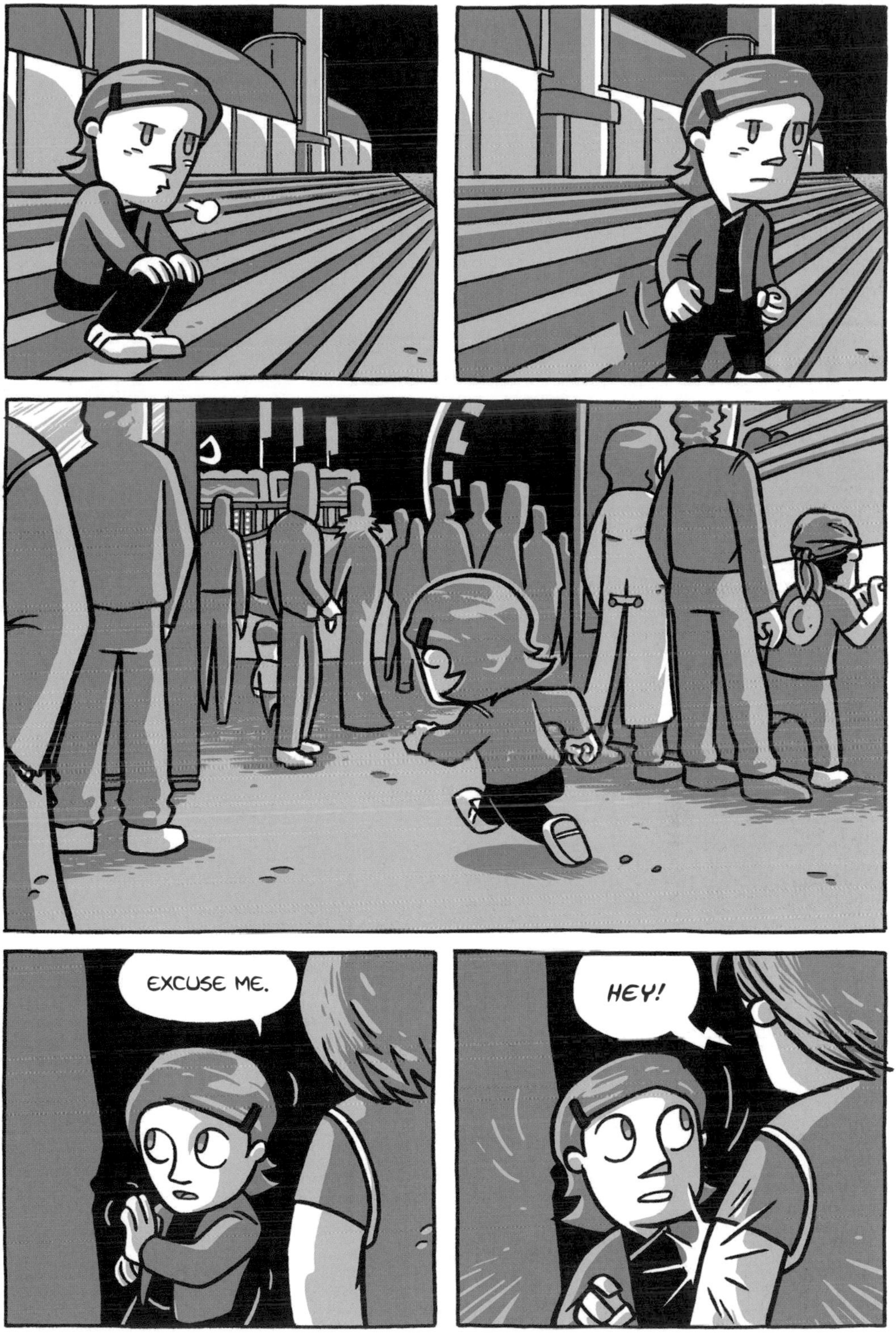
EXCUSE ME.
HEY!

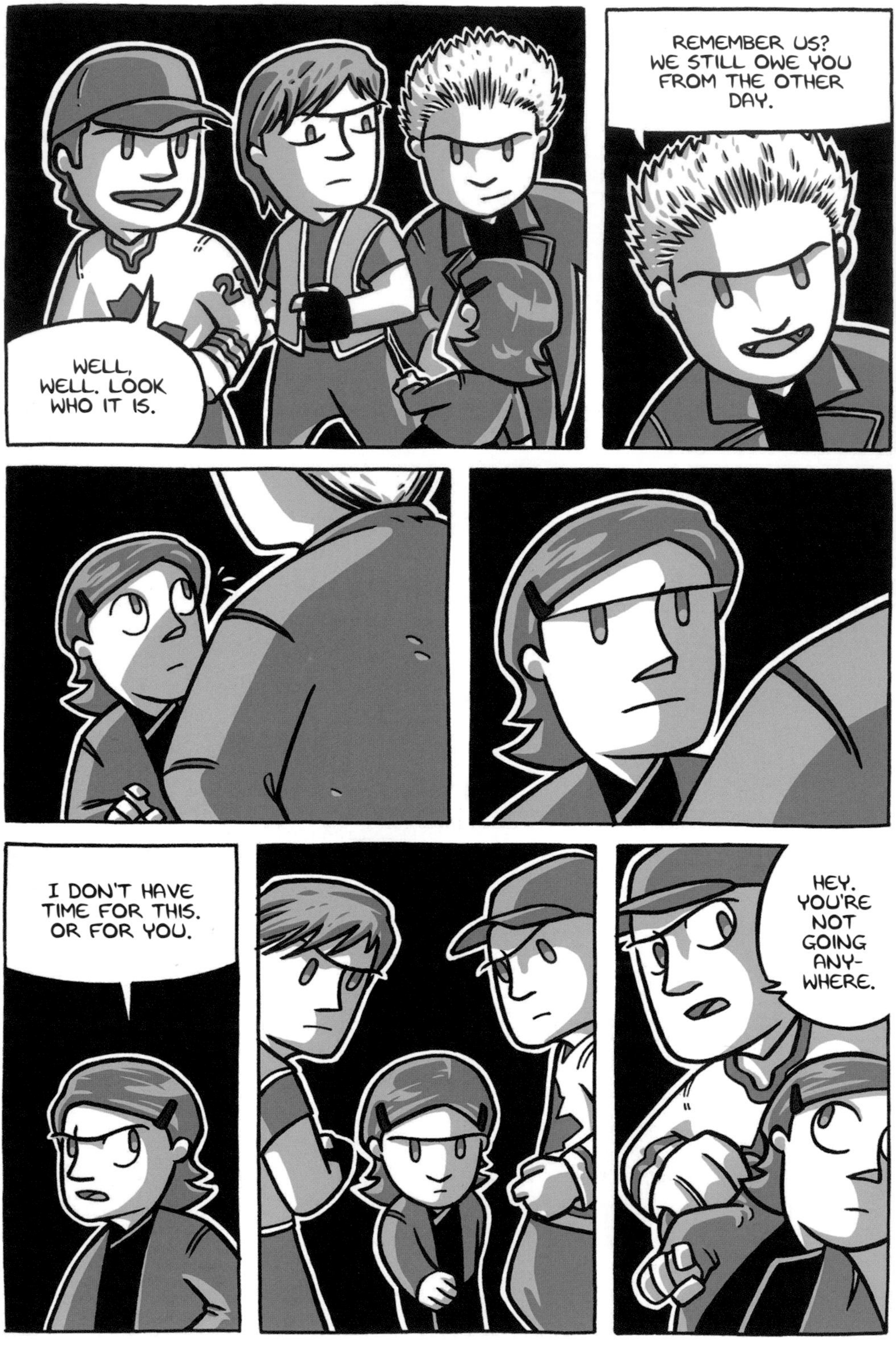
WELL, WELL. LOOK WHO IT IS.
REMEMBER US? WE STILL OWE YOU FROM THE OTHER DAY.
I DON'T HAVE TIME FOR THIS. OR FOR YOU.
HEY. YOU'RE NOT GOING ANY-WHERE.

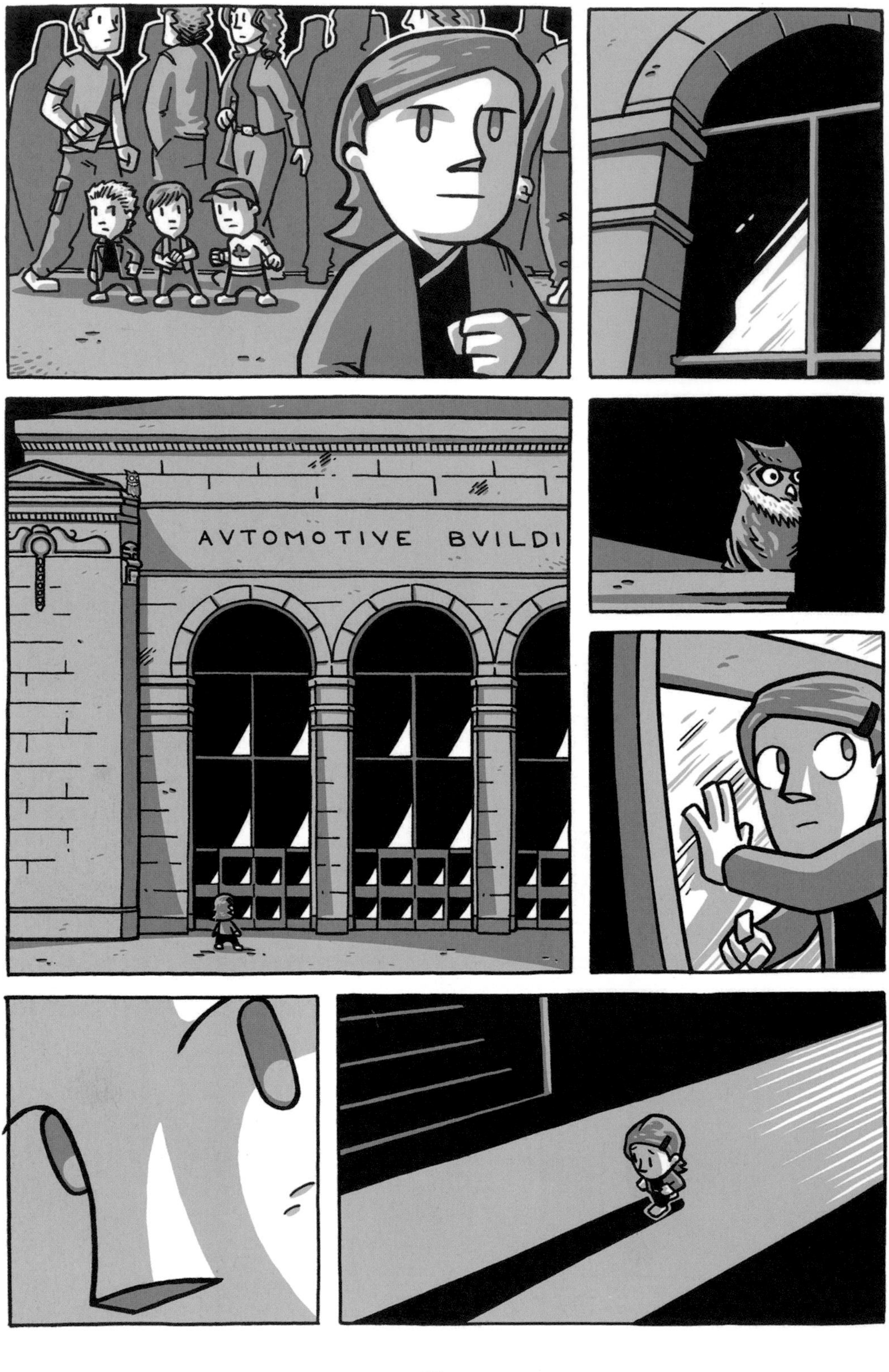
AVTOMOTIVE BVILDI

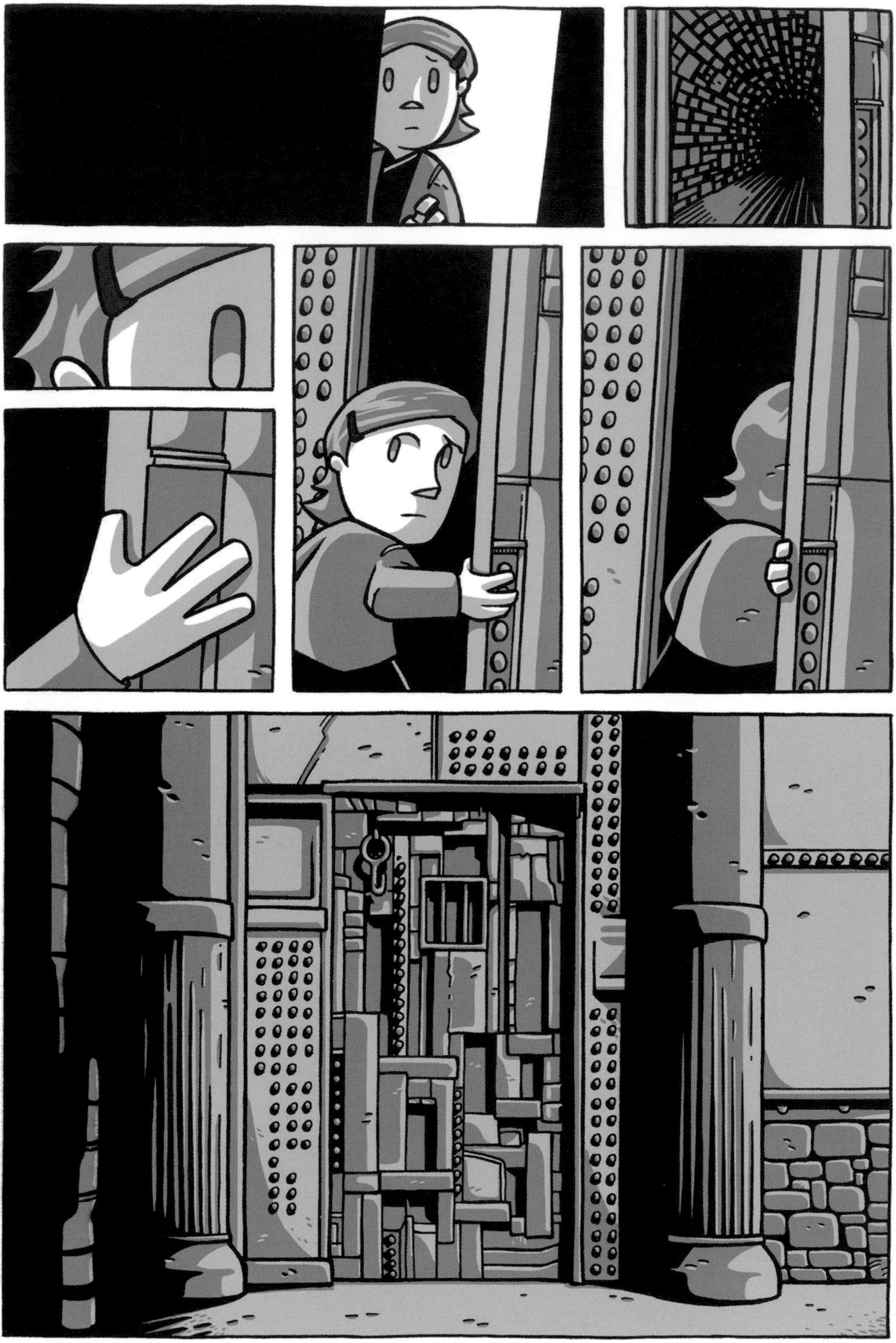

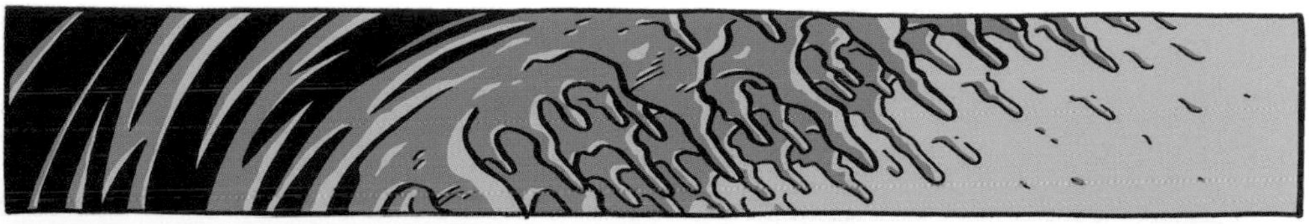

CHAPTER FOUR

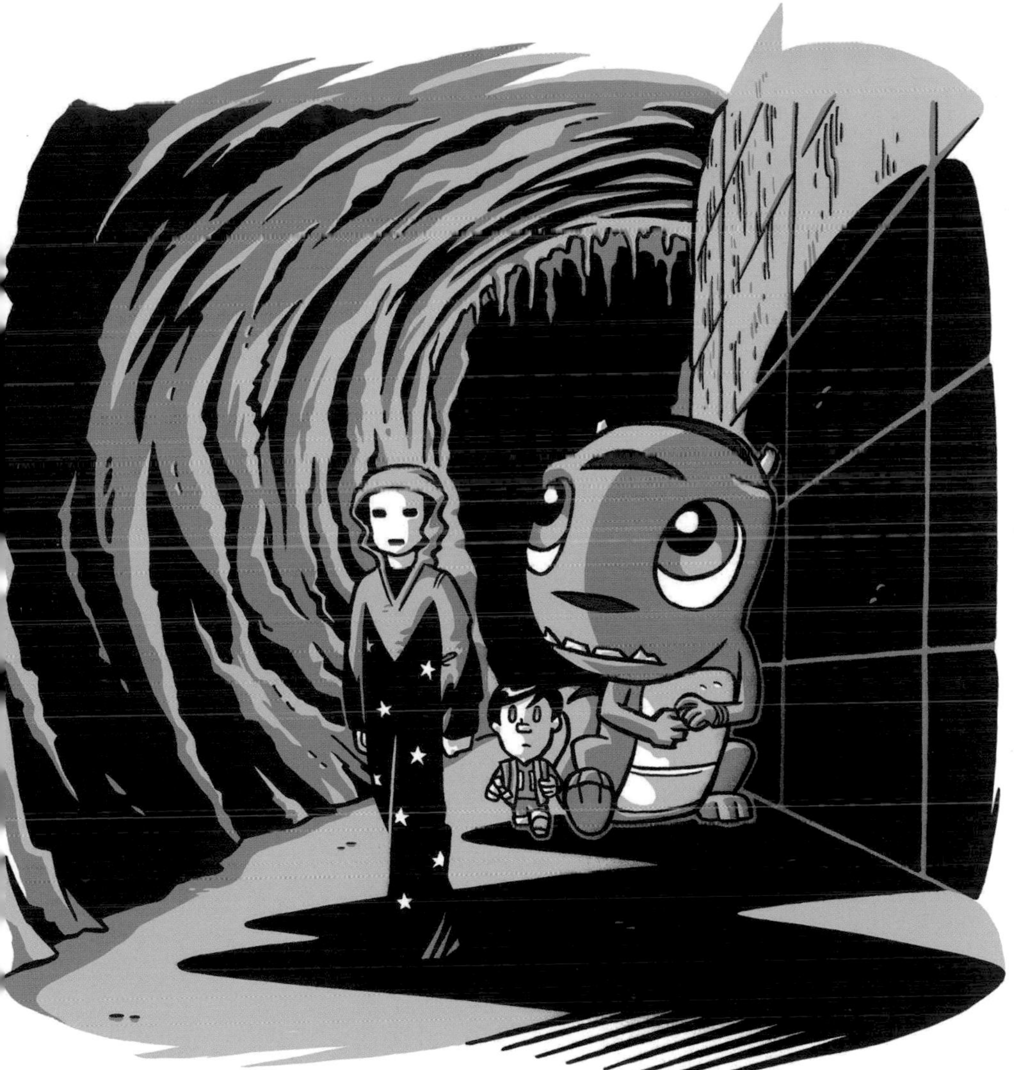

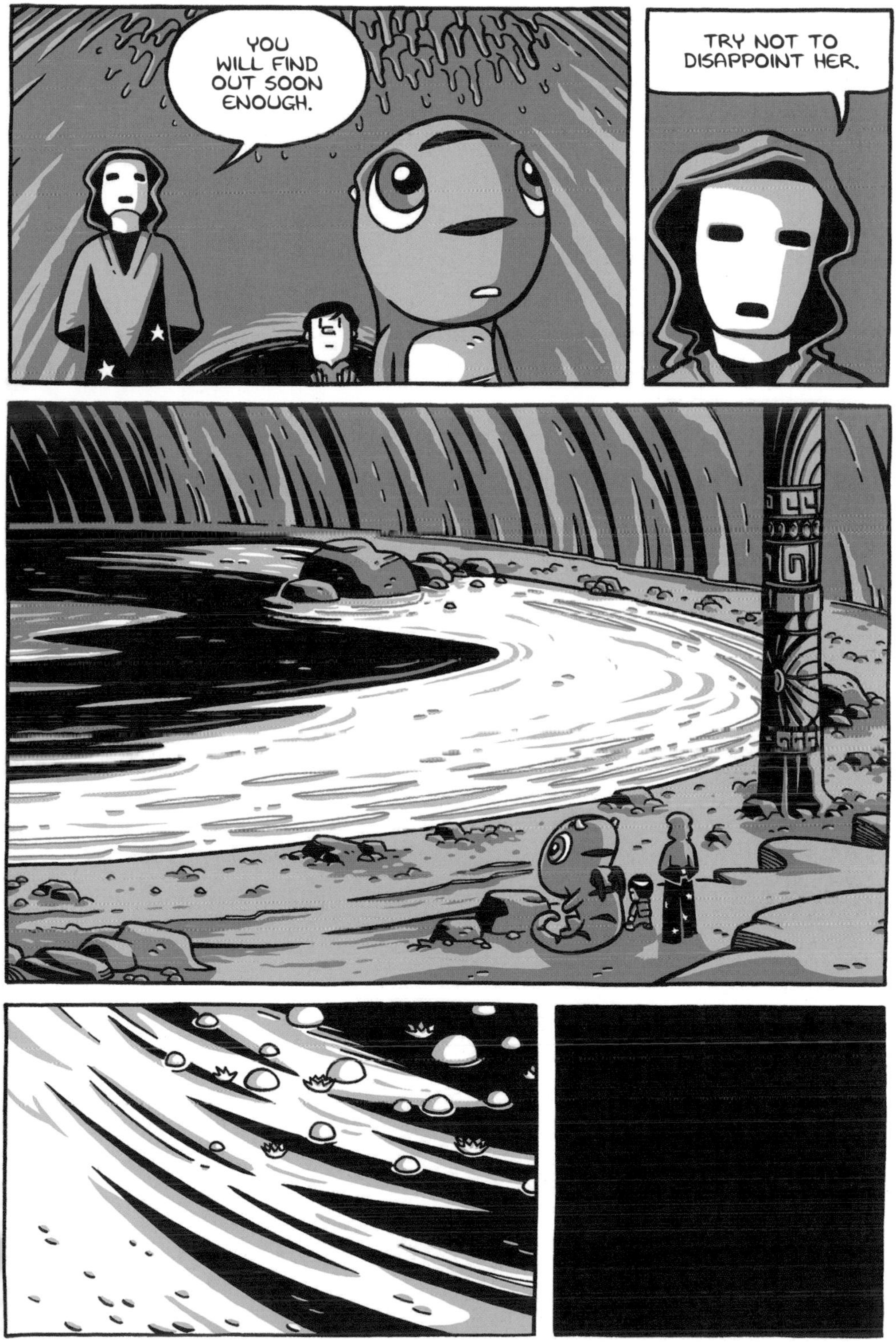
YOU WILL FIND OUT SOON ENOUGH.
TRY NOT TO DISAPPOINT HER.

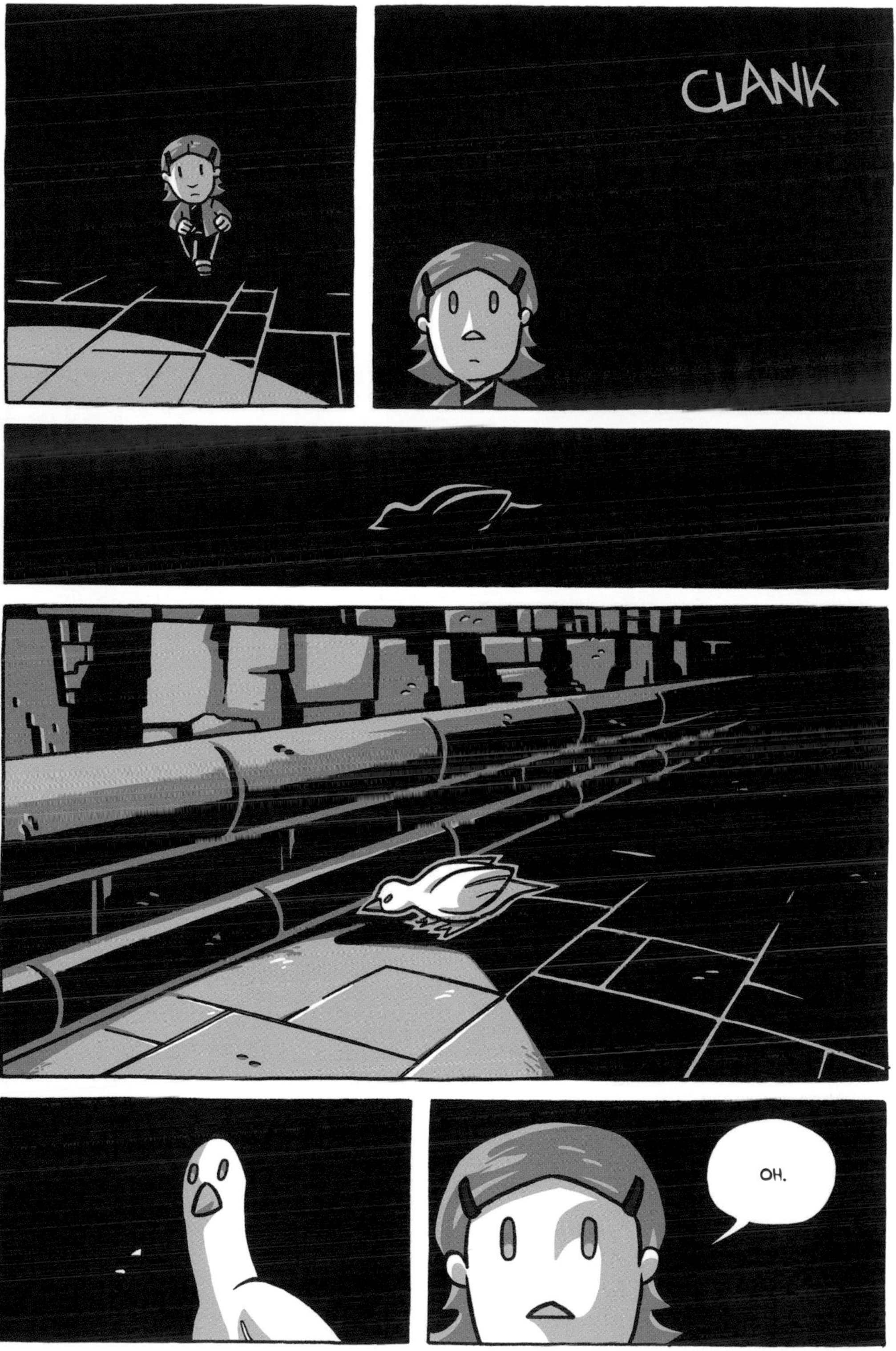
CLANK
OH.

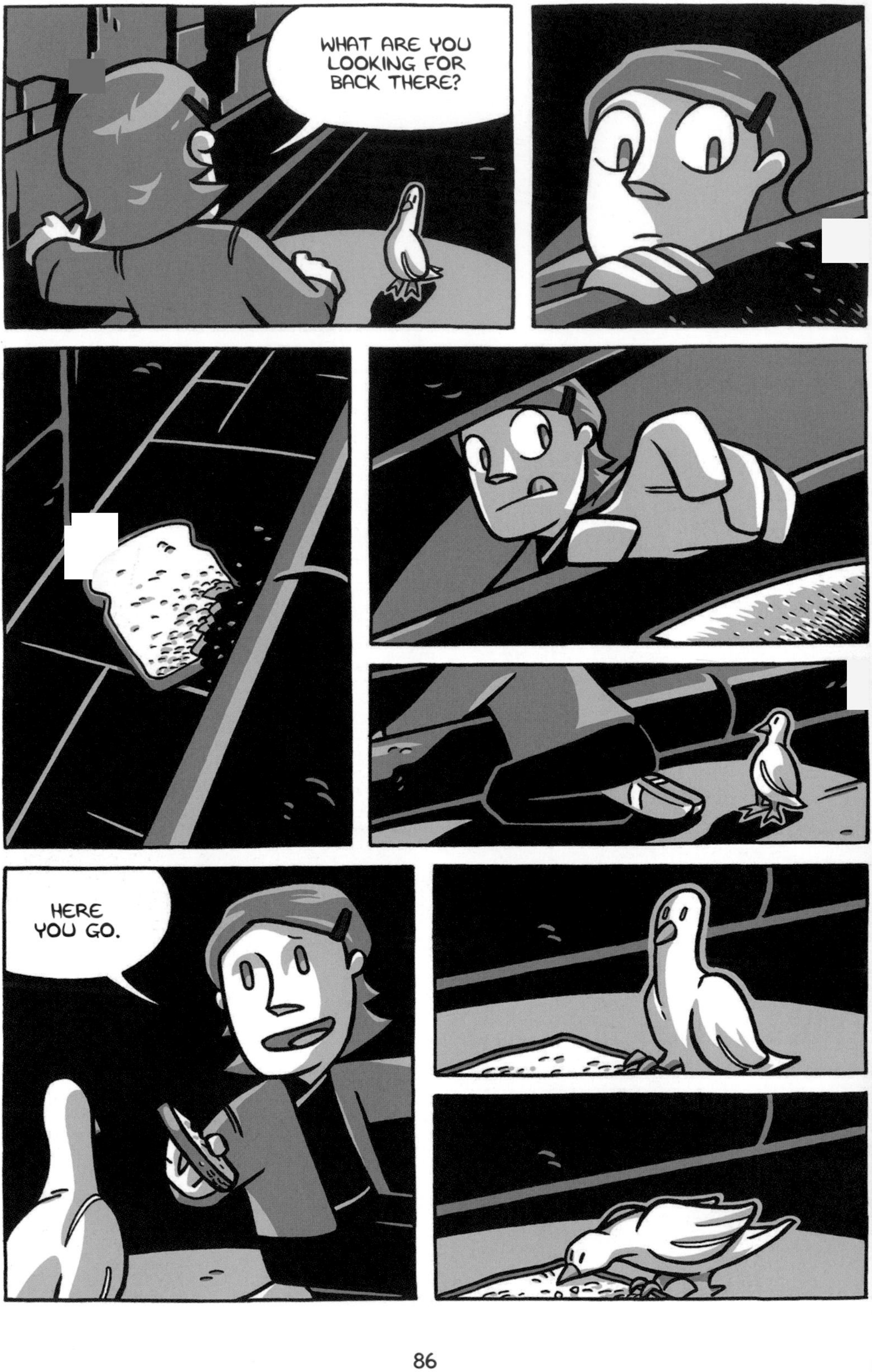
WHAT ARE YOU
LOOKING FOR
BACK THERE?
HERE
YOU GO.

88

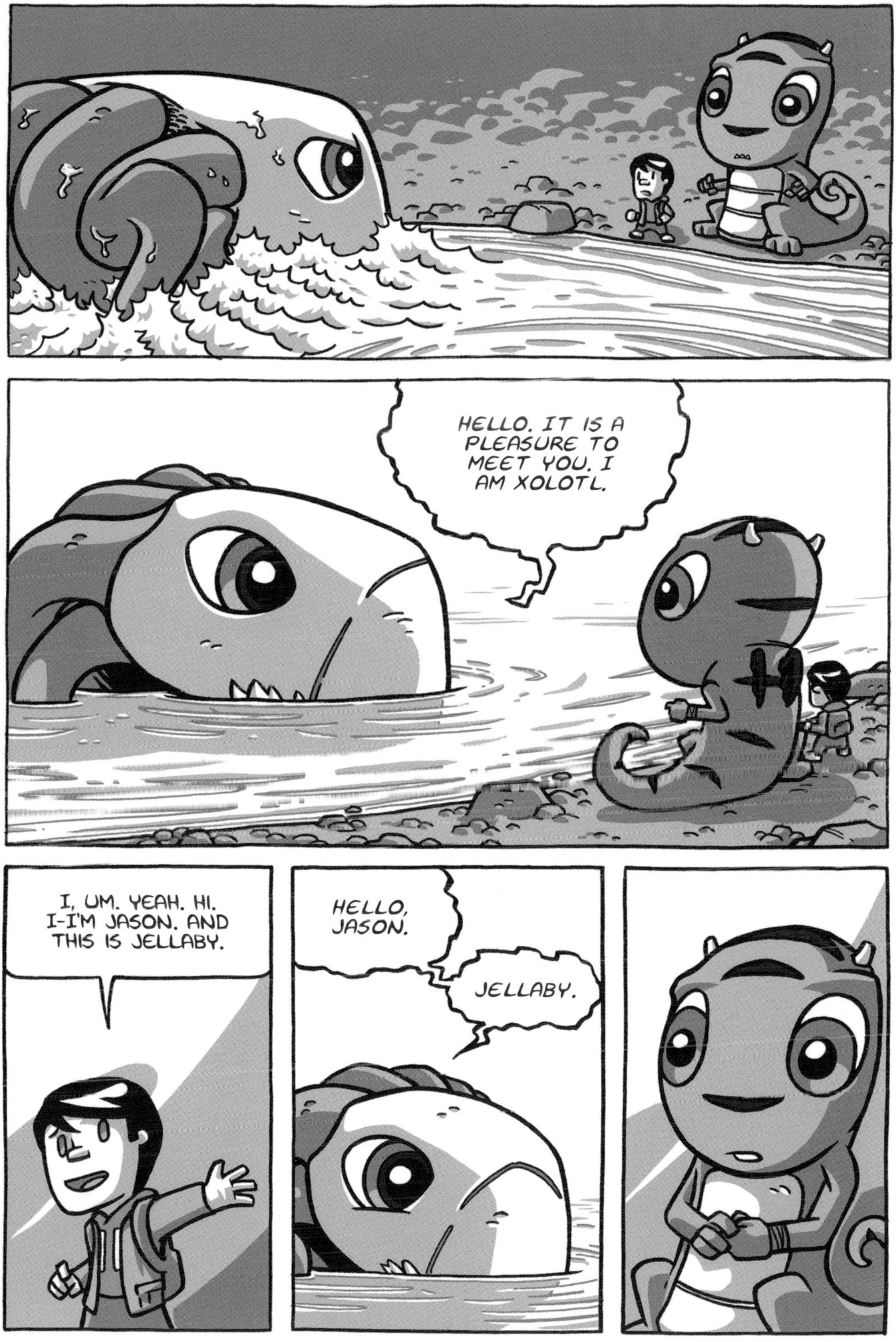
HELLO. IT IS A PLEASURE TO MEET YOU. I AM XOLOTL.
I, UM. YEAH. HI. I-I'M JASON. AND THIS IS JELLABY.
HELLO, JASON.
JELLABY.

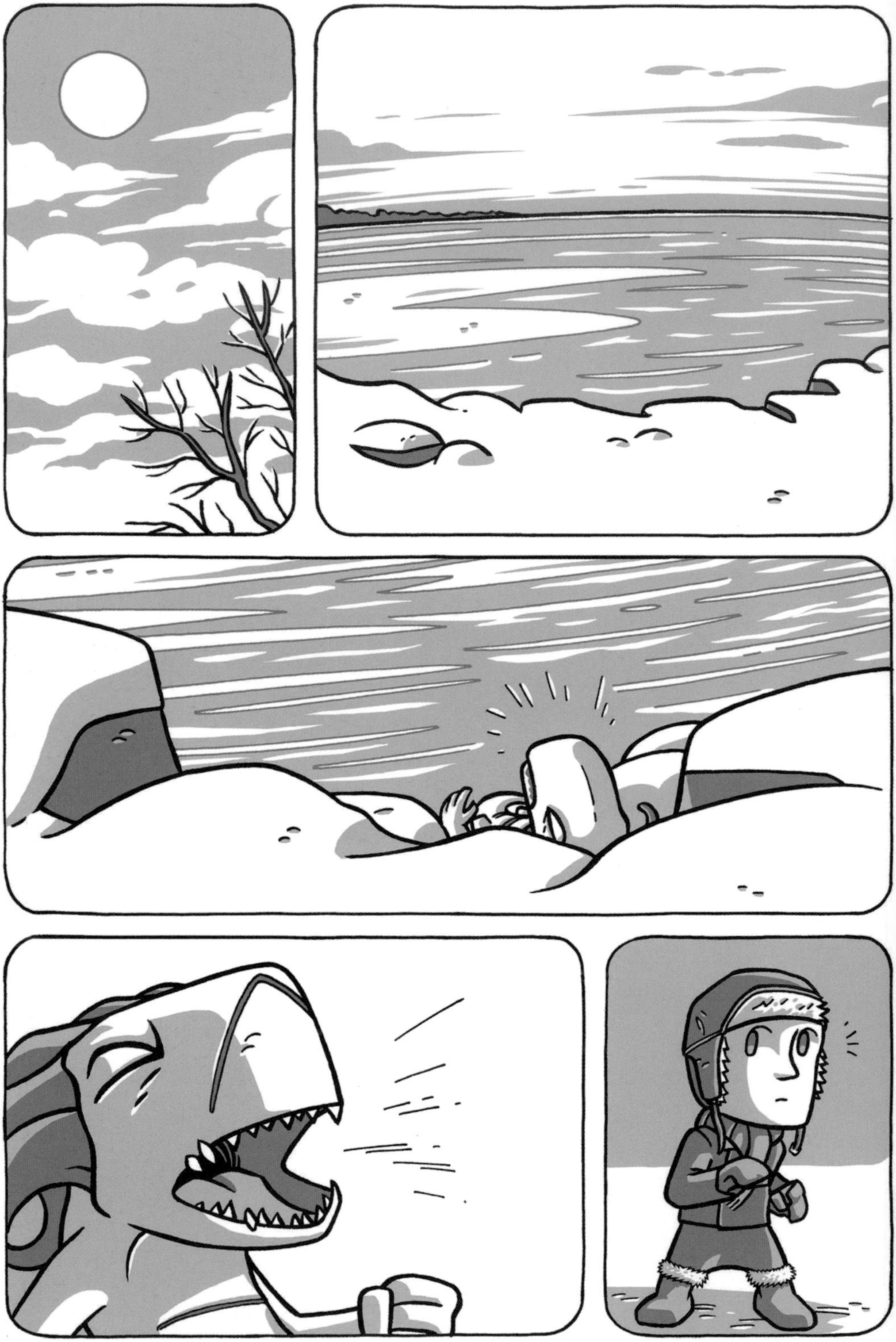

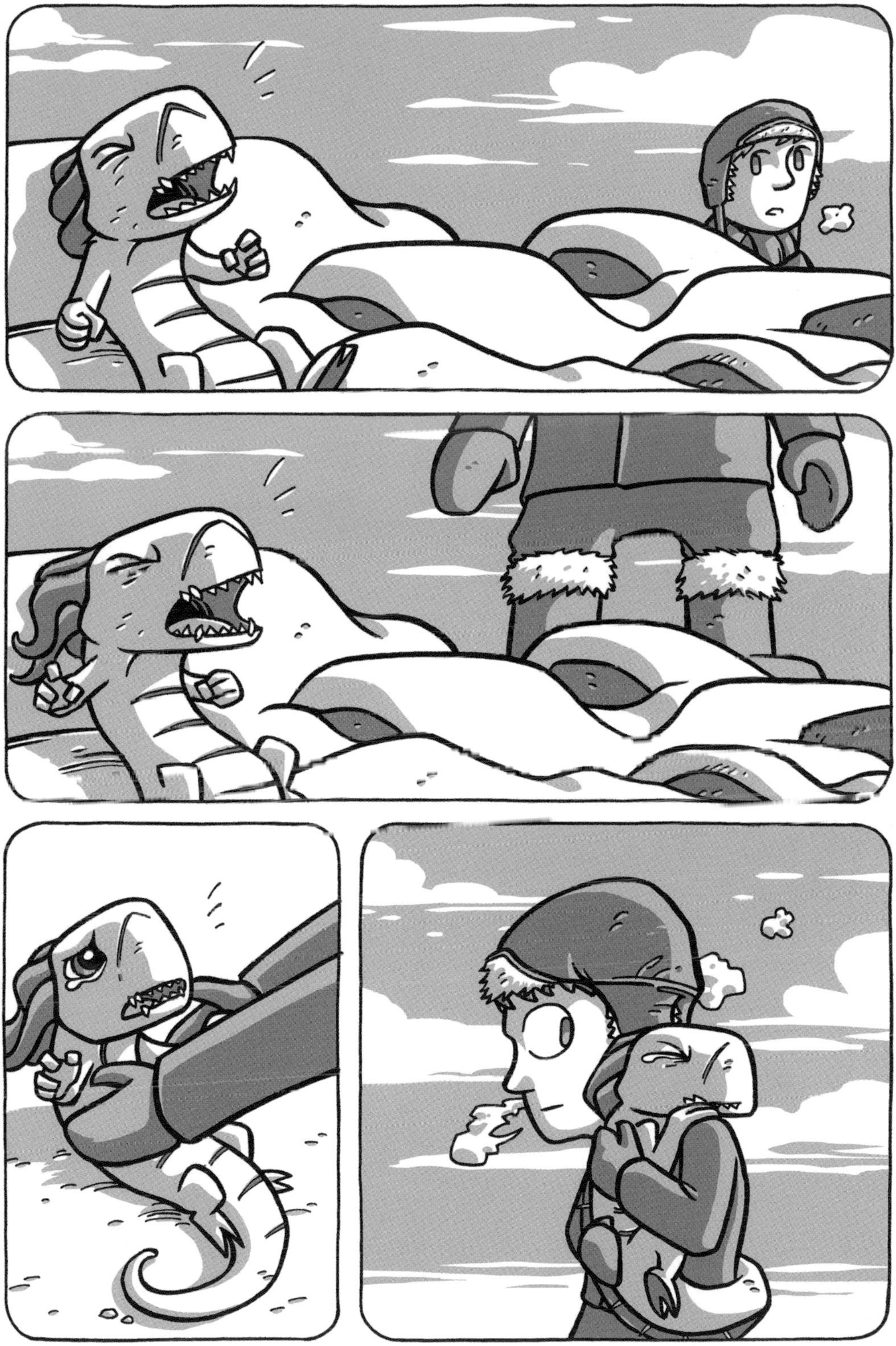

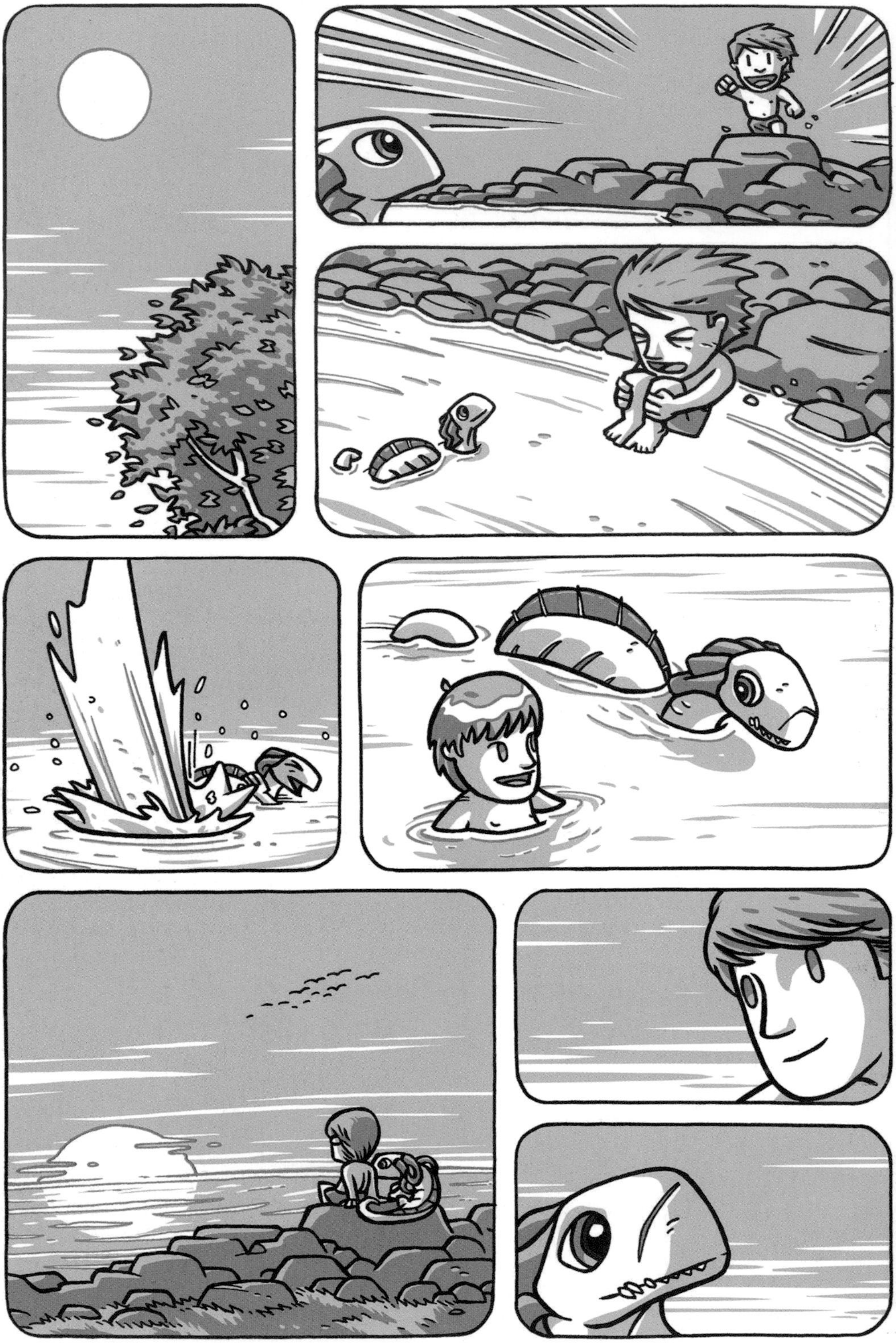

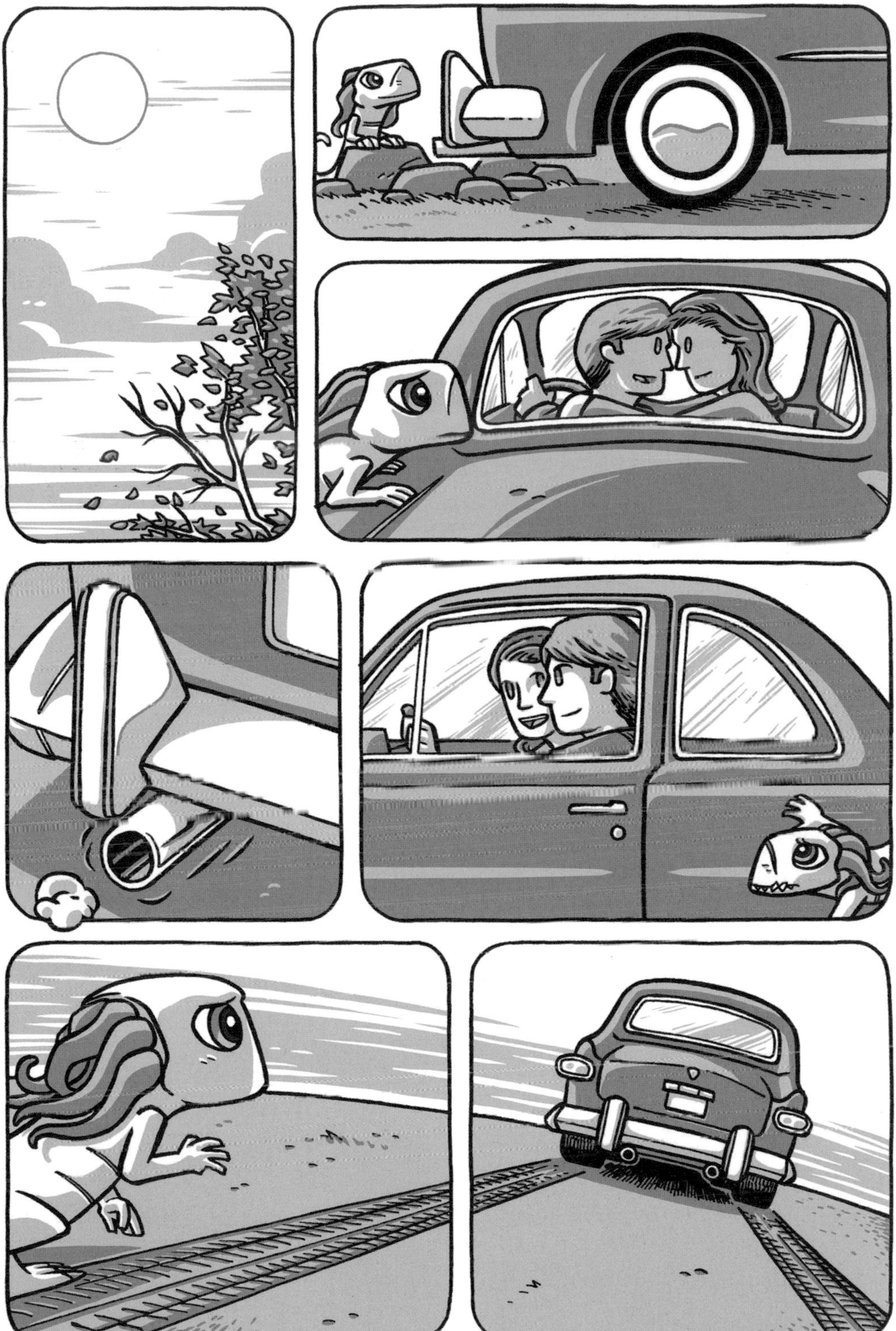

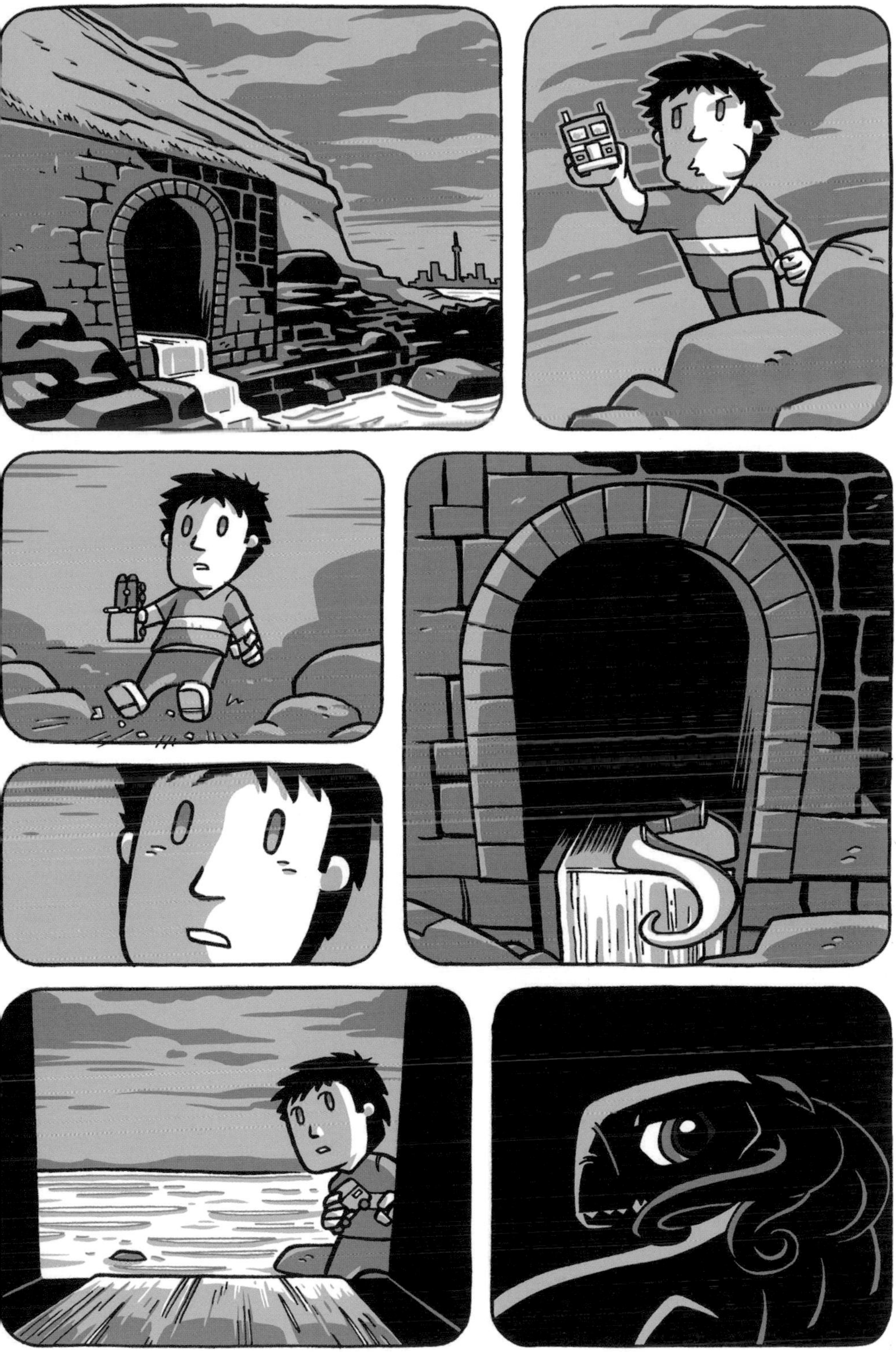

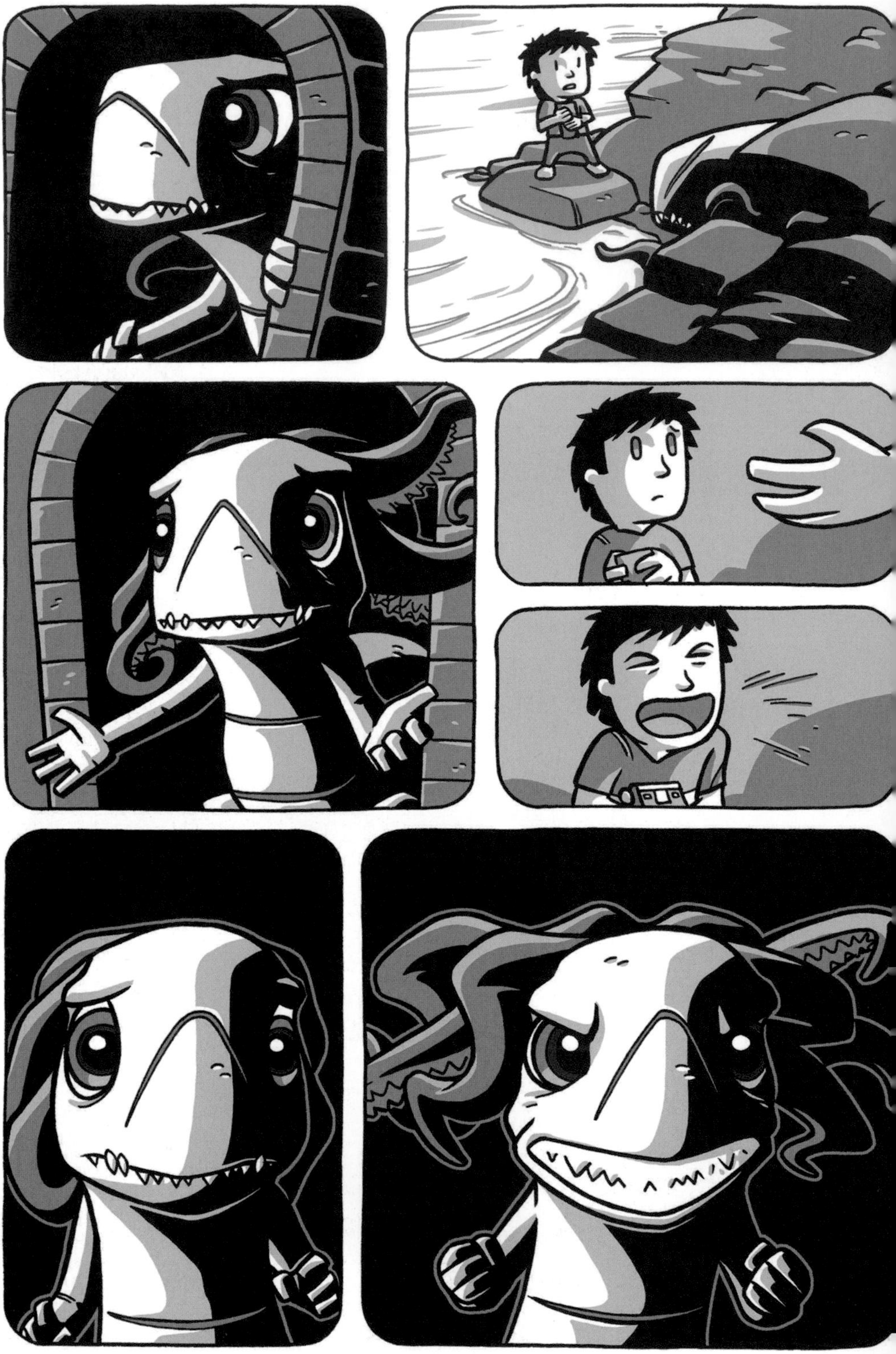

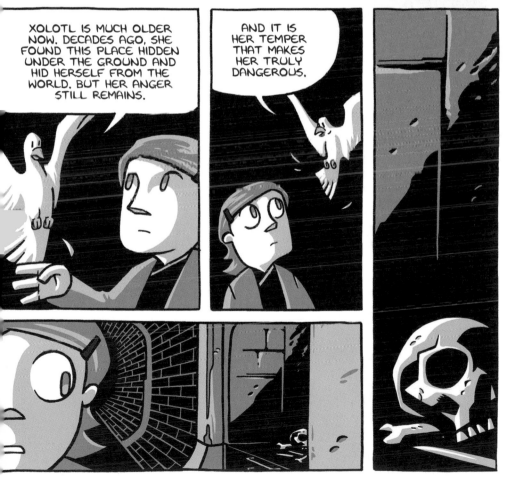

XOLOTL IS MUCH OLDER NOW. DECADES AGO, SHE FOUND THIS PLACE HIDDEN UNDER THE GROUND AND HID HERSELF FROM THE WORLD, BUT HER ANGER STILL REMAINS.

AND IT IS HER TEMPER THAT MAKES HER TRULY DANGEROUS.

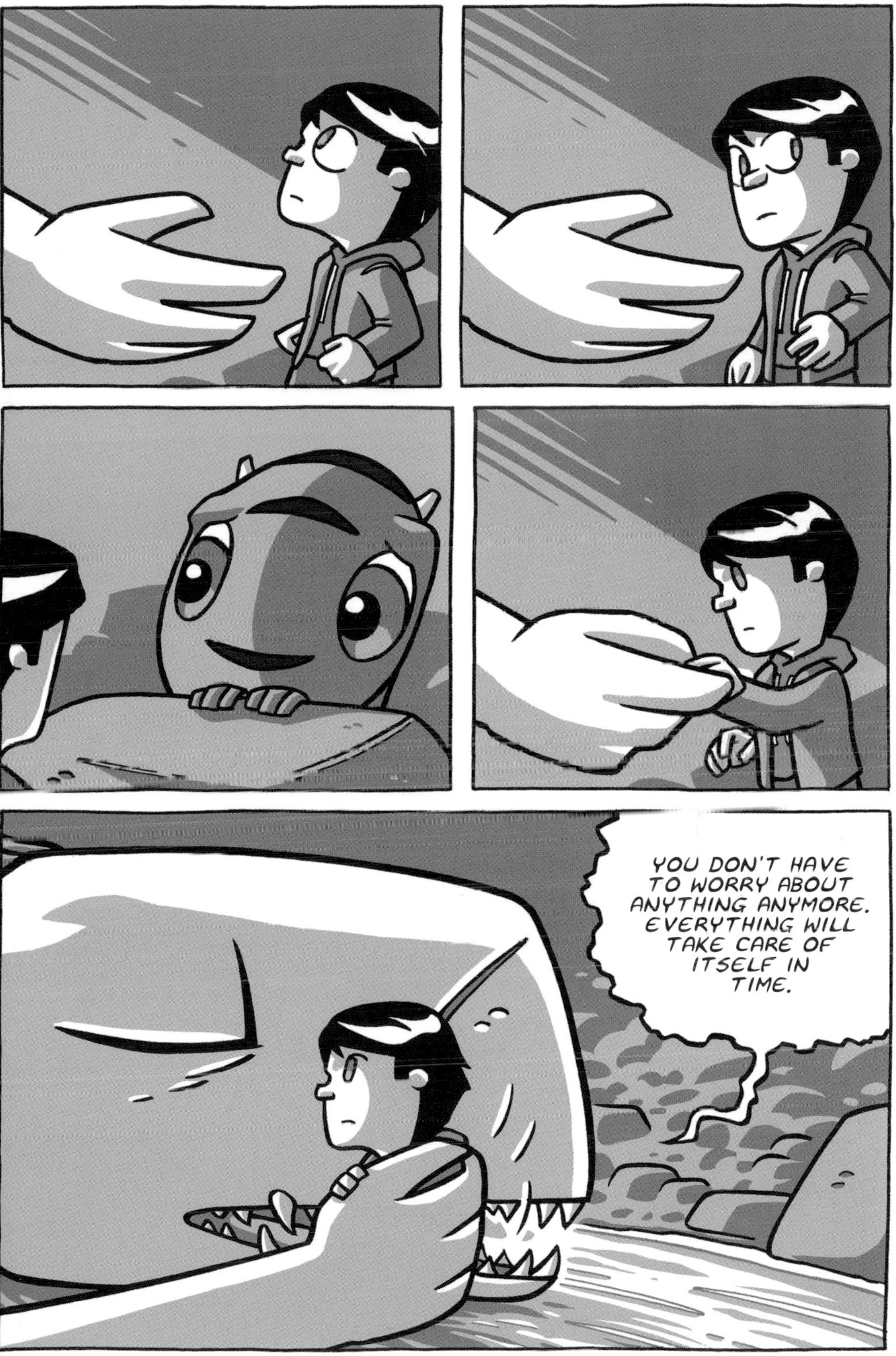
YOU DON'T HAVE TO WORRY ABOUT ANYTHING ANYMORE. EVERYTHING WILL TAKE CARE OF ITSELF IN TIME.

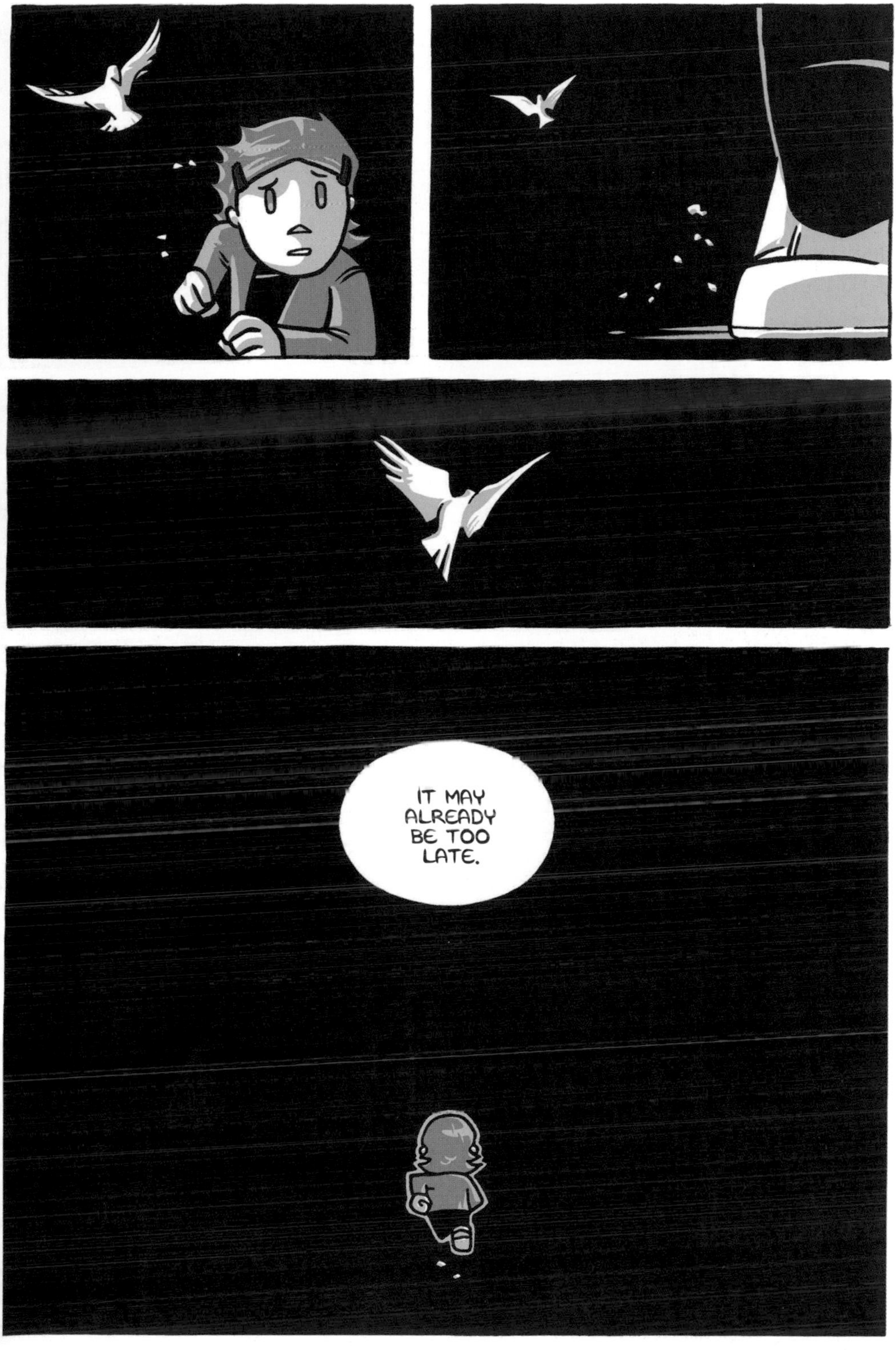
IT MAY ALREADY BE TOO LATE.

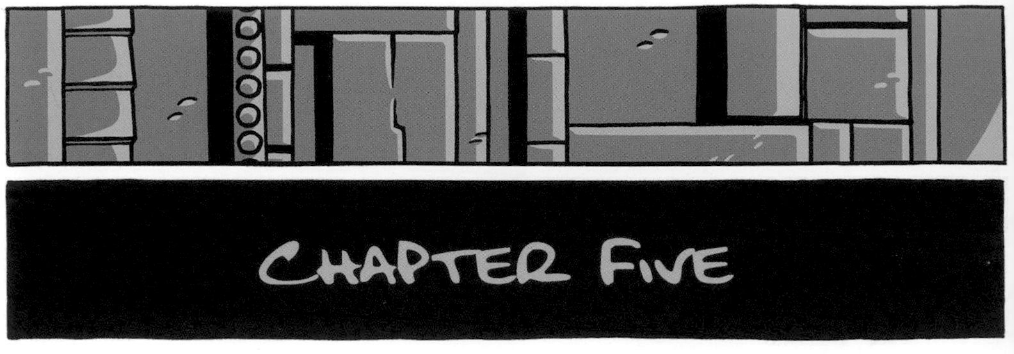

CHAPTER FIVE

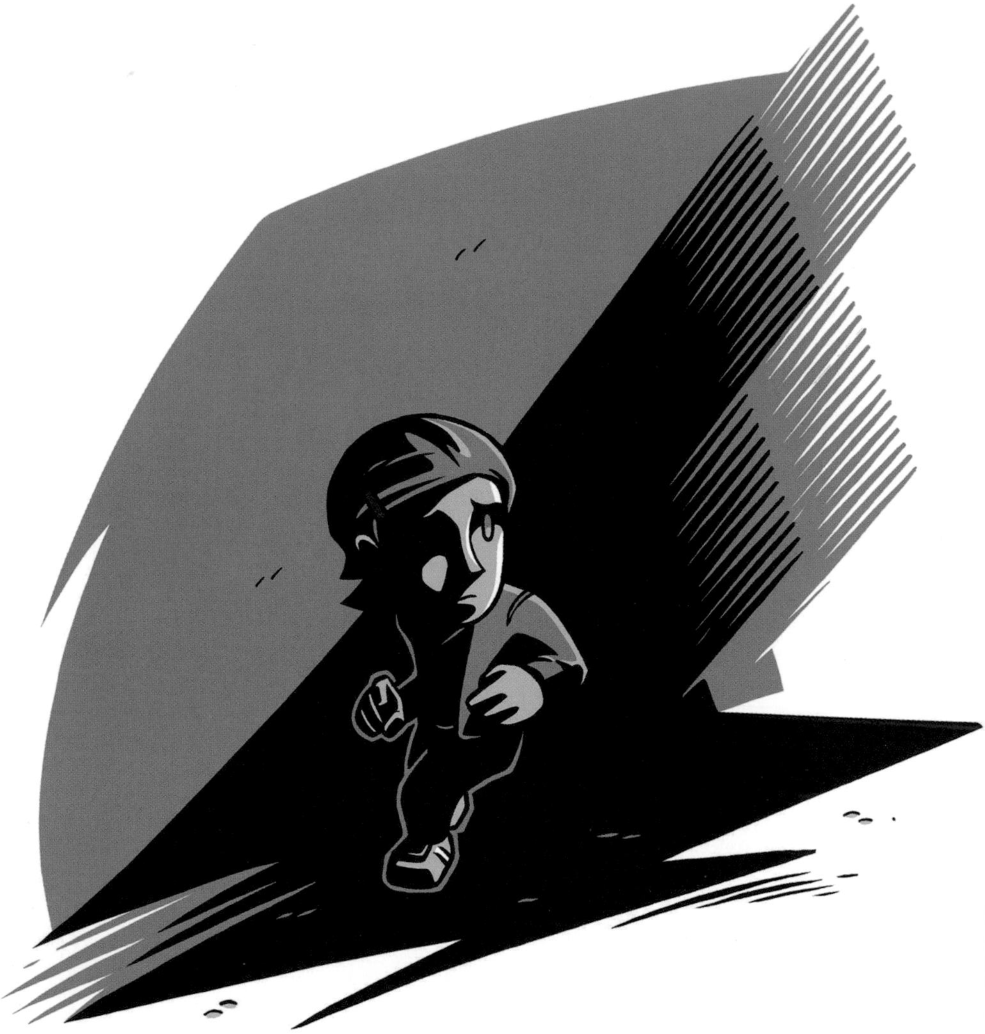

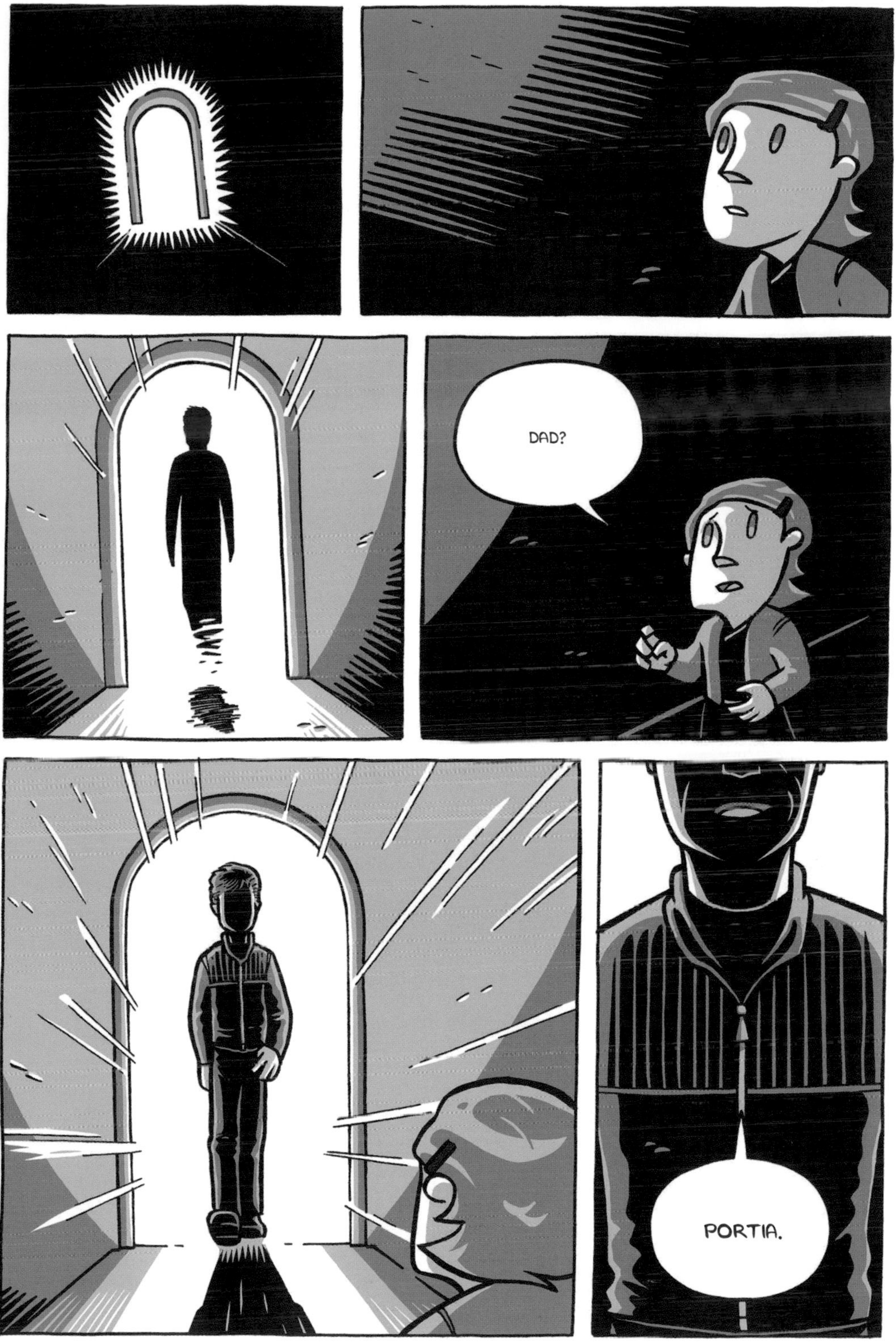
DAD?
PORTIA.

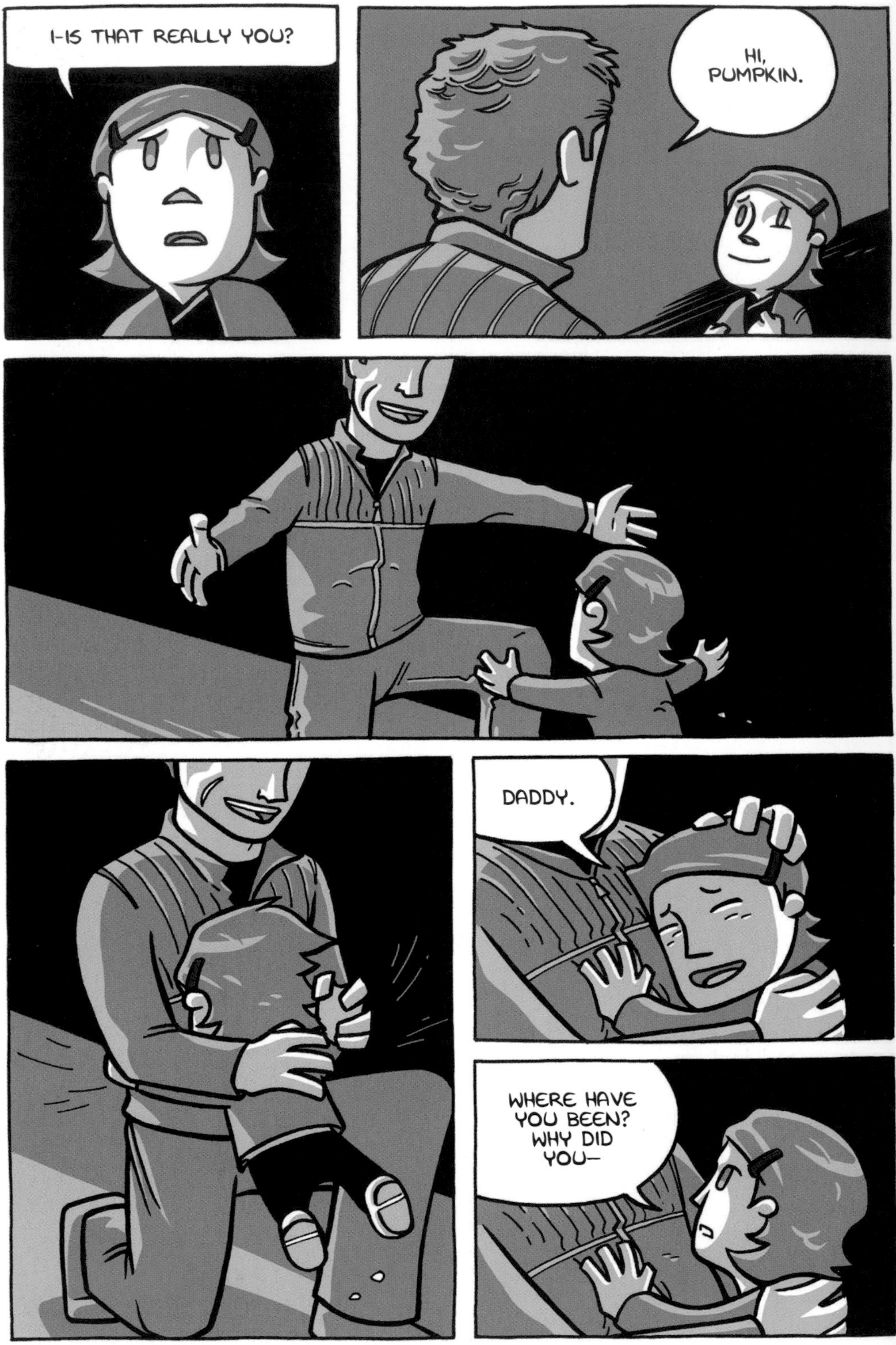
I-IS THAT REALLY YOU?
HI, PUMPKIN.
DADDY.
WHERE HAVE YOU BEEN? WHY DID YOU—

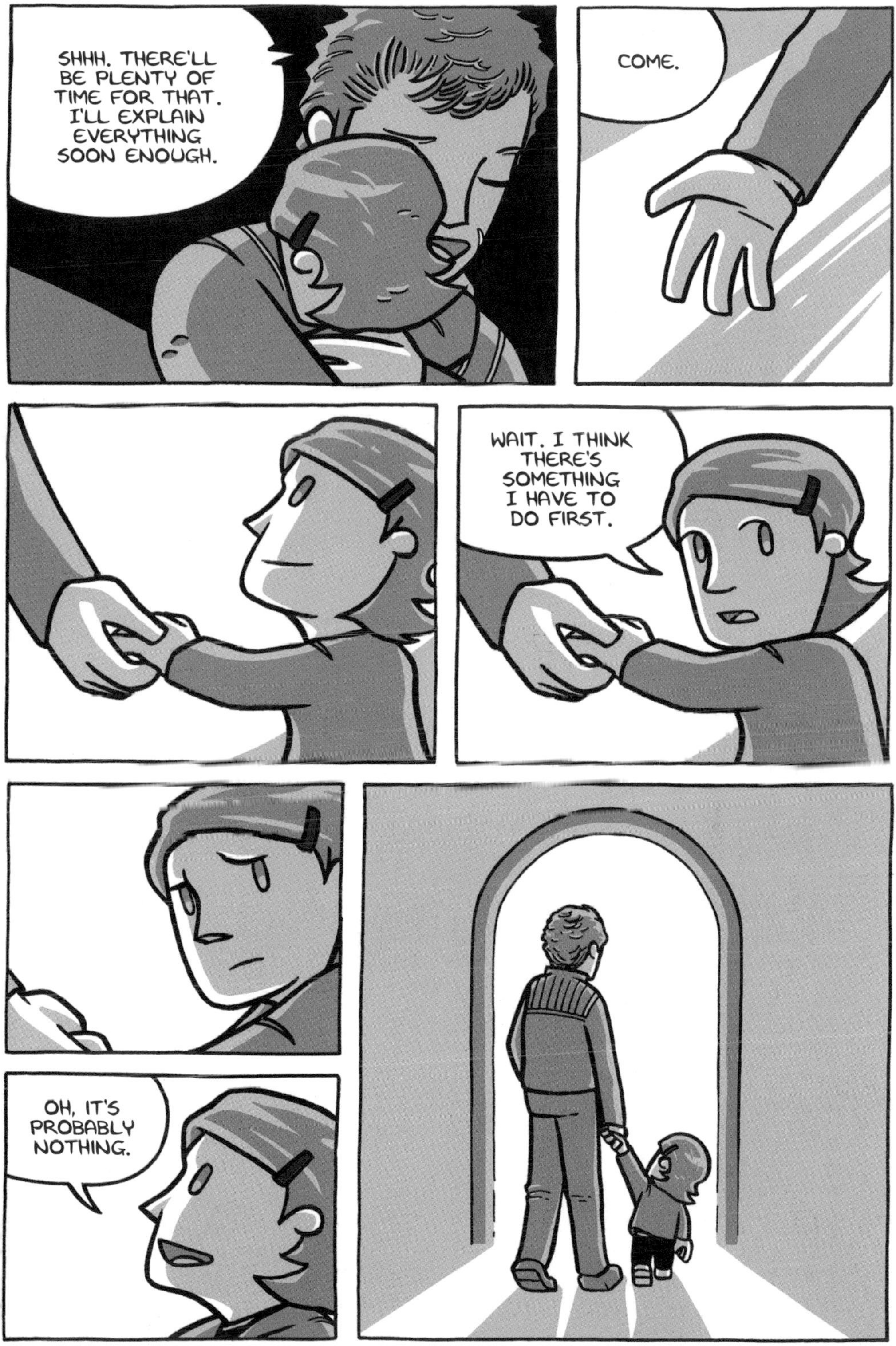
SHHH. THERE'LL BE PLENTY OF TIME FOR THAT. I'LL EXPLAIN EVERYTHING SOON ENOUGH.
COME.
WAIT. I THINK THERE'S SOMETHING I HAVE TO DO FIRST.
OH, IT'S PROBABLY NOTHING.

108

110

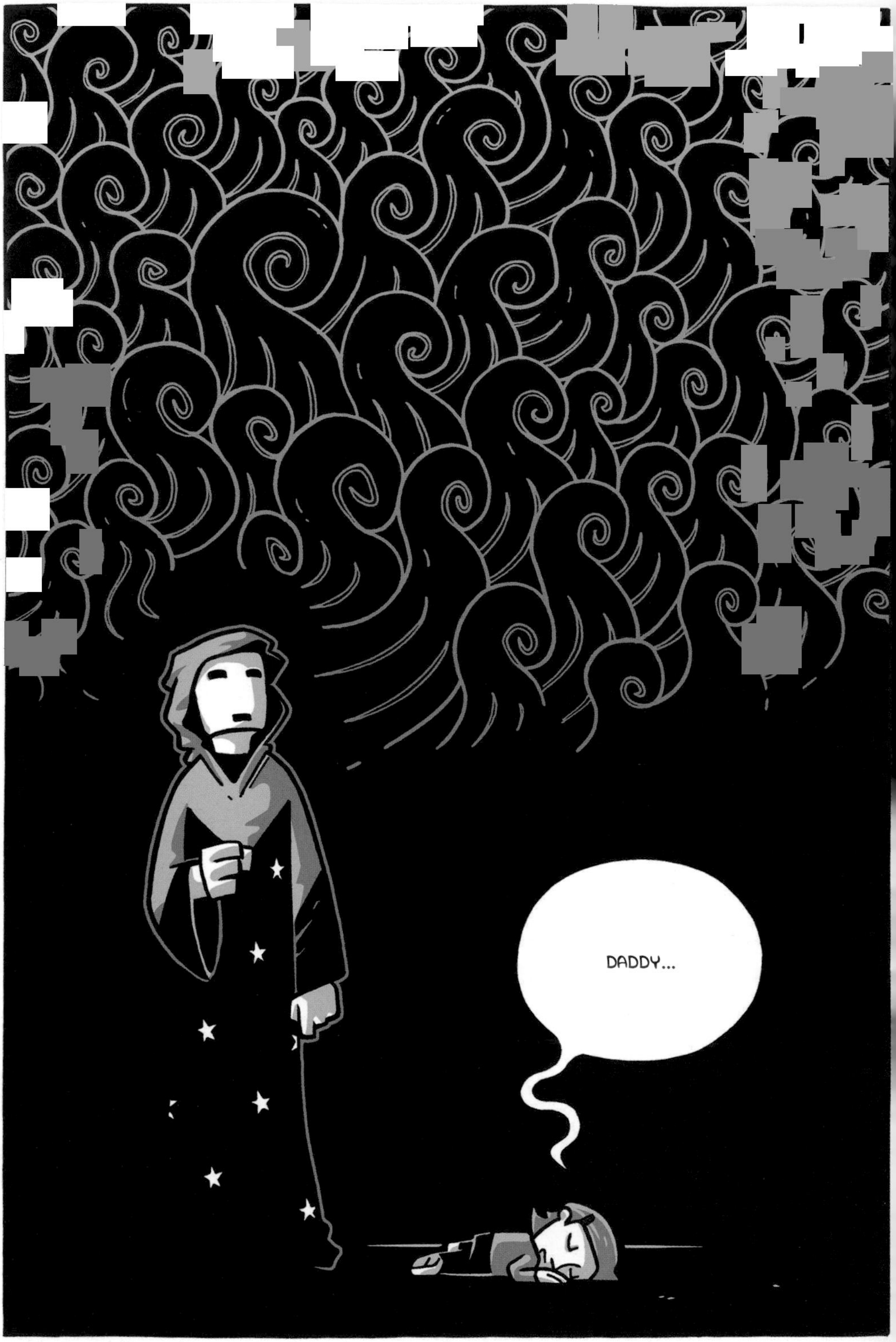
DADDY...

114

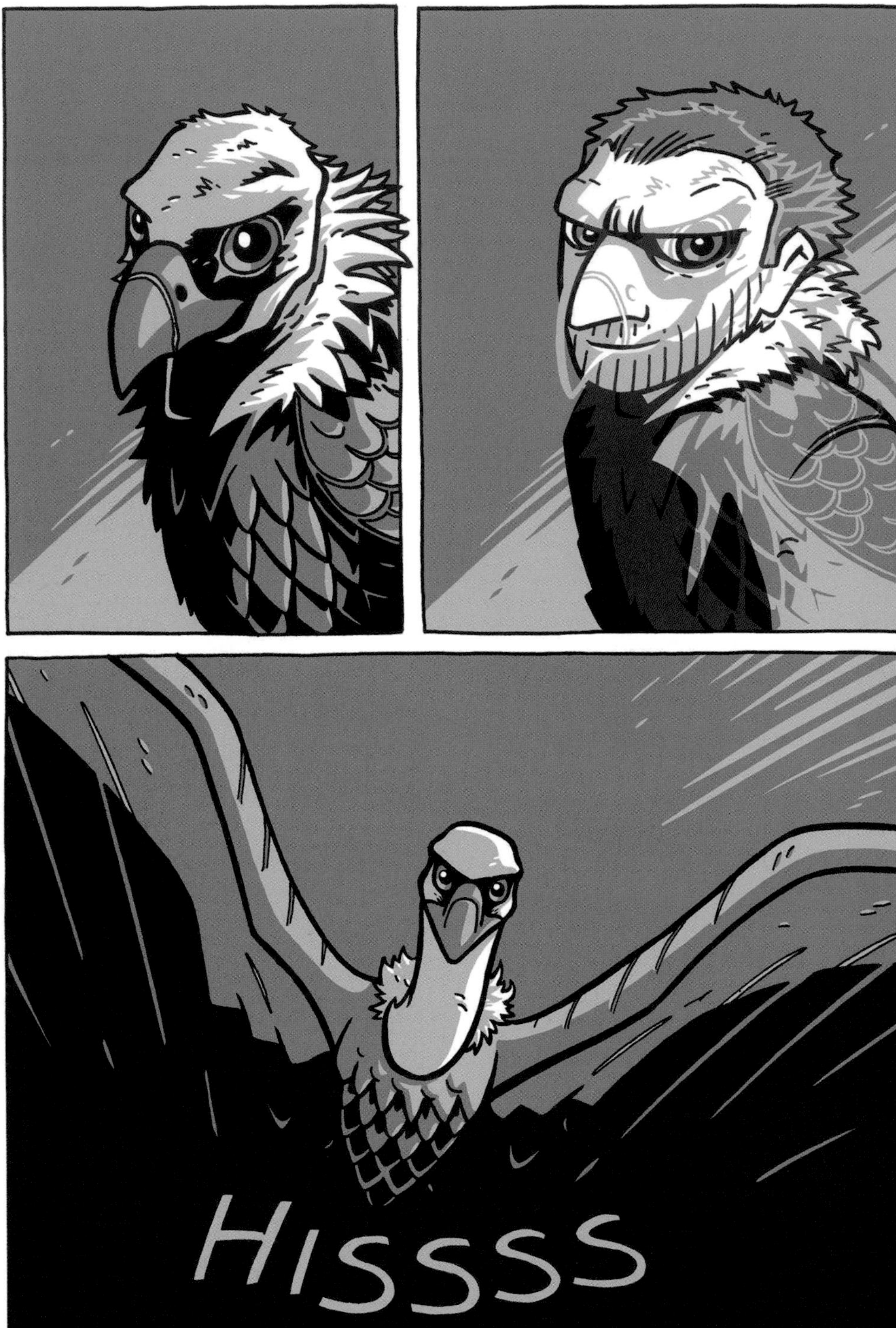
HISSSS

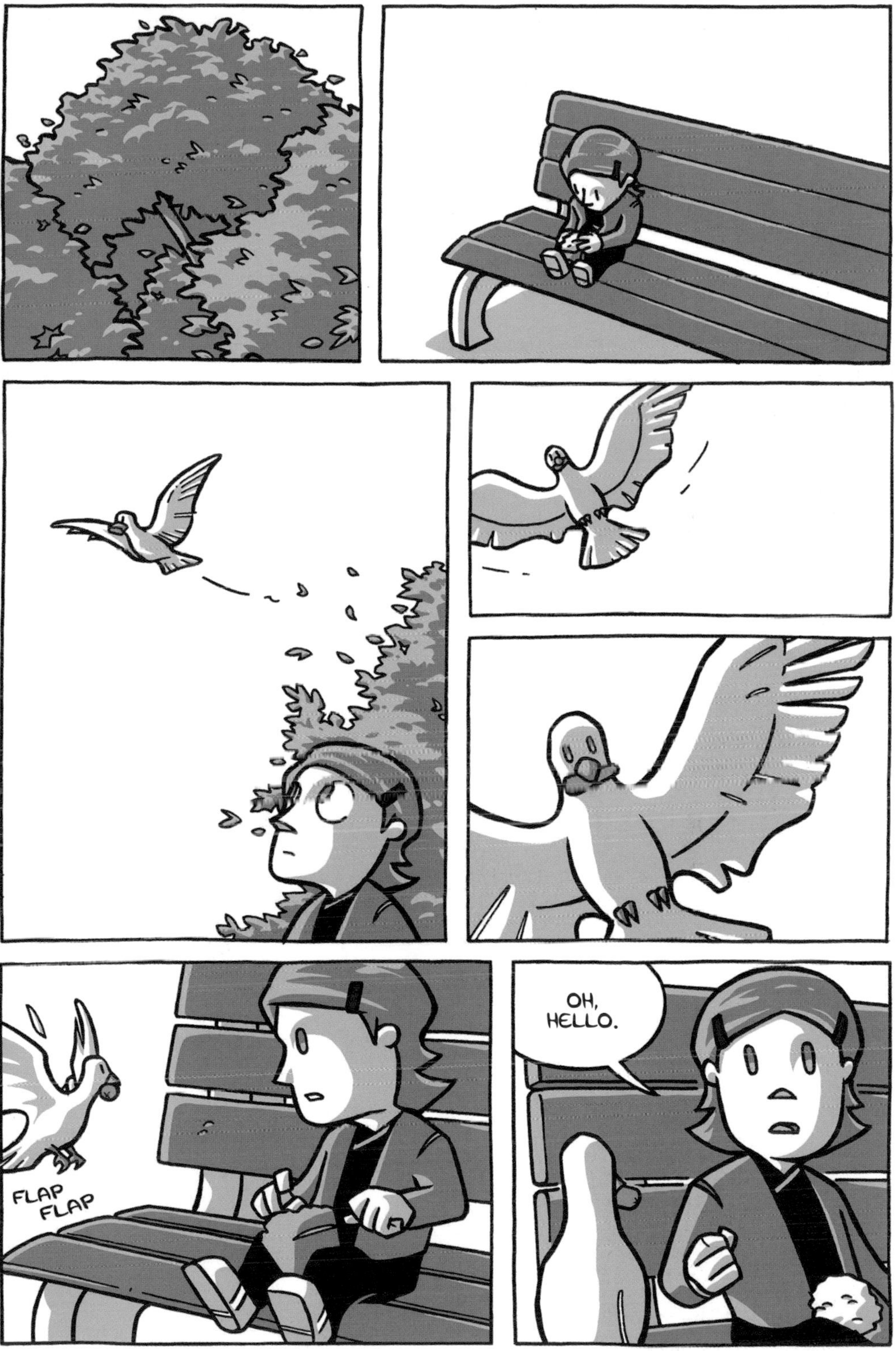
FLAP
FLAP
OH, HELLO.

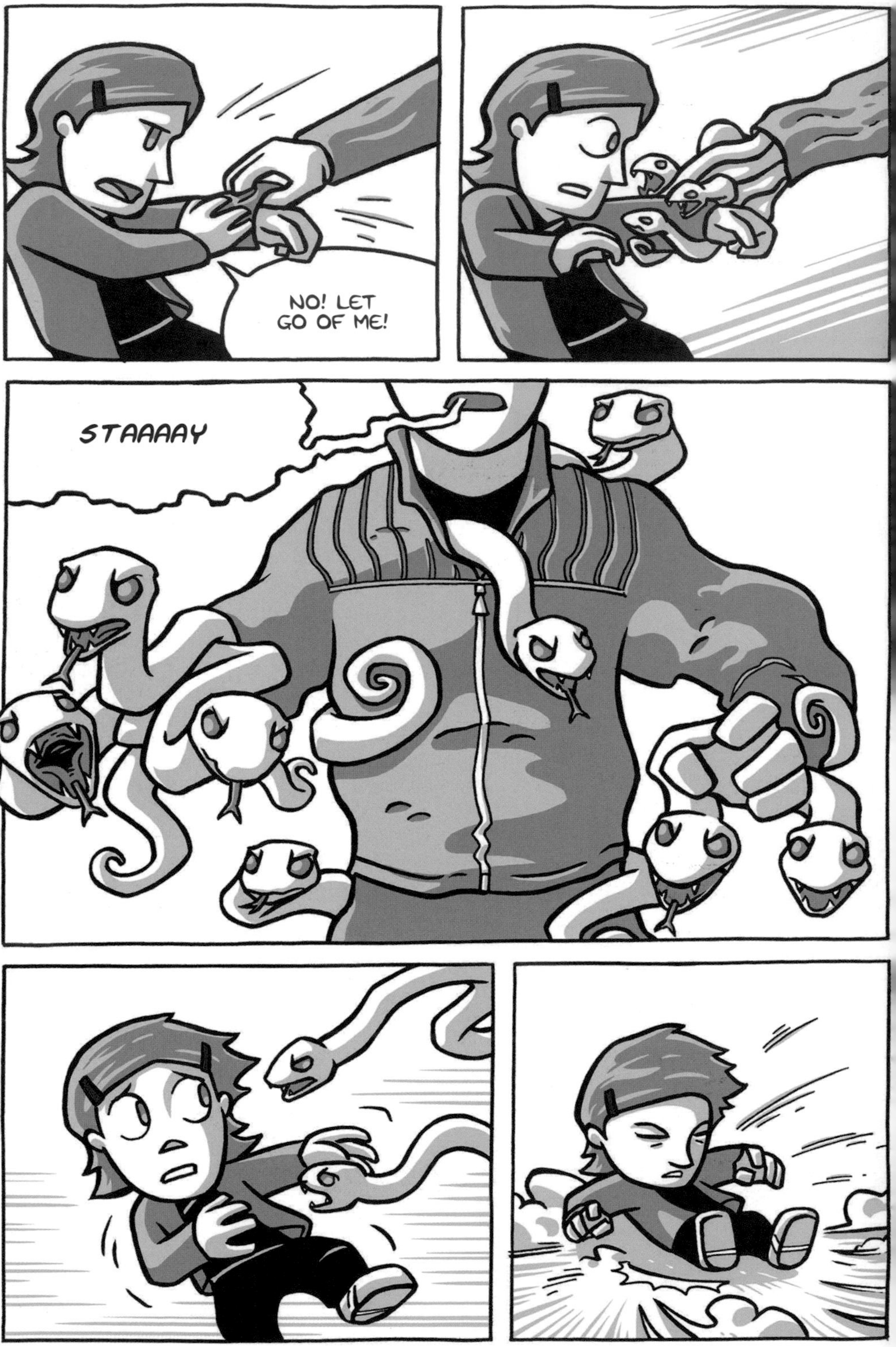
NO! LET GO OF ME!
STAAAAY

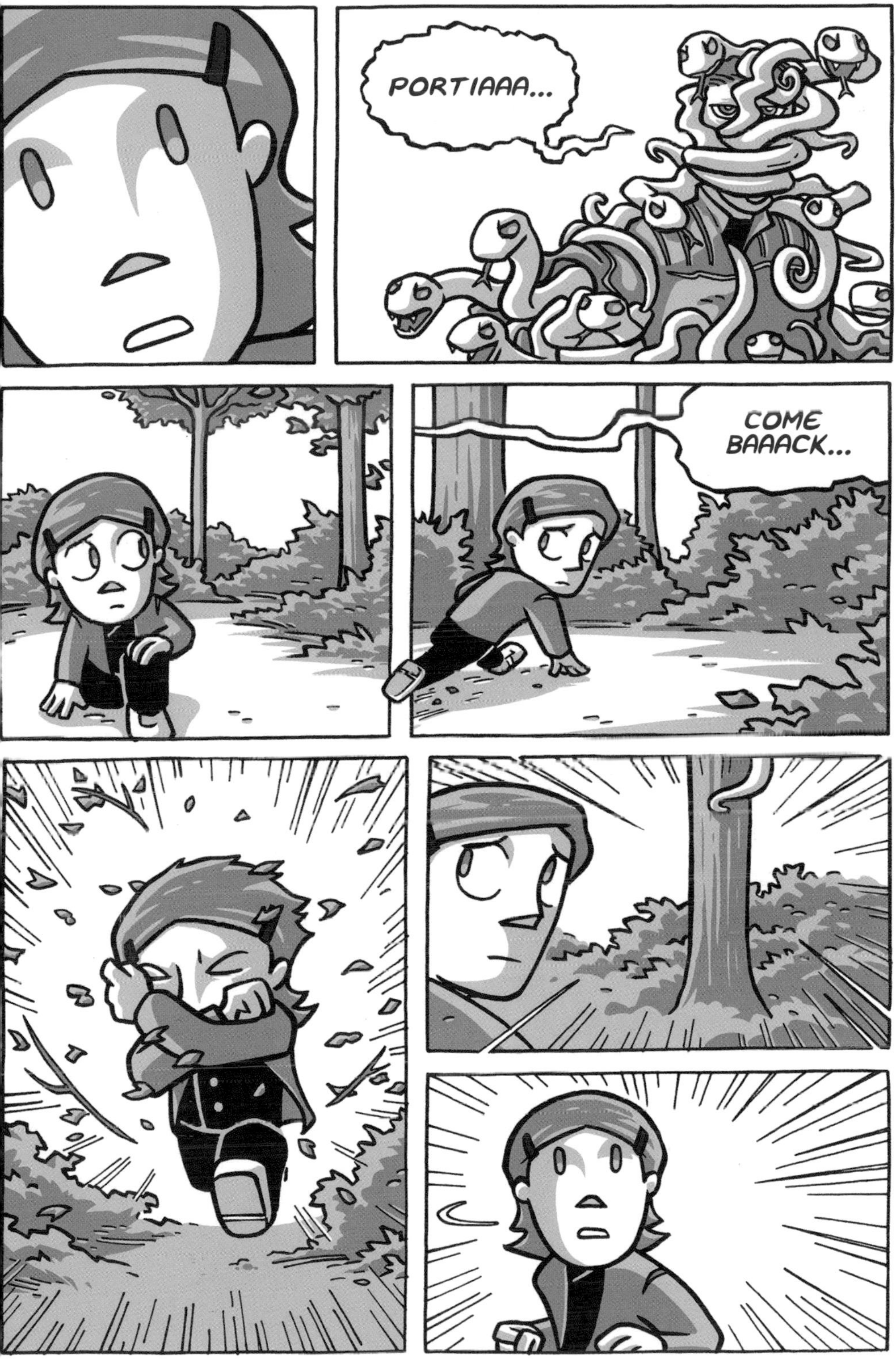
PORTIAAA...
COME BAAACK...

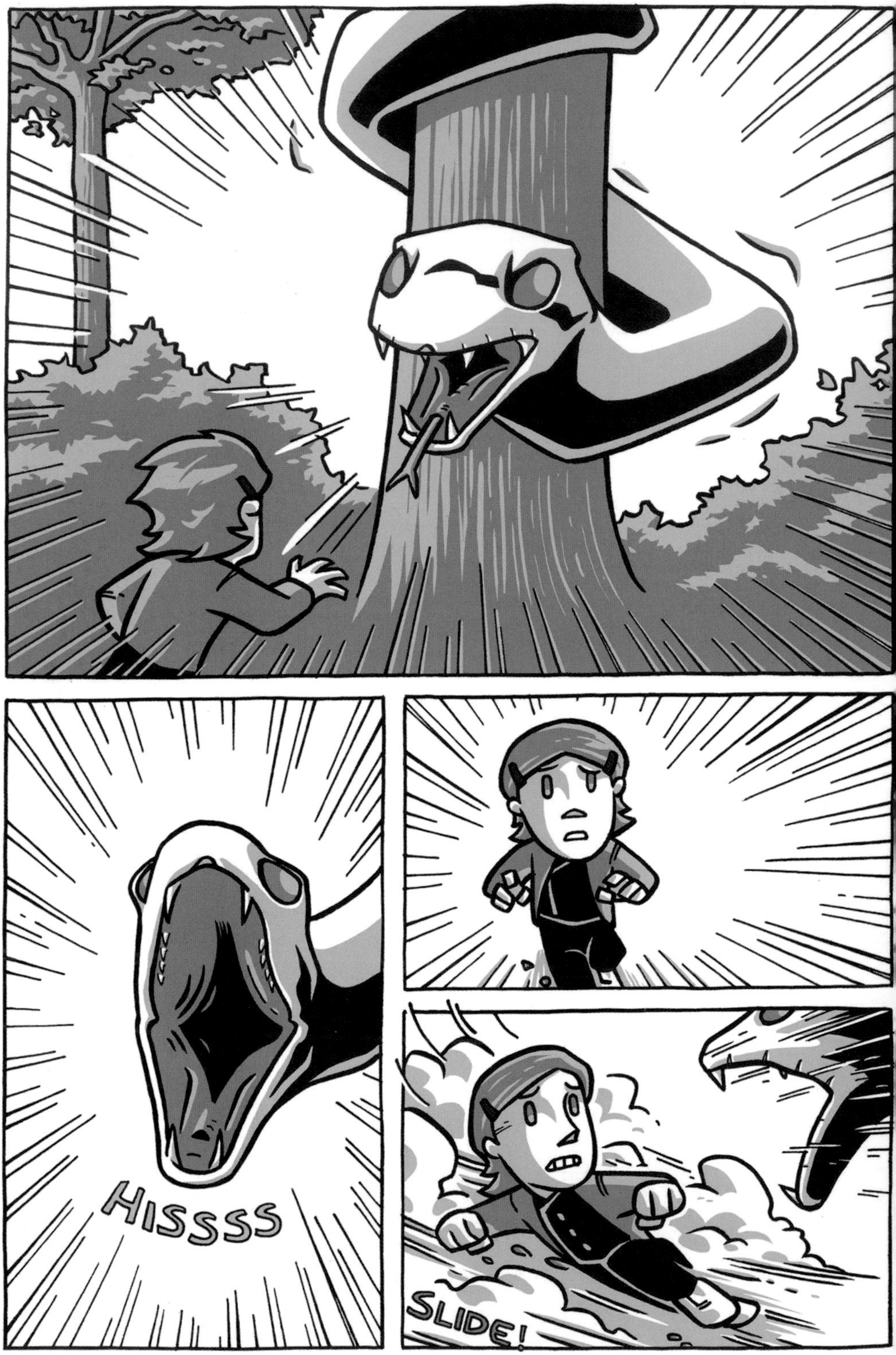
HISSSS
SLIDE!

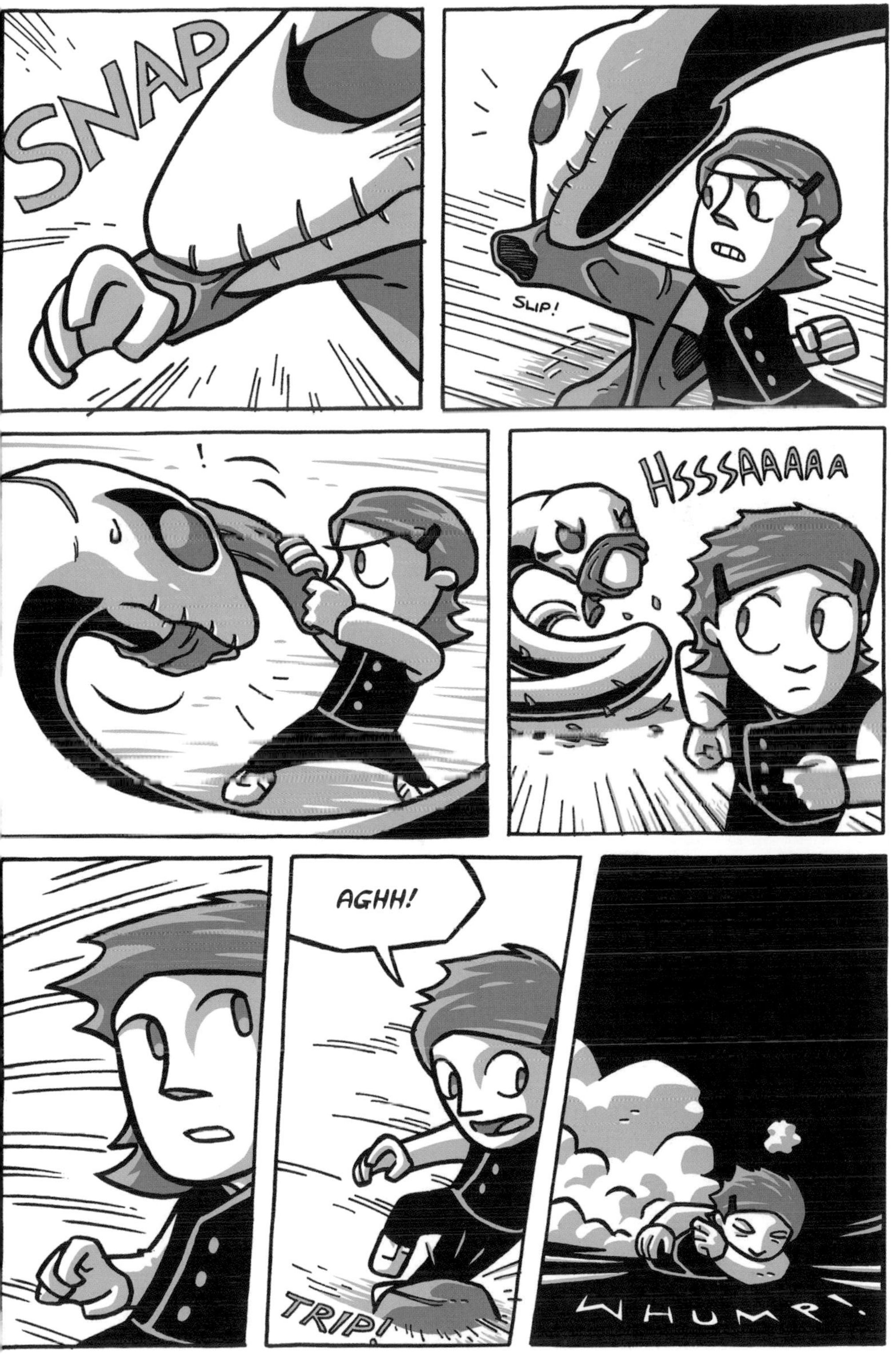
SNAP
SLIP!
!
HSSSAAAAA
AGHH!
TRIP!
WHUMP!

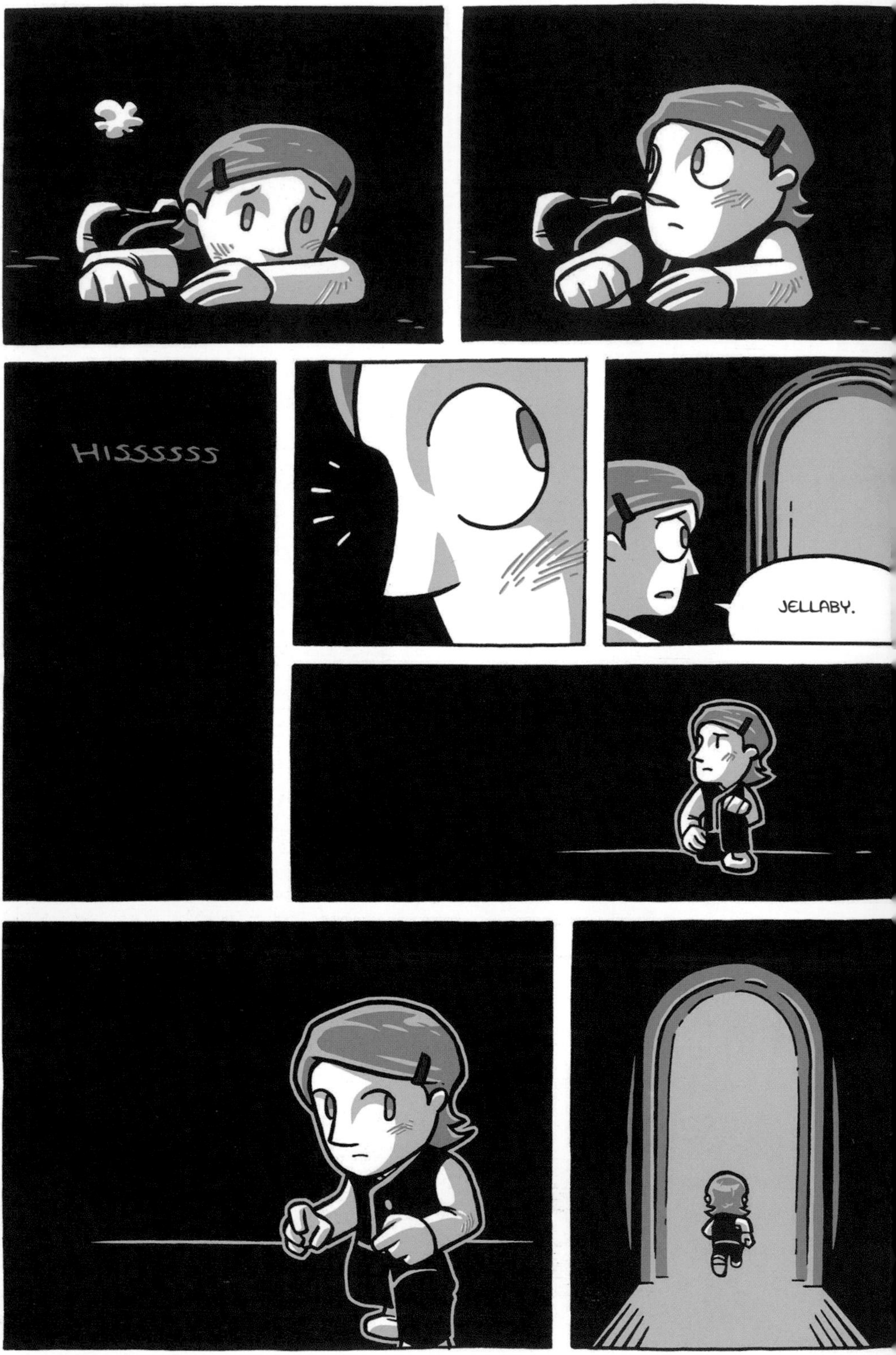
HISSSSSSS
JELLABY.

128

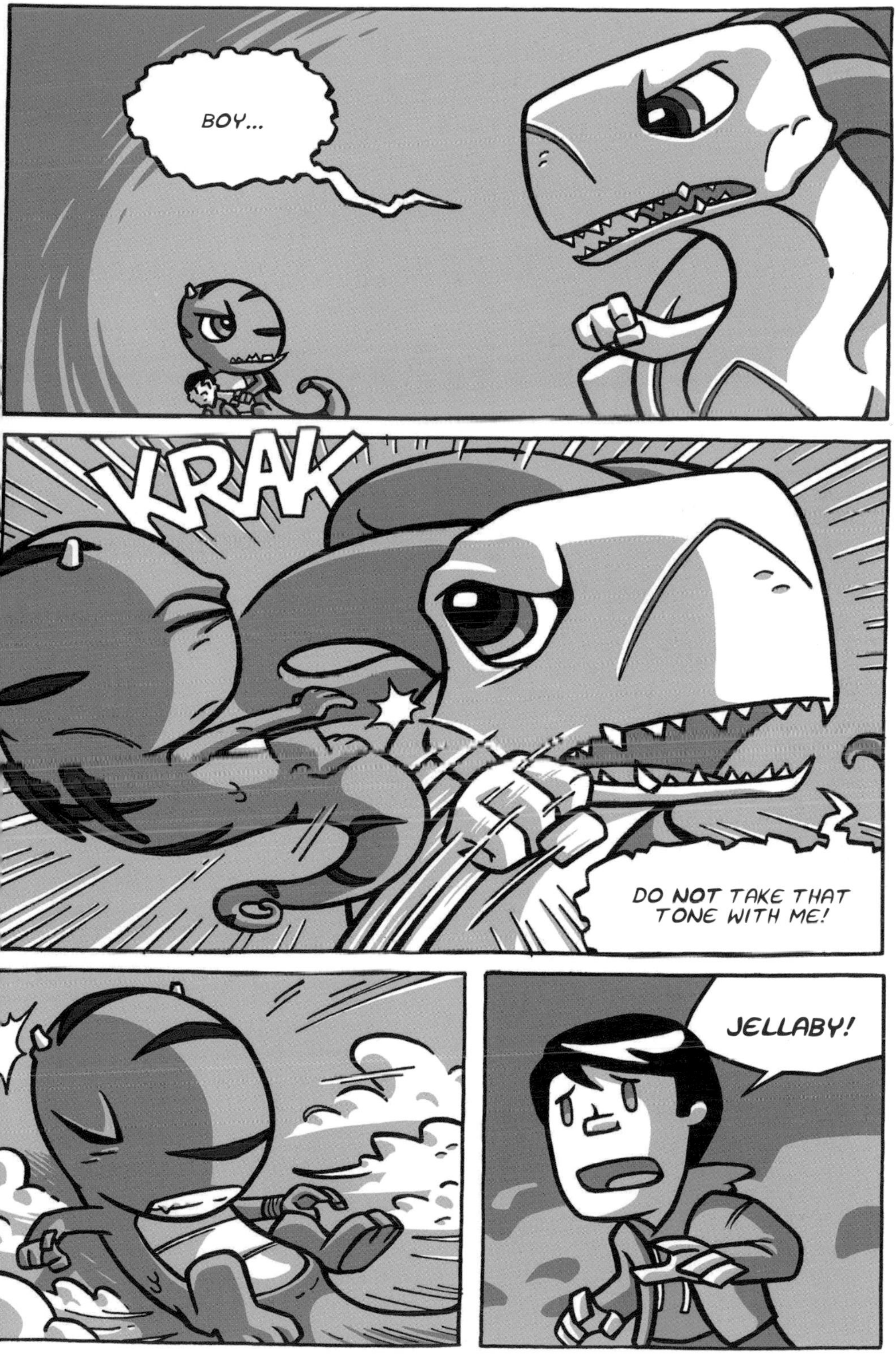
BOY...
KRAK
DO NOT TAKE THAT TONE WITH ME!
JELLABY!

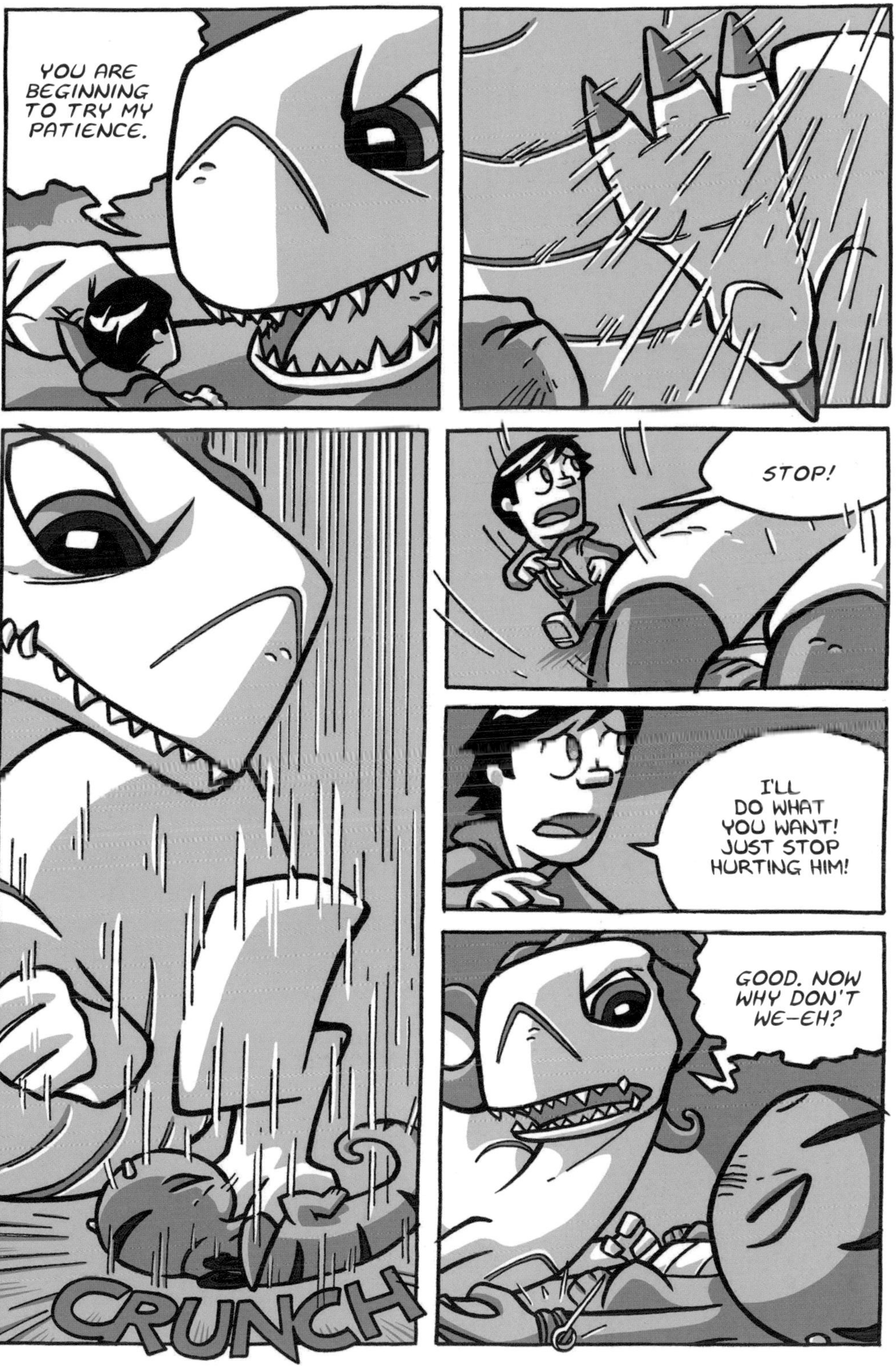
YOU ARE BEGINNING TO TRY MY PATIENCE.
STOP!
I'LL DO WHAT YOU WANT! JUST STOP HURTING HIM!
CRUNCH
GOOD. NOW WHY DON'T WE—EH?

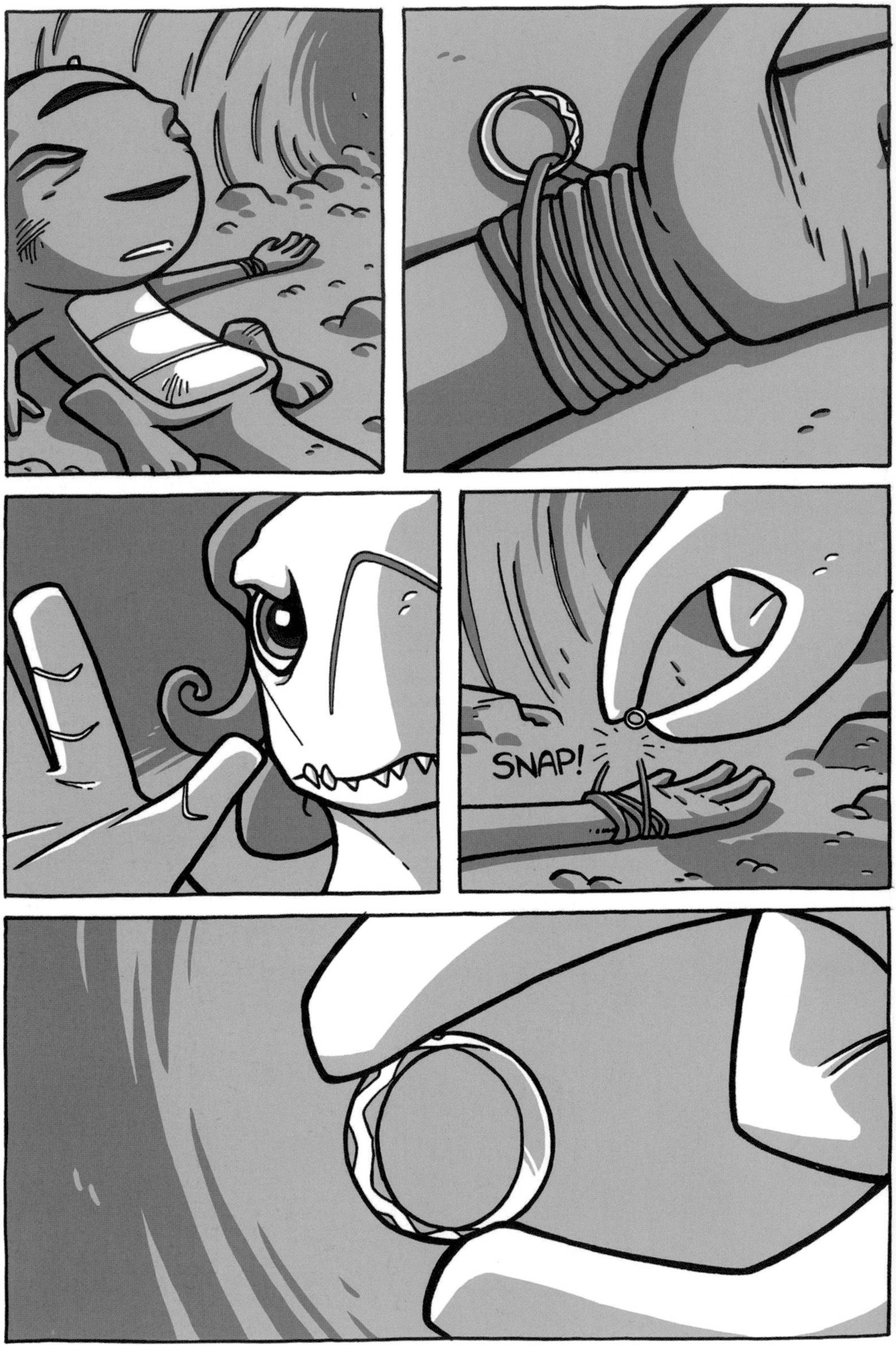
SNAP!

133

134

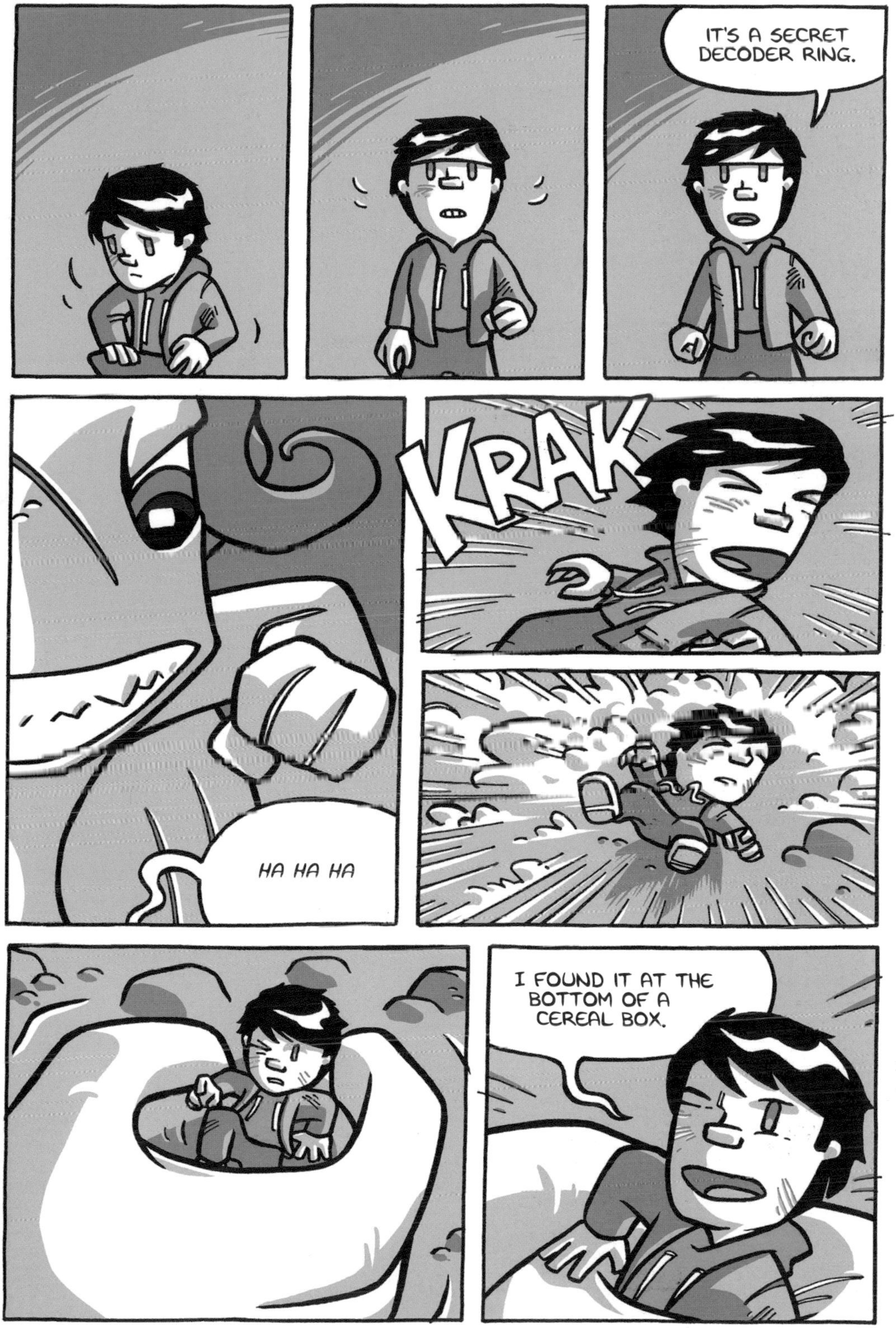
IT'S A SECRET DECODER RING.
KRAK
HA HA HA
I FOUND IT AT THE BOTTOM OF A CEREAL BOX.

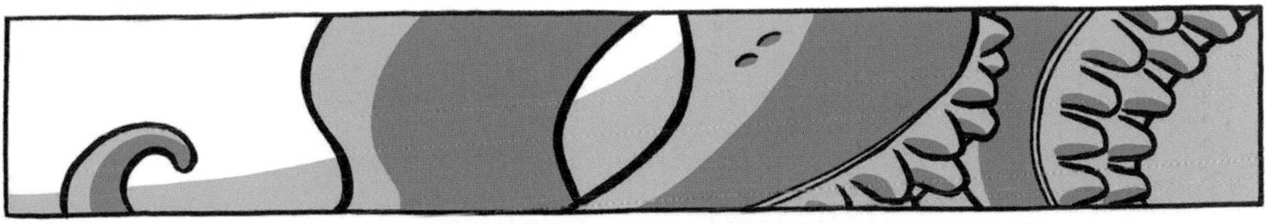

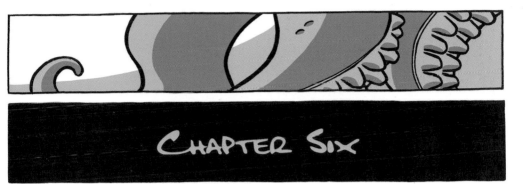

Chapter Six

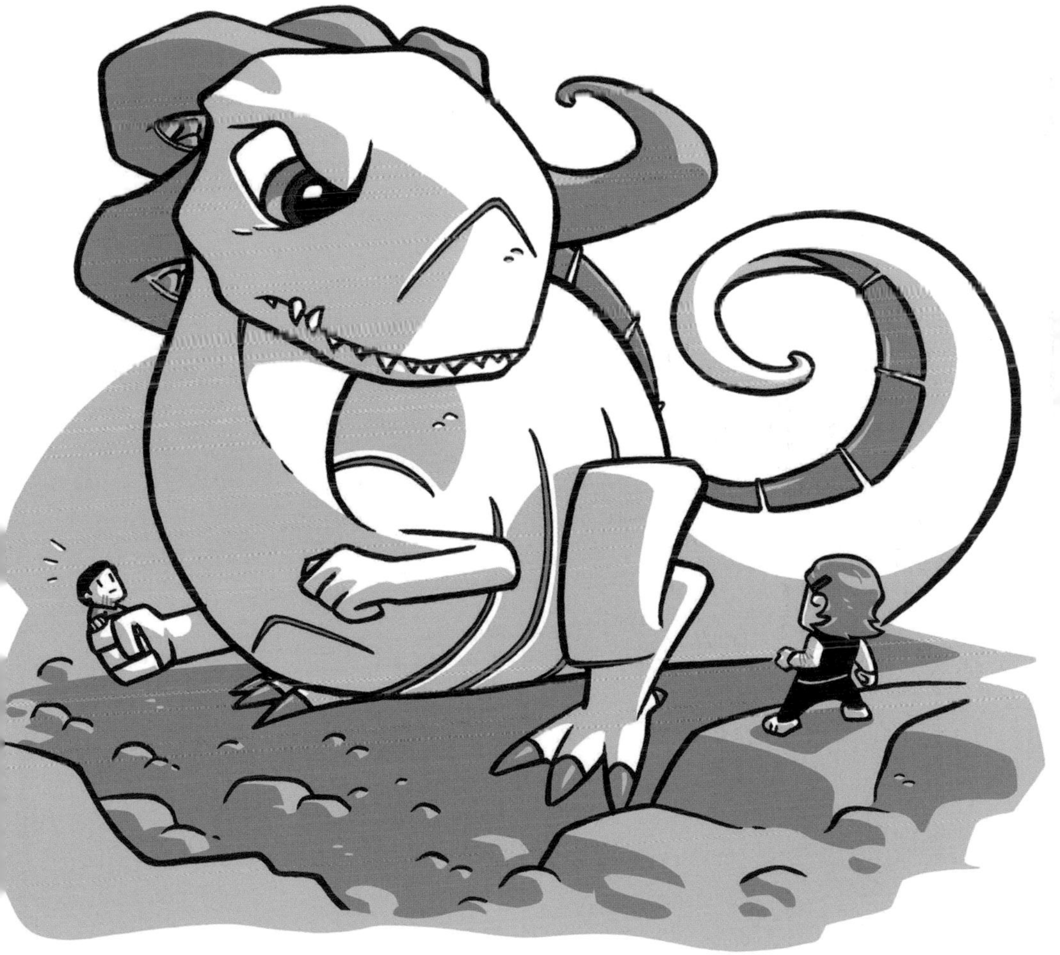

140

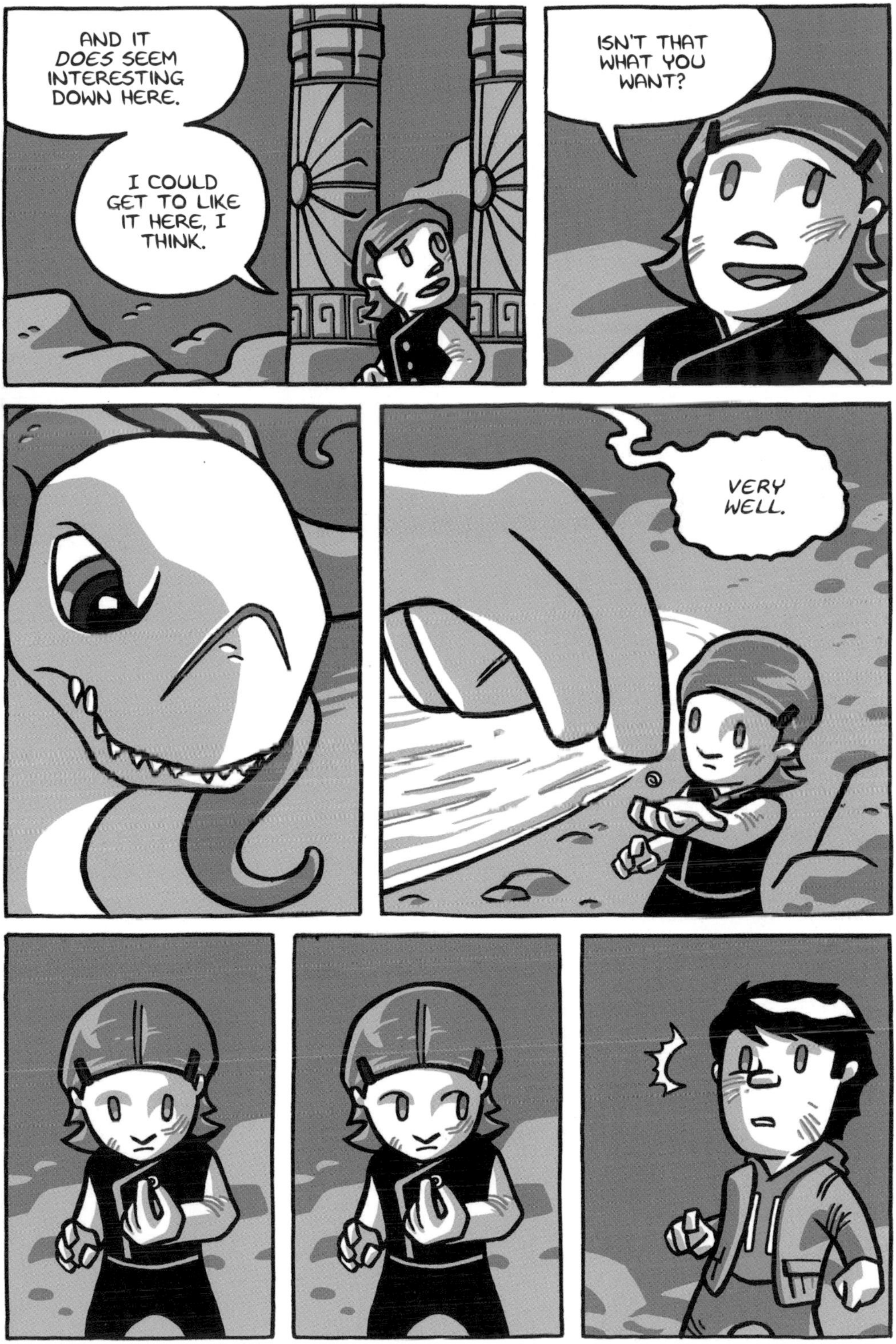
AND IT DOES SEEM INTERESTING DOWN HERE.
I COULD GET TO LIKE IT HERE, I THINK.
ISN'T THAT WHAT YOU WANT?
VERY WELL.

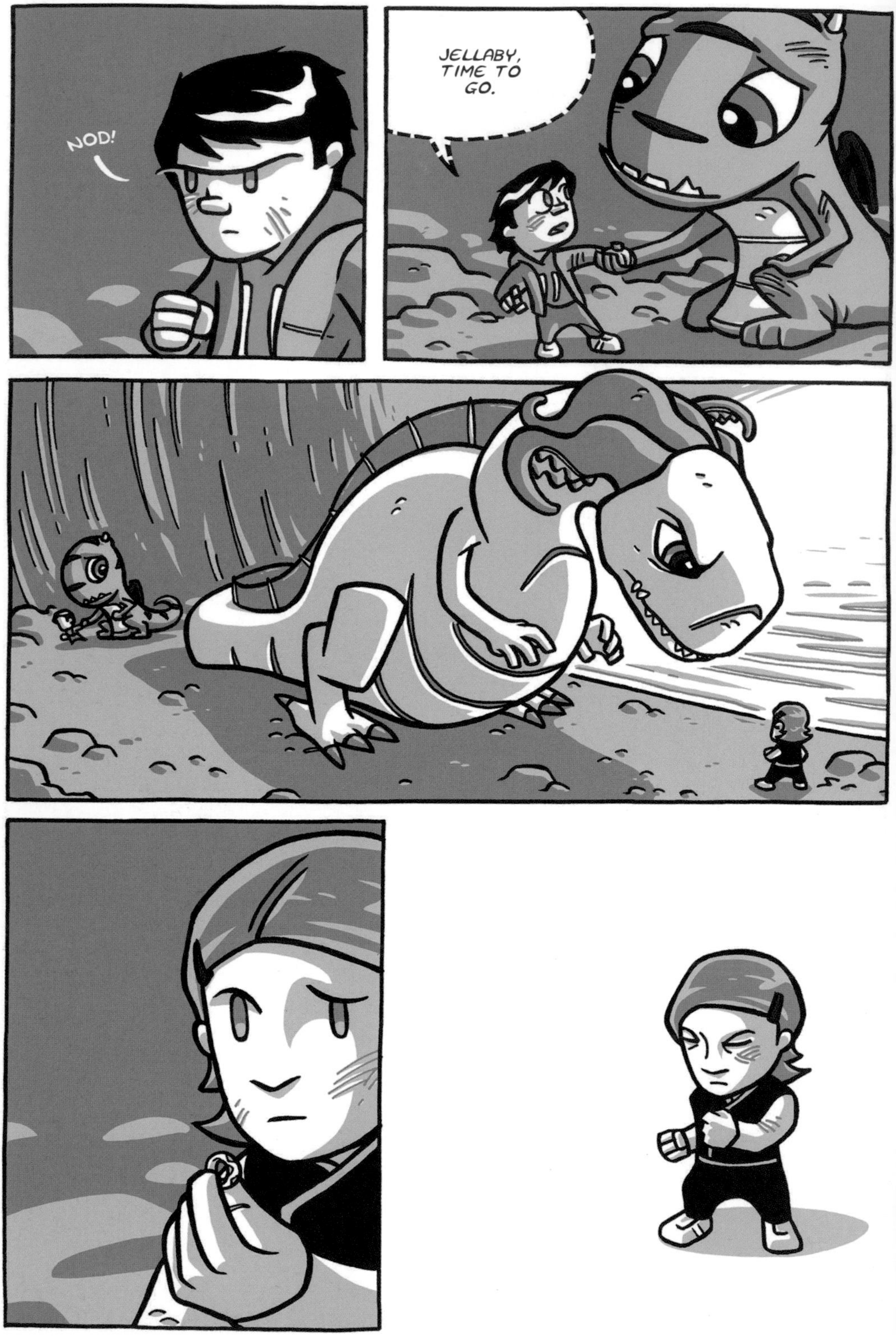
NOD!
JELLABY, TIME TO GO.

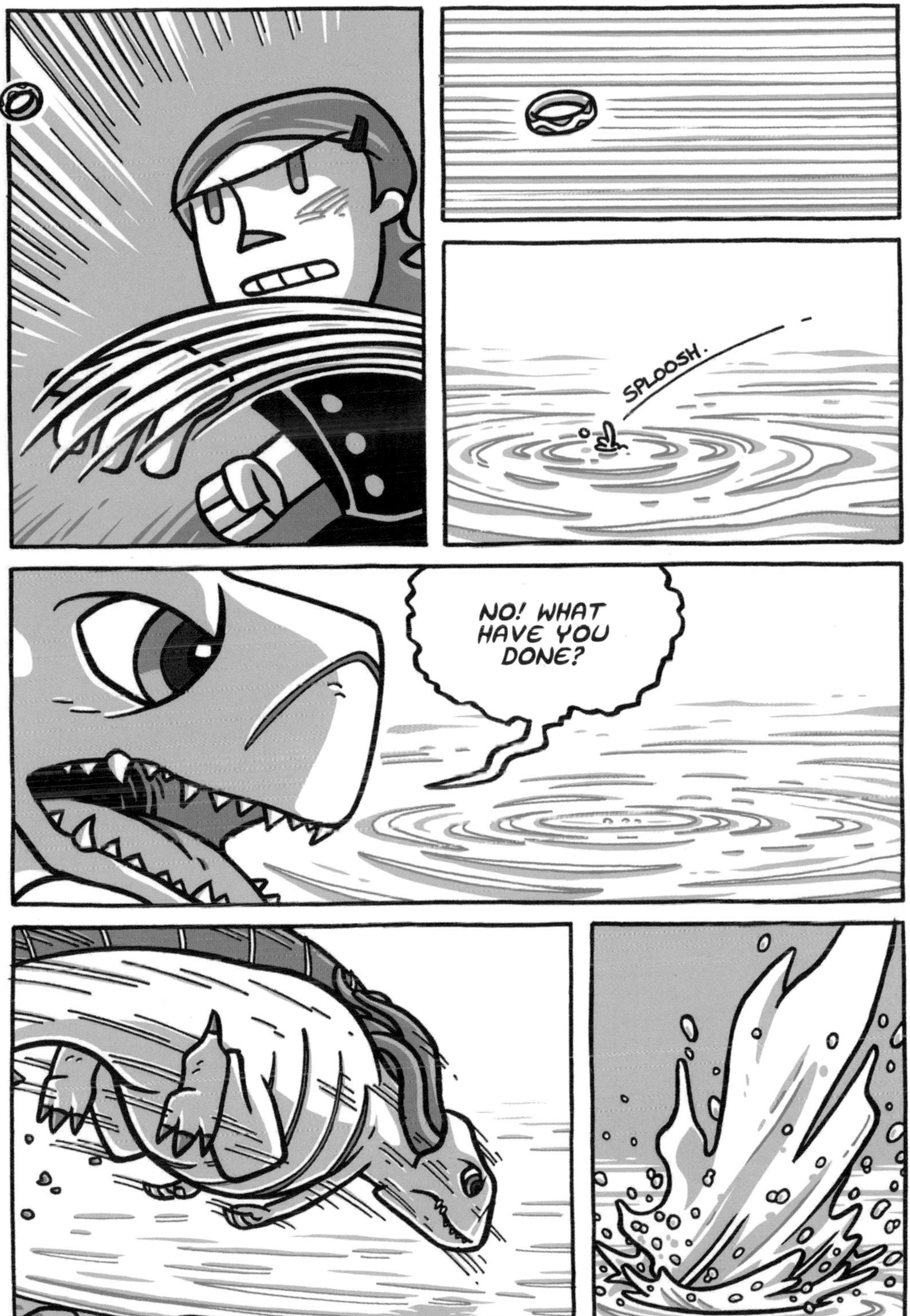
SPLOOSH.
NO! WHAT HAVE YOU DONE?

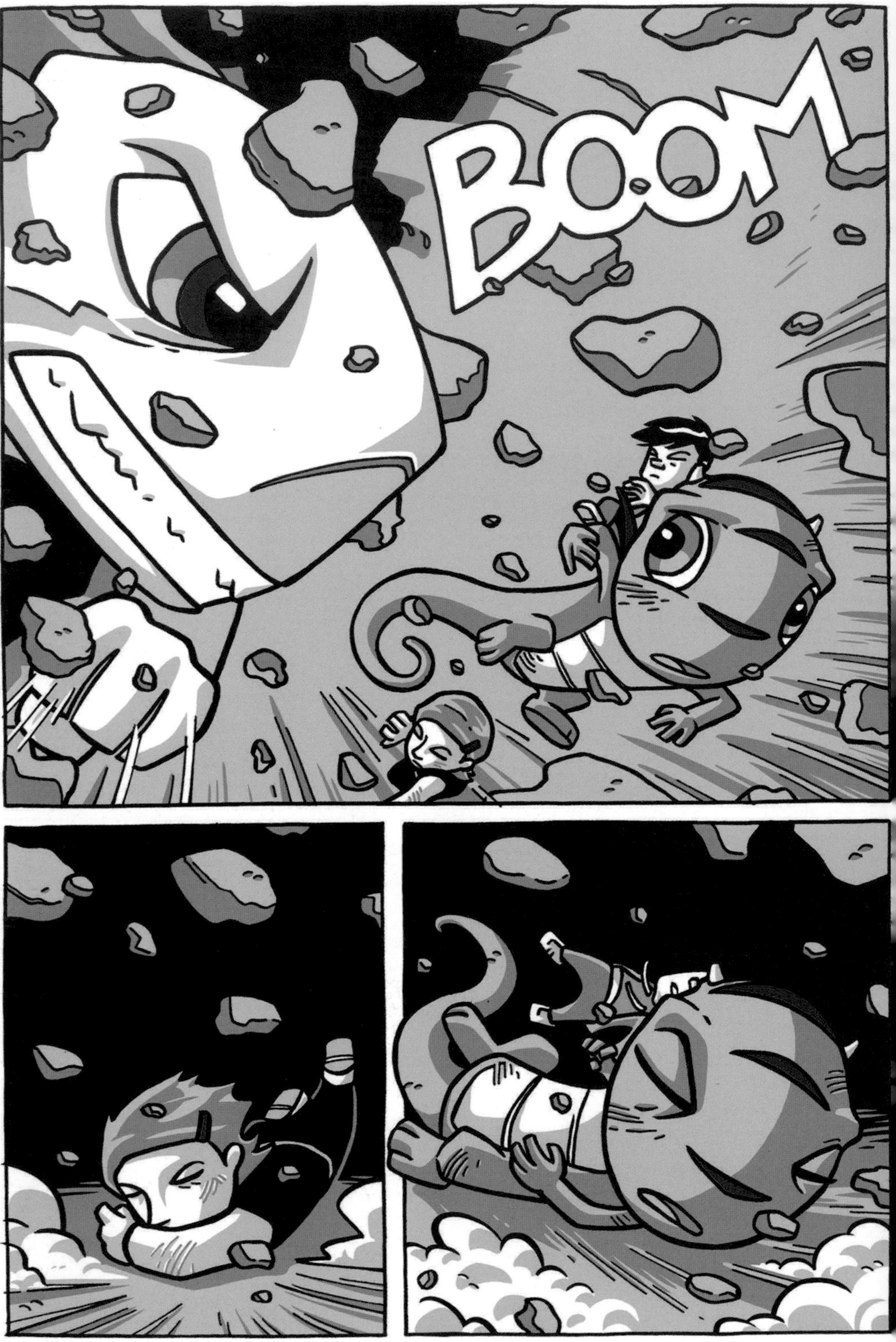
BOOM

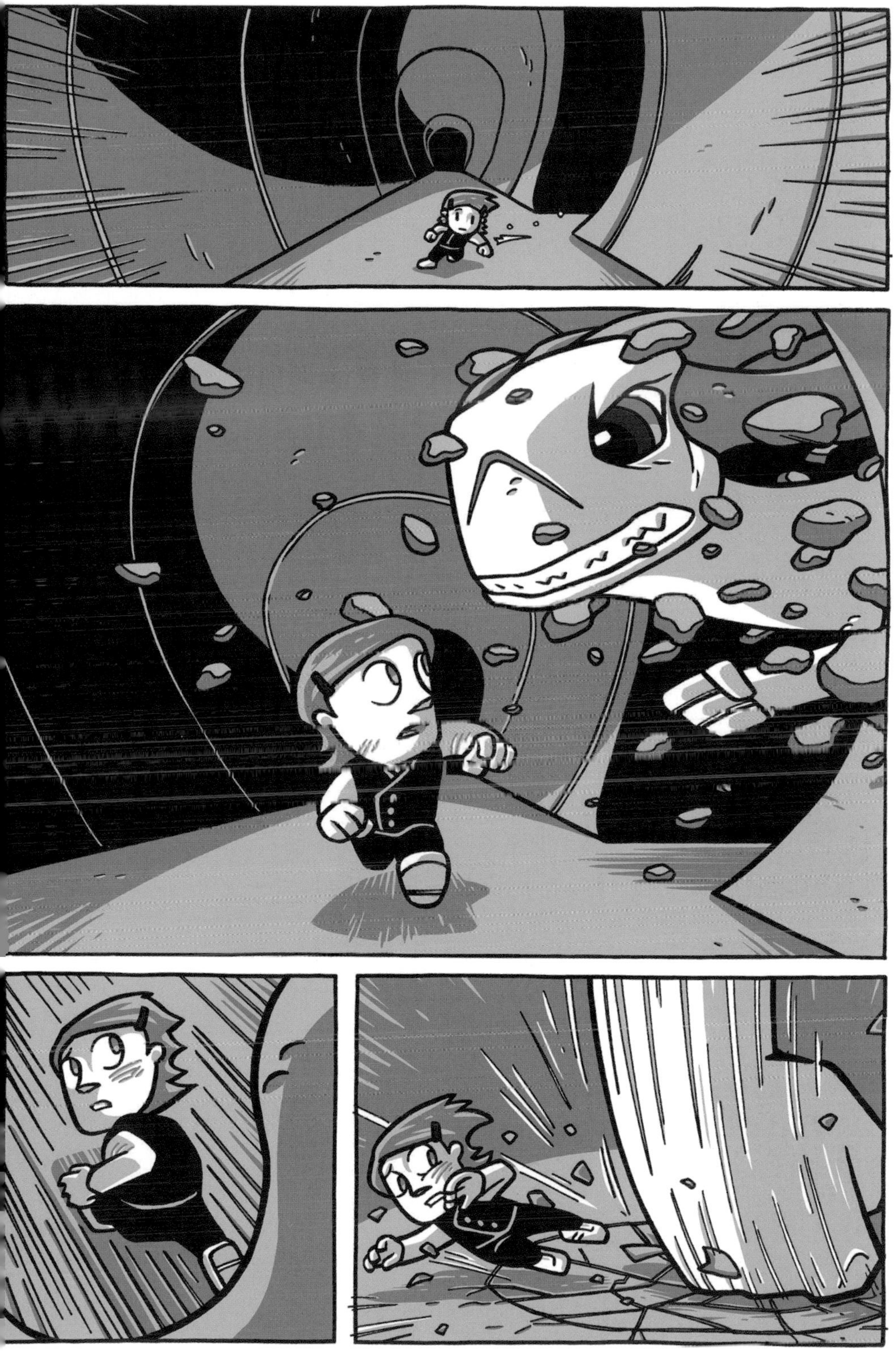

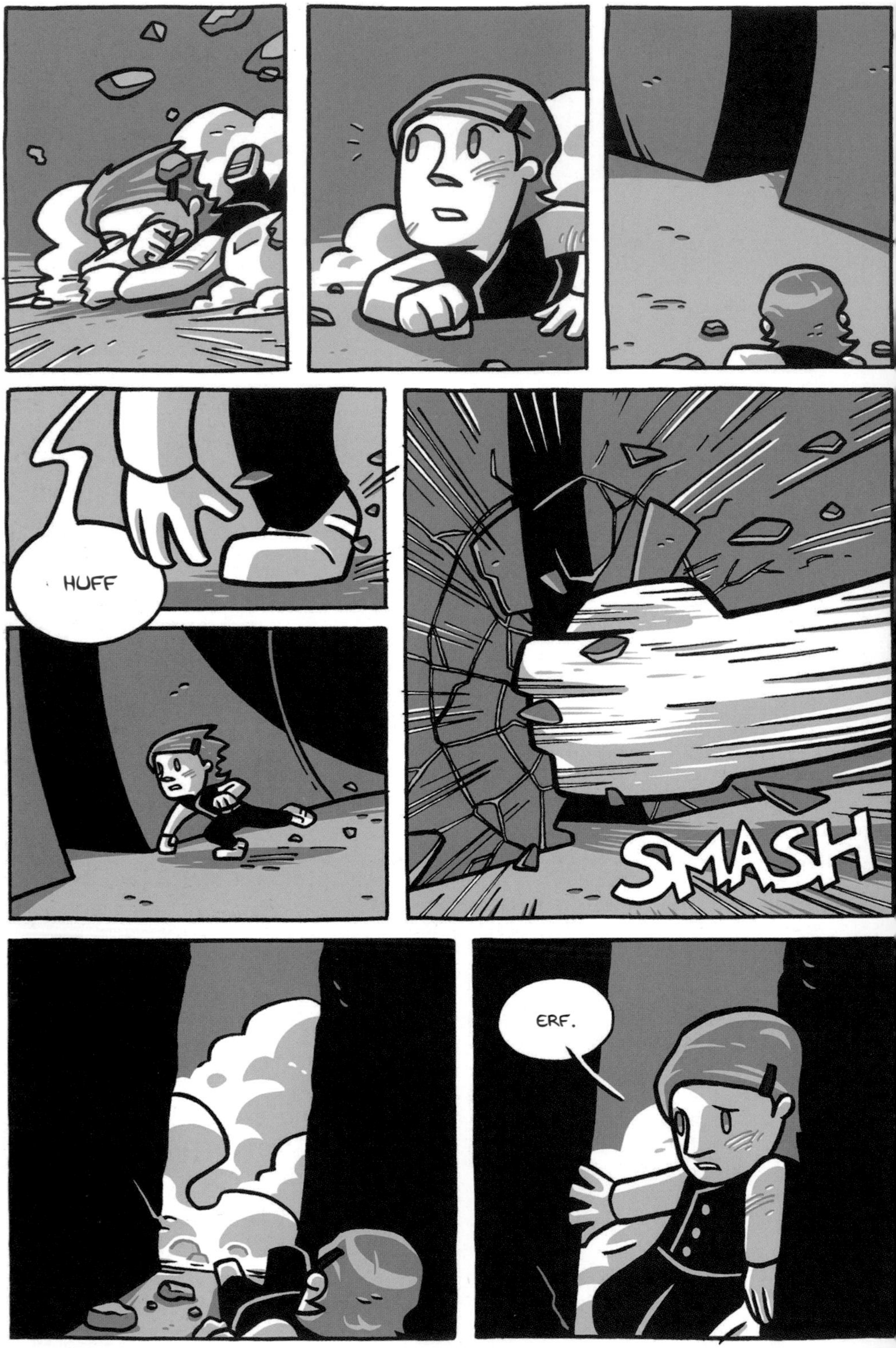
HUFF
SMASH
ERF.

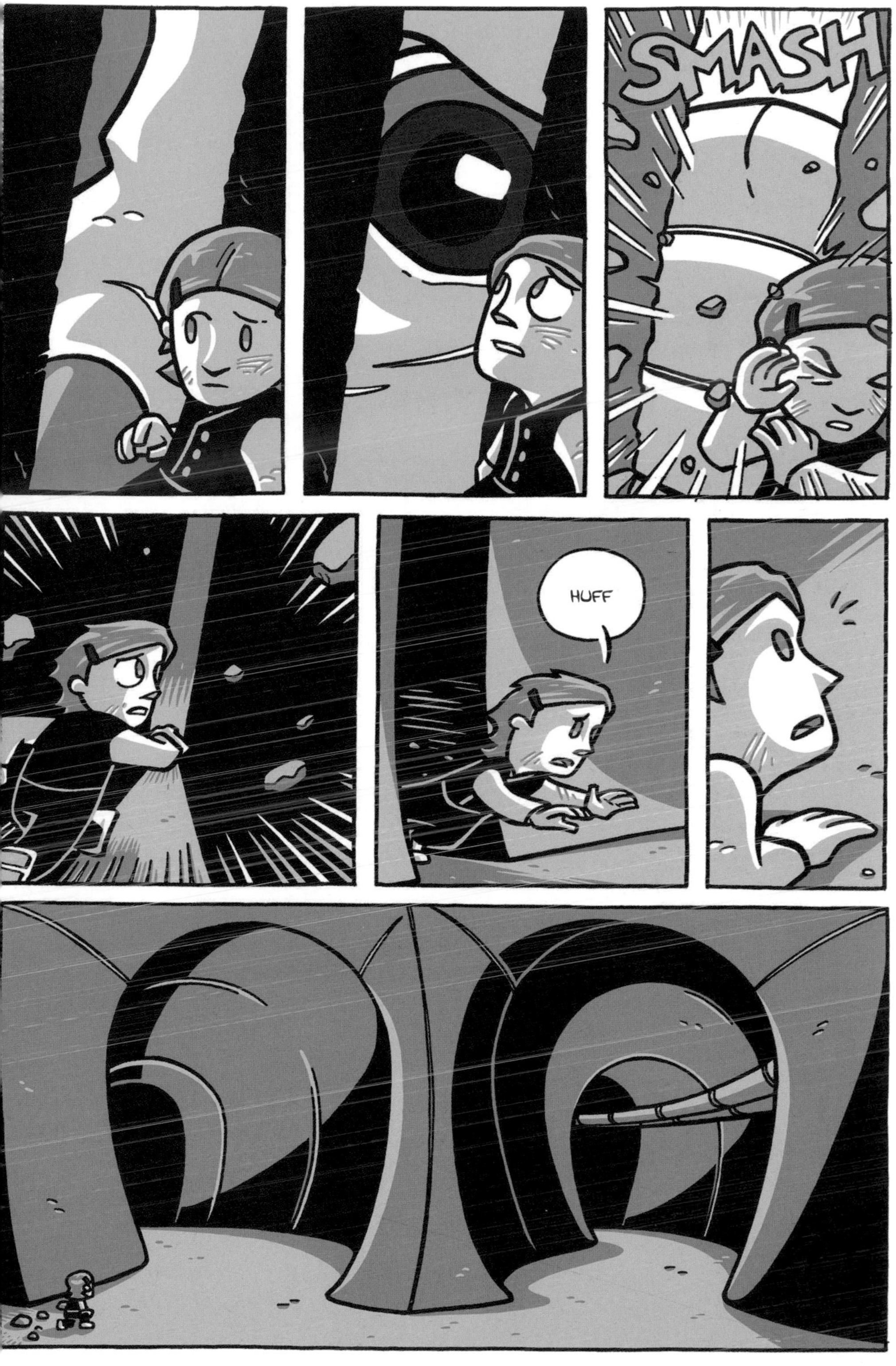
SMASH
HUFF

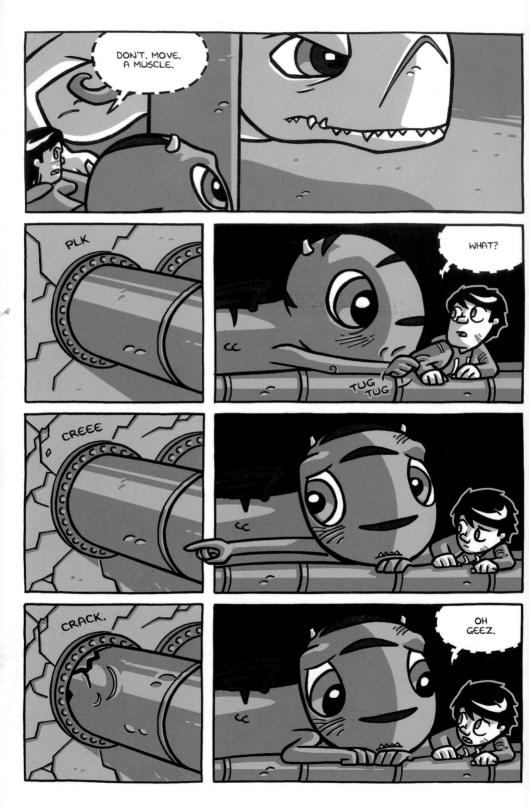

155

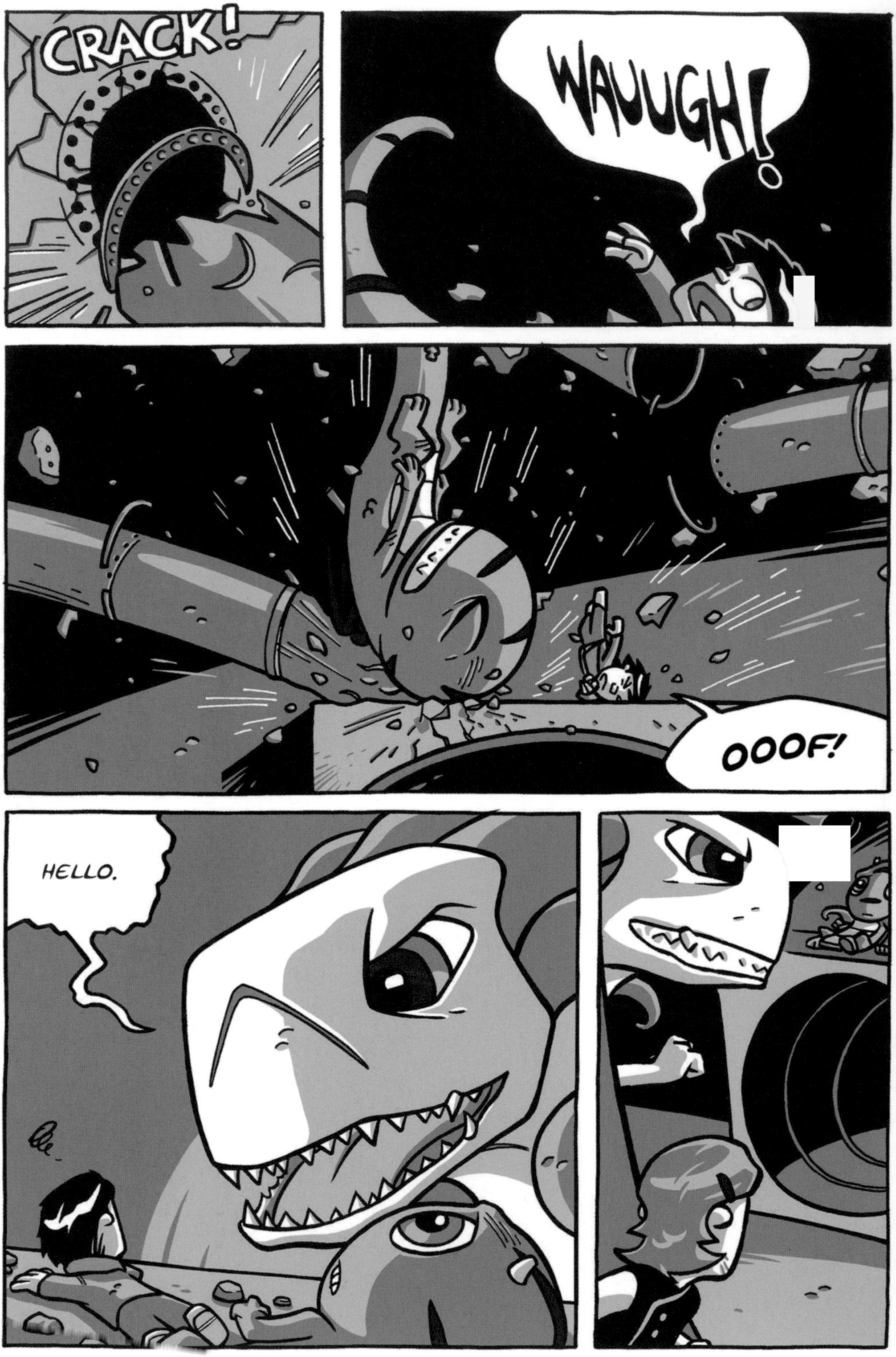
CRACK!
WAUUGH!
OOOF!
HELLO.

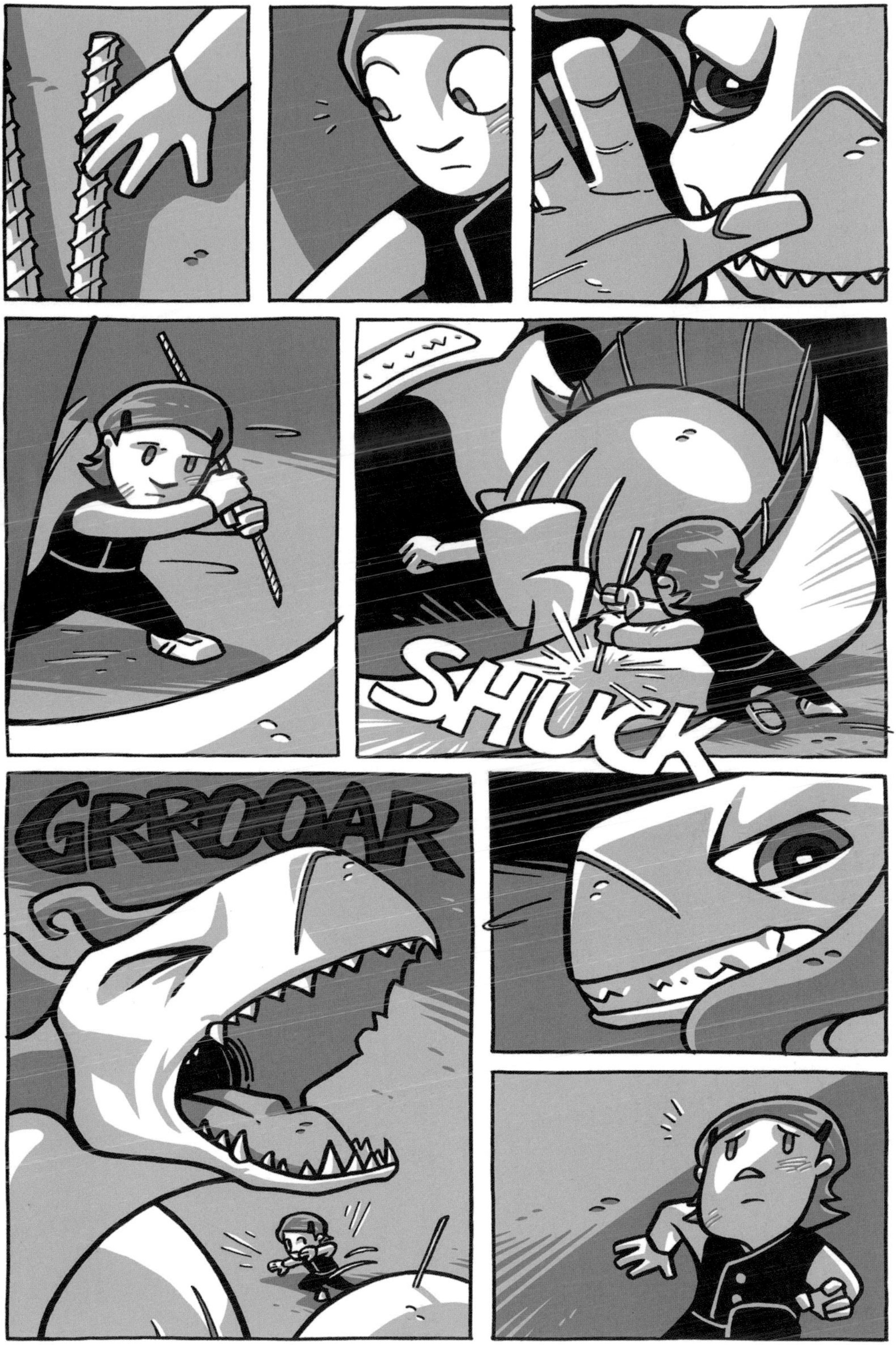
SHUCK
GRROOAR

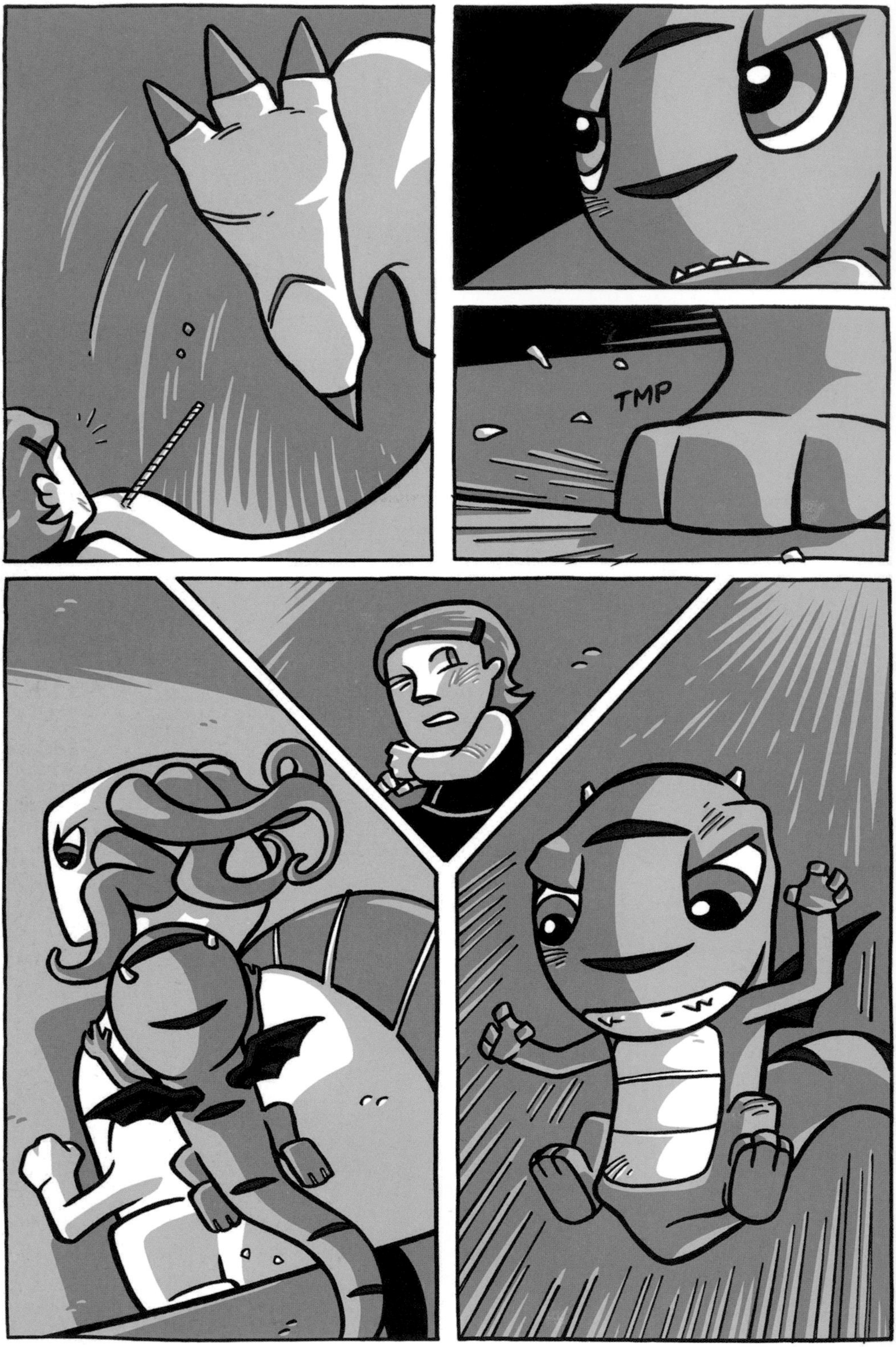
TMP

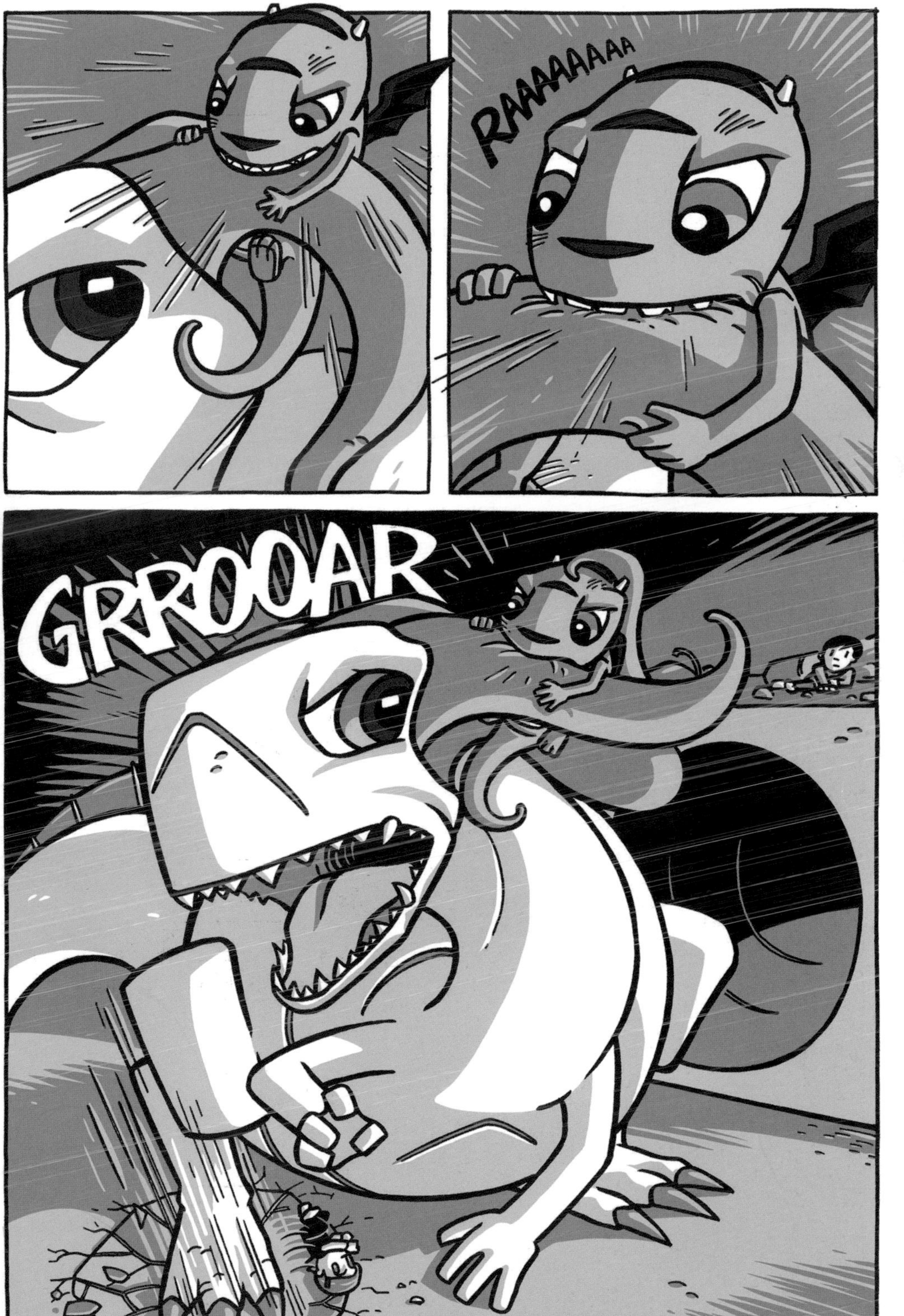
RAAAAAAAAA
GRROOAR

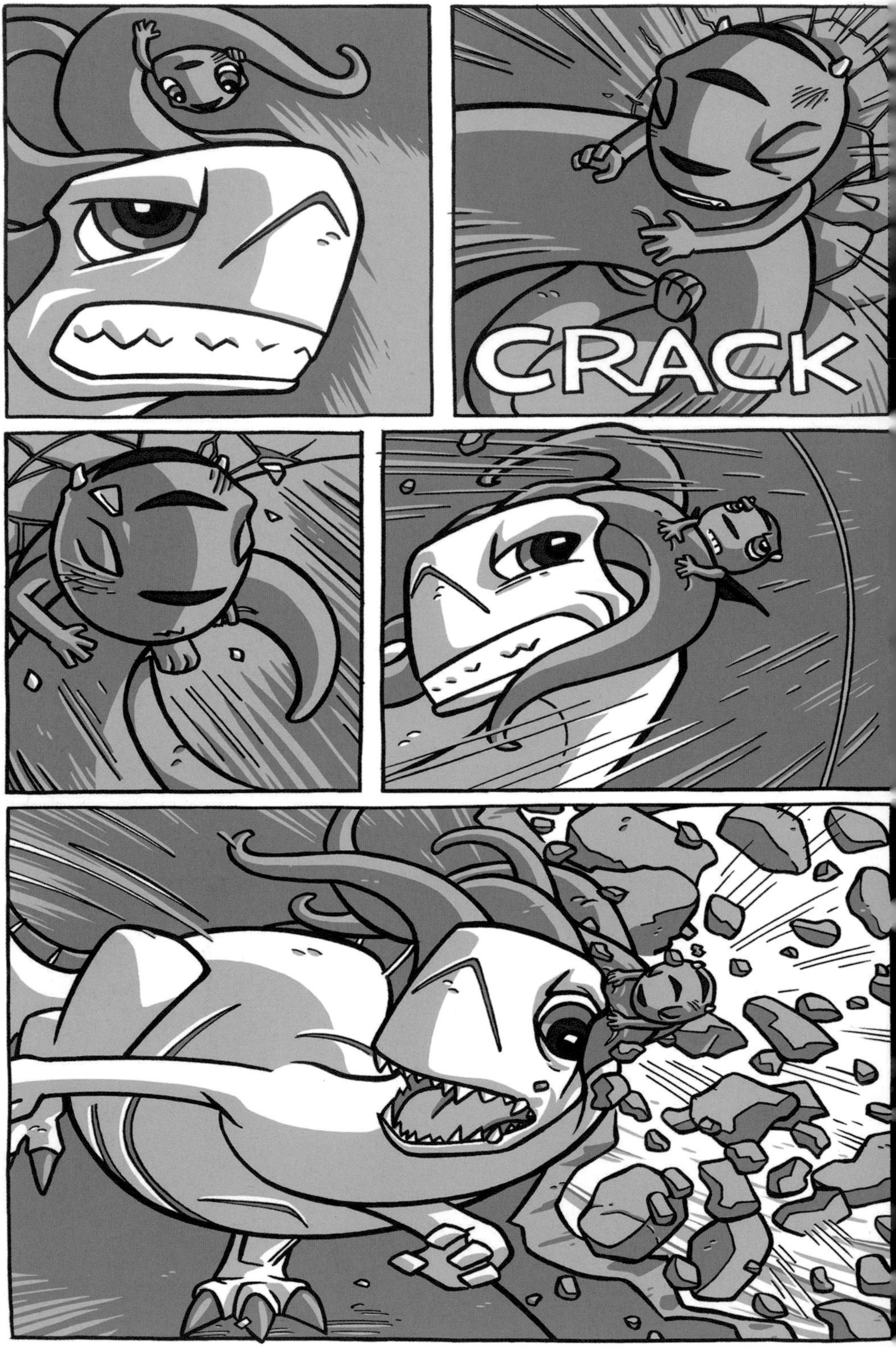
CRACK

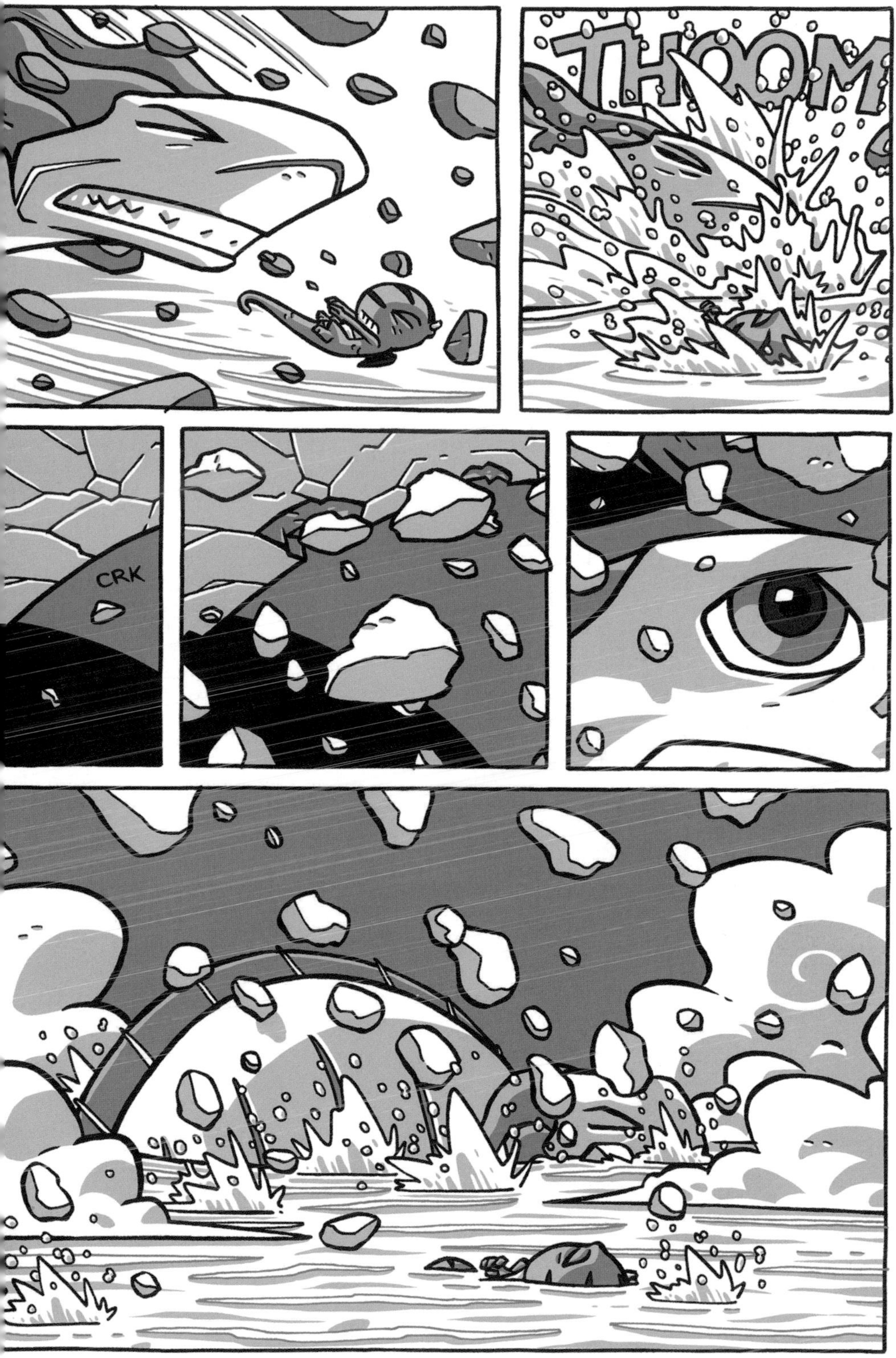
THOOM
CRK

162

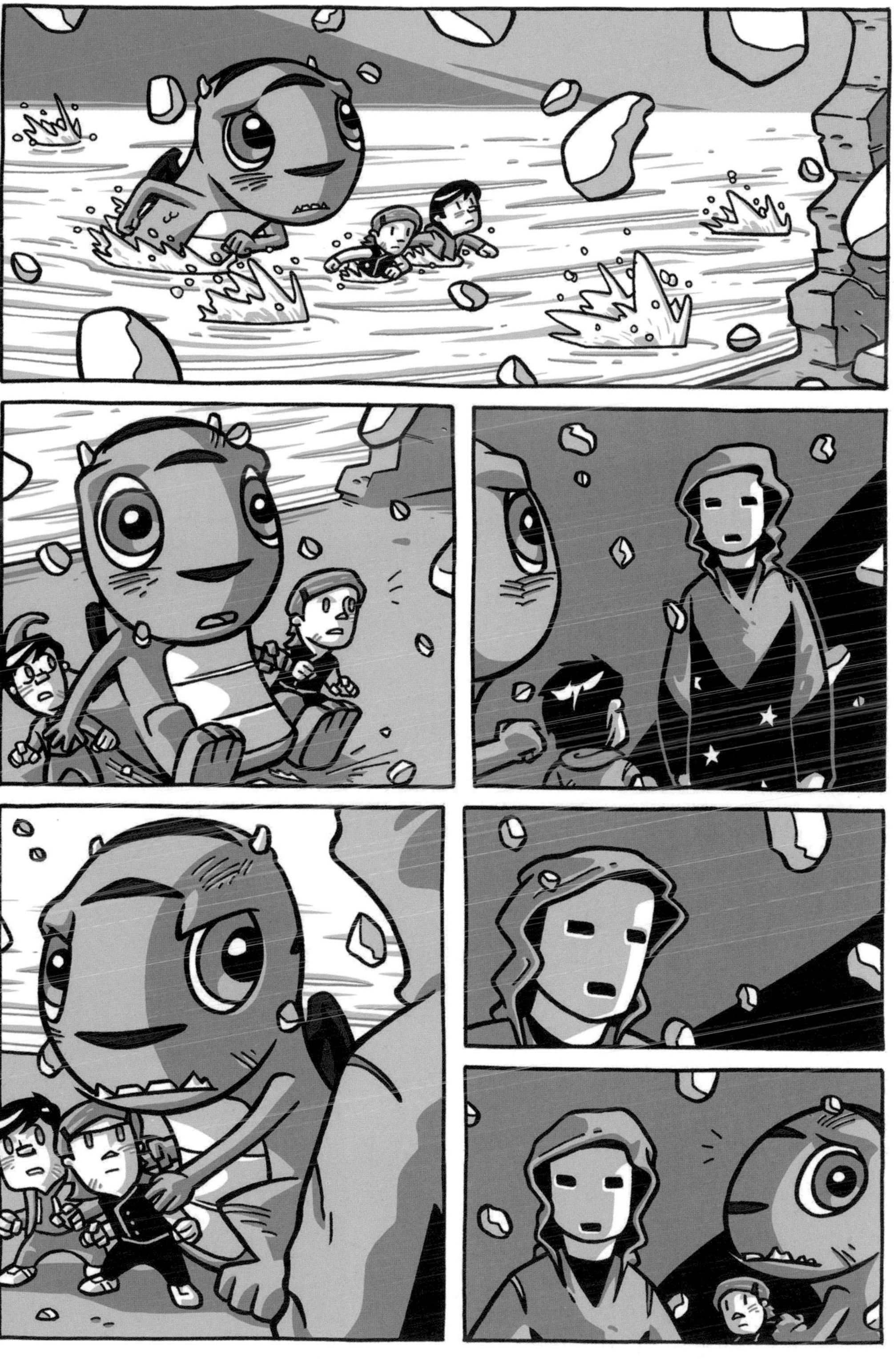

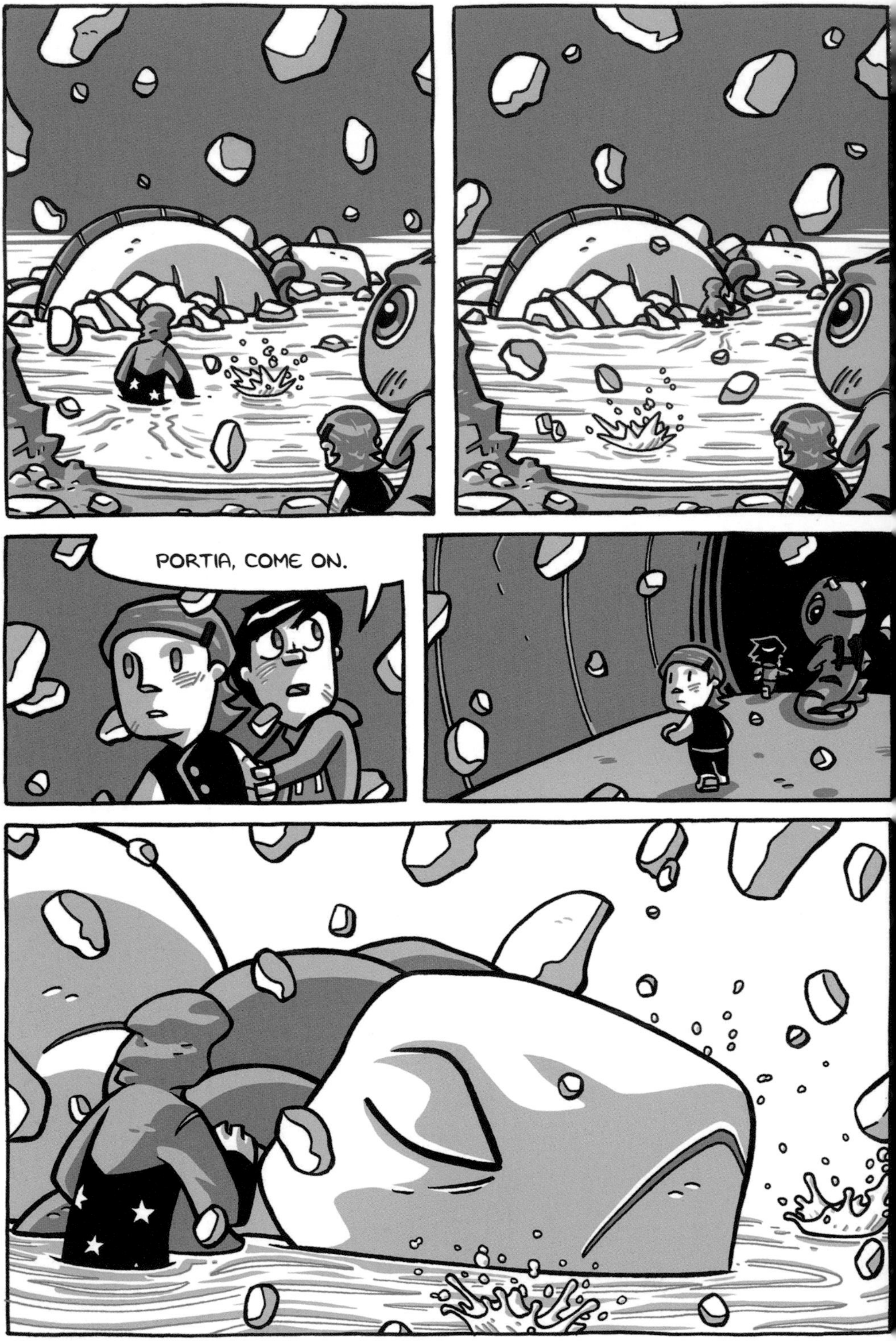
PORTIA, COME ON.

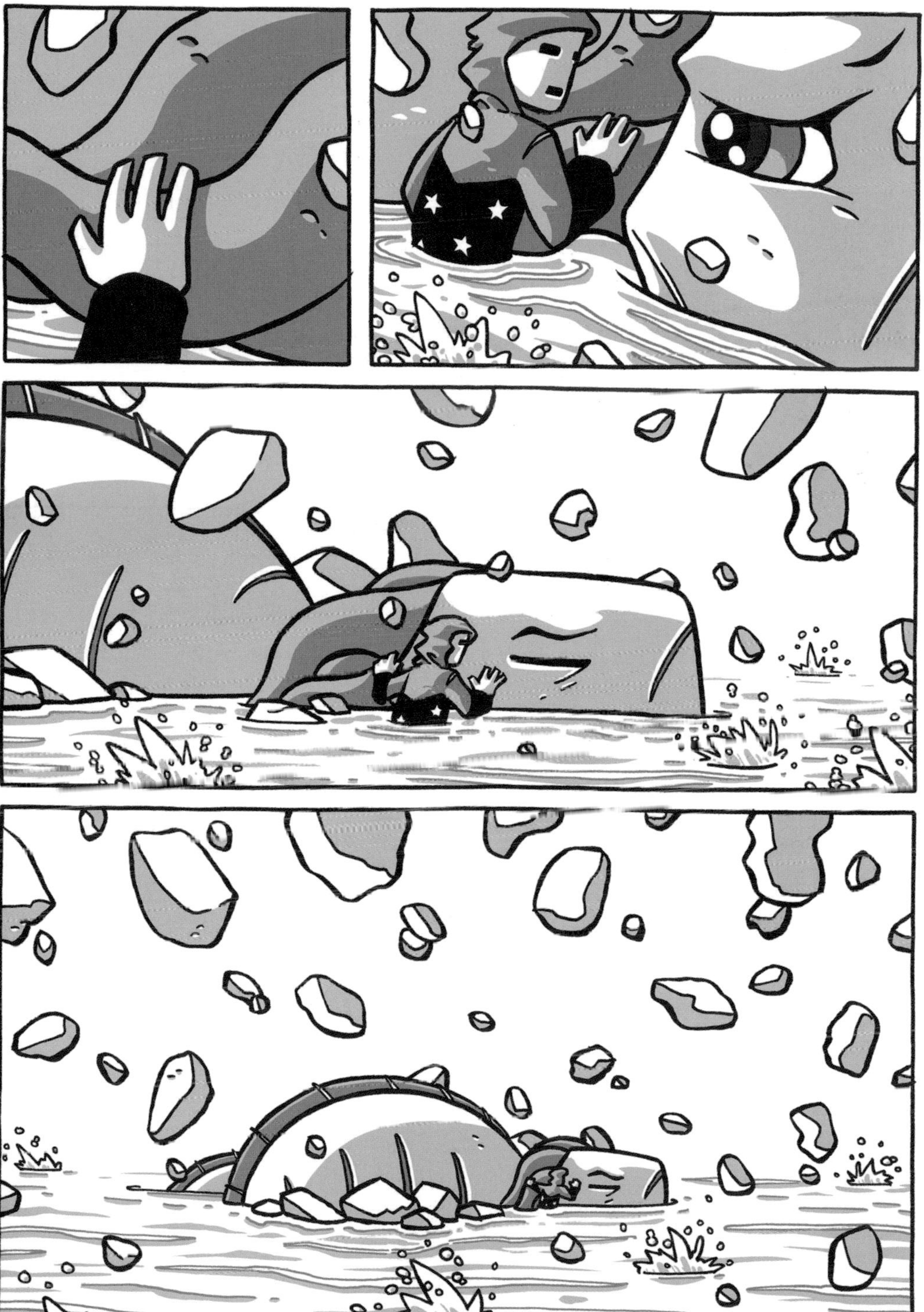

169

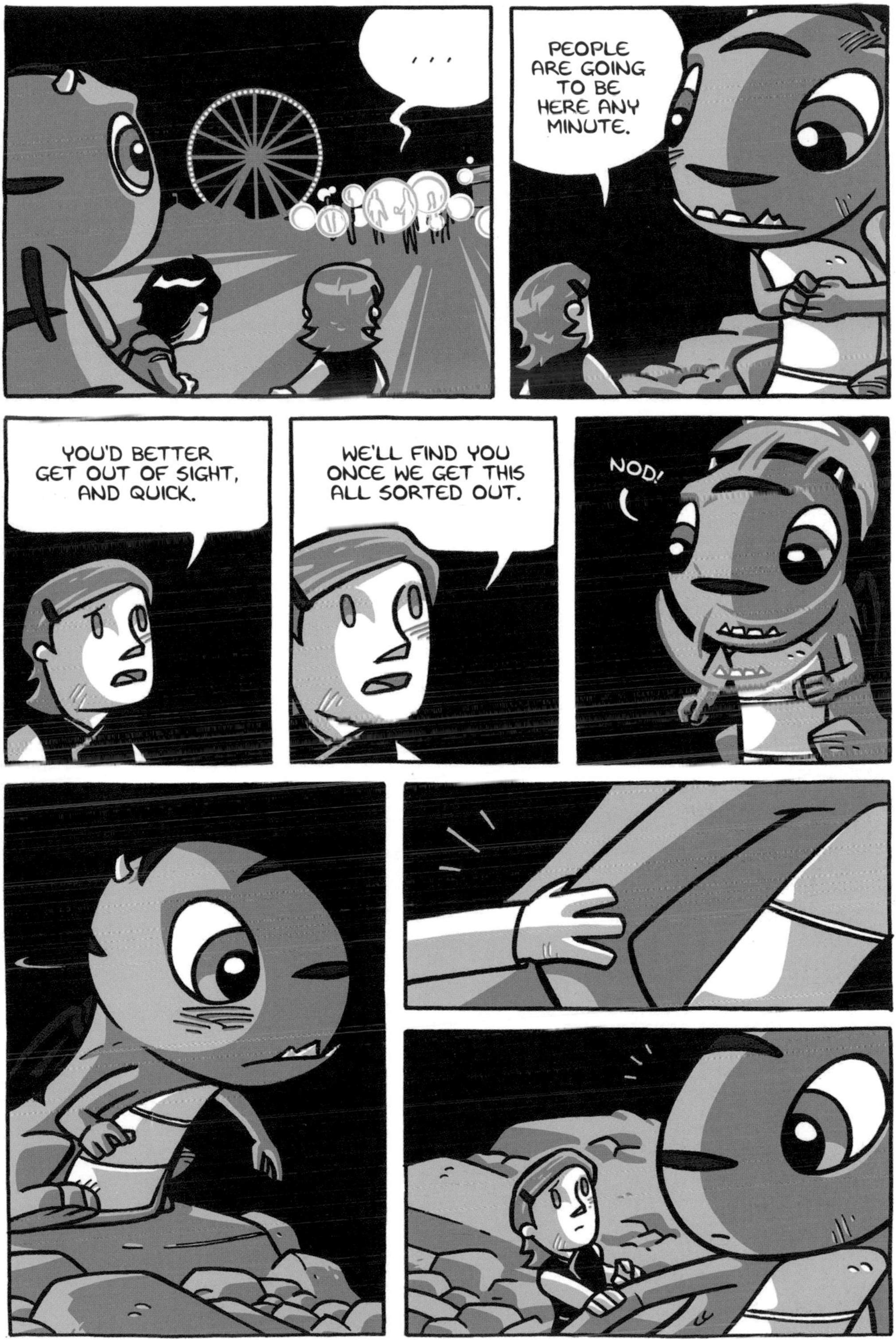
. . .
PEOPLE ARE GOING TO BE HERE ANY MINUTE.
YOU'D BETTER GET OUT OF SIGHT, AND QUICK.
WE'LL FIND YOU ONCE WE GET THIS ALL SORTED OUT.
NOD!

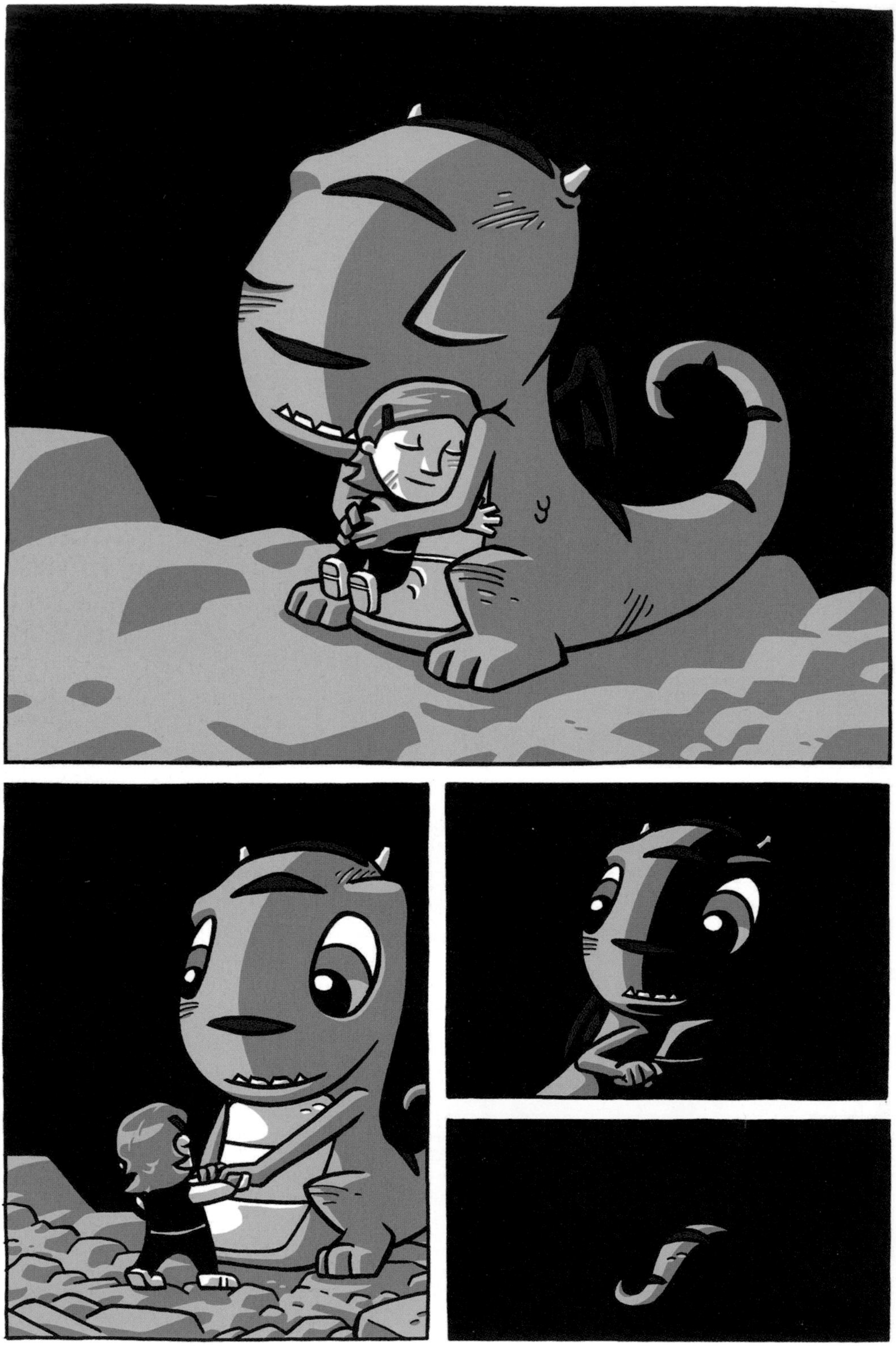

EPILOGUE

176

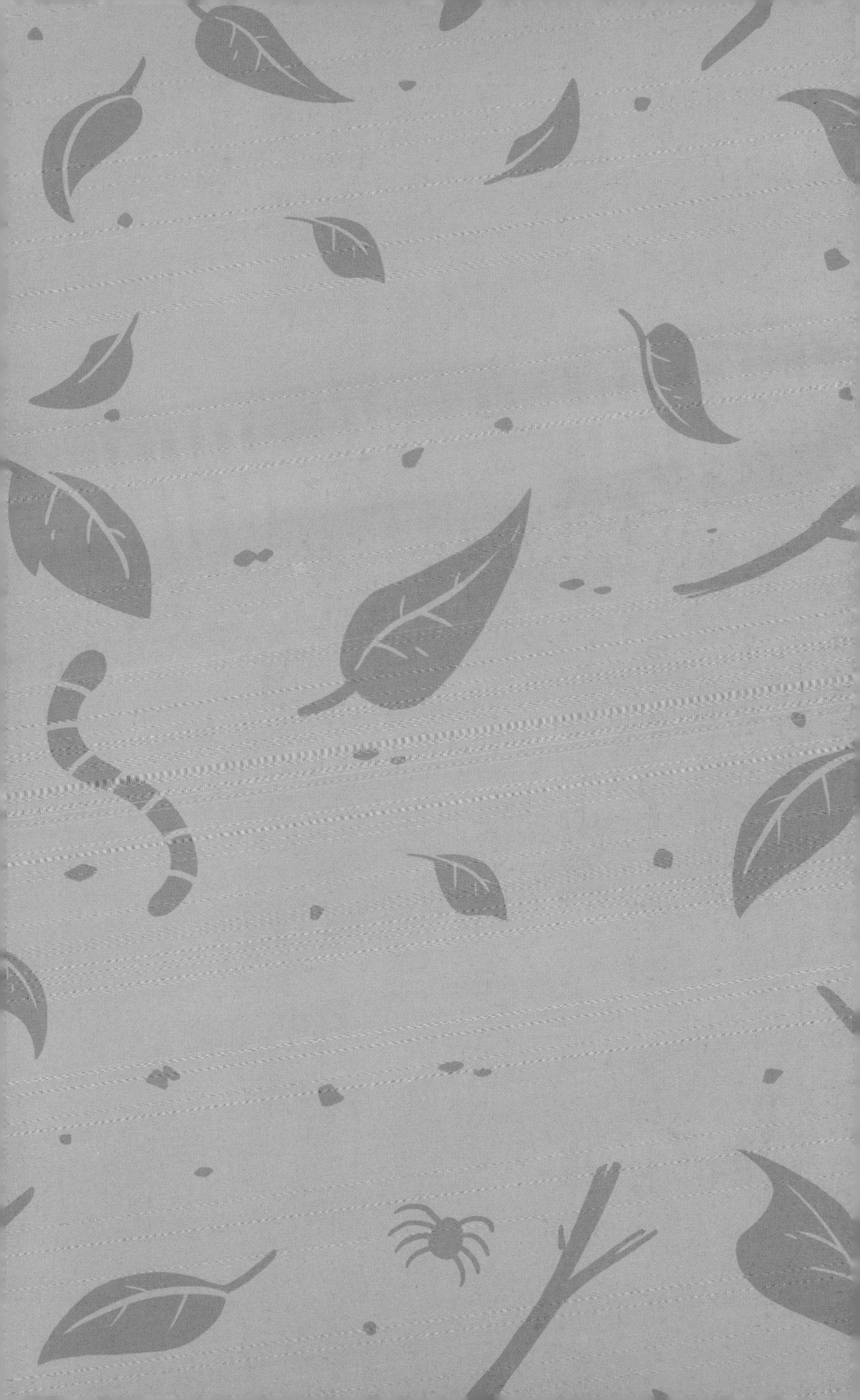

About the Author

Born in England and raised in Hong Kong, Kean Soo settled in Canada, where he planned to embark on a career in electrical engineering. However, he discovered that he'd rather draw comics instead. Kean began posting his comics on the Internet in 2002, and later became an assistant editor and regular contributor to the all-ages *Flight* anthologies. Kean was nominated for an Eisner Award and received a Joe Shuster Award for Best Comics for Kids for his work on *Jellaby*.

Kean still loves going to the CNE (the Canadian National Exhibition) for the tiny donuts and the rides. He enjoys riding on the Wave Swinger, but his absolute favorite is The Zipper, which is probably the only ride that makes him genuinely fear for his life.

Portrait of the author by Hope Larson

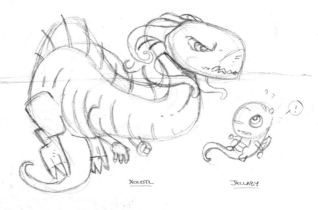

XOLOTL   JELLABY

Top: Some early sketches of Jellaby and Xolotl. I based Xolotl's design on the Mexican axolotl, a type of neotenic salamander, which has since become a critically endangered species.

Left: An early study of the underground setting for Monster in the City.

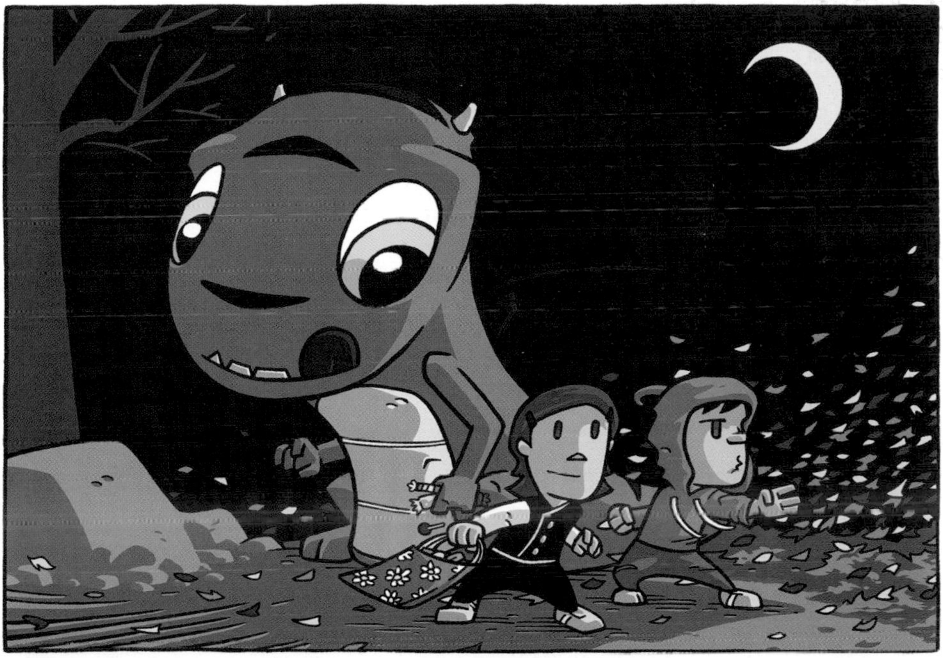

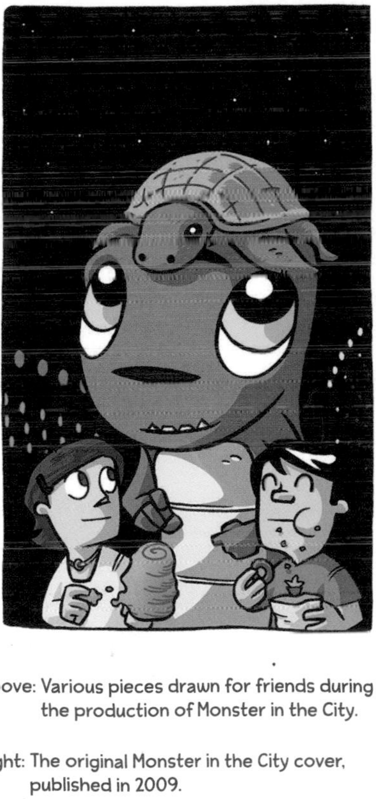

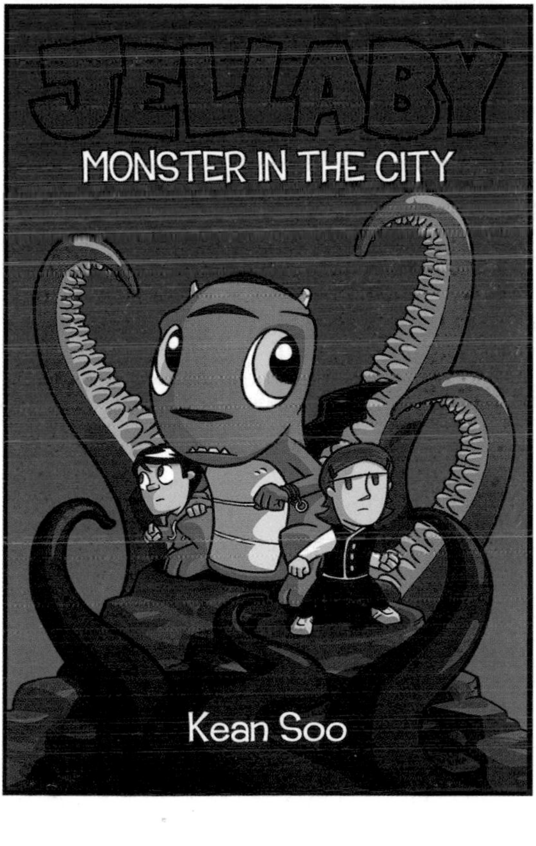
JELLABY
MONSTER IN THE CITY
Kean Soo

Above: Various pieces drawn for friends during the production of Monster in the City.

Right: The original Monster in the City cover, published in 2009.